Praise for *The Maze at*  W9-BJA-226

"An intricate creation you'll happily lose yourself in." —*People*

"Staggeringly brilliant . . . An extraordinary demonstration of narrative dexterity. Moving up and down through the strata of history, Smith captures the ever-changing refractions of human desire. . . . The cumulative effect of this carousel of differing voices is absolutely transporting. . . . Looking up from this remarkable novel, one has an eerie sense of history as a process of continuous erasure and revision. You'll start *The Maze of Windermere* with bewilderment, but you'll close it in awe."

—*The Washington Post*

"Pitch-perfect . . . The different strands of the narrative are skillfully braided."

—*The New York Times Book Review*

"Once you read Gregory Blake Smith's *The Maze at Windermere*, you'll understand why Richard Russo calls it 'a dazzling high-wire act.' It's a labyrinthine, layered novel that spans three centuries while following the exploits and experiences of a compelling cast of characters."

—*Southern Living*

"*The Maze at Windermere* is a dramatic and interesting look into the past of a town and the lives of those who've dwelled in it."

—*New York Journal of Books*

"Smith's vibrant mix of beautiful writing, clarity of voices, flow of history and storytelling, and philosophical reflections had me slowing my pace to stretch out its pleasures."

—*Minneapolis Star Tribune*

"Dazzling . . . An impressive achievement."

—*The Emerald City Book Review*

"This novel is, in a word, excellent. . . . Beautifully drawn . . . Gossamer filaments connect these plotlines; duplicity in all its dismaying forms is a major theme, along with the brilliant contrast between substance and shadow, superficiality and depth. There are moments of wry humor, suspense, gut-wrenching human exchange. And through it all, an honesty—capturing life as people live it—that is made to appear easy, but is very, very difficult to actually achieve in fiction."

—Historical Novel Society

"It is just so vibrant, so fun, so mesmerizing."

—*Bill's Books* on NBC New York

"Gregory Blake Smith's *The Maze at Windermere* is a dazzling high-wire act. I turned every page with a sense of wonder and excitement."

—Richard Russo, Pulitzer Prize–winning author of *Empire Falls* and *Everybody's Fool*

"*The Maze at Windermere* is thrilling. This novel restored my faith and made me laugh out loud. It's rare that a novel comes along that is broad ranging, so very funny, profound, provocative, literary, and page turning, and also word perfect. I went right back to the beginning when I'd finished, marveling again at the radiant mind of Gregory Blake Smith."

—Jane Hamilton, author of *A Map of the World* and *The Excellent Lombards*

"Not since *Beautiful Ruins* have I read a novel with such breadth of imagination or depth of heart, nor a cast of characters so real, so varied, so compelling. In five exquisitely braided tales spanning nearly four centuries, Gregory Blake Smith illuminates the everlasting power of our passions and the hazard of our follies—in essence, the many ways we mortals strive and yearn toward the center of the maze we each call life. This book is a tour de force: gorgeous, suspenseful, cunning, and wise."

—Julia Glass, author of *Three Junes*

"*The Maze at Windermere* is an astonishing book—prismatic, continually surprising, daring not only in structure but in its investigation of the human heart. Somehow it manages to be both ruthless and tender. On top of all that, it's wildly, hurtlingly entertaining."

—Leah Hager Cohen, author of *The Grief of Others*

"Compelling . . . The changing language, landscape, and mores of three centuries of American history are depicted with verisimilitude, highlighting what doesn't change at all: the aspirations and crimes of the human heart." —*Kirkus Reviews*

"Intricately designed and suspenseful . . . Though references to James's work, particularly *The Portrait of a Lady*, abound, readers don't have to be familiar with his novels to relish the well-differentiated voices and worlds or to enjoy the way the novel's five story lines subtly shift and begin to merge." —*Booklist* (starred review)

"Taken individually, each story is dramatic and captivating, but as the author makes ever-increasing connections among the stories and shuffles them all into one unbroken narrative, the novel becomes a moving meditation on love, race, class, and self-fulfillment in America across the centuries."

—*Publishers Weekly* (starred review)

"Compelling . . . Award-winning novelist Smith moves nimbly among his tales' various settings and diverse characters within the confines of Newport. . . . [An] intricate tale." —*Library Journal* (starred review)

PENGUIN BOOKS

THE MAZE AT WINDERMERE

Gregory Blake Smith is the award-winning author of three previous novels including *The Divine Comedy of John Venner*, a *New York Times* Notable Book. His short story collection, *The Law of Miracles*, won the Juniper Prize and the Minnesota Book Award. He has received a Stegner Fellowship at Stanford University and the George Bennett Fellowship at Phillips Exeter Academy, and grants from the National Endowment for the Arts, the Bush Foundation, and the Minnesota State Arts Board. Smith is currently the Lloyd P. Johnson-Norwest Professor of English and the Liberal Arts at Carleton College.

Look for the Penguin Readers Guide in the back of this book. To access Penguin Readers Guides online, visit penguinrandomhouse.com.

GREGORY BLAKE SMITH

The Maze at Windermere

PENGUIN BOOKS

PENGUIN BOOKS
An imprint of Penguin Random House LLC
penguinrandomhouse.com

First published in the United States of America by Viking Penguin,
an imprint of Penguin Random House LLC, 2018
Published in Penguin Books 2019

ISBN 9780735221932 (paperback)

THE LIBRARY OF CONGRESS HAS CATALOGED THE HARDCOVER EDITION AS FOLLOWS:
Names: Smith, Gregory Blake, author.
Title: The maze at Windermere : a novel / Gregory Blake Smith.
Description: New York : Viking, 2018. |
Identifiers: LCCN 2017025390 (print) | LCCN 2017028123 (ebook) |
ISBN 9780735221949 (ebook) | ISBN 9780735221925 (hardcover alk. paper)
Subjects: | BISAC: FICTION / Historical. | FICTION / Sagas. | FICTION / Literary.
Classification: LCC PS3569.M5356 (ebook) | LCC PS3569.M5356 M39 2018 (print) |
DDC 813/.54—dc23
LC record available at https://lccn.loc.gov/2017025390

Printed in the United States of America
1   3   5   7   9   10   8   6   4   2

Set in Dante MT Pro
Designed by Francesca Belanger

for Laura

What is it then between us?
What is the count of the scores or hundreds of years between us?
Whatever it is, it avails not—distance avails not, and place avails not.

—WALT WHITMAN

The Maze at Windermere

I

Duplicity

→ Summer 2011 ←

He was trying to explain to her how he'd gotten to be where he was. The condition he was in. His state of mind, the state of his bank account. His heart, his soul, whatever. They were in the Orangery at Windermere, Aisha newly naked beside him, the salt air coming in through the window, and this was the sort of moment when he somehow felt compelled to *tell all*.

What had gotten under his skin, he found himself saying, was the way the guy kept bringing up the *Tennis Life* article. "Lacks the killer instinct to break into the top fifty," he kept saying, drunk, obnoxious, smiling that smile that men smile to show they're just kidding even when they're not just kidding. Who was this bozo anyway?

At which Aisha leaned over and kissed him like "poor you," her dreadlocks spilling across her lovely shoulders.

This had been last August, he told her, a real low point in his life. His knee was shot and he'd just retired . . . or was on the verge of retiring . . . or wasn't sure whether he was retiring or not—but his right knee was messed up, his life was messed up, his ranking had dropped below two hundred for the first time in eight years, and the only options were to drift back down into the Challengers circuit, or pack it in and try to land a college coaching job, or failing that a gig at some luxury resort instructing Fortune 500 types on how to hit a slice backhand.

"Sandy Alison," he imitated the guy, the bozo, the guy with the motorcycle last August. "Out of Duke, a great shotmaker but lacks the killer instinct to break into the top fifty."

Thing was, that past August was the second year running he hadn't qualified for the US Open. It had been the beginning of the end. And even if he *had* qualified, he wouldn't have been able to play—his knee again—so he'd come to Newport to the Hall of Fame Champions Cup as a hitting partner for Todd Martin. (A tagalong, a hanger-on: was that his future?) His money was beginning to run out and he knew he had to make a decision, and soon, but in Newport a little of the old life beckoned, and after the semifinals he'd gone to the Champions Ball with the idea of catching on with some of the local wealth (this was *Newport*, he didn't have to remind Aisha), but the evening had degenerated from the waltz to the bossa nova to the Watusi until the surviving couple dozen partiers—the Champions had left a long time ago—had gone off barhopping down along Thames Street and ended up at this . . . this . . . he couldn't even remember where they'd ended up but the bozo, the guy with the antique motorcycle, just wouldn't let up.

What he didn't tell her was how that phrase—"lacks the killer instinct"—had eaten at him for nearly a decade. It came from a year-end issue of *Tennis Life*, a Future-of-American-Tennis sort of thing about the new crop of guys making the transition to the pro tour. This was back in 2002 and he had just made it, as a freshman no less, to the NCAA Semifinals, and some of the things they had to say were cool. They called him "the Southern Gentleman," said he had an artistry on the court, was well liked in the players' lounge. But that last summing up had seemed to doom him to the hinterland of Almost-But-Not-Quite, which, if he was completely honest, was exactly where he'd spent the decade of his pro career. He *had* in fact cracked the top fifty (Sandy Alison, 2006, #47 in the world, you can look it up), had made it once to the third round of Wimbledon, twice to the second round of the US Open, had a dozen Challengers titles to his name, the courts back at his Charleston high school named in his honor, but somehow none of that was good enough. He was, somehow, in spite of all that, a loser. It didn't matter that in 2006 he could beat *all but forty-six freaking players in the whole freaking world*. It didn't matter that whatever town he drove into he could beat whoever their best tennis player was, could beat him left-handed for Pete's sake (and he *could* too; he used to mess around on the court playing left-handed when he should have been doing drills)—none of that mattered. He was—even while people wanted to know him, wanted to hang out with him because he was a professional athlete—somehow he was still a loser. He hadn't been a winner—*he lacked the killer instinct*—and therefore he had to be a loser. That was how it *felt* anyway, although he didn't ever tell that to anyone. Certainly not to the woman lying beside him.

So yeah, the motorcycle. Maybe all it was, was just that the guy was a bad drunk. Maybe he was just a bad drunk and it just happened to have been Sandy who had gotten in his way. But the guy started calling shit at him across the room the Casino party had settled into, the women in their cocktail dresses and the men in their dinner jackets with their ties undone. It got bad enough that everyone started getting embarrassed for Sandy. The women wouldn't look at him, or they'd shush the bozo—there was this one British woman there who kept saying, "Oh, what rot!"—and the men had that look men get when one of them is being singled out. The challenge, the appraisal, the are-you-just-gonna-sit-there-and-take-it? look.

Earlier in the evening the motorcycle guy had been friendly enough. Sandy had stood with him on the sidewalk in front of one of the bars down on lower Thames Street and they'd talked tennis. The guy knew who Sandy was, knew his career, had himself played for Williams twenty years earlier, and Sandy had complimented him on his motorcycle parked alongside the curb—an antique red Indian Chief with those deeply valanced fenders and the whole Steve McQueen look—complimented him not because he cared about motorcycles but just because he was a nice guy, right? Hadn't *Tennis Life* said so?

Anyway, inside the bar it got to a point where Sandy had to answer the guy, had to say something, *anything*, so he called back over the tables and chairs that separated them: "Dude, I could beat you left-handed!"

"Dude?" the guy had said. *"Dude?"* Like it was the sorriest-ass thing anyone could say. And he had this way of spreading his hands about himself, gesturing toward the others as if to include them on his side, as if it was the lot of them who'd paid a thousand dollars a plate against the tennis pro who lacked the killer instinct. There was no way Sandy could beat him

left-handed, the guy said, and when Sandy challenged him again, the guy had said okay, he was on. One set. Sandy left-handed. Him right-handed. He'd put up the Indian.

"No Indian," Sandy had said. "We just play."

The bozo went *"pfft,"* like what kind of loser was this? Of course they had to play for something. That's how it was done. "The Indian," he said again. "You were drooling over it an hour ago, pretty boy. It's yours if you can beat me."

He had tried to keep his own nonchalance, but the faces on either side of him began to swim at the edge of his vision: the low-cut necklines, the pearls and spaghetti straps, the men with expressions of wanting to look away.

"Lacks the killer instinct," the guy said and gazed around the room with an easy gesture like *voilà.*

"Okay," Sandy had said. He tried to make his own easy gesture, like okay if that's what you want.

The guy turned back to him. *"Okay."* He mimicked Sandy's accent, making the word sound like it had three syllables, and then after a few strategic moments had passed: "And what're *you* putting up, champ?"

And that, he told Aisha, was when he got it. When he understood. The motorcycle was appraised at 30K, the guy was saying. What was Sandy going to put up against it? He had walked right into it, he told her. It hadn't been about tennis. It wasn't even the drunk-former-college-player-who-thought-he-could've-been-a-pro thing. He'd seen that before. No, this was about something else.

"Dude?" the guy mocked.

He could feel the heat coming into his face. The whole room began to swim. He had enough presence of mind not to smile, but that was about it.

"What rot!" the Brit tossed out again.

"Thirty K," the guy repeated, "give or take a couple. I'll accept stocks, bonds, traveler's checks"—he was having fun now—"a new bow thruster for my thirty-meter—"

And that was when Margo had saved his ass, he told Aisha, who propped herself up on her elbow like this was the part she wanted to hear about. This classy-looking woman who stood up and ring-tossed a necklace down on the table in front of the bozo. Sandy had noticed her earlier in the evening, tight black dress, super-short hair, maybe available if it weren't for this girl with—what? cerebral palsy?—this girl who was always at her side. Who was even now staring at him with her pale, strained face. The guy looked at the necklace like a grenade had just landed in front of him. The classy-looking woman had turned to Sandy with that hard face he would come to know.

"You *can* beat this asshole, right?" she said.

So there had been no other way out. He had stood up and the whole room had broken into a buzz. They had loaded into their cars (the Brit lady on the back of the Indian, it turned out), and because there was no way to get into the Casino now, had driven out to the high school, where there were lighted courts, but of course it was two in the morning and the lights were on a timer so they had to maneuver some of the cars alongside until their headlights lit the courts. Half a dozen racquets came out of various trunks. Someone popped a new can of balls.

And what could he say? He had destroyed the guy. There was a big difference between a drunk forty-year-old former Division III player and a drunk thirty-one-year-old international touring pro even if the international touring pro was playing left-handed in his stocking feet and lacked the killer instinct, you tuxedoed douchebag. The guy had a big first serve that was a bitch returning left-handed, but it became clear after the first couple of games that everything else he had was strictly 4.5. And once the freaky nerves were gone, Sandy had started totally messing with the guy, moving him back and forth along the baseline and then drop-shotting him, moon-balling him just for fun, spinning the ball, cutting it, slicing it like a Harlem Globetrotter. He even pulled out this hilarious serve he'd learned from Jimmy Arias. He'd toss the ball up and swing at it like he normally would do, only he'd miss it—a total whiff!—and then all in the same motion, just when the ball was about to touch the ground, underhand it right into the service box. Only he had to do this right-handed, but by then nobody cared, not even the bozo douchebag who Sandy had to admit had carried the whole thing off better than he would have expected.

When it was over, they met at the net. The guy was holding out the key to the Indian, telling him something about how it had a suicide shifter so he'd have to watch out. The Brit lady was saying she'd always hated the bloody thing anyway.

"Forget it," Sandy had said. "You're drunk. I'm drunk. Everybody's drunk. Forget it."

But as soon as he'd said it he knew it was the wrong thing. Margo took the key and threw it into his chest, gave him a look like don't be a loser. (Cripes, he said to Aisha—he said things like that: cripes, geez, smart aleck—it was part of being a Southern Gentleman—cripes, it was like he couldn't get anything right that night!) He'd at least had the good sense to wait until people were out of earshot before he admitted he didn't know how to ride a motorcycle. Margo had rolled her eyes, held out her hand for the key, and Sandy had followed her home in her SUV with the thin, intense-looking girl sitting silently beside him in the passenger seat.

And that's how he'd met Margo. That's how it'd all started, if "all" was a word he could use for an affair that was more off than it was on. Or rather, an affair that was only on when Margo said it was—a phone call, a meeting place, and then nothing for days. Or months, as it turned out once he'd left Newport that past September. Not a text or a phone call or an e-mail the whole winter while he was down south at Saddlebrook.

In truth, he didn't know why he had come out to the house that morning. He hadn't intended to, had arrived back in Newport a couple of days earlier with the thought that he'd let sleeping dogs lie. But something about being back on the grass courts at the Casino had triggered the whole feel of that past summer, and he had found himself that morning gunning the racing-red 1946 Indian Chief past the Gilded Age mansions along Bellevue, in and out of Ochre Point, and then down to Windermere, where he'd entered the key code Margo had given him the previous summer ("Let's keep this to ourselves, eh?"), just to see if she'd had it changed. When the wrought-iron gate slid open, he'd guided the Indian down the sweeping moss-covered drive, in between the lovely old oaks and ashes, into view of the great house with its beautifully weathered shingles and century-old brick, its seven chimneys, countless windows, and the squared-off hedge of the maze on the south lawn that led down to the ocean. The house had the look of being taken out of mothballs, carpets draped over the knee wall on the veranda and the whine of vacuum cleaners through the open windows. A groundskeeper, caretaker, whatever he was, came out of somewhere and asked could he help, sir, and Sandy had pulled out their names—Tom and Margo du Pont, the girl Alice—so that he wouldn't seem quite the interloper he felt. He was swinging a leg back over the Indian when he saw her—Alice's friend, the black woman with the dreadlocks, the jewelry maker or sculptor or whatever she was: Aisha, wasn't it?—coming out of the Orangery down the lawn where she had her studio. She had called to him, waved like they were old friends, and he had left the Indian on its kickstand under the porte cochere and started across the thick turf toward her.

She had on this tight sleeveless leotard thing and he was in a tank top and shorts and they were, he thought, right from the start conscious of their naked limbs. The du Ponts were still in New York, she had told him, weren't due until the ninth. She herself had only arrived yesterday, was still unpacking. And he, was he back teaching at the Casino Tennis Club for the summer?

For half an hour they had strolled under the trees, past the glass-walled Orangery, and down toward the ocean, where the great sweeping lawn began to turn into ribbons of rock, and where a fence running the length of the Cliff Walk kept the tourists on the other side of things. In the distance was Alva Vanderbilt's red-and-green Chinese teahouse perched absurdly over the pounding surf, and farther out on the bay the sleek white sails and scudding clouds, and in their faces the salty, cool, expensive breeze. When they reached the boxwood maze on the south side of the lawn—the house was famous for it—they stopped at its entrance as if feeling each other out, and then Aisha had gone in and Sandy had followed. But he kept getting lost in the maddening thing, turning first into this dead end and then that, until finally with a laugh she had taken his hand and guided him toward the maze's center.

They were catching up, was what they were doing, even though they had only been in each other's company—what, maybe half a dozen times the previous summer? He remembered they'd talked once, bonding over their both being blue-collar kids who had gone to fancy colleges on scholarship, Duke for Sandy and Vassar for Aisha. And he remembered something Margo had once said that had seemed to imply that Aisha was being semi-supported by Alice, the thin girl who was an heiress or something. "Semi" because she really did design and make her own jewelry. He'd even seen her work in one of the chic Newport stores. Strictly upscale, he'd gathered.

Aisha had made a few sly comments about Margo like she knew what had been going on the previous summer and wanted him to know that she knew—but it was okay, *she* wouldn't tell. She was small—maybe five-one or -two—but her parts all fit tightly together the way they did sometimes with small women so that there was a quickness and a brightness and an athletic ease about her. Her dreadlocks had this lovely way of brushing across her shoulder blades as she walked. And then there was this overbite she had that struck Sandy—maybe he was just being generous, falling into the mood—as cute. Her skin was dark enough he couldn't quite make out the tattoo that ran up the inside of her arm. (Snake? Dragon?) From time to time as they talked she gazed up at him with a look he knew.

And so it was that when they entered the Orangery (she'd asked if he could help her move the oxygen and acetylene tanks) and she'd turned to him as soon as they were inside the door and lifted herself onto her toes and kissed him on the lips, he had said to himself, *Well, okay, here we go.* She had made room for them on the little narrow bed that was set against one glass wall and they had fallen onto the cold sheets in the living part of the studio and the whole time he had tried to make out just what her tattoo was. A mermaid, he finally decided. Only instead of a fish's it had a serpent's body that started in a coil down near her wrist and ran up the inside of her forearm until it turned into the breasts and neck and face of a woman. *You're beautiful!* he heard her whisper under him more than once. *I can't stand you being so beautiful!* He leaned his head over and kissed the mermaid's tiny lips, her breasts, the coil of her tail. Outside they could hear the aluminum rattle of a ladder against the side of the big house. There were the cries of seagulls coming in at the door, and the sound of the surf. And when once he lifted her on top of him—she was so small!—he could see the blue sky through the glass roof.

And then it was over and he had—lovemaking had this unfortunate effect on him—he had started telling her about the state he was in. Which he was still doing (though she'd pulled on her top, was calling Manny's Gourmet Pizza).

Truth was, the girl—Alice—made him nervous. It wasn't just the cerebral palsy—as those things went he figured hers was pretty mild—but driving her home in the SUV that first night he found it hard to talk to her, even just to say something the way you do because you're in a car with a stranger. She answered his questions in a manner that seemed to border on rudeness—her name was *Alice*; she'd *grown up* in Newport; she didn't *do* anything—sitting kind of crumpled into herself, not looking at him when he glanced across at her. And there was that wrist of hers, bent and useless, lying in her lap like a strangled kitten. She told him where to turn, and when they got to Windermere directed him up the drive between the massive tree trunks to the porte cochere, where Margo stood with the Indian on its kickstand. There were lanterns behind her on the side of the house, all soft and Gilded Age looking, the brick and granite in shadowy repose, the ornate beams, the fluted copper downspouts. He hit the SUV's lights and shut the engine off, opened the door so the cab light went on.

And that's when he saw the scars, he told Aisha. (They had gone back outside, back onto the lawn to make sure the gate was open for the pizza truck.) Unmistakable, he said, and he made a slicing action along his wrists as if asking for confirmation. In the cab of the SUV he'd shot a look at the girl's face and from her expression he could tell that she'd seen him, she'd seen him see. He tried to act like he hadn't, but she kept her own eyes on him as if daring him to say something. Her whole manner was this mix of pain and humiliation and at the same time fierceness, resentment. They sat like that for a time. And then he did this thing, this Southern Gentleman thing. He reached out and placed his hands over her wrists and pressed. Nothing more than that, but it made her drop her gaze and soften into her seat. Half a minute went by—through the windshield he could see Margo striking the impatient fist-on-the-hip pose—and then he had taken his hands away and that had been that. They'd gotten out of the car. The girl had said good night and with her hitching gait gone inside, and Margo had driven him in the SUV to his hotel where, you know, things had happened. But hey, he said to Aisha now, he was right, wasn't he? Alice had tried to kill herself?

They were walking down the pebbled path that led toward the house, waiting for the trees to give way so that they might catch sight of the gate onto Bellevue. She didn't answer at first, kept her face forward. Some pickup trucks had shown up, and there were three or four ladders now against the exterior of the house and workmen retrieving lawn chairs and porch stuff from the carriage house. He had the thought that he had over-stepped, that the scars were there for anyone to see but you didn't talk about them. He was about to apologize, say he understood, change the sub-ject, but Aisha stopped walking, turned to him, and looked up into his face.

"I've known her for ten years," she said. "She's tried to kill herself three times to my knowledge. She can be very difficult. And very special. She's my best friend and I love her."

He had the good sense not to say anything. Perhaps because he couldn't tell whether he had just been granted access to some inner life of hers or warned away from it. He turned and let his eyes roam over the house on its crest, over the rich brick and the mossy shingles and the tiny leaded panes. The caretaker he'd first seen that morning stood a ways out from the house, supervising the workers.

"Sorry," he heard beside him, "that was a bit much."

He inclined his head slightly, touched her lightly at the small of her back. He knew how to say things with his body. She moved against him and for a minute they both looked up at the beautiful house coming awake in the spring sun.

"You ever been inside?" she asked, and when he shook his head: "C'mon, then."

So he followed her up the lawn. And while they walked she said she didn't want him to get the wrong idea about Alice, she didn't want him to think that she was a total basket case or something. Because she was really smart, super-smart, and she could be really funny. She had this really dark sense of humor. Like after the wrist business, lying around sighing like a Southern belle, calling the bandages her corsages.

"Funny in her Alice way," she said. "Which I guess means dark and manic-depressive and suicidal. But funny all the same. Wally, my man!" she called out as they passed the caretaker. "Keep an eye out for Manny's, yeah?"

The caretaker did this little salute thing. One of the workmen watched them—watched Aisha in her tight top and her bare legs and her ropey dreadlocks—as they went up the wide granite steps onto the wooden veranda that wrapped around the ocean face of the house.

"And there you go," Aisha said, turning and making a sweeping gesture at the view. He turned and looked too.

Well! He'd been around the rich before. And the famous. Had hung out in the players' lounge with Agassi and Hewitt, after the Italian Open had been invited to stay in a villa outside Lucca. But this was something different. This was like you owned the summer itself—the breeze, the salt-spray roses, the sailboats like props out on the sparkling water. He said "wow!" and Aisha said "yeah" and then she was telling him he was in luck because she'd been a student docent at the Vassar College art museum and was a pro at giving tours of stuff you wanted but couldn't have, but all he could really see, all he could really take in was the deep ease of the house and the grounds, the sense he had that under the rich patina of the shingles and the dark brick there was a century of life that was as good as it got. Lime rickeys, he remembered some of the women—his middle-aged students—ordering at the Casino in their post-lesson lassitude. They would invite him to join them and he would have his stupid Sam Adams. This was the life they had: lime rickeys and Adirondack chairs, the sound of children playing croquet and a date later in the afternoon to go riding, or play mixed doubles, or go sailing out on the bay. And yet even as he was thinking it, *feeling* it, some voice in him was saying, *What rot!* Hadn't the house seen a poor girl try to kill herself? Not to mention Margo and Tom's marriage. And yet standing there he couldn't quite shake the feeling that *here* one might give up trying to *be* something, that the house and the

workmen, the warm breeze and the rich brick would vouch for one—
would *authenticate* one—and one could let go, a poor schmuck of a has-
been (never-was?) tennis player could let go and simply let life *be*.

"The seagulls are on retainer," Aisha was saying. She was standing
along the knee wall looking out at the gliding birds. "Like me," she said,
turning back to him, "just part of the picture."

For the next half hour they strolled through the lower floors of the
house, into the library and the drawing room, down into the massive
kitchens in the basement, rooms with brick floors and stone walls where
there'd once been servants and which now were mostly closed off except
for one remodeled space with its Frigidaire and its Amana range looking
like middle-class stowaways. He got the story of Aisha and Alice at college
together, the Thanksgiving Aisha had come down to Newport for the first
time, the first time she'd met Tom (how to get her nineteen-year-old black
scholarship ass married to him? she said with a laugh), the first suicide attempt (horse tranquilizer, stomach pump), the European tour she and Alice had gone on the summer before their senior year—(here she got a
bottle from the wine cellar, poured them each a glass)—the money Alice's
mother had discreetly sent her way, the travel, the visits, the art openings,
the vacations.

"It took me a while to realize they saw me as a kind of employee," she
said, throwing him a look like maybe the Casino's International Touring
Pro understood what she meant. "A paid companion, au pair girl, attendant, chaperone, nurse, whatever."

They had just come back into the massive hall with its coffered ceiling,
Aisha carrying the wine bottle by its neck. Somewhere above them a vacuum cleaner was running.

"At first I thought it was just because they loved having me around. I
was the college friend." She stopped and leaned back against the newel
post. Behind her, the wide stairway climbed with its dark wood and bur-
gundy carpet to the second floor. There was a workman on a ladder on the
other side of the big window on the landing. "The daughter wanted to go
to Europe. She wanted a friend to go with her. The friend's father was a
pipe fitter at the Bath Iron Works and couldn't afford it. Gosh, what the

heck, let *us* pay your way! And I was such an innocent, twenty years old, I thought everybody just loved me and wanted me around."

"It could've been both," Sandy said in his nice-guy way. "They could like you *and* want you to help take care of her."

She peered at him as if maybe he was putting her on, then crossed to him and kissed him on her tiptoes. "You're sweet," she said like it was a quaint personality trait. She filled his glass, gave him another quick kiss, and crossed to the window that looked out onto the porte cochere. There was a window seat there with a tufted cushion and she sat and pulled her bare legs up under her. Through the wall they could hear the rough sounds of the storm windows coming off the dining room windows.

"You know it was Alice who put up the money that night, don't you?" she said after some time had passed.

"Alice?" he said and shook his head like that wasn't possible. And then: *Wait, what?*

"The drama was all Margo," she said, "but the necklace itself was Alice's. It was her money on the line."

"She told you? Alice told you about that night?"

"She said she felt sorry for you."

He felt a sudden heat rise from his neck into his cheeks.

"She also said you were the most beautiful man she'd ever seen."

He had an idea he must look silly—injured vanity, a suicidal girl feeling sorry for him—but he had the good sense to keep quiet, keep his face expressionless. Aisha fixed her eyes on him, maybe looking to see how he took it, and then with a toss of her dreadlocks turned from him and looked out the window at the Indian on its kickstand.

"You have to keep this quiet," she said after a minute. "You and me, I mean. Do you understand?"

He raised his wineglass to his lips, drank from it cool as a cucumber. "You mean because of Margo?"

"Yes." And she tracked him to see if he understood. "I mean if you want to see me again."

"I'm not even sure it's still on with Margo," he said a little stiffly. "And if it is, I can break it off. She'd hardly care, I think."

She shook her head with this sorry amusement and stood up. "These people," she said, putting her wineglass down on the wide sill of the window, "*they* say when things are over." And not convinced he understood, taking a step toward him, she added: "She could make things difficult for me. My situation here." And again, did he get it? "For you, too. At the Casino."

He pursed his lips—Margo was on the Casino board of directors—and then bowed his head as if conceding.

"And then there's Alice. I don't want her to feel—" And she searched for what she meant, and then said simply: "I don't want her to feel bad."

She had crossed to him and set herself small and barefoot before him. She took the wineglass out of his hand, set it down, and with the edge of her palm caressed where his hair grew out of his temple. "*Sandy Alison,*" she murmured like his name meant something to her. She lifted herself on her toes and said something in his ear, which made him direct his gaze up to the big triple window on the stairway landing where the workman could see in from his ladder.

"It's all right," she whispered, her breath exploding in his ear. "They're on the *outside*. We're on the *inside*."

☞ Summer 1896 ☜

As Franklin told Mrs. Belmont—the former Mrs. Vanderbilt—(and the dear monster thought he was joking, of course) he liked to pretend to be looking at the young girls when in fact he was looking at the young men, their silly suitors, dressed in striped jackets and straw boaters, and panting like hounds in heat. Dogs were so much more attractive than cats, didn't she find?

She didn't know *what* she found, she said. But she was sure he was very, very bad!

They were drinking lime rickeys (he'd managed to get some gin in his), sitting outdoors at the Casino overlooking the grass courts where some inexplicable contest involving racquets and balls was going on. There was a net that kept getting in the way. Why on *earth* did they not simply *remove* it? he kept asking. Well, of course he *knew* . . . but he liked to pretend he was at a loss in matters of the world, posing questions to Mrs. Belmont and Mrs. Auld concerning who was serving whom, eh? and who was an ace at love and who was a deuce, in ways they chose to find delightfully absurd. It was part of being a lapdog, which was his most recent sobriquet in the scandal sheets. *Mrs. Richard Auld was seen at the Horticultural Society taking Mrs. Oliver Hazard Perry Belmont's lapdog out for a walk. Might there be canine jealousy a-brewing along Fifth Avenue?* But he was a lapdog with a bit of a bite, he liked to think. A cheerful, brown-eyed, wet-nosed, tail-wagging, lamppost-peeing lapdog who when you weren't looking might take a piece out of your hide.

"Marriage!" cried Mrs. Auld. They had been talking of this the last half hour. Indeed, the last six months. "*That* will cure you of this wickedness!"

He was sure it would, he told them.

They were sitting up in the Horseshoe Piazza, which at least had the advantage of being above the damned sea of parasols so you might actually catch a glimpse of the lawn tennis. Which was to say, a glimpse of the young men in their white pants and their bare wrists and their hair falling about their flushed temples. It was one of the perquisites of being a lapdog. One was given the best seats. One was invited to Newport for the summer season, invited uptown for winter evenings (even though one's own apartments were down around Fourth Street, below which *nobody* descended), and there was the occasional tour, some Mediterranean sailing, quantities of foie gras and salmon terrine. Woof, woof.

"For purposes of efficiency," Mrs. Belmont said—she was having a high time; plotting his engagement was a favorite divertissement; indeed he sometimes thought she was using him to reestablish her precedence after her own shocking divorce the previous winter—"we might divide the candidates into widows and debutantes. The two rough categories will serve. Which would you prefer, dear?"

"Oh, a widow by all means," he answered. "Someone wrinkled and quite desiccated. Then I needn't water her."

It was safe for them to be seen with him. Because he was seen everywhere, with everyone. He was handsome, and witty, and sunny, and well dressed, and he always knew the right thing to say. Even when the right thing was wrong, if it was *he* who was saying it—he with his fair color and his ready smile and his slight, elegant frame—it *became* the right thing. Even TOWN TOPICS had remarked upon it. Mr. Franklin Drexel, they said—this was before the lapdog business—Mr. Franklin Drexel was the Skeleton Key of Fifth Avenue, for he opened all locks.

Though the sort of locks they seemed to mean in their snide, vulgar, insinuating, insulting way were most certainly not the sort he opened.

It was not lost on Mr. Franklin Drexel that his days as a lapdog were numbered. He was thirty-three. The mange was beginning to show itself in the form of little gray hairs which this past winter he had begun to color with a light tan shoe polish but which would eventually be too numerous to disguise. He knew who he was. He was the boyish, handsome type. He wasn't the distinguished, gray-templed type. Nor was he likely to effect the transmogrification from the one to the other with any grace. It would be a slow slide, he knew, but sometime before he was forty he would have ceased to appear in TOWN TOPICS or any of the other scandal sheets. His invitations would slip from Mrs. Belmont to Mrs. James to Mrs. Beaulieu and then to the fringe knocking on the doors of the great Newport cottages, and then to those who weren't even coming up the walk and who, for a time, would consider him a catch—Mr. Franklin Drexel and his stories of drinking lime rickeys with Alva Belmont and Irene Auld at a Casino outing—but then those invitations too would cease to make their way down to Fourth Street. He was not a fool. And he kept his eyes open. And this he knew: the social blasphemy that was charmingly risqué in an impish *jeune homme* would prove coarse and repugnant in a man of middle age. The impish *jeune homme* must take care to land feet first on Fifth Avenue before he became an out-at-the-collar *vieillard*.

"I am not quite sure, my dear Franklin, what you mean when you say you would not need to water a desiccated widow. Would she not need watering more than a young girl?"

But he had a few years yet in which to turn around. His tailor had yet to increase the measure of his waist. No one knew of the shoe polish. He had time to appraise just what the best *carte de visite* might be, the entrée that would not be subject to revocation by the whims of bored women or a slight distension of the jowls. But there should be no mistaking that such an entrée needed to be secured. He had neither money nor name—or at least not enough of either. He had rather his looks and his wit and the studied luck of having charmed the right women at the right moment, but all that would evaporate with time and familiarity. If the thing needed to be done, he sadly realized, *now* was the time to do it. Now when he was the *Register*'s lapdog—petted and fondled and fed.

"If called upon to water a wife," he responded with a dignified elevation of his chin, "I will of course do so. I am a man of duty, as you both know. Indeed the name of Drexel is acknowledged as a synonym for Duty all along the Atlantic Seaboard. I insist you stop laughing. Point me in the direction of a lonesome Lily and I will show you—I will souse her with spray! She will beg you to rescue her!—though really I must repeat that I should much prefer, for my boutonnière, a dried Daisy."

And then there were the men—the husbands. They had yet to concern themselves with him. He was their wives' plaything—an embellishment of Newport and not of New York—and it was the wives who ruled Newport. But should he rise in their field of vision so that they inquired about him, they would—at the very least!—come to know him as a remittance man. And it was only one step from being found out as a man who was kept by his family with a monthly check to being seen as a cad or bounder or worse. He could not afford to have the men communicate a view of him as a fortune hunter to the women. His campaign of deft parries, his witty deflection of the topic of marriage, his careful sculpting of the Free Young Man Unwilling to Submit to the Connubial Yoke would be lost on the men. They would cut through that particular Gordian knot with one swift slice. He knew men. Indeed, he knew men *and* women. It was one of the compensations for being who he was.

"Or perhaps, after all," he mused, "I should prefer a Dollar Princess. That is, if I could elbow aside the English Barons and the Italian Counts."

And as soon as he'd said it, he knew he had gone too far. Mrs. Belmont let her eyes rest fully on him. She had herself famously succeeded in marrying her daughter Consuelo to the Duke of Marlborough the previous November. It was a subject that could only be spoken of as a testament to her power and her status. Not to her wealth. Any suggestion of the Duchess of Marlborough as a Dollar Princess—and she was, after all, the Dollar Princess *ne plus ultra*—was beyond the pale. But as he had so often done before when he had gone too far, he found the best route out was to go even further.

"Or have you used up all the Dollar Princesses?" he asked. And when Mrs. Belmont continued to fix him with her gaze: "Surely you have one in your pocket or hiding under the bed. I should like a wife who had the good sense to hide under the bed. Indeed, I should set her up with reading material and a pot of tea. Oh, *now* what are they doing?" he cried, turning back to the court below as the spectators burst into applause and one of the young men leapt the net. He made an exasperated face and threw his palms in the air as if the world were just too much—didn't they agree?—and then rose and held his white linen arm out for Mrs. Belmont to take, and the dear monster, with a sigh at the utter impossibility of the dear young man, took it. And then he held his other arm out for Mrs. Auld and the three of them made their way along the curving piazza down the steps onto the grass where under its parasols and straw boaters the *beau monde* milled and observed itself.

He had a welcoming word for everyone, and a ready smile, and when the time was right he left the two women to fetch them each an ice. He allowed himself a bit of loitering—breathing a little easier now and keeping an eye on the men retiring into the Casino. He greeted those he knew, smiled at the young girls who smiled back at him, watched the hubbub surrounding the tennis players.

After a quarter hour, laden with ices, he rejoined the women only to find they had, in his absence, conjured a desiccated widow.

"You know Ellen Newcombe, I think?" said Mrs. Belmont, and indeed he did. He had made Mrs. Newcombe's acquaintance this past winter, he believed. He smiled and offered her his ice, made it seem as though he had known she would be there and had brought the extra ice just for her.

She was dressed smartly in a bicycling costume, a lavender affair with an almost masculine shirtwaist, leg-o'-mutton sleeves, and blousy Turkish bloomers that gathered high on the shin. She was thin and though the line of her was, he supposed, not unpleasant to look at, she had, he thought, an unfortunate face. It was a face that somehow managed to look permanently in pain and at the same time hopeful of release—rather, he thought, like a mistreated dog. He supposed the pain had something to do with the loss of her husband three years earlier. He supposed, too, that he was not the most generous arbiter of woman's faces. But if nothing else, it was a face that had yet to realize it was too old for the bicycling dress.

"You will not tell us, my dear Mrs. Newcombe, that you rode that preposterous machine of yours all the way in from Windermere?"

She certainly *would* tell them. She found bicycle riding marvelously invigorating. Were it not for her young children, she would utterly dispense with her carriage. Did not Mr. Drexel share her love of bicycle riding?

Mr. Drexel did not, but said he did. *Children?* he thought.

They talked of the things they were wont to talk about, of the highlights of the coming season, of the Hobbyhorse Quadrille of the past winter which had not yet lost its piquancy, and of course of Mrs. Belmont's renovations at Belcourt. She was inundated with architect's elevations, she said, with marble and drapery samples. Mrs. Auld didn't know *how* her friend kept her head above things, but she was a whirlwind of energy, they all knew. Indeed, the whirlwind had in ten months managed to divorce her husband, to weather the scandal that that divorce had caused, to get her daughter married to the Ninth Duke of Marlborough, and then herself married to the renowned horseman Mr. Oliver Hazard Perry Belmont (whose father had been a Jewish banker, but never mind that). She was now mistress of two of the most famously lavish cottages in Newport, her own Marble House, which had been a birthday present from her first husband, and her new husband's sixty-room Belcourt. The latter somewhat infamously had stables for its ground floor. Franklin had not seen them himself, but he could imagine they were no ordinary stables.

"Alva, I think you are only happy when you are up to your elbows in mortar," said Mrs. Auld.

"I like to build things," Mrs. Belmont said with a firmness to her round face—it always put Franklin in mind of a pugilist's. "I like to make things happen." And she looked at Franklin as if to gauge his understanding.

"If I had a calling," he remarked, "a calling to *miss*, I mean, it would be that of an architect. Don't you think I would make a fine architect, Mrs. Newcombe?"

"*You*, my dear," Mrs. Auld interrupted, "were made to *inhabit* beautiful homes, not to build them."

"*Ah!*" he said with a sad inward smile as if this—alas!—were indeed his fate.

Some others came over and the conversation turned general. From time to time Franklin thought he could feel the woman's eyes on him, the woman for whom he would have to forge his charm into a trap if he wanted her Sixty-second Street mansion, and her bank account, and—delightful development!—this Windermere she spoke of. He tried to hold himself as he thought a potential husband ought to look. Clean line about the jaw, shoulders square, serpent's tail well hidden. His ankles were beginning to sweat with the effort when he heard his name called over the tops of heads.

"I say, Drexel! Come have a smoke!"

He smiled an excuse to Mrs. Auld, to Mrs. Belmont, to Mrs. Newcombe. "The fairer sex calls," he said with a polite bow, and then with just a tint of intimacy: "Charmed to see you again, Mrs. Newcombe."

"Don't forget tea," Mrs. Belmont reminded him. She gave him her own meaningful look. "You're coming of course."

"Madam," he said as he backed away.

"At the *old* house! At Marble House!"

A tactical stroke, he thought as he turned and started across the smooth grass toward the Casino, not to appear too eager to drape his dressing gown over Mrs. Newcombe's newel post.

⤳ Summer 1863 ⤳

~For my twentieth birthday Father presented me with this lovely bound notebook. He has written on the inside leaf in his formidable script *"From Henry James, Sr. to Henry James, Jr. May you make upon these pages an impression of the person."*

I will try, though I think the person whose impression these pages show may not be to Father's liking.

For I have taken to "hanging about" the hotels this summer watching the leisure population. As there is a sharp divide between the Newport summer people and those who live year-round, there is no need to worry that someone of Mother's or Father's acquaintance will observe me. In that sense I am a spy, loitering about the hotel piazzas, just another idling young man who has managed to avoid this terrible war, one whose head is perhaps slightly too large and whose stature is slightly too small (and there's the unfortunate stammer which he does his best to hide), but with a touch of elegance, standing around and observing the world.

And what I see I jot down in this notebook (I shall be taken for a journalist!), ideas for characters, *situations*, complexities, the melting look of Miss So-and-So as she gazes out from under the brim of her bonnet.

Here's a budding novelist's question: Can the *appearance* of people suggest their reality? Do we "read" the psychological in the tilt of a lady's fan, in a pair of spectacles askew upon the bridge of the nose? And could one let those appearances, the dress, conversation, postures of the Newport *beau monde*, suggest their inner lives, and so make of them subjects that one might "work up" in sketches or stories? If I am really to embrace the writer's life, might not such a Notebook serve as a fount into which one might dip one's pen time and again?

I must work up the nerve to inform Father that I shall not be returning to Cambridge in the fall. I can no longer pretend to be studying the Law. Odious enterprise!

~I have seen the young lady several times now and feel I must note her here. (Why one person gives us an impression and another does not is a mystery, but so it is.) What is perhaps most striking about her is her height. For she is very tall, taller than most men I suppose, certainly taller than poor Harry James! And she is thin, without the usual local places of volume I believe it is considered desirable for young women to possess. She has a sleekness and a bearing most striking. And since the first time I saw her was on the archery field at the Atlantic, she had I thought a look rather of the goddess Diana, a regal chastity that was suggestive. She was a novice at the sport, yet she was able to draw back the bowstring and let loose her arrow with considerable determination.

This is the subject I have spun about her. The business of Newport, it is said, is flirtation. And I have heard it suggested (it is a conversational shuttlecock among Newport residents) that there are young women of the working middle classes who save year-round in order to stay at one of the finer hotels that they might be "thrown in" with a better class of people. The hope then is that she will bewitch some man whose wealth, while not of the first rank of course, would be beyond what she might expect had she stayed home in Hartford or Trenton. We have here a game of presentation and withholding, of infatuation and discovery, a social campaign just on the perimeter of malfeasance.

So what is the necessary *matériel* for such a campaign?

First of all, the young woman must be beautiful. For that is what she is "selling." Secondly, she must be able to dress well enough so that her antecedents, for a three- or four-week period at any rate, are hidden. (This is no mean challenge, for the denizens of the hotels are forever changing: morning clothes, riding habits, clothes for tennis and croquet, and of course gowns to be worn for supper followed by dancing or a concert.) Thirdly, she must be able to converse intelligently, and to have enough sense to smile charmingly when the conversation turns to matters beyond her, and her accent, if she has one, must be part of her charm, and not reveal her father as a shopkeeper. But most of all (it bears repeating) she must have a physical splendor that would make a widower (who ought to know better), or a young second son (who oughtn't), care only about having her, and quickly.

The whole enterprise is predicated upon the glow of her beauty prompting a proposal which, later on, when the antecedents *are* known, there will be no withdrawing.

And those are the brushstrokes I painted her with, observing her, first in the ladies' archery, where her posture was superb and her sleek flanks on display; and then the next afternoon on the veranda, listening to her converse with a woman who appeared to be her mother (I shall make her an aunt), the spy sitting at a little wicker table pretending to read the *Revue des Deux Mondes*, she standing at the railing overlooking the gardens.

Perhaps I might make her a dressmaker as a way of accounting for her fashionable clothes, and ground the conceit by having her take apart imported French gowns so that she can use the pieces for patterns (revealing detail!). However it is managed, the writing must be charged throughout with the atmosphere of the Newport summer, with the unreality of society at the hotels, the meringue of artificial talk against the ruddy glow of hidden motives, and for the girl and her accomplice-aunt, the awareness that the clock is ticking.

~Today she was in the company of a rather vulgar young boy I take to be her brother and whose name, if I heard aright, is Harry. Odd coincidence.

Question: to have names which signify (as Mr. Hawthorne does), or to allow them to be "merely" real as in life?

The thing is to *see* them, to see one's characters in all their complexity, all their blind groping, engaged as they must be in the hubbub of connection and courtship and "getting on" where clarity lies remote, and to represent them without stint, yet without embellishment, to have them feel the beat of their hearts though they may not know for what their hearts beat. The *feeling* must be all theirs, the *clarity* all mine!

Ruskin says that the greatest thing an artist can do is to see something and to tell what he sees simply and honestly, and that to do so is poetry, prophecy, and religion, all in one.

As to the subject of the designing dressmaker: I must endeavor to understand (that is to say, to *imagine*) the condition of her heart as well as the magnitude of her ambition. It will not be enough to present her merely as a "climber." The reader must be made to understand the forces that impel her, the mother's resentment, the father's discontent, the jealousy she feels for the Washington Square women she attends in the shop, their slighting treatment of her, the beauty she catches glimpses of when she travels to the wealthy homes to fix a hem or take in a bodice, and which she dreams of having about her always.

~Now, after some several days of spying (I shall be taken for a pickpocket!), here is my sense of the Newport hotels and their clientele, along with some details that may prove useful, for my story's setting must have the perfume of the real world.

My Diana and her mother are staying at the Ocean House on Bellevue Avenue (the extension of what used to be called Jews Street), which is the most massive of all the new hotels with its four stories and three hundred rooms and its full-length verandas at both the first and third stories festooned with gothic tracery. The Ocean is accounted as catering to the best clientele (one day I saw delivered in wagons about thirty trunks, one of which, I heard one of the draymen exclaim in his Irish burr, was the size of a Dingle shanty). They sound a Chinese gong for supper, and afterwards the musicians of the Germania Society play while the guests promenade in their fashionable dress. They have a large saloon for concerts, and a wide central hall 250 feet long where balls are held and from which the servants take their name of "hall boys." Perhaps too elegant (and expensive) for my dressmaker.

The Atlantic House, of the style called Greek Revival (though of wood and white paint so bright it blinds you in the sunlight), is said to have rivaled the Ocean for elegance and the fashion of its clientele, but since the bombardment of Fort Sumter and the loss of Annapolis it is taken over by the Naval Academy.

In contrast to the stately balls held at the Ocean, the Aquidneck House offers more democratic "hops." Each morning a wagon appears outside after the breakfast meal with a sign announcing it is "For the Fishing Ground Direct." They seem to hire only Negro servants, and the sight of their dark skin against the white of their collars and cuffs produces an effect. Notable for its indoor roller-skating rink, which might serve as a most original setting.

Behind all of these great hotels there are the little alleys and *couloirs* that act as service lanes. In these are found the stables and carriages houses, quarters for servants and hotel personnel.

Among those who live year-round in Newport there is some talk that these great hotels, though they are not yet twenty years old, are in danger of losing the very best of their clients to the private houses that are being built up and down the Avenue. The war has calmed that building paroxysm, though even now one can hardly walk anywhere in town without the sound of hammering or of a planing mill incessantly in one's ears.

~Observed today the Huntress at the hunt. For my Diana was much engaged with a young gentleman of the barber's block type, so fashionably turned out and shaven was he! He wore his hair parted in the middle *à la* Fremont, and had a cane with silver embellishments which he used to point at this and that, illustrating his conversation like an impresario, and when once I was close enough to see, a thin little mustache that looked like some theatrical assistant had painted it on with a rigger brush. They were of a party that left the Ocean House to walk down to the harbor, where there was to be a steam organ concert from on board one of the great yachts at anchor. There were other such parties from the other hotels. They went out to the end of Da Silva's wharf, talking and laughing and heedless of their finery amidst the workaday iron and casks and the pier toughs watching them. I followed at first at some distance, and then as the crowd gathered, ventured closer. The mother-aunt was there, as was the brother (about twelve years old, I think), and altogether some hundred or so music lovers to provide me paling from behind which to observe.

I jotted some notes of his manner toward my dressmaker: his way of inclining solicitously toward her as they walked; his placing of his hand behind her back (but never touching her); his way of being aware of the figure he cut by such gallantries; his taking the liberty of pointing the tip of his cane first at one of her shoes, then at the other, illustrating some witticism (to which she lifts her chin in lovely renunciation!); the carnation in his gray lapel, the silver sleeve-links, the way the white uppers of his camp shoes flashed out now and then from under his trouser cuffs; and always about his person a look that he knew just what he did, and what effect it was intended to produce, for (he seemed always to be saying) was not one fortunate to be invited to partake of the luxury of his manner?

As to the steam organ, Balzac has none such! It sounded a most burlesque note: the wind whipping the wheezing music to and fro, and the laughing, blabbing crowd. All quite in contrast to the blue of the sky and the harbor dotted with yachts whose candy-colored streamers winked in the wind, and beyond, the sun-flecked bay melting into the horizon.

⇀ Spring 1778 ↽

I went this morning to Pettibone's Wharf that in my capacity as Master of Genl Pigot's spies I might view the maps. A detachment from the Hessians was pulling up the planking of the Wharf next over. I was lately informed the Army needs 400 cord a week. At this rate there will not be a House or Tree standing on the Island by the end of Summer.

Indeed the British Army has gone about the Destruction of Newport with no want of Enthusiasm. What was Twelvemonth past a lovely prospect has suffered an ignoble Devastation. Our chief Duty would seem to be to overawe and terrify the Inhabitants of this place, and by our Contempt to ruin their homes and their places of employ. When first we came it was said there were 9 thousands of Population and now that number is more than halved. And where there was Business and Commerce there is Inactivity and Rebellion. The Navy is anchored in the Harbour and there is no Merchant shipping, and the Chandlers & Coopers & Distillers & all the sundry other trades that depend upon the sea are Gutted & Ruined. 'Tis the Colonists' fault of course, this Blight, at least the fault of those who are disloyal. But all the same it is a sight to see this city that is reputed to be the most Comely of all the American Seaboard looking like a Drunkard in a ditch. Tho' the Superior Officers are billeted in lovely if quaint wooden houses along the Harbour and on the Point, the Fusiliers and other Reg^t of foot are otherwise Barracked wherever they may fit, in sugar Refineries, tallow-works, sail lofts, Warehouses & Distilleries all of which have fallen into disuse and are ill-treated by the troops. Houses that have come empty are dismantled for firewood, as are the Wharves, so that the face of the town appears as scarred from the Smallpox. The Redwood Library, which

I am led to believe is the first and most Elegant of its type in the whole Country, is plundered, its books taken, and Furniture scattered. Indeed the other night I saw Bradshaw lighting his Cigar with a page of Voltaire. The Churches & Meetinghouses, of which there are many, are taken over for Barracks & Hospitals. Even the Synagoge, again the first of its type in this country, is seized. All the Jews are fled, except Da Silva who shows no anger over the fate of his people's House. Tho' that may be but further Smoke on the Jew's part.

Leaving aside the merchant Aristocracy (of whom there is not one in five left in the town) the remnants are a Motley rabble of impudent boys, Irish teagues, Negroes and Molattoes, and brassy jack tars.

Tho' the Whores have stayed. 'Tis their Golden Age.

Mar 3

Fair. Wind SW. No birds seen yet except such as remain here for the Winter. I will make a hunt of it when the Spring birds come through, go out to Doubling Point and pretend I am back on the grounds of Clereford and my damned elder brother, the future Lord Stevens, the Victim of an unfortunate Accident.

Smithson very amusing this evening, says he is to blame for the Inaction of the Reg^t, says wherever he goes looking for War, he finds Peace. He is bad luck, he says, a regular Jonah. Pitch me overboard, fellows, he says, 'tis the only way.

Mar 4

Saw her today, a most Fortuitous meeting. Evidently the Gods of Love disport themselves even here in the midst of War.

It happened as I was coming down the Wooden planking of Thames Street in the company of Smithson and two or three of the others with whom we are Quartered. I paused for some Trifle, and when I looked up, who should be before me, just coming out of one of the Shops and looking herself Stricken at the sight of me, but the Jewess!

She was in the company of a Negroe Servant laden with Parcels, a boy whom I had seen about Da Silva's house, and who I took to be about her own Age. We recovered ourselves and asked Politely after each other, but it seemed to me we had each Betrayed ourselves, that as she inflames my Thoughts when I am away, so do I hers.

She with her Dark Jew's eyes and her exotic Complexion! No Devonshire Rose, she!

I left her with a promise to call upon her Father soon, voicing the Gallantry that even the Exigencies of War would not keep me from the Pleasure of her family's Hearth, and with such a look in my Eye as to have her know that these Social calls were but a Ruse that I might be yet again in her Company.

And all the time forbidding myself the lowering of my gaze to the Swell of her magnificent Bosom!

Mar 8

Tonight we had one of the Colonial rags which was full of news of Gen[l] Burgoyne's arrival in the eastern Massachusetts. Smithson expresses the opinion that Gentleman Johnny, having lost 1000 men at Saratoga and surrendered another 6000, should be feted by the Colonials. Says the Rebels have no General themselves so adept at assisting their Cause. Says Burgoyne ought to be placed over Washington, and look out then, boys, he says.

The surrendered Army is also come into Massachusetts, shorn of their Arms. The Newspaper makes a high time of calling it the "Convention Army," Burgoyne having insisted upon calling the terms of his Capitulation by that name instead of the Surrender it was. It is rumored he will be escorted here to Newport from where he is to sail on his parole to never return to the Americas. He will have to find some other War to lose.

Have not seen the Jewess since I recorded in these Pages our encouraging Colloquy four days ago. On the Chessboard we call this a Quiet move.

Mar 9

This afternoon in the Newport Cemetery the body of Corp[l] Whitcomb was interred without Ceremony, no Prayer allowed. I went and stood in the rain to make a show of it. Smithson is of the mind that Whitcomb is but the beginning if we do not move soon. The inaction of the Reg^t is its own worst Enemy, he says. How d'ye make a Noose, he says.

The rain froze as it fell.

In the late afternoon word came that the merchant Mr. Goldthwaite is found guilty of Insolence by the Garrison Court-Martial. He had publicly abused a Lieu^t Kersteman of the Engineers whose conduct the Court found had in no way warranted such Abuse and is so ordered to pay 5 pounds Sterling for the use of the Poor.

We had a good fire and smoked and had some Idle discussion of this, and of the late Sheep-stealing incident that led to the execution of three of the Colonists. Richards maintained that a sterner sentence was needed to which Smithson responded sterner than hanging? He meant the fine levied on Goldthwaite, Richards said, which was no punishment at all for a Slave-trading, rum-smuggling Merchant of this town. Insolence to a British officer was worse than sheep-stealing, the way he saw it. It is open Rebellion and ought to be dealt with as such.

The Colonies were as a Child to a Parent, I answered. One does not execute a Child for misbehaving.

If they be Children, Richards countered, yet they are children who have Cannon and Firearms.

I said then what I had been thinking of late, that the only Immoral action is to treat an Inferior as an Equal. All other actions if they be between Persons of adult Intellect and Power are moral, even those that Religions call immoral, or that the Courts call illegal. But to treat any Inferior with force or Guile or Cruelty or any other adult Manoeuvre, because one *can*, is to be guilty of the Immoral. Addison said he had never realized I was such a sentimental soul, to which all laughed, but I persisted. The only Immorality is to take advantage of an unequal Contest, I said, *that* and only that is immoral. To betray, trap, trick, gain the Advantage of, that is the Life we are engaged in and all who are of Age should quicken themselves and be on their Alarm. 'Tis a game of Chess, I maintained, equal Forces arrayed. Victory to the skilled.

Surely, the others objected, I did not mean that all actions as long as they be between those of Age are equally moral.

I said I did. I said we are Men, and have about ourselves our full Faculties. We know the moves of the Chessmen. We know their relative Strength & Weakness. We know 'tis a Game of feint & trap & capture. Let all be on their lookout.

Was it moral, in the playing of this game of Chess, to cheat? Smithson said as if he had caught me in an Illogic.

It was, I said. Indeed I said there was no such thing as cheating. Cheating was just another Tactick available to each side, dependent upon each side's Skill, to be used or discarded as the Position on the Board demanded.

And the whole time I had Da Silva in mind. For it is my Nature (and my Pleasure) that I must have an Opponent, and in this Godforsaken land it is the Jew who has sat down across the board from me. It is against him I strategize, against him I deploy my Pieces. His young daughter is but the luxuriant Prize!

Mar 10

Several letters have come today aboard the *Lark*. Mother tip-toes around the matter of the Scar on my throat. Asks in her roundabout way if I have been well, has the Melancholia returned? Says she has spoken in confidence to Doctor Edgerton who has informed her that such Ebbing & Flooding of Mood, and any Injury the Patient inflicts upon himself, are held to be the result of a Disturbance of the Soul due to inner moral Conflict. Asks delicately what inner moral Conflict I might have.

Damn my eyes but I should have told her I'd been in a Tavern fight!

That I am subject to these Fits with their great Upheavals of mood is but a Testimony to the Force of my Passions. I would not have it any other way. Yet there is a part of me that quakes still at the Memory. The Razor, the Rage, the Sinking, the slashing Madness: What was it?

Mar 11

Went finally to Da Silva's with my best Gentleman's manner only to find Judith out with the Negress Phyllis on some errand. Had to mask my Disappointment. Played Chess with the Jew and was somewhat irked to find him with a strong Kingside attack. Did he find this Symbolical? I pointedly asked, to which he just as pointedly laughed. Could not hold him off.

Afterwards he brought out his Port and as we drank and smoked he spoke some of his youth in Portugal and in the West Indies as he has done of late. I cannot imagine an English Jew so presuming. But I am at pains to present myself a tolerant soul. 'Tis a Gambit that I hope later to show he should not have accepted.

Interesting History of his family being of those Jews who were forced by the Papists to convert to the Roman Faith or face Persecution and likely Death. Indeed, he said, all the Jewish families of Newport, and they were many tho' they are nearly all now fled, were of this history of forced Conversion. Of these Marranos or Conversos, as they are variously called, many gave an outward show of Christianity but practiced their Judaical beliefs in secret. He told one story that was a legend in his town of the Inquisitor taking the Regent of Aveiro into the tower of that city to show him the Heretics that he lived amongst. When the Regent protested, the Inquisitor pointed out house after house, each a Marrano household, he said, Heretics from great-grandfather to babe, for you saw no smoke rising from any of their Chimneys, in spite of the cold, for the Jews have no fire on their Sabbath.

He had me understand that this was no new state, that his family had been Christian for two hundred years before he was born, that they had kept their Judaical practices in secret those two Centuries, that he was himself christened Sebastiao, tho' he bore the secret name Isaac. When I asked how he as a child understood these Strange things, by which I meant going to Church as a Christian and practicing these other ways at home, he said a child did not need to make Sense of things. The world just was, to a child, he said. And so he had been Sebastiao outside the house, and Isaac inside.

One other thing he said of interest, I remember now. He said he was taught to ignore the Tortured figure on the cross in his Romish church, and instead to pray to the Holy Ghost. For this was a way of performing an act of Devotion meaningful to his private self, while seeming to enact the

Worshipful motions of the larger world. Is this not the mind of a man steeped in Duplicity?

Marrano, of course, means pig in Spanish.

Mar 12

Played Chess, played Loo, slept, stared at my second-son face in the Glass.

I must wait a decent Interval before I go again to the Jew's, and content myself with the mere Memory of her Face & Figure.

Mar 15

Summoned the Negress Phyllis without anyone in Da Silva's household knowing. Brought her back to the room, gave her half a Crown and had her wake up the Snake and then put him well-exercised to bed. The damned one-eyed Fellow. I'd take a razor to *him* if I could.

When she was gone I sat and smoked and looked out the window at the Fleet. It was quiet & pretty, the Masts and Spars in the moonlight, and the forge-fires of the Engineers out on Goat Island. There was a Sloop coming in, its sails luffing as it came nearer the wind. Someone in the streets was singing *The Vicar of Bray*.

The Jewess is sixteen. Is she a Child or a Woman? She has a woman's body and a woman's look in her eye, but does that signify?

Mar 19

Took the bottle of Amontillado I won off Smithson and carried it (along with Smithson that he might prove a diversionary Tactick) to Da Silva's in the early evening. This time Judith was at home and we all sat in the drawing room with a good fire. Phyllis came in to set an Impromptu treat. The Negress is a skilled Actress and performed her Duties without giving me a notice.

Da Silva's house is one of the three or four best in Newport. Best, I should say, in relation to other Colonial houses for I have yet to see a house made of Stone in either Massachusetts or Rhode Island, and the wood which in Devon we might make an Outbuilding of is here used as a Principal material. The better Houses have a rude elegance to them, as the

Classical elements are here in evidence, tho' greatly reduced in scale and Ornamentation. Most unusual in Da Silva's house are a Quartett of Cherubim which face onto the mantelpiece in the Drawing room, carved in high relief representing the Four Corners of the Earth, with the central panel a painting of a merchant ship in its Voyages. The wood is not the limewood that such an Ornament would be made of back home, but it is a goodly Imitation. There are reputed to be very skilled Cabinet-makers in Newport, tho' those of that Trade are distressed and dispersed by the Hostilities as are so many others.

Judith was sumptuously dressed in a Silk frock over a slip of peach-colored Satin with drooping sleeves. Smithson, of course, is stupid around women, and the prettier they are, the stupider he becomes, and so he sat beside the girl most awkwardly while Da Silva showed me a Portuguese rapier we had talked of the last time I visited. I asked how his Wife & Sons were, for I knew that they had gone into the Interior as many others had done to escape the Strife, and then turning to Judith asked did she not wish she could join them? To which the girl replied that she was not afraid of Deprivation, or of life during War. Indeed, she considered it a rare Education. But you must miss your Mother and your young brothers, I continued, at which she gave me a look, for her own mother died when she was young, and she had told me once that there was no Love between herself and the second Mrs. Da Silva, and the three boys were but her half-brothers. I gave her a small smile to let her know that I was but referring to our Confidence.

As Smithson had never before visited Da Silva, the Jew said that if we did not mind the Roughness he would give us a tour of his Warehouses, tho' due to the occupying forces and the cessation of Trade he maintained they have been mostly bare these Twelvemonth. Yet he had obtained from Admiral Howe a Passport for a ship to go to sea and would like to check on his Sloop, the only vessel docked at the wharf. We might bring the Amontillado along, he smiled. So we made to go out, Da Silva putting on a cape and Judith a scarlet cloak. We were accompanied at some backwards distance by an African servant named Hannibal in a white powdered wig and carrying the bottle of Sherry with a great deal of Dignity. Phyllis stayed behind.

Such are these Colonials that even their wealthy Merchants do not mind their houses being situated upon their wharves so that their families are within bowshot of the Tars & Toughs & Stowadores that rat about the Harbour environs. I let Smithson take the brunt of Da Silva's showing of his Warehouses and Jib cranes and with a casual air fell behind with Judith. I told her how smart she looked in her scarlet cloak and didn't it match the Royal Welch Fusiliers, holding my forearm up to hers, even pressing against her to show the match. Indeed, I teased, since she already had the Uniform would she not like me to gain her a Commission? She was sure to raise the Quality of the Regiment, particularly if we could effect the Plot underfoot to drum out Smithson and his damned Whiskers. Look, the Spying fellow was glancing back at us even now! She laughed and with a brazen look, called me wicked. Damn my eyes if the girl doesn't know she is beautiful!

When we entered the Counting-house there were some of Da Silva's men there gathered around a fire. They seemed disconcerted by the sudden appearance of their Employer, and bowed their heads and went quickly out to the Wharf. Through the windows we could see the Sloop they were readying moored alongside, a mere Coaster by the look of her. Da Silva had a word with one of his men and then asked might we try the Sherry, and got out glasses. He noted the bottle was from Spain and said it was good, but the very best Amontillado he liked to think came from his home Portugal, tho' he had left that country too young to have tasted it. Judith said then that surely he did not wish the same Deprivation upon her—did not Major Ballard just say she was too deprived?—and was she not to be allowed a sip with the men? At which Smithson and I laughed, but then exchanged a look, each of us, I suppose, imagining her making such a Remark in front of our Mothers & Sisters.

Da Silva talked then in a relaxed manner of how we should have seen Newport (the Venice of America she was called, he said) before the Hostilities. The shipwrights & draymen, the smell of tallow & tar, cordage & casks, the half-mile long ropewalks which are now torn down for their timbers, the rich smell from the rum Distilleries. And in the midst of all this commerce were to be seen Negroe footmen in powder-blue livery the equal of any in London, carrying the Nabobs and Grandees of the town in sedan chairs over the cobbled streets. Everything in the town was either being sold or being bought. His own ships brought in molasses, sugar, cotton, nankeen, brass and pewter ware, and carried out rum, candles, lumber, fish, rope. He said once he had a cargo of Narragansett Pacers and had to have his men rig Harnesses in the hold of one of his Brigantines to carry the Beasts without their breaking their legs. The Oeconomy of the town was such that you had to be a Fool or a Gentleman not to grow wealthy.

And how much of this wealth, I felt called upon to ask as the only Gentleman present (Smithson, I said, could do for the Fool), had come from the Smuggling of goods? For we had heard that the merchant Da Silva had been a great Smuggler in his time, tho' he professed himself loyal to the Crown now.

He was not above unloading Hogsheads of molasses in the dead of night, Da Silva said, pouring us each more Sherry and fixing us with a look. The Navigation Acts which forced upon him Inequities of Commerce were an Abomination, he said. He considered himself an Englishman. Yes, a Portuguese Jew, he said, yes, he spoke with this accent, but he was an Englishman all the same, a Freeman, he had papers to prove it. He was a Subject of the King, and as such should not be saddled with Acts that treated him otherwise.

I looked at Judith to see if this was a shock to her, but she had about herself a look of Pride & Defiance.

It was worthy of thought, wasn't it, said Smithson, that those amongst the Colonials who were loyal to the King saw themselves as Patriots, and that those who were disloyal, and were rather loyal to this new Confederation, saw themselves as Patriots too. Whoever should prevail in this Struggle will consider the Patriots of the other side Traitors, would they not? Which group of Patriots, he wondered, would end up at the Extremity of a rope?

Do you say that to frighten us? Judith asked, and the directness of her Question disconcerted Smithson so that he stumbled about saying he had only meant to draw attention to the Vicissitudes of war, victors, spoils, &c., and that surely the King's forces would prevail, he did not doubt it, and that Miss Da Silva would be returned to the comfort of her former life.

And the whole time Judith had the full force of her Beauty upon him like a Broadside from a Man-o'-war.

On the way back to the house in which we are Billeted together, Smithson was full of compliments to the Jew, and said what a handsome woman Miss Da Silva would be someday, to which I responded, what did he mean someday? Well, she was but a Child still, he said, and there was an attitude about him of sounding me out. She doesn't look like a child, I told him coldly, nor does she act like one. At which, he gave me a look, but I would not Satisfy the damned Dwarf.

⤙ Fall 1692 ⤚

5th Day, 6 viii mo.

I felt this morning a Motion of Love to speak of those moments of Grace which I have felt in my Heart. And as I have heard that true Worship consists of an Inward life, I am determin'd to set down on these pages the Map of my Heart and of my Mind, tho' these be Weak and a girl's only. By such Employment I might keep Mother's ink from moulding, and so from wasting. She will not again use it herself.

Yet now that I am embark'd, and have trimm'd my pen, I can not think of how to say what I meant to say. For I had hoped to record this morning's strong Exercise of Light, whereby I felt such a Sweetnesse in me, that I might read of it later and profit of it. We were in the Kitchen and Dorcas was playing on the floor when it happen'd. Yet now I can think only of the Ants we discover'd had got in the sugar. For Ashes and I were about the stewing of apples and needed the Sugar to abate the tartness.

But now that I write that, I am minded of their fruity Odour and how the Light seem'd to come to me *through* them, so that if I would speak of the Light I must speak of the Apples. I stood there a good moment, and while Ashes continued her peeling, I smell'd in the air and tasted on my tongue the tart Sweetnesse of God's love. Yet it was not just on my Tongue but was felt over my whole body. And in the whole Kitchen. And out the window, as if the whole world, tho' it was eighth month, were wimpling as in the Summer's heat. I saw the Ants and the Sugar and knew One was not more Sweet than the Other. And I saw Ashes's black hand gripping the white Apples and I knew that their being of a different Colour matter'd not. The slave's hand was as a Sister to the Apple, and the Apple was as a

Sister to the Slave's hand. Oh, I am a poor Writer and know not how to say this. Yet it was so.

May God keep me, and little Dorcas, and may Father yet return to Newport safely.

7th Day

Martha Coggeshall and Hannah Carr visited me today. Hannah is not a member of the Society of Friends and so does not keep plain. But she is of a good and warm Heart, and an old friend, and she took me by the hand and kiss'd me on the cheek and call'd me her Prudence with much love. We took up some yarn and play'd at cratch-cradle and then went into the Dooryard and mark'd in the hard earth the boxes for Scotch-hoppers. I tried to be as I was before, for I knew they had come out of Concern for me, and out of Love for our old Sorority. But such are the Afflictions that have burden'd me, and so the Worries, that tho' I tried to be Prudence their old Playmate yet I could not. And it made me feel that I had lost myself, that the old Prudy had gone away. And that verse of Corinthians sounded over and over in my ear: that when I was a Child I had spoken and understood as a Child, but now I had been made to put away childish things.

We soon gave over our Games, and sat on the stone wall, which was cold coming through our clothes, and talk'd as we were wont to do, and that made me more at ease. Then we walk'd down to the Harbour, leaving Dorcas with Ashes.

It was a bright day, with some Bluster so that the leaves were showering down, yellow and brown and scarlet. And there was the autumne Smell that I love. Hannah who always has a little Money bought us some Gingerbread Men at Sarah Wilson's shop on Thames Street and we ate as we walk'd. We pass'd the slave Barracks at the head of Bullock's Wharf. Martha does not like going past it, but I told them there were no Africans there now, Captain Easton's having been sold off the week past, and those that hadn't sold being taken to the south. We went to the water's edge and look'd out at Goat Island. There were five Ships in the harbour, and they baited me to tell them what they were, for they know Father has taught me. Thee are such a know-all, Prudy Selwyn! they cried. And so I told them: two Bermuda sloops, a Snow, a Dutch fluyt, and a Ketch, tho' that latter I could not be sure wasn't a Yawl. And there were several wherries for going up the Island, but they do not count.

From the second-floor door of his Warehouse William Reed call'd out in his hearty manner that he was glad to see I had for once brought my friends with me, which dismay'd me for I would not have them know that I have the Habit these past Weeks of coming down to the waterside to watch for Father. It is such a stupid thing to do.

We then teas'd Hannah about Henry Whitlow, and that was diverting and I hope not mean, for her cheeks were burning but she was all alight with Humor and Secrets. Martha and I took leave of her at her House and then return'd to the Point, Martha kissing my cheek good-bye and saying she would see me next first-day at Meeting.

Today, my friends did cheer me, and I take this moment to thank the Lord for sending them to me.

3rd Day

This morning when I went out Jane Beecher was next door in her Yard, and she ask'd whether we should not set a Day for our soap-making, for the Snow would be coming before long. This pleas'd me, for she had always done so with Mother, and now it seems she means to do so with me.

We did not speak of Father, or of her husband James. Though each of us surely knows the Fear in the other's Heart, there is nothing to be had by speaking of it. We must pray and wait.

4th Day

I read from the Holy Scriptures to Ashes today and then took up Dorcas and we walk'd to Mother's Grave. I had to carry her upon my Hip for some Part of the way for tho' it is not so far, yet it is too far for her infant's legs. We went through the narrow streets of the Point uphill to the Burial Ground. I was tired when we arrived for I am not strong, or am still too much a Child to carry a Babe for long.

Dorcas knows Mother's grave, for the colour of the slate is more blue than the others, and the grave bed is not yet sodded over. She says Mamma to it in a most piteous way. I have tried to tell her our Mother is in Heaven, but she saw the men put Mother's corpse in the box, and then the box in the ground, and she will not give up the Surety of her babe's eyes.

There is no Inscription on the Slate for I did not think I should spend so much without Father's Approval. When he returns we will have one made. O! I was downhearted and felt an aching Sorrow that Father does not yet know his belov'd Wife is dead!

In the Scriptures, Dorcas is rais'd from the dead. And this for her good works in the World. Would that it could be so with Mother!

I did try to comfort Dorcas and tell her our Mother is in Heaven and watching us. And when she was calm'd we lay down together on the turf and look'd up at the sky, which is all I could tell her of where Heaven is. She kept asking Where? and all I could say was that she was in the Blue of the Sky. And I said that tho' we could not see her, she could see us.

The Ground was cold. The Lord keep us.

5th Day

Today Ashes would not answer to her name as she sometimes is wont most annoyingly to do. She says her name is Ama. She says if I want her help, I must call her Ama as her mother and sister did. If Father were here he would fix her for that, I know, but he is not.

She has a pock'd face for which I have heard Father say more than once he purposely selected her that she might not die aftertimes of the Small-pox. He accounted it a sign of sound Oeconomy. Yet I think her pocks are but the type for her most spiteful and horrid Heart. She will be difficult!

In a few days it will run out of her as it always does.

6th Day

I returned today some books Henry Dodson was good enough to loan me and have borrowed some others. I have read in Mr. Williams's *The Bloudy Tenent*, and in Mr. Cotton's answer to him, and in *The Pilgrim's Progress*, and now I have Mistress Bradstreet's *The Tenth Muse Lately Sprung Up in America* and a book of the Ancients' stories of the pagan gods and of the Heroes.

This last was given me with some Anxiety by Ruth Dodson who is herself a lover of the pagan stories, tho' she admits it is a weakness, yea, a Wickedness she says, tho' with a rueful smile at herself. They give them to me that I may be educated, as I am no longer at school. And for this favor I am most grateful, for the reading fills me with a type of Light, and transports me from the Troubles and Sorrows with which I am beset.

2nd Day

This morning a most lovely Indwelling of Light. There was a black-capp'd Titmouse in the bush outside the Kitchen window and it sang its simple two-note song and I felt the whole of Creation was in those two notes. It was as a Truth reveal'd to me. There were those two notes, one high, one its lower neighbor, and all else was but the noise of our Confusion.

It is gone now I write it. But I did feel it, and it gave me a deep Peace.

3rd Day

I have had a second Visit from John Peele. He came this time with John Cole who is much esteem'd in our Society and with Esther Pennington who has often I thought look'd kindly upon me. We sat in our small Parlour. I had Ashes serve us Cider. They ask'd did I not want to be back at the School, did I not miss it? To which I answer'd that I had my penmanship and my sums and that I had begun to keep Accounts for Father as Mother had done, and that I was reading the books that I had borrowed, and my Schooling was enough for that. But thee are accounted a fine Scholar, John Peele said with a smile I suppose at such lavish Praise, and might assist the schoolteacher in her duties, he said, helping the younger girls. To which I replied I had the running of my Father's Household and the caretaking of Dorcas, and I could not put that aside. He smil'd as with Apology and was silent.

Esther Pennington then ask'd was there anything I needed that the Friends might help me with. I thank'd her and said no, that for the time being our wants were supplied.

John Cole, not having said anything to this point, sat forward in his chair and drew himself together as with an Intention to speak. I had a sudden fore-knowledge that he would tell me Father was lost. He spoke in a solemn voice and said that the sloop *Patience* had return'd yesterday from Barbados and brought with it news that Father's sloop had yet to make the port at Bridgetown. I was at the moment reliev'd that the news was not worse, but of course in another moment I understood the Import of what he said. But there is no news of the *Dove* being lost, I heard my voice bravely saying. No direct news, said John Cole. But it has not arriv'd, he repeated. After which we were silent. I look'd at Esther Pennington and her face was so gentle and tender of me that I could not keep myself, and I was overcome with tears in a way that sham'd me, and makes my Face grow hot even now when I write it.

They moved to comfort me but I made it known I did not wish it. To hide my Agitation I spoke several hurried things I know not what. They did then urge on me that there were Several among our Society who had experienc'd a Motion in regard to Dorcas and me and had offer'd to take us in. To which I said that I would not have Father return to find that we had deserted his Household. They said it need not be so, for when he return'd, they said, we would surely be reunited. And much more of the like. Their faces were pain'd and urgent. I thank'd them but I did not submit. I told them I would await the Lord's Light on this matter, as in all Matters.

5th Day

At Night sometimes I am afear'd of such things as do not run in my mind by Day. I hear strange Noises and account them the presence of Spirits, or of Thieves, or mayhap someone of our town who has set his Sights on me. Then it is I wish most awfully that Mother was in her room with Father. I try to quiet these Fears with Prayer, hoping thereby to be deliver'd from the Dark. And I do sometimes talk to Mother, that she might know I am still here. Sometimes the thought of her listening to my Voice quiets me.

I am put in mind of a most dreadful Incident of some weeks back while Mother was lingering sick. I know not how to explain it for it is like an Apparition to me. I lay in bed and in the middle of the Night woke and became convinc'd that a shadow in the hallway just outside the Doorway to my room was a malevolent Presence. It moved only slightly, as in a light breeze, and I could not tell what it was, but I knew that I must not move or make a sound or it would know I was there and it would come and have me. How long I stayed in this State as in a Trance, I know not. But I was long frozen in Terror. Only when Daybreak came and the Shadows slowly chang'd did my Spirit relax that I might fall asleep. But to this present time I know not whether some Person or some strange Specter was there, or whether it was all my Fancy.

~ 2011 ~

They had a few days before Margo and her husband came up from New York and Alice returned from Santa Fe. The weather was good and since Aisha's studio was not a place you could hang out for long—and the bedroom she had in the mansion felt off-limits—they took to riding the Indian around southern Rhode Island in the late afternoons when Sandy was done at the Casino. They'd meet as inconspicuously as they could and then head out over the Newport Bridge to Conanicut Island or Narragansett Pier, or once as far west as Mystic, where there was a clam shack famous for its whole-belly fried clams. They tried their hand at windsurfing, drove up to Wickford Harbor to check out the fishing boats, had steamers and a couple of lobsters. Afterwards, in bed, he pretended to have Paralytic Shellfish Poisoning, one of the symptoms of which was a stiffening of the extremities, ha-ha.

He had hoped that when Margo came back she might just let the thing they'd had drop, smile at him on the tennis courts, say "Hey, champ!" and that would be that. But her first day back at the Casino she'd invited him and the others from her doubles group up onto the Horseshoe Piazza, where they'd all had gin and tonics and the women had flirted with him, teased him about his retirement, about having to find a wife and kids for him, maybe a rich widow. Afterwards she'd come by the place he was renting—a vacation condo overlooking the Newport Shipyard that the rental agent had said was a hot potato in a divorce settlement and so only available week to week—and then, *sheesh!* It all came back to him. Being in bed with Margo was like being in a close-order drill. Stand fast! Column movement! Sound off! She took down his cell phone number, conspicuously neglected to give him hers. The next day he'd felt some sort of obligation to tell Aisha what had happened, but she'd only smiled, patted him on the stomach, said that these things had to run their course.

He got used to seeing Alice in the afternoons. She was doing research—writing a book or something, Aisha said—at the Redwood Library just a couple of blocks down Bellevue, and she would come down to the Casino in the late afternoon, and sit and watch the play, the lessons, waiting to catch a ride with Margo. She wore these funky clothes—big-brimmed hats, loud sundresses, scarves you'd expect Isadora Duncan to wear. As for her cerebral palsy, there was the one hand bent in on itself, the one laggard leg, and this strained intensity to her face, but, as cerebral palsy went, all pretty minor, he supposed. Really, he found himself telling Aisha once when they were talking things over, she was kind of pretty in this nervy, brainy, hopeless sort of way. She'd sit at a little iron café table just in front of the pro shop with a thermos of coffee, book or notebook or laptop open, scrunchie holding her long hair back. He thought he could feel her eyes on him, watching him in his shorts and T-shirt as he fed balls, or as he paced alongside calling out coaching stuff, but whenever he turned—casually, nonchalantly—she was always looking away, watching one of the other courts, or turning her face up to the sun or down to her laptop.

The couple of times she caught *him* looking at *her*, she'd said: "And what do you *see*, Mr. Winterbourne?"

Which he totally didn't get.

And then there was Margo's husband, Alice's brother, Tom. Sandy had met him a couple of times the previous summer. A big guy, he'd been a second-string safety for Stanford. But since then—what, he was maybe thirty-five now?—since college he'd put on a bit of weight. Tried to keep it off with racquetball, he said, Sandy ever play racquetball? He seemed an okay kind of guy, maybe with a little of the arrogance you could have if you were rich, had gone to Stanford, had a nice-looking wife and an unas-sailable job, even in the recession—Credit Suisse in Tom's case—but he was okay. The few times Sandy'd talked to him the previous summer they'd talked sports, guy stuff, including Tom's story about how Roger Federer—who had a major deal with Credit Suisse, Sandy knew that, right?—had come by the New York offices that past August and given some face time to top management. Federer seemed like a good guy, Tom said, had Sandy ever met him? (Indian Wells, 2006, Sandy was thinking, 6–1, 6–1.) But okay, he wasn't trying to make Sandy feel bad, rub it in that he wasn't Roger Federer—who was?—he was just making talk the way a life of Newport and Stanford and Wall Street had taught him to do. Smooth, confident, a smiling slap on the back any minute now.

So what was the proper deportment toward a guy whose wife you were screwing, not to put too fine a point on it? It wasn't the sort of thing Sandy was used to. He kind of wished there was somebody he could talk to about it, someone he could sound out on just how much of this was he responsible for? Morally speaking, he meant. But he didn't feel right talking to Aisha about it. And it was definitely off-limits with Margo, who seemed to want to pretend she didn't *have* a husband. And who knew, maybe she and Tom had some kind of understanding, an arrangement. Sandy had heard of such things. But still he didn't like it. Sleeping with someone's wife was a dickish kind of thing to do, and he prided himself on not being a dick. It wasn't who he was. You could ask anyone.

There was this one day toward the end of May when Tom was up from New York with two clients for the Memorial Day weekend and he'd shown up at the Casino with Aisha and Alice because it was the first truly hot day and they'd had an idea to round everyone up and go out to Bailey's Beach. Sandy was invited too—hey, why not? said Tom. But Sandy had had another class to teach—he was a working man, he'd said with a smile— and he'd gone off to his Intermediate Doubles over on Courts 5 and 6. But instead of heading out to the beach, the group had settled onto Crowley's deck where it overlooked Court 1 and started in on the gin and tonics. When the hour was up, Sandy went to join them, found them a little drunk and animated on the subject of Clarendon Court, the place—Alice was explaining to them—where Claus and Sunny von Bülow had lived until Claus sort of accidentally injected Sunny with an overdose of insulin. Which brought up the tobacco heiress Doris Duke, who had killed her chauffeur/lover back in the sixties, drove her car right into him ("Silly me!" said Alice. "Is *that* the accelerator?"), and whose estate, Rough Point, where it'd all happened, was just a few houses south of the du Ponts'

Windermere. And hey—back to Clarendon Court—did they know that it had been the set for the movie *High Society*? Louis Armstrong, Bing Crosby, Grace Kelly? Had Sandy never seen the place? Had the two friends from Credit Suisse?

So they dropped the idea of going to the beach and instead headed off to their cars to descend on Clarendon Court, and then maybe over to Windermere for some more drinks, or maybe the beach after all. At the sight of the red Indian parked at the rear entrance of the Casino, Alice had said hey, she'd never *been* on a motorcycle. At which Sandy had shot a look at Aisha, then had the presence of mind to say he didn't have an extra helmet.

"That's all right," the girl had said, handing her laptop and stuff to Margo. "I'm *already* brain-damaged." And she hobbled over to the bike and swung her good leg up over the seat. "Last one there's a murdered heiress!"

And for the rest of the day, while they stood outside the gates to Clarendon Court, and then later out at Bailey's Beach wading in the surf with their pant legs rolled up, she called him Mr. Winterbourne. ("Oh! Mr. Winterbourne!" she said when he helped her off the bike. "I never dreamed a mere physical experience could be so exhilarating!" That kind of thing.) Back at Windermere drinking cocktails and playing croquet on the front lawn with the sun going down and the Atlantic out there like it was the du Ponts' private ocean, he smiled and asked her what was with the Mr. Winterbourne stuff?

"That's for me to know and you to find out," she said with this look. Which pissed him off because he had been trying to be nice. He'd said it like okay, you got me, so what's the joke? And it seemed to him the proper response to that was to clue somebody in, not to continue to keep them on the outside. Keeping them on the outside was like what you did in high school when you really *wanted* them on the outside, when you wanted some loser to know that hey, you are *so* not one of us.

So a couple of days later at the Casino, when she asked in this coy sort of way when was he taking her on his motorcycle again, he told her not until he found out who Mr. Winterbourne was. Which he hoped communicated to her that he didn't need to be made to feel out of it by suicidal manic-depressive heiresses. And to punctuate that, he did this thing he could do, which was to bounce a tennis ball off his biceps, back and forth—*bump-bump-bump*—like his biceps were playing catch with each other.

"Oh, Mr. Winterbourne!" she said, as though she were overcome with sexual arousal.

In your dreams, he said. Or would have said. If he was a dick. Which he wasn't.

To get away he went up to Brown on his day off and hit with their top singles player. The guy was not quite good enough but it was nice at least to be hitting the ball with some pace, kicking his serve, keeping the ball deep. And his knee didn't feel too bad. Afterwards he went out for hamburgers and a beer with the guy and his girlfriend and it felt nice, almost like he was back at Duke and things were still in the future. On the drive home he resolved to take up his old training regimen. Not that he'd ever play competitively again, but he was an athlete all the same, he needed to stay in shape. Weights, shuttle sprints, ladder drills. As long as he took it easy on his knee. No long-distance running.

Back at the condo there was a package from Amazon but he was used to getting stuff that wasn't for him, was in fact filling a cardboard box that one of these days he'd haul off to the rental agent so that she could pass it on to the divorcing/reuniting couple, whoever they were. He was about to throw the thing from Amazon in the box—just another reminder of his interloper status—when he noticed the package was addressed to Mister Winterbourne. "Mister" like a first name, then "Winterbourne," then the condo address and number. He pulled the zipper thingie and inside found a book. *Daisy Miller.* Henry James.

What? he wanted to say. He turned the thing this way and that, and then chucked it into the box anyway. Whatever the game was, let the divorced couple wonder.

But half an hour later he couldn't help himself. He opened the book and sure enough the main character was a guy named Winterbourne, an American living in Europe whose chief occupation seemed to be watching Daisy Miller—the pretty American flirt, as one character called her—to see if she was socially acceptable or if she was—as another character called her—"a horror." It was short and he read it through in one evening, puzzled at just what the correspondence was supposed to be. Okay, he and Winterbourne were about the same age. The story took place at Vevey, which he took to be a kind of European version of Newport. And the two girls were both heiresses—rich, young, marriageable. And he, he supposed, *had* been looking at her the last couple of weeks, *watching* her if you would. But that was because—what could he say?—she had cerebral palsy and she dressed like she was hitching a ride to Woodstock. He had been *curious* about her, is all. When he finished the story proper he read the afterword, which made a point of their names—Daisy fresh and flowerlike, Winterbourne cool and blighting—and that it was Winterbourne's watching her, evaluating her, the blindness of his moral insight, his inability to see the worth of Daisy's true self, that caused her death at the end of the book. He figuratively freezes her to death, the afterword said, like a September frost on a summer flower. The afterword also mentioned that James had lived in Newport.

"Lots of murdered heiresses in my neck of the wood," he remembered Alice saying when they were standing outside the gates to Clarendon Court.

Back at the Casino he wondered whether he was supposed to mention the book or not. Was it just a game, a joke? Or did she mean something by it, some warning not to misunderstand or manhandle her, not to be *morally blind* around her? And did it matter? Why should he have to concern himself with her?

So he didn't say anything.

What he did do—when she went to the bathroom and he had the chance—was sneak a look at what she was writing. Aisha had said it was some sort of Newport history thing, and that's why she spent her days at the Redwood Library. The part he'd read was about somebody marrying a Dollar Princess—which was a weird coincidence because that's what the afterword had called Daisy Miller. He asked Margo about it, but she just shrugged, said it kept Alice occupied, kept her from Googling how to make a noose.

"Slow reader, are we?" Alice asked a couple days later, pulling these Lolita sunglasses down and looking over the tops of them. "That's a hint, son." Which he didn't take.

It was around this time that he pieced together from Margo and Aisha the story of the night Alice had slit her wrists. It had been Aisha who had found her. She had woken up in the middle of the night and had come out of her bedroom, following the sound of opera down the hall to this semi-circular alcove with a big bay window that looked out onto the ocean. And there was Alice unconscious in the moonlight, blood all over the couch, and *Tristan und Isolde* on the CD player. ("Leave it to Alice to cast herself as Isolde," Margo had said. Sandy nodded, like he knew who Isolde was.) The ambulance had come and they had pumped her full of blood and she had lived, depressed for a long while after, lying around the house with these big bandages on her wrists. Tom had asked her for the umpteenth time to go back to having professional help, begged her really, get *professional* help, to which Alice had said okay, she'd make an appointment with her dentist.

At the Casino Alice wanted to know when she was going to get her motorcycle ride, now that he'd found out.

"What did I find out?" Sandy asked.

"You know," she said.

He kept his gaze on her steady and not-to-be-tricked. If she saw things that weren't there—Sandy Alison as the handsome but shallow Mr. Winterbourne—made up things in her squirrely head, was he responsible for that?

"Look," he said like he was going to level with her, like he meant to tell her she had the wrong guy, "I'm just a tennis player. All this—" and he made a gesture at the stuff in front of her, at an invisible *Daisy Miller*, at her own weird self—"this is all beyond me."

She picked up her notebook and laptop and her papers and held them to her chest like a schoolgirl. "No, it's not," she said.

"Yes, it is."

She smiled like she knew something he didn't. "Let's go anyway," she said, and when he shook his head: "Mr. Winterbourne! We're young and alive!"

"Sorry," he said. "I've got something on."

But he felt like a creep saying it. Maybe she wasn't making fun of him. Maybe all this—what his mother would have called being a smart aleck—was just long-ingrained self-defense.

"Maybe tomorrow," he said and tried to smile. "If the weather's good."

She let her face light up. "I'll be sure to wear my biker-babe outfit."

Which turned out to be jeans with these metal studs on them and a fringe leather jacket, outrageous mascara, and no helmet. They stowed her laptop in Sandy's locker and when he was finished with his lessons took off together down Wellington Avenue, past the yacht clubs and Fort Adams, past the turnoffs to Eisenhower's house and the Castle Hill light-house, and then out onto Ocean Drive as it made its long curve around the point. All the way they kept the water on their right, the sun slipping be-hind as they went eastward. The girl had her hands clasped around his waist as she'd had that first time, but now he thought he could feel in her, in her body pressed against him, the thrill she felt, the sting of speed and wind and the danger of it all. When once the road curved he caught sight of their shadows on the tar, the Indian long and low, his own arms cow-boyed out in that motorcycle posture and the girl hugging him with her good hand locked onto her bad wrist and her long hair streaming behind. They must've looked like a video for Youth and Freedom, he thought. And Sex, he supposed. Well, maybe it was all right: life was made up of mo-ments when you almost made it, when you *almost* got a third game off Roger Federer, when you *almost* were with a guy who had a bright red motorcycle. It didn't hurt to come close, did it? In the long run? Surely she understood what was what.

When the parking lot for Brenton Point came into view he pulled the Indian over, not into the parking lot but onto the strip of turf between the road and the ocean. He helped her off. In the park behind them there were dozens of kites flying—box kites, parafoils, Felix the Cat. They watched for a while and then made their way along the rocky edge of the land toward the breakwater. She seemed uncertain of the uneven ground, held on to his arm as they walked, the fringe on her jacket swaying be-tween them. There was a sailboat some distance out on the water, and way out on the horizon what looked like a container ship. When they got to the stone stairway that led down to the breakwater, they stopped and just watched the people in the distance navigating their way over the huge black boulders jutting into the ocean.

"Can you make it out there?" Sandy found himself asking.

She let her eyes sweep along the length of the breakwater. "No," she said.

Closer in, in the embrace of the little bay that curved toward the Castle Hill lighthouse, there were half a dozen smaller sailboats tacking and coming about in the wind, and on the rocks that lay like black rags along the shore, fishermen with their poles and tackle boxes. On the breakwater two high school girls in shorts and tank tops were holding hands and letting out mock-terrified screams each time they reached a new rock, and out at the very tip a man and a woman were sitting with their legs hanging over the edge of the last stone. Above them the seagulls squawked and swooped. It was all so bright and beautiful.

"Come on," he said. "Let's give it a try."

She shook her head.

"Come on." And he took her hand, stepped onto the first of the stones that made a rough stairway down to the water. She held back and he was aware suddenly of the differential between the brashness of her mind and the timidity of her body. "It's okay," he said. "I've got you. We'll see how far we can get."

She made a face but let him lead her all the same, first slowly down the steps, then up onto the first boulders of the breakwater. From there they went carefully from stone to stone. He held her hand, let her come along at her own pace. She kept her face down, watching her feet, keeping away from where it might be slippery. When once they came to a spot where some rocks had tumbled away, he put one of his arms behind her knees and lifted her and carried her across to the next boulder. He expected her to cry *Oh, Mr. Winterbourne!* or something, but she didn't, had instead this look of thrilled concentration.

When finally they reached a break in the stones that was too much for them, they stopped, found a spot to stand, and without saying anything just looked around at everything there was to see: the big sailboats out on the ocean, the smaller ones upcoast, the hazy arc of the Claiborne Pell Bridge in the distance, the coastline as it swept south, and the horizon where blue met blue. After a time he felt her squeeze his arm and then point at a racing yacht in the distance. It had just unfurled a bright red spinnaker, the huge loose sail filling so that the boat suddenly heeled. She smiled at the sight of it. The wind whipped her hair so she did that thing that women do, dragging her hair back from her lips with her fingernails.

"Sometimes," he heard her say after a minute; she had her head turned from him, upwind so the breeze took her voice, "sometimes just being alive is enough."

Back on the Indian they continued around the point, the mansions on their left with their many-windowed facades facing oceanward, and after a couple of miles the private beaches on their right, first Gooseberry, and then Bailey's Beach, where they'd gone that Clarendon Court day. They banked in and around the inlets and finally onto Bellevue, shooting down the long avenue toward Alice's house. But when they reached the gate he didn't turn in, gunned the engine instead so she screamed behind him, and kept on down Bellevue until he could turn onto Thames Street where the evening crowds were beginning to gather. He guided the Indian along the wharves, past the tourists looking for a place to eat, the college kids waiting for dark to start drinking, and then pulled the bike up onto Da Silva's Wharf where he knew of a not-quite-illegal place to park.

"Are you allowed to drink?" he asked. She fixed him with a what's-that-supposed-to-mean look. He hoped he wasn't doing the wrong thing.

They were seated at a table on Da Silva's Terrace with its canopy and trellises and where there was an outdoor wet bar. He was aware of people's eyes on them and he had the thought that it must be like that for her all the time, people looking and pretending not to be looking. The waitress came and they ordered a bottle of wine and a dozen oysters. When she left, Alice leaned across the table and, pointedly keeping her eyes from looking at the people around them, whispered: "They can't figure out why

a fella like you is with a gal like me." After a couple of minutes the waitress
came back with their bottle of wine. Alice lifted her glass, waited for him
to lift his, and then as they clinked said:

"Here's to your and Margo's cheatin' hearts."

Well, geez.

He looked past her, out through the terrace trellis at the busy wharf, at
the kiosks and boutiques and scrimshaw shoppes, then out over the rooftops of the old warehouses and chandleries on Pettibone's Wharf toward
where the tall yacht masts swayed at anchor. Maybe the thing to do was to
just not respond, let her know that she was crossing some line and that it
was not okay. There were half a dozen wind-speed thingies spinning atop
half a dozen masts, gulls and pigeons standing hunch-shouldered on the
roofs of the buildings. Just to drive the point home he ran his eye slowly
along a banner that was spread across the width of the wharf advertising
the 12-Metre Worlds. Out in the harbor there was the deep, loud bark of
the Providence ferry.

"I'm not sleeping with Margo," he said finally. "If that's what you mean."

She eyed him a moment with something like a bemused expression,
then made a forget-it gesture with her good hand. "I don't care if you are,
you know."

"But I'm not," he said and then, as if to mitigate the lie, said something
about the night of the Champions Ball—that crazy night, he said: afterwards, after they'd brought her home and Margo had to give him a lift
back to his hotel because he didn't know how to ride a motorcycle back
then—well, that night, he said, but not since.

"What you do is your own business." She still had the look of saying forget it. She shrugged herself out of her fringe jacket. "But just to put you on
notice: I make it a rule not to sleep with men who have slept with Margo."
She lifted her hand, palm out as if to ward off his protestations. "I know that
limits my options considerably—" and here a so-be-it gesture—"but I consider sleeping with Margo a sign of moral infirmity in a man." She drank
from her wineglass, set it firmly on the table. "Not to mention bad taste."

He screwed his mouth up, like ha-ha.

They sat and sipped their wine and ate their oysters, and when the oysters were gone, decided they'd make a dinner of hors d'oeuvres, since the wharf was getting crowded and they were lucky to have a table. The sun was setting and the lights were coming on and there was music from somewhere. The more wine they drank, the more Alice talked, first about local girl Jacqueline Bouvier marrying that Massachusetts senator at St. Mary's—you could see the steeple from here—and then Edith Wharton and her unhappy marriage, and then about the Da Silva of Da Silva's Wharf and Da Silva's Restaurant and Da Silva's Terrace where they were seated *even as she spoke*. A Portuguese Jew, she said, that was his house over there, and she indicated a clapboard building right on the wharf that Sandy could see had the lines of a Newport Georgian even though it was a restaurant now with modern windows disfiguring its facade and kitchen vents like brain tumors. Slave quarters on the third floor, she said.

"So what I do at the Redwood," she said, changing gears, "is I put on these white cotton gloves and I paw through all these old documents and stuff. Letters, diaries, receipts. Even Da Silva's account books. A Jew surrounded by Christians. I identify with him," she said, again with the wry smile.

"But you're not Jewish," he felt called upon to say. She looked up at him from under her brows.

"You need to approach the world more metaphorically, Mr. Winterbourne."

But she said it kindly, with none of the smart-aleckness of the last week. She sat back, slouched so the nape of her neck touched the chair back, closed her eyes. She's drunk, Sandy thought.

"Sometimes I imagine what Windermere was like when it was first built," she said, still with her eyes closed. "Such a big pretentious house, and the husband dying within a year of the young couple moving in, and the maze they'd designed and planted because they'd loved the one at Hampton Court on their honeymoon. Or I imagine I'm poor little rich girl Consuelo Vanderbilt being bullied by her mother into marrying the Duke of Marlborough, or the young Henry James with a life of celibacy ahead of him. You ever do that?"

He kept an attentive expression on his face. Do what? he was wondering. She sat up again, leaned over the table all confidential.

"And *sometimes*," she stage-whispered, "I get drunk late at night all by myself and call a taxi and I get down here and I just walk around the city. I'll start with the seventeenth-century houses out on the Point, and go up to the Quaker meetinghouse, and then the Jewish graveyard—and I just imagine a different world, I imagine it's not *now*, it's *then*. It helps if it's foggy. You ever do that?" she asked again.

He shook his head *no*, smiled. "No," he said.

"Not even up at the Casino? Never think about the US Open being held there a hundred years ago? René Lacoste? Bill Tilden?"

"Sure," he said, "okay."

"The wooden racquets? The long pants? The spectators sipping their gin daisies?"

He smiled, nodded.

"See?" she said, like she'd revealed something about him to himself. And she started to close her eyes again and then just as quickly was getting to her feet. "I gotta pee," she said. She took a step away from the table, set her sights on the restrooms, but then she was turning back and leaning toward him. For one awful moment, he thought she was going to kiss him.

"In France," she whispered instead, "they have a crime called *abus de faiblesse*. Which is exploiting someone's frailty or weakness for your own gain. A kind of killer instinct," she said, fixing her eyes on him, whether serious or mocking he couldn't tell. "Woe to him who is guilty of *abus de faiblesse*."

And she made a pistol with her thumb and forefinger and shot him.

Later, after they'd found a cab for her—she was too drunk to ride a motorcycle, she'd said—instead of going straight to where the Indian was parked, Sandy let himself fall in with the crowd strolling along the wharf. He remembered something he'd said to Aisha that first day, that Alice always looked like she was being electrocuted. Like she was being perpetually electrocuted, he'd said. There was something about her, something about the curved fingers and the bent wrist and the ungraceful gait and the self-consciousness that went with it all. It was as if with the condition, with the misfiring nerves and muscles, there came an inability to keep the world out, like her body was an open circuit and the world traveled through her like electricity. She was *open*, he found himself thinking, and she could not get herself closed.

At the end of the wharf he stood and looked out over the harbor, at the hundreds of masts rocking gently in the dusk, and he tried to imagine what it was like a hundred, two hundred years ago. He closed his eyes and tried to picture—what, frigates? schooners? clippers?—but he couldn't do it. Not really. The present was too strong, had too fierce a claim on him. He lacked the imagination to overcome it, to loosen its grip. Or maybe he just lacked the need.

1896

The rooms inside the Casino were done in dark paneling so it took a moment for Franklin's eyes to adjust to the light. Whoever had called him to come have a smoke and drawn him away from Mrs. Belmont and the other women—Hobson he thought it had been—was nowhere to be seen. He milled about with the men in their summer jackets and their cigars. One of the tennis players was standing in the embrasure of a window with a circle of admirers. Franklin added himself to their number so he wouldn't look conspicuous. But the talk was so tiresome that he peeled off after a few minutes and strolled toward one of the other rooms where there was the clack of billiard balls. He stood a ways back from the table, hands clasped behind, and watched.

Children, he thought. How had he missed that? True, he had not given much thought to this Mrs. Newcombe after the winter—there were half a dozen Mrs. Newcombes to whom he had been introduced in the past half year—but he did not like being taken by surprise. He did not like not knowing what was arrayed against him. What he had to contend with. And what he had to contend with evidently was *children*. Two at least, he should think. And what to make of that?

He had always envisioned a woman weakened by widowhood, by loneliness, by the sight of herself in the mirror. He imagined, in short, an invalid who would be hungry for the sun of his attentions. Onto such a battlefield—always keeping a path of retreat in view—he might indeed stride and conquer. His lack of wealth, his respectable but by no means exceptional family—if the invalid were weak enough, none of this would matter.

But children. Children gave the widow an obscure heft. How did they alter matters?

The thing he knew—had always known—in the deepest part of himself, was that he could not make love to a woman. He could *not*. He could not even do what some of the men he knew from the Slide could do: make love to their wives once a month, have children by them, turn their wives' naiveté to their advantage, keep a loving smile on their face as they went out the door Saturday nights. No, if he was going to do the deed—*and he must*—if he was going to lure a woman into the trap of marriage with him, he would have to do it with the private understanding—an understanding with *himself*, he meant—that he must be prepared to destroy her. To tell her after the wedding that theirs would be a public marriage only, that he was prepared to treat her in the presence of others as admirably as any husband treated his wife, that he would dote and fawn and caress—she would have his word on this. He would not rob her of *that* dignity. But she must understand that in private they would be—how would he phrase it? as brother and sister? as *friends*—well, however he managed it, she must understand that in private she could not expect attention from him of the other sort. He would be polite and pleasant in private, but not more than that. If he could phrase this kindly, he would. If not, so be it.

And who knew, perhaps children could be his allies in this. He was not un-fond of children, he supposed. He could picture himself winning their little hearts, and by that their mother's affection. He could turn the little so-and-sos into his advocates. And then afterwards, after the deed was done, would they not provide the woman with an emotional reserve? She would have her children at least. And she could comfort herself with the thought that her husband appeared to adore them. Would that not serve?

"Drexel!" he heard behind him. He turned—it was Hobson and the others, all dressed in their smart summer suits. He smiled his hail-fellow-well-met smile.

"I say, Parrish, pour the man a brandy!"

They circled around him, put a snifter in his hand. Was he going sailing? they wanted to know. Briggs had the *Dolphin* outfitted, and there was going to be an evening party, was he coming? Alas, no, he had made a promise to Mrs. Belmont for tea.

"Oh, break it," they all cried. "Come sailing!"

"Yes, that's right," Hobson said with some sort of meaning. He had planted himself opposite Franklin with his chest out in that way he had. He was smoking a cigar. "You don't mind breaking the rules, do you, Drexel?"

"As long as they're not Mrs. Belmont's rules," he smilingly replied.

Hobson knocked his ash into his empty snifter. "Parrish here tells us you were breaking the rules just the other weekend. Isn't that right, Parrish?"

Parrish just grinned. He was dressed in a rather undergraduate-looking jacket, all wide stripes and cheeky naiveté.

"He's given us to understand you've set yourself up as something of a cicerone. A docent of the demimonde. Is that true?"

"I shouldn't mind a tour of the demimonde," put in Phelps with his British accent and with the tops of his ears reddening. "Ladies of the evening, don't you know."

"It isn't ladies of the evening that form the chief attraction of Drexel's sightseeing, as I understand it. At least not the sort of ladies *you'd* like, Phelps."

"I like *all* the ladies," said Phelps. "And they like me."

At which the others guffawed.

"As to that," Hobson went on, "I have no doubt, *these* ladies *would* like you, Phelps. But come clean, Drexel, we've got it from Parrish here."

"*I* had it from Simmons," Parrish added somewhat sheepishly. "He said you took his set down into the Bowery. Ghastly, he said. He said it quite undid him."

"Ah, *that*," Franklin found himself saying with his easy smile around. "It's become quite the Fifth Avenue fashion, didn't you know? Rather like Virgil and Dante, I should say. A tour of the demimonde—why, it's better than the zoo!"

"Simmons said there were these places where—! Well, I *say*," Parrish said and stopped.

"What?" the others cried.

"Yes, spill it!"

Parrish looked helplessly about himself. "These places where there were men with—! Well, with girls' names."

"All part of the tour!" Franklin managed. He smiled around as if daring them. As if he were in the know, had stolen a march on them, the donkeys.

"Next time we're all back in town, what do you say? Shall I give you my Baedeker's for the Bowery? If you think you've got the stomach for it. Eh? But don't be telling your mothers!"

They all laughed and then someone mentioned a story in the *Mirror* about a police raid in the Village—had they seen it?—and then it was off into newspaper gossip. After a few minutes the billiard game broke up and Phelps and one of the others began to play. And then it was back to Briggs and the *Dolphin* and whether there would be any young ladies at the evening party. Franklin drank his brandy and listened, dimly aware that he had managed to step back from the precipice. Indeed, he was so preoccupied with looking unimpeachable—Parrish had offered him a cigar—that it took him a moment to realize the others had stopped talking and were looking at him. It was another moment before he realized that someone—Mrs. Belmont's footman—was waiting beside him for his notice.

"Ah, Wells!" he said, turning.

"Thank you, sir," the footman responded. "Mrs. Belmont wishes me to communicate to you that Mrs. Newcombe will be accompanying Mrs. Belmont in her carriage to Marble House for tea. As you are expected as well, sir, she is wondering if you would be so good as to return with Mrs. Newcombe's conveyance."

"Mrs. Newcombe's conveyance?" he found himself saying. "You mean her bicycle?"

"Yes, sir."

He was aware of the others' eyes on him. Was he going to be twice in ten minutes held up for scrutiny? "Look here, Wells"—what else was there to do but make light of it?—"did you dream this up yourself?"

"No, sir."

He let his accusing smile grow even broader. "Not trying to do me a mischief?"

"No, sir."

"Ah! Then Mrs. Belmont is." He wagged his cigar in the air. "But I shall outflank her. I shall prove to her that I am an excellent cyclist. None better!"

"Very good, sir. I understand the bicycle to be somewhere adjacent to the pavilion."

"Thank you, Wells."

"Very good, sir."

He stood a moment longer smoking so as not to look like he was at the beck and call of a footman, and only when the billiard game ended said his good-byes all around, said he'd try to make it down to the wharf before Briggs's lighter ferried them all out to the *Dolphin*, but not to wait for him, and then turned and left the Casino. Outside, the crowd had thinned. The sun was a little lower in the sky. He crossed the grass courts toward Berger's Pavilion.

He was obscurely aware that he had been insulted. That as playful as Mrs. Belmont's request was—he could so easily imagine the laughing conversation and the importuning of Mrs. Newcombe: she must *not* ride her bicycle all the way back down Bellevue Avenue, rather she must come in Mrs. Belmont's carriage at once—why, they would get *Franklin Drexel* to ride her bicycle back (the young man claimed to be such a lover of bicycle riding!)—yes, playful as that was—indeed, he could imagine making the joke himself—still, to be summoned by Mrs. Belmont's man there in front of the others . . . ! Well, he supposed he must take refuge in its being Mrs. Belmont who was doing the summoning. Hobson and Parrish could whistle into the wind until *they* were so summoned.

There were three bicycles outside the pavilion but just as he drew up a young man and woman wheeled two of them away. He sauntered over to the remaining metal contraption and eyed its pedals and wheels and its chain drive. He supposed it was not so very difficult to ride. Women managed it, after all. He took the thing by its handlebars as he'd seen others do and walked it away. He would start down Freebody Street, where he would be out of view until he had gotten the hang of it and then come out onto Bellevue.

But how the deuce did one mount the thing? He supposed he might use the curbside as a mounting block as women did when mounting a horse. There was that box hedge to watch out for. One foot on one pedal, push off—he believed it was necessary to have a certain initial speed—swing the other foot around onto the other pedal and . . . and . . . oh, good lord!

He inspected the bicycle first to see if there was any telltale damage.

The end of a handlebar had dug into the sod, but the machine appeared otherwise unscathed. Not so his leg! His trousers were not torn but there was a deuce of a scrape on his shin! He became aware of some children laughing at him from across the street. He righted the bike and without looking at the nasty creatures began walking it away.

It was a good two miles to Marble House.

But damn that Simmons! What was he doing blabbing about their slumming expedition? It was indeed becoming fashionable among the younger set to tour the Bowery and the tenements—but really! one needn't broadcast one's divertissements. Especially to a knucklehead like Parrish. And what had made Franklin suggest the tour in the first place? Was he so perverse? So indifferent to exposure? It had been dangerous and foolish.

He had at least had the good sense to keep the party out of Bleecker Street and Washington Square, where he had his own haunts. They had instead threaded their way through the tenements along Mott and Spring and Hester Streets, marveling at the throngs of people, the carts and laundry hanging between the buildings, the smells and the spray of incomprehensible languages, the Italian women with babies riding on every hip and the Jews with their absurd ringlets and ridiculous clothes. He had taken them into a couple of the taverns along the Bowery where the drink-mollies plied their trade and the prostitutes showed their wares. And then—what had he been thinking? really, he had wanted to force their muzzles into it, hadn't he?—he had steered them into the Paresis, where Simmons and that fool Chauncey went quite white. Well, if Hobson and Parrish and the others took him up on his offer—and he wouldn't be back in town for any extended stay until September and there was a good chance the whole matter would have blown over by then—but if they *did* importune him, he would confine himself to showing them the tenements and the prostitutes—let them wonder where the mincing Mary Anns were.

He was coming up on the broad face of the Massasoit Hotel, where he had his rooms. The resort with its wide veranda and striped awnings had been fashionable in the fifties and sixties just before the great years of cottage building and was still discriminating enough, but it was no longer frequented by the best society. Mrs. Belmont, for one, never inquired as to where he was lodging. She no doubt knew—Wells or one of the other foot-men had no trouble finding him—but she did not wish to have the matter acknowledged between them. Because really, when one came right down to it, he was lodging with parvenus and Jews and with families from Scran-ton and Albany, and with the occasional shopgirl who had saved all year to spend two weeks in Newport where there were lawyers and brokers who might be induced—by the double-barreled testimonials of her beauty and her being able to lodge at the Massasoit Hotel—into marriage. One of these girls had the previous year, he believed, set her sights on him. He had been kind enough—comrades-in-arms!—to set the poor dear straight.

Now, wheeling Mrs. Newcombe's bicycle along as fast as he could with-out looking ridiculous, he wondered whether he might not turn in for a drink of water—he was devilishly thirsty!—but he was already on thin ice for his remark about the Dollar Princesses; arriving late would have the ice cracking under him. There was nothing to be done but to keep going.

⇥ 1863 ⇤

~I have tried to keep from these writer's notes any day-to-day record of young Harry James's life for I am not engaged in the writing of a diary. But news came today that Will Temple has been killed in the late battle at Chancellorsville and I am pitched into a gloom. I must summon the courage to go see Kitty and Minnie and the others for I can only imagine how distraught they are. The six Temple orphans, as the world calls them. Now they are one fewer. And oh! Gus Barker with his red hair, showing off his beautiful muscles! His laugh never to be heard again!

These friends from my childhood, they have done something with their lives, committed themselves to an action noble and terrifying. What will I do with mine?

~When we first lived in Newport—before Father whisked us off to Geneva—the little Rhode Island seaport was known as the Carolina Hospital, so common was it for Southerners to flee the "country fever" they were subjected to in the summer. There were in the city in those days planters from Savannah and Charleston and the Indies who brought their household servants with them without a second thought given to the sensibilities of the Northerners. Might not a story be made of that? One in which the rich past underlies the present?

I have read somewhere that curators of antiquities have discovered that oftentimes parchments of the Dark Ages have underneath their present writing an older writing incompletely effaced, and that by careful investigation, the older writing can be read beneath the newer. Such a layering of writing is called (Mrs. Browning, I believe, uses the word in one of her poems) a palimpsest.

Ah, to be able to read both the surface *and* that which is below the surface!

~O! I am exposed and my life incognito (at least as regards the Huntress) is at an end!

It happened thusly: I was at the Ocean, seated on one of the wicker chairs that dot the playing lawns. There was a tennis match being contested between two young men dressed all in white and a goodly number of guests observing their exertions, my Diana and her brother among them. This latter came over at one point and dropped himself in the chair beside me. He had a tennis ball which he exchanged from hand to hand in a little tossing motion. I kept my head down, looking into my notebook, so as not to excite notice. Diana stood off a short distance, parasol held over her head, watching the men play.

The following is a simulacrum, reconstructed without the aid of notes. (For how could I have been taking notes? It was life lived!)

"Say!" I heard the boy say beside me. "You're that one always hanging about writing!"

I looked across at him as if he were a nightmare I had endowed with the faculty of speech. And as I did, his sister turned to ascertain what her charge was doing and, seeing him safely in a chair, did a most remarkable thing. She closed her parasol, pointed it at him from her shoulder as if it were a rifle, and shot him. Then she reopened it and turned back to the match.

"Yes," I said, at a loss.

The boy tossed the ball back and forth between his hands. There came the sound of rackets striking a ball, and polite applause for a point. We sat like this for several such exchanges, and I began to collect myself.

"I play base-ball," the boy said sullenly after a minute. "Base-ball's a good game. Not this."

That last opinion expressed with a wrinkled nose at the athletic spectacle before us.

"I have never seen a base-ball match," I ventured.

"Blazes!" he said, getting a good look at me as he might an animal in a zoo.

Blazes! I wrote down in my notebook.

"Hey!" he cried. He leaned over toward me. "You can't be taking down what people say!"

Again his sister turned toward us. I wondered, should I get up? Make my escape while I still had the chance?

"Let's not bother the gentleman, Harry," my Diana said.

"It's that one that's always writing!" the boy called with a tone that partook of both discovery and tattling. I was chagrined to see several of the guests turn to us.

"Let's not bother people anyway," she said, crossing over and standing before us, without quite acknowledging me. I had no choice but to stand and bow.

"Watch out! He'll take down what you say!"

Thinking that I had been, after a fashion, presented, I stepped forward with a second little bow.

"Hello."

"That's my sister Alice," the boy said; and then, disgusted: "She's always blowing at me."

I smiled agreeably, said hello again, said my name, and when she didn't seem to recognize its eminence, was sufficiently in possession of my Geneva manners to ask did she enjoy the lawn tennis, though I stammered on the "t" in tennis. She answered that she had never seen the game before and had been attending to the play so as to deduce how the score was kept, the deuces and loves and faults and advantages. Curious, wasn't it? Did I understand such obscure nomenclature?

She has the most unusual eyes, the quality of which I had never before been close enough, or rather had never been sufficiently the recipient of, to notice. They seem to be of a gray-blue hue, yet not quite, rather more violet, if such a thing is possible. Or better said: they seemed to melt in and out of their color as if there were some molten substance inside her onto which her eyes "gave," and which was always dissolving and remaking itself as she gazed at you.

She asked was I staying at the Ocean, and why did they never see me at dinner or supper, to which I responded that I was an interloper, that I was of the town itself, and only came to the hotels out of a sorry need to amuse myself.

"You amuse yourself at our expense?"

I told her the *beau monde* must make itself useful in some fashion or other (which made her smile) and then, because she had gazed pointedly at my notebook, told her she beheld a young man in search of a profession, one who thought he might "work up" an article for one of the journals on the life at Newport, the resort life I meant, and so took notes of what I saw and heard, and "lines" I might take. I hoped it might provide an entry into the life of writing *pour les revues* (that last to avoid the treacherous "m" of magazine).

She asked did I remember the scandal a few years back, just before the war, when a newspaperman had pretended in print to be a young belle giving herself over to the follies of the Newport social life? She hoped I was not going to be so duplicitous as to pretend to be something I was not.

We went on in this manner for some time, eventually moving toward the hotel veranda when the dinner gong rang, talking as we walked, "feeling" one another out. She was not, of course, a dressmaker on the lookout (though I may still use her as such; there's *that* much duplicity in me). She said she was from Waterbury (did I know it? I did not) where her father, Mr. Taylor, looked after a brass mill, a position so consuming (she said) that he would not be free to join his family until the end of the month. And then to reciprocate, she asked the question which William and I have dreaded ever since we were school-boys about Washington Square. She asked what my father "did." I pulled a face and told her what Father had told me to say years before when I complained that he had no profession as the other boys' fathers had (and which I could *never*, of course, have actually *said* to those boys), to wit, that he was a Philosopher, a Seeker of Truth, a Student, a Writer of Books. Ah, she said, for I think she now recognized my name, was my father not the great thinker and were we not friends of Mr. Emerson's? I told her that indeed I had that weary pleasure. And then told her how we had of late sojourned in Europe, and that Newport, being the most European of the Northern cities, was meant to be a country, as it were, halfway between the two, in whose atmosphere we might live whilst we changed out of our European attire into our American.

"For like the smallpox," I said, debarking from one metaphor and embarking on another, "one must be inoculated against America if one is European, and against Europe if one is American."

She looked at me then as if I were, indeed, a rare animal, and then said she wondered that an American might need to be inoculated against America. Indeed, if I had been inoculated against *both* America and Europe, then who was I? Did I mean to be an Arab? And she peered at me (*down* at me, it needs to be said) with a look I can only describe as satiric, as if to see if I were up to returning the tennis ball she had just batted at me. I stammered something in response (alas! no figurative stammer!) but she shook her head and smiled at me, softly and beautifully, so that I might understand that she had meant no harm, that she had been teasing me as if we were great friends—indeed, were we *not* great friends? She folded her parasol and stepped up onto the first stair of the veranda.

"Thank you for rescuing me, Mr. James," she said, and when I gave her a quizzing look, explained herself by saying that the conversation in the hotel could be dreadfully conventional. She hoped she might see me and my mysterious notebook about the place again some time. She would even consider serving as my Epeius (really, she said that: not a dressmaker) some day in order to get the Trojan journalist inside the citadel of the Ocean that he might thereby observe the *beau monde* at their consommé. What did I think of that invitation, her looks seemed to ask, was I bold enough? She then called to her brother—Harry!—told him to throw the tennis ball back, and then, holding her hand out for me to shake in the forthright American manner, turned and started up the steps into the hotel.

Was this, then, an example of the business of Newport? I must say I do not believe I have ever been flirted with before!

1778

Mar 26

It has been in my thoughts, one story the Jew told the other evening. I understood it at the time as just part of his Reminiscence, but now I wonder did he mean more by it?

He related a story of a fellow Merchant, tho' I think he meant us to understand the story was of himself, who, before the present Hostilities had commenced, had happened at night upon a Tidewaiter in the hold of one of his ships looking for smuggled Goods as they were charged to do. And that this Merchant, who as I say I take to be Da Silva himself, had snuffed out this Tidewaiter's lantern and had caused him to be removed from the ship, yet then had treated him to a Whisky at one of the low Taverns that front the wharves. He lulled the fellow with Bonhomie and then, as they were leaving, looked around at the riffe-raffe in the room with them, the molattoes and wharf Rats, and said did the Tidewaiter not think that £10 would buy the Violent hand of any one of them?

He is not a man to be trifled with. I know this even without the Evidence of this story. His family survived the Romish Inquisition through Guile & Duplicity, and he himself made his way by his own wits first to the Netherlands and then to the Dutch West Indies, where he rose to Prominence and has still trading Interests & Properties. A man who buys and sells other Human beings, even if they be Africans, is not likely to scruple in his private Affairs, notwithstanding his pleasant aspect and his snug Abode and the dark eyes of his Daughter.

And withal I wonder just how I am to advance. These first moves have been easy, for we have our Parts to play: I the visiting Aristocrat, she the colonial Flower. We are thrown together by the Exigency of War, and the

Rules which otherwise govern are for a time suspended. But how to progress? What plausible Plan to employ? If she is naïf enough to think that someone of my Class might marry a Jew, then her father is not. So I cannot pretend to court her as I otherwise might. But if not that, then what?

As to employing Phyllis, as was my original Intention, how do I know that she is not already a Spaniel, reporting my moves to her Master? She speaks no love for Da Silva, or for her Mistress, and I fancy she might enjoy seeing them played, yet might not these same dislikes be but Feints & Ploys? Indeed, the very Hatred she expresses toward the family may be a Masquerade, or it may be no Masquerade but why should she not have hatred as well toward me and my Purse? If she does not object to getting her Knees sore for half-a-crown, would she not sell her Loyalty to whoever would Pay?

Mar 27

A Colº Benjamin came in last night and is released on his Parole to return to England. A month past there was a pinnace-full of Rebels brought in, sick each one, and released too on their Parole. Are we to believe the word of these Rebels not to rejoin the strife? If War is to be fought should it not be fought to Win, and to the Devil with these Grace notes and Curtsies?

Heard from an aged Resident of this city that the Jews of Newport in years past were wont to fling open their doors and windows at the onset of a Thunder-storm, and to employ themselves in the midst of the Storm with prayers & singing. This was a Superstition of their Race that the Messiah would come at just such a Calamitous moment and this was their way of welcoming him into their homes. Curious.

Have had no recurrence of my Melancholia, nor of those Fits that sometimes follow upon. Tho' he is the type to keep the Confidence, still I regret having told Smithson of the Circumstances of my Scar. I sometimes catch him gazing at me with something like fraternal concern, as if he were gauging me, measuring my Mood.

Apr 1

The news at breakfast was that two vessels laden with Oysters and blue crab and Flounder from Long Island Bay had entered the Harbour and were selling their fish to whoever could pay. I was sure this was someone's clever All Fools' joke (*poisson d'avril* the French call such pranks), but no, there were Oysters to be had. I sent Private Stephens to procure five bushels. And then to alleviate the Dullness these last days have put me under followed after him down to the Harbour.

When I drew up to where they were unloading the fish I had the surprize of seeing, in the midst of the gathering, Judith accompanied by Hannibal and a Negroe boy also of the Jew's house. When I expressed my Wonder at seeing her, she said that she would have me know that with her Step-Mother gone, she was charged with running her father's Household. It was too dull not to have employment, she said. We colonial women, she said, are not the delicate flowers you English raise in your Orangeries.

Did she not, then, consider herself English as her father did?

Indeed she did. If she was not English, then what was she? She hoped she was not an Arab! But she ventured to say that she was an American Englishwoman.

This bewildered me. I wanted to ask did she think she could be a Jew and an Englishwoman at the same time, but of course I did not. Instead I found myself relating how a German friend of my family who had visited Newport before the War had remarked that the Jews of the New World were not known by their Beards & Clothes but dressed like other men in colorful silk and white wigs, and that their women were in the same French style as other women. To which she responded, But we are as other women.

Indeed you are not, Miss Da Silva, I had wit enough to say. And I followed the remark with some further Gallantry I will forgo reproducing here.

But I did not fall into the Badinage that has become the mode of our usual Intercourse. For I had the Inspiration that it might no longer do to take up that bantering way, even if that Banter brought with it the Vivacity of her eyes. Instead I saw clearly that from this point on, the way forward lay in Sincerity and in the evidence of a Troubled Heart. So I let my voice grow thoughtful and told her that it sometimes saddened me that we had met under the Dreadful circumstance of War, for I held it a Privation that I might not enjoy her company under more Civil circumstances. And I sighed and accounted it a lack that in Devon where I grew up it might be permitted us to walk among the shops or to have a Pic-nic upon the Meadows. But here there were eight thousand pairs of Military eyes upon us. Was that not a Hardship, Miss Da Silva?

She said I was not Bold enough, that if she wanted a Pic-nic, there was nothing that would stop her from having one.

Did she want me, then, to be more bold? I asked her.

To which she answered that I was an Officer in the Royal Welch Fusiliers, was I not? Attach'd to General Pigot's staff, in charge of marshalling his Spies? She supposed I was bold enough.

I told her I would endeavor to be as she wished.

When her slave boy return'd with his basket I noted it had only Flounder in it, and remark'd to Judith that it was a pity she was forbidden the eating of Shellfish, and did she know that the Romans considered Oysters an Aphrodisiak? And that they used to put them in Saltwater pools and fatten them with Wine & Pastries for some weeks before enjoying them?

Apr 3

Word comes this morning that at Genl Pigot's order I am to accompany a party charged with a Survey of the island's Defences. I am to take some of my Spies with me and distribute them as I see fit that they may report on the Locals. We shall be gone several days. I shall take this Opportunity to show a crest-fallen face at Da Silva's this afternoon. Parting is such Sweet Sorrow, &c.

Had coffee that was part of the lading of the rebel Schooner lately taken by *The Maidstone*. Bradshaw managed to place his hands upon it. I took a cup in Satisfaction of his debt. Delightful aroma.

And now just returned from Da Silva's. Learned there that Smithson has called upon the Jew under his own sail. Extraordinary. What is he after? I wonder.

Da Silva being still at his Counting-house when I arrived, I had occasion for some private talk with Judith in which I mentioned the writing of this Journal. Told her I wrote it with the Imagination that years hence I would read it and remember my Youth. Perhaps it would form the basis of a Memoir, for were these not Historical times? She asked did I write about my visits with her, and did not Blush asking it. I told her oh yes, I did. Told her our Conversations before her father's fire were my chief respite from the unhappy Duties of War, and more of the sort. Told her I would remember them, and her, wherever Life took me.

A good move, letting her know the Impression she had made upon me, and that I carry that Impression with me. It prepares the way for more Intimate confession.

But Smithson! The man sees me shave every morning, sees the Scar upon my throat, knows its origin. Is the damned Fellow telling tales behind my back?

When Da Silva returned I could not keep myself from goading the Jew about his Loyalties, did he not work both ends of the Conflict? There was a Suspicion to that effect amongst Admiral Howe's staff, I told him. Was he not a kind of Sebastiao to the Loyalists and an Isaac to the Rebels? Contemptible mood that only grew worse with every sight of Judith's bosom. Imagined myself forcing the girl. Upon leaving, signaled to Phyllis to come later. She is just left. Treated her roughly, but with great Pleasure.

❧ 1692 ❧

6th Day

Ashes told me once that when she sleeps, her Spirit travels back to Africa. There she finds her Village and her mother and her sister with whom she talks as if she had never come away. It is then her Spirit is happy, she says. Someday, she says, her Spirit will stay in Africa. And we will see her no more.

I had once, shortly after Mother died, said to Ashes that we were both orphans now. I meant it I know not how, but as if it was my Fear speaking that it might not be so. And that she would say it was not so, that Father would yet return, as to comfort me and to reassure me. And indeed she answer'd that we were none, but it was not as I had meant her to answer. For she then said that her Mother and Father were still alive, and I felt the Force of what she said and was shaken. And I thought, too (why had I never consider'd it before?), how she must feel the loss of her Mother. For now it has come to me to know somewhat of that. And it is not so clear to me as it has been beforetimes that God has given it to us to be above the African Race as I have heard it said. But I do wonder now.

2nd Day

In Meeting yesterday, John Pettibone would stare at me so! Every time I look'd across at him his eyes darted away!

We used to throw Mussels at one another down along the breakwater.

3rd Day

Oh, those first Days when we learn'd that Father had yet to make port! I would lie in bed (and Mother suffering so!) and I couldn't help but picture the *Dove* engulf'd in Storm, the rolling deck, and the Waves breaking over the bow, and the Sails shredded! Yet whatever pictures my Fancy would conjure I would just as quickly counter them with a Saving. Oh, they had got the ship turn'd into the wind just in time! They are not stove as they had thought! They made it into the dory and might yet brave the storm! It was as if I were there aboard the ship and could alter what was fated, tho' I lay in my bed still. As if (as Ashes says!) my Spirit travel'd to Father that I might save him.

Is it not possible that he is wreck'd upon one of the lesser islands of the Indies? He and James Beecher and the others? And that in time we will hear of it, that he is Saved, that he returns aboard a Newport vessel any day now?

If his Soul is with the Lord, yet I do feel such Fear and Dread. How low I am in my Understanding!

4th Day

Jane Beecher and I have had our soap-making. She is such a handsome and yet I think forbidding woman. But I am grateful to her for making a Party of the soap-making as she used to do with Mother, for it is the most unpleasant of the household Chores.

She is taller than me, and strong, and altogether what is accounted a buxom woman. I feel so very slight when she is around. Her two young children were there to play with Dorcas, and I brought Ashes to help. She cannot understand Ashes, who speaks as do the Negroes of the Islands. Again we did not speak of her husband James or of Father.

We set the leach and she show'd me that it must be strong enough to float a potato so that a part just the size of a Ninepence stands up out of the Lye. Like a woman's nipple, she said with a look that embarrass'd me. The work took us all morning. We were in the Dooryard and we had to keep the children away for it is burny stuff. And then we boil'd and boil'd, but we had luck and the soap was soft and good and without Grease. Toward the end there was some light Snow. We heard it falling in the dry brown leaves that were still on the oak, and we look'd at one another with Satisfaction.

When we were done we divided the Soap and I sent Ashes home with our share.

Jane then spread a Supper for we were tired and hungry and cold from working out of doors.

She was very soft of me. She ask'd did I not miss Mother, and was it not hard to have no Woman to speak to? She told me that she had seen John Peele and John Cole come to the House third day last and said she knew why they came for they had come to her too. I told her they had brought as well the news that some of our Society had put themselves forth to adopt Dorcas and me. She ask'd whether a Match had been propos'd, which made me Blush but I answer'd that there had been None, that doubtless I am accounted as yet too young. To which she said I was come into a Woman's body and that there would surely be a man would not mind my Youth. There was always such a Man, she said. I mark'd the tone with which she spoke, for I had heard her do so before. A girl's body is like a Garden that ripens, she said, and there will always be someone who will want the harvest of it.

She says too that she will not remarry if it is the case that her James is lost. That she will turn her hand to sewing for others, and if she needs to, she will get a small shop of Fabric and sundry sewing Articles and become a Mercer. But she will not remarry.

1st Day

After Meeting today I had a Visit at the house of Henry and Esther Pennington which tho' I try not to write on first days I must set down. For the news is of the late witch Trials in the Massachusetts. There are some two dozen hang'd we are told and more awaiting, but now the dissenting minister Mr. Mather has spoken against spectral Evidence. We talk'd much of whether the Townspeople there, even their Magistrates and Divines, have been laboring under a delusion of Satan.

John Peele then express'd the Idea that if there is a Light that comes to us, may there not be also a Darknesse? I was greatly work'd upon by this Conceit. For I have always thought, from my own Experience, that the opposite of the Light was an Emptiness, or as I may say, an Absence. It is, for me, a lack of Light that I live in most. But this Conceit of John Peele's has struck me with great Force.

Are there, then, those among us who have Visitations of Darknesse, as we of the Society hope to have Visitations of Light? Is there, if I may follow out the Conceit, a type of Inner Darknesse as there is the Inner Light? This is most terrible to think of! For as I hope to live my life by the Instruction of God's Light, are there those around me who live their life under the Influence of a Darknesse? And who are they? For the news from the Massachusetts is not that these Witches are the Thieves of the highway or the Water-rats of the wharves, but they are Members of the Community, tho' they be not Friends. There is an Awe in that, I think, a Dread that makes me quail at the World around me.

And now that I write this I am struck that the Matter may be even more subtile. For these Townspeople of the Massachusetts, did they not think they were acting in a Brightnesse, and now that Brightnesse is reveal'd as Darknesse? Can the Devil act so to perplex us? Can our Spirits be so bewilder'd that our Minds and Hearts are as a Maze?

I walk'd home with Jane Beecher and we did talk much of this news.

4th Day, 2 ix mo.

I have been all the way out to the land which is call'd Doubling Point, past the farms and the old Narragansett sites. I walk'd and walk'd as if I would outwalk Affliction. When the land gave out I stood and look'd at the blue bay and the great blue sky with the gulls crying all around me. There was one sail on the Horizon, and for a moment my Heart leapt, but I soon saw it was not sloop-rigg'd. I sat on a rock and look'd across the water.

A Conviction has come into me as an Intruder who has taken up a seat at our Hearth and will not be moved: there can be no more denying Father is lost. That we can not be certain of this is no Reason to go about in blind Belief. As Jane Beecher says, it is the nature of the Sea that we often do not know a vessel's Loss for a Surety. And to hope in the face of such Likelihood seems a Blindnesse.

I have known this without admitting it, but now it seems to me as a Child's thing that must be put away. I must admit it so that I may set a Course based on the Apprehension. Dorcas and I are Orphans, and God has seen fit to place my little Sister in my Care and I must find a way whereby she may be saved.

What are the Difficulties? What is the End to be aim'd at?

The Difficulties may be named. We must have Firewood enough and flour and corn and fish. And tho' there is enough money in Father's Bible-box for this Winter, it will run out and then what? I might let out Ashes to another Family. I might even sell her outright. That would increase my work, but not, I pray, beyond what I can do. And it might earn enough that we might have our Wants taken care of. I shall have to think on this.

And the End? Are there, as Jane Beecher says, men who would have me? She says I own a House now, and a Servant, and she says I am pleasant enough to look at, what Man would not take this? But I would not have a Man who wants me for my House and my Chattels. Is that not suspect? Yet all others are but Boys and I am not sure Dorcas and I can manage until they are Men.

John Pettibone is throwing Mussels at girls still, I fear.

I must be strong. I must look to Jane Beecher and her Strength, for I am amaz'd that she is able to face the Prospect of her Husband being lost with such belief in herself and her Abilities.

2nd Day

This morning I went out to Abraham Levi's shop with Dorcas. When we return'd there was on the door-stead a neatly folded-over scrap of muzlin and inside some several Coins amounting to 1£, 8d, 4p. This anger'd me, and sham'd me, and made me thankful all at once.

6th Day

Over the course of the last few Days, Jane Beecher has come to the house to look over our Stores, and our Firewood, and much else. And she was stern with Ashes, and brought her a new broom when she saw how unfit ours was become. She has given Dorcas some of her Ruth's gowns that have grown too small. And today she brought over two of her own stays that she said have become too small for her. She ripp'd out the stitches, and had me standing before the fire in my smock that she might lay the Pieces against me and measure them to fit. We cut and sew'd and I was endlessly putting on and taking off my Petticotes and waistcoat. She watch'd me as a Mother might, I suppose, tho' she would say now and then, that yes she could understand a man's being interested in me. She pull'd my Smock tight against me, against my waist and elsewhere, as if she meant to show how I have chang'd. After a while I stopp'd smiling at this, for she did not do it as Hannah or Martha might.

Still she is become a great Friend, and a Strength to me. She calls me Prudence, and it is so nice to hear my name spoken by one who might love me.

⇀ 2011 ↽

The more Sandy saw of Aisha—and their getting together always had to be clandestine—the more he appreciated how her life in Newport required a certain tiptoeing finesse. From the outside she seemed so free and self-assured, her summers spent working in the Orangery while in her Brooklyn studio a couple of MFA students from Pratt Institute were knocking out a retail year's worth of what she called her donkey designs. But she didn't quite make a living from her business, she let him know. Between the salary she paid the interns, and her Brooklyn rent, and the fact that she wasn't, you know, famous yet—no, she couldn't really support herself. And the gems she used for her real pieces—jade, malachite, lapis lazuli, not to mention the gold and platinum—were expensive. If something were to happen to her situation here—and someday, of course, it *would* happen; surely she and Alice couldn't be college roommates forever—well, she needed time to establish herself, to get her high-end designs into the shops on Newbury Street, Bloor Street, Rodeo Drive: that's what she was shooting for. She was ambitious, she admitted.

Okay, if she didn't hire the Pratt students each summer to do the donkey work, instead spent the better part of the year doing it herself, then yeah, she could probably support herself. But that wasn't what she wanted. What she wanted was to design and make stuff that was hers, hers alone, unlike anyone else's. Beautiful, expensive stuff that would be bought and worn by beautiful, expensive people. And fate or luck had put her in this unusual situation where she had the freedom to design and make what she wanted and she wasn't going to wreck it. She never quite declared to Sandy just exactly what her unusual situation was, but if she admitted she couldn't support herself then money was coming from somewhere, wasn't it? So it presumably wasn't just the residual habit of looking after Alice as it'd been during their college days. Well, he wasn't going to be holier-than-thou about that. And he had to admit her designs were beautiful in an edgy kind of way. He'd seen a couple of them in the display cases at All That Glitters, an upscale store down along Thames Street, and more of them on her website, all professionally photographed in moody light and shadow. The snaky mermaid figured in a number of them.

One long weekend when the du Ponts were off at a wedding down in Delaware he got to watch her work. They had risked his coming out to Windermere because the caretaker and his wife had gone off on a jaunt of their own, and that left only the two Salve Regina college girls that Margo hired every summer to help with the housework—Mitten and Rachel were their names this year—who presumably didn't know what was what. So they had hung out for the three days like regular lovers, and he got to watch her sit at her long workbench against the glass wall of the Orangery, hammers and files and jeweler's saws arrayed in front of her. He asked her questions—he knew nothing about soldering, casting, about tripoli, rouge, all the different hammers and anvils and stuff—and she explained things to him, even let him tap away at some silver wire to see what it was like. It struck him how capable and efficient she was, how much she knew what she was doing and where she was going.

Beautiful as it was, with its walls of glass looking out over the broad lawn at Alva Vanderbilt's crazy teahouse perched on the distant rocks, the Orangery wasn't really habitable. It had only a makeshift kitchen and no bathroom and no heat. So though Aisha tried to keep a low profile—tried to keep out of Tom and Margo's hair, she said—she still had to go up to the house to shower or fix herself something to eat or go to the bathroom. She had her own room on the second floor—the third floor was the servants' quarters, where the college girls lived—but she only slept there on occasion, on nights when it was cold, or if she'd hung out with Alice after dinner, maybe watching a movie, and it would seem odd for her to head back to the studio for the night. She kept tabs on when Tom and Margo were home—or would be home—always trying to minimize her presence. She didn't want to wear out her welcome.

But for that three-day weekend they had free use of the house. There were still the college girls to look out for but they had their own door in and out and used the servants' staircase, and Margo had them pretty much trained to stay on the third floor except when they were cleaning the house or whatever. So they cooked in the big kitchen, ate at the stupendous dining table in the stupendous dining room with its shimmering wall sconces and massive fireplace, had late-night cocktails on the veranda overlooking the dark water of Doubling Point Cove, and made love, it seemed, in every room of the house. ("Six down," Aisha said once, "twenty-two more to go.") They stayed up all hours, drank Tom's scotch, walked around half dressed, and when they'd had their fill of each other's bodies, lay on whatever bed or couch or rug they found themselves on and talked.

"Join the club," Aisha said when he told her about the Mr. Winterbourne business. They were in the upstairs sunroom with its wicker furniture and fat pillows, naked, letting the sun warm them. "She used to call me Merton Densher. From *The Wings of the Dove.*"

This had been in Italy, she said, in Venice, on that trip they'd taken after the first suicide attempt. The time Alice's mother had paid Aisha's way. The novel was about this guy Merton Densher, who was supposed to woo a dying heiress so that he might inherit her money when she died, and then marry the woman he was truly in love with. The whole plan being this other woman's.

"We were staying in a room across the Grand Canal from the Palazzo Barbaro, which is where this dying heiress is staying in the novel. I don't remember it bothering me at the time. It was just a joke. Although I do remember pointing out to her once that she wasn't, in fact, dying. She said she could fix that."

It had been over a boy, that first time. He was a senior and Alice had been a freshman. He had been her first-ever boyfriend. Aisha had never really gotten the full story of what had happened. Had the guy just wanted to break up with her? Slept with someone else? Jesus, had he done it—slept with Alice, she meant—on somebody's dare or something? Whatever it was, the breakup came right during finals week and just as a testament to something or other, Alice had finished all the work she had to do, took her calc exam, handed in her term paper on the *Symposium*, packed her side of the dorm room up, left her room key on her bureau, and then did it. Horse tranquilizer. Whether she'd gotten it out at the Red Hook stables or on the street—cat valium, it was called—she never said. But it was no suicide gesture. If Aisha hadn't found her, she would have died.

It was there in Venice, while they were gondoliered around with *The Wings of the Dove* like a guidebook, that Alice and Aisha had developed the Theory of the Heiress's Dilemma. Which was how to know someone loved you for yourself alone and not your golden bank account. The dilemma in Alice's case being further complicated by the fact that you had to go at it with the presumption, the a priori thingie had to be that they *didn't* love you. Because, as Alice put it, what normal twentysomething guy wanted a retard for a wife, eh? This was the rare variant known as the Retarded Heiress's Dilemma, she'd said, sucking on an ice as they went under the Accademia Bridge. Perhaps one could devise a test, insist that the candidate agree to share the retarded heiress's condition, like Isolde dying a sympathetic death with Tristan. The candidate would have to contract cerebral palsy is what he'd have to do, drink a draught, a potion or something. Instead of Tristan you could insert Romeo here, kneeling beside the poisoned Juliet in her family's tomb, taking the poison himself to share Death's Darkness with her, although of course once you drank the potion—this was Aisha talking now—it was Windermere you got to share.

Because Windermere was Alice's, she said, did Sandy know that? Windermere—the whole amazing place—was Alice's, not Tom's. Their mother had seen to that. Tom had inherited the apartment on the Upper East Side. Twelve rooms. Alice had gotten Windermere. Twenty-eight rooms. That way there would be no having to sell, no splitting the family legacy. Tom and Margo were there by Alice's sufferance. And don't think Margo wasn't aware of that.

"I want you to be nice to her," she unexpectedly said, and when Sandy responded, hey, he was nice to everyone: "Especially nice. Like with the motorcycle and Da Silva's that day." (Ah, he'd been wondering if she knew.) "Because she's always on the edge. For all her wiseguyness, she's always just this far away. And I love her. Life would be a lot less fun without Alice. Okay?" she said, and she began kissing him again. "Okay?"

He found himself after that weekend—whether as a result of the motorcycle day or because Aisha was orchestrating things, he didn't know—
but he found himself spending more time with the two of them, casually
included for dinner, for an ice cream cone, rounded up for a jaunt over to
Mystic Seaport, and once when a new Netflix arrived, out at Windermere
eating microwaved pot stickers and watching a Cary Grant movie. Halfway through the film Margo had drifted in and he had felt weird sitting
there in the dark with the three of them, Margo shushing Alice, who had
to sigh theatrically every time Cary Grant did a Cary Grant thing.

"Keep an eye on her," Margo told him a few nights later when she'd
come by his condo. He thought she had meant Alice but then realized it
was Aisha she was talking about. "She has a way of wanting things," she
said. And he had to hear about how back in college Aisha had dated Tom,
did Sandy know that? Sandy did know that, but it was safer to say he didn't.
"It didn't go anywhere," Margo resumed. "But let's not be naive about
what she was after. I know a little something about that."

"But I'm not rich," he smilingly said, trying to deflect the insinuation,
trying to keep back the urge to defend Aisha.

"No," Margo said then, starting to unbutton his shirt, "but you have
other assets."

Which she knew a little something about as well, she added.

At the Casino, preparations were under way for the Campbell's Tournament, which would take place in the second week of July and which would
include the induction of Andre Agassi into the Tennis Hall of Fame on the
Saturday of the semifinals. It was a big deal, sold out since January. There
were the courts to get into perfect shape, media requests to attend to, ac-
commodations for the VIPs who would be attending. Sandy did his bit, serving as docent for this or that sponsor, showing them around the grounds,
taking them into the beautiful buildings of the old Casino where the Tennis
Hall of Fame was now housed. He even managed to work in some of the
stuff Alice had told him of the early days of the Casino—the billiard rooms,
the men smoking cigars, the women in their Parisian gowns—and no, he
always had to tell them, it had never been *that* kind of casino.

He found himself wanting to ask Aisha what it had been like back when she was dating Tom. Being a young black woman and Tom a rich white guy, he meant. And he wanted to ask whether she and Tom had, you know, slept together, but he knew that that was one of those stupid guy things he was supposed to be curing himself of so he didn't. When they talked once, she described it as a time of confusion for her. She had never loved Tom, nor he her as far as she knew. But maybe, yeah, she had been trying to talk herself into loving him, or at least believing that she *could* love him. She had been nineteen. She was on a scholarship. Her father came to the supper table each night still in his overalls. She had never experienced anything like Windermere, or that trip to Venice, or the apartment on the Upper East Side. When that kind of money was involved, that kind of privilege—Sandy should have seen the palazzo they stayed in on the Grand Canal—could anybody really be sure of their motives? How do you separate love for a person from your experience of them? And when that experience includes twelve-dollar martinis at the Waldorf-Astoria bar? And you're this black kid with a pipe fitter for a father, helping Vassar up its diversity quotient, what then?

(It struck him, listening to her sometimes, that he didn't know whether she was complicated or simple—psychologically speaking, he meant. Whether this business with Tom and her account of it—the struggle, the second-guessing, the insistence on looking at things squarely—was because she was honest with herself, undeluded about the complexity of her motives, or whether it was just that, as Margo said, she wanted things.)

One feeling he could never quite shake was the suspicion that she actually welcomed his involvement with Margo. It had something to do with the lack of jealousy, the continued insistence on secrecy. Sure, okay, he could understand how her situation might get a bit dicey if Margo knew about them (not to mention his own situation), but still, he couldn't rid himself of the feeling that it afforded her a pretext, and that what she really wanted was not to keep their affair secret from Margo, but from Alice. He couldn't explain it, couldn't prove it, and sure, maybe it was just him being paranoid. But once when they'd been talking about her finding out, it'd dawned on him that they were talking about two different "hers," Sandy meaning Margo and Aisha Alice. Did she have a history of keeping her boyfriends secret out of concern for Alice? he wondered. Surely Alice didn't begrudge her a normal romantic life.

As it turned out, there was no ticket for him to the Hall of Fame ball. There were just too many in-house requests this year, the superintendent of the Casino told him a little sheepishly. This was at the hundred-dollar Meet and Greet at the beginning of the tournament. When Margo found out, she said she could get him one, but she said it in a way that made him think she didn't really want to, so nah, he said, he didn't have a tux anyway. But then Alice said hey, she needed an escort, someone to protect her from the riot of suitors.

"How about it, sailor?"

So on the evening of the ball, after the semifinals and the induction ceremony earlier in the day, he went out to Windermere in his rented tux so the four of them could ride to the pavilion in Tom's car. Aisha stood with them under the porte cochere in her work overalls and took photos like they were headed to the prom. He felt a little weird. Not just being Alice's date—if that's what he was—but because he'd had no chance to see Agassi earlier and he dreaded some humiliating moment when Agassi didn't quite remember him. They'd played once at the beginning of Sandy's career, had hung out during a rain delay once playing Hearts, but while these were highlights for Sandy, they were nothing to Agassi. And Steffi Graf would barely have heard of him. Ugh.

But as it turned out, Alice had no interest in elbowing her way into the great man's presence. She was content instead to stand off to the side and just watch. So that's what they did, drinking wine, snagging hors d'oeuvres, and making comments about everyone. Behind them the pavilion windows were open to the ocean and there was a lovely night breeze coming through the screens. A band was playing nineties hits, but it was so crowded you couldn't dance. Which was okay with Alice: she only danced when she was alone, she said. Or with Aisha if she was very, very drunk.

"*Very* drunk," she emphasized.

They went outside once, onto the deck built above the rocks and below which the surf curled and broke. It was less crowded there and a few couples were taking advantage of the elbow room and dancing. There were these two teenage boys over by the door horsing around, one of them imitating Alice's gait and the other busting a gut laughing. Sandy managed to turn Alice away in time, guiding her toward the railing that overlooked the ocean. It was chilly, he said, and asked if she was all right—had she seen? he was wondering—but she just smiled and said yes, it was beautiful.

Out over the water, a half mile off, there was a wall of cloud, fog. He'd heard of such things but had never seen it, not a wall like that. It was just hanging there, right above the water, not moving, like a curtain, faintly lit by the lights from the shore. They gazed at it in silence.

"You look very handsome," he heard beside him. She hadn't turned to him, had her eyes still out to the fog bank. He wanted to say something in turn, to say that she looked nice in her gown. It was green—brocade, he supposed—with these thin straps that showed her shoulders nicely.

"Are you drunk enough to dance yet?" he asked instead. She kept herself turned to the ocean, closed her eyes, lifted her face to the breeze.

"I don't want those boys to hurt themselves laughing," she said.

Ah, he thought. Yet she had said it with something like amusement— serenity, tolerance, forgiveness: he didn't know what. It made him feel suddenly the commonplace of the experience for her. The Chemical Heiress, Aisha said she'd heard her called at Vassar. Sometimes the Plastics Princess. Who knew what else.

When it grew too chilly, they turned to go back inside. Sandy held the door open for Alice, and then found himself leaning over the boys and telling them to smarten up. And when that didn't seem enough: "Assholes."

For the rest of the evening they stood and chatted with people they knew. At some point Andre and Steffi left and the room relaxed. Sandy danced with Margo, with some older women he knew from this and that. Alice chatted with the director of the Redwood Library. Around midnight when they'd had enough the four of them got in Tom's car and headed back to Windermere, where Alice thanked him for a lovely evening in her Scarlett O'Hara voice and Tom said: "Nice moves, big guy." Margo merely twiddled her fingers good night. There was no invitation for a nightcap.

Back downtown at his condo building, instead of going inside he went across to the fish pier with its stacks of lobster traps and commercial fishing gear. He could see the pier from his living room window, and the contrast it made to the Newport Shipyard next over with its million-dollar yachts in dry dock always made him think of Aisha and her father the pipe fitter. More than that: of Aisha as a black person in the midst of all this white wealth. He walked in between the coils of rope and the plastic bins and buoys, past where the commercial boats with their unlovely booms and winches were moored alongside the pier. Out beyond the harbor the fog was still there, still like a curtain someone had drawn. The Pell Bridge disappeared behind it, and the mainland lights that should have been across the way had vanished. He watched the cars rising up into the darkness and disappearing into the gray cloud. It was weirdly unnerving.

He turned and started back down the pier. Ahead of him on the block-long face of the complex he could pick out the windows of his condo. For the umpteenth time he wondered how much it was worth. It was just a one-bedroom but it faced the harbor, and the complex itself was upscale: it had that shingle-style look, and the courtyard was beautifully landscaped. Half a million? He supposed at least that, and he wondered how long it would be before he could afford such a place. Would he *ever* be able to afford such a place? He hadn't used to think that way, had never been one to covet things. Was it Newport or just the age he'd reached? The fact that he had to find some way forward?

He entered the lobby, nodded to the concierge behind his desk, and took the elevator up. Inside the condo he went and stood at the window, looked out to where he had just been, at the rusty, ungainly fishing boats, and then at the yachts in the shipyard next over. He undressed in the dark, climbed into bed. He would have to do something. It was all right to tread water in Newport for a year while he got used to his career being over, but now he needed to figure things out. Surely he would be a viable candidate for a college job. A Division I school would grab him in an instant, although he'd have to be someone's assistant at first. Or maybe Division III. Williams, Trinity, heck, Vassar: those kinds of places would go for him, wouldn't they? And he was personable. If he got to the interview stage, how could they not hire him? Would that be okay, he wondered, Coach Sandy? Maybe a women's college, heh. Were there still women's colleges? Mount Holyoke? Sweet Briar?

When his cell phone rang he felt like he'd only been asleep for a couple of minutes, but when he looked at the clock on his nightstand it was three thirty. He scrambled out of bed, flipped open the phone. There was a young woman downstairs who wanted to see him, the concierge said. No, she didn't want to come up, she wanted him to come down. So he pulled on his clothes—Margo?—went down the hall, and got in the elevator. He dropped the two floors and when the doors opened—a few seconds before he actually saw her—he knew it was going to be Alice.

"Hey," she said when she saw him.

"Hey," he said. She was still wearing her green gown, but she had on a plastic see-through raincoat over it. And absurdly, a deerstalker hat, her long light-colored hair pulled behind and down her back. He walked her a little ways away from the concierge. "You're drunk," he said.

"I've come to fetch you."

"You're drunk."

"A necessary ontological state," she said, and she pulled a pint of something from her raincoat pocket. "Necessary for you too." And she handed him the bottle. He handed it back.

"I was sleeping."

"The game's afoot, Watson."

"I was sleeping."

"I've come to awaken you. I've come to awaken you from your benighted state." And she took a step toward the door that opened onto the courtyard and held her hand out to him. "The fog's come in," she said. "The ghosts are walking. I've come to fetch you." And she waggled her hand in the air. "Come on."

He let her lead him out into the courtyard, but stopped once they were outside. The winches on the boats at the fish pier had vanished. There was no traffic and the quiet was eerie. Every ten seconds the foghorn out on Goat Island sounded, and then in the distance like an echo, a second horn.

"That's the Newport Bridge horn," Alice said. Then: "Ssshh." They listened. She raised her brows like: *Did you hear it?* But he hadn't heard anything. She waited and then raised them again, and this time he thought he had heard something.

"That's Fort Adams," she said and started down the street. When he didn't follow, she waggled her hand again. He had either to make a fuss or give in. Beneath the hem of her gown he saw she was wearing orange sneakers.

"What are we doing?" he asked when he'd caught up to her.

"We're walking."

"Where're we walking?"

"From the twenty-first century backwards," she said. She fished in her plastic raincoat and handed him the bottle of bourbon again: "This helps the ghosts come out."

He touched the bottle to his lips, tilted his head back, but he didn't actually drink. He didn't want to be drunk; he wanted to be back in bed. He was going to have to humor her and then somehow get her back in a taxi.

They went out to Storer Park where it overlooked the harbor and the Pell Bridge. But there was nothing to see, no bridge and no harbor. Sandy could barely make out the basketball court where some nights after work and a frozen pizza he came and waited for the townies—mostly black guys who called him Larry and tolerated his jump shot—to let him play. It was one of the spots Aisha and he had arranged as a kind of meeting place: weeknights, at dusk, with plausible deniability should someone see them. Now Alice led him over to the seawall where they stood on one of the huge granite blocks looking out into the gray nothing.

"Do you hear that?"

He didn't hear anything. Just the three foghorns. Close. Far. Farther.

"What?"

"That," she said. Again he listened. "That's the Rose Island bell. Hear it?"

He didn't hear any bell.

"Taken down in 1912," she said. "Replaced by a steam-powered horn, in turn dismantled in the early seventies." She turned her face up to his, smiled—was he going to play or not?

"Look," he said. "Why don't you come back to my place. I've got a pull-out couch." And when she lowered her chin, gave him a disappointed look from under her brows: "You're drunk. I'm tired. And this is a little nuts."

"Not nuts," she said. "Adventurous. Stimulating. An unconventional yet memorable evening spent in the company of a charming young lady."

And she snugged her deerstalker hat down on her head. "I didn't think you'd be such a buzzkill, Watson."

He held his breath, looked down at her like he was going to give her what-for, then blew out his cheeks like okay, fine. "Whatever," he said, and he swept his hand in an after-you gesture. "Lead on, Sherlock."

And for the next hour he let her take him through the narrow seventeenth-century streets of the Point, in and out of the driftways and along the buckling sidewalks under the gaslights. She had a story for every spot: the pirates hanged on Gravelly Point, the Depression-era nuns living in Hunter House, the Quakers in their prim, small-windowed homes. Every so often she'd take out the bottle of bourbon and drink—"The trick, Watson, is to maintain a steady state of inebriation"—and then carry on. She showed him some of the houses her grandmother had been involved in saving, one of them the house where the Vicomte de Noailles had lived during the Revolution, another a tiny building on Willow Street where there had lived an infamous Jamaican slave who announced to anyone who would listen that she was a witch. At one point they walked out the length of the Elm Street Pier until the shore vanished behind them and there was nothing but vacant gray in front of them and the bleating of the foghorns. They stood and listened. It was eerie, even for Sandy.

"We might be the only two alive," Alice whispered.

They just stood and peered into the emptiness. Somewhere in the gray a dog barked. Alice seemed to have stopped breathing.

"We can't see them," she said after another minute, "but they're there."

Back on the Point she conjured for him the carriages and oxcarts, the cobblestones, the high tides that crept up the driftways, the wharves with their hogsheads and wheelbarrows. He had to forget tennis, she said, forget the Casino and the Hall of Fame and the houses along Bellevue: they hadn't been built yet. "Forget the rich people," she told him, "forget you and me." They didn't exist. There was nothing but sheep out on the Doubling Point meadows. He needed to imagine that this was the world: these little houses, the narrow streets, the Quakers thee'ing and thou'ing each other and the slaves speaking their creole. It was a foggy night in—oh, 1706, she said—and everyone was sleeping. Up there, she said, and she pointed to the little half-windows of a third floor—slaves sleeping three to a bed and dreaming of their homes in Africa. Of their mothers and fathers. Of the village girl they used to watch.

He looked down at her when she said this.

"It's a moral obligation," she said. And she peered up into his face to see if he understood. "They're dead. We're alive."

At which she slipped her hand under his arm, started him down the narrow street.

From the Point they went out to Battery Park and then across the railroad tracks and across Farewell Street into the North Burial Grounds. They passed the modern headstones ("Cheap thrills," said Alice) and then wandered in and around the older grave markers with their slate death's-heads and angels' wings. It was too dark to make them out, Alice said, but there were gravestones that had soul effigies with African features—noses and lips and hair—and up behind God's Little Acre there was a string of small stones that marked the graves of Isaac Da Silva's servants, nominally Jews, she said, but not allowed in the Touro cemetery. It was hilarious, wasn't it? That a crypto-Jew in Portugal should have slaves who were crypto-Christians in Newport, hey? Outcasts all, she said. And she closed her eyes, seemed to sway on her feet. And then without warning she plopped over backwards onto the cemetery grass, sat there on her fanny with a stunned look on her face and her expensive green dress hiked up around her knees.

"Ever been an outcast, Watson?"

He took a step toward her, stood over her. "Let me take you home," he said.

"Motorcycle too noisy," she said, wagging her index finger in the air like no, no, no. "Mustn't wake Margo."

"Then let me walk you to the taxi stand."

"I'll just take a little nap here," she said, and she leaned back, laid her head on the ground so the deerstalker hat went askew. Sandy kneeled down beside her. The grass was wet.

"You can't sleep here," he said. She was going to pass out. "Let's get you a taxi."

At which she smiled, still with her eyes closed, said something he couldn't hear. A minute passed. There was the sound of a car going past on Farewell Street. Then there was a dog barking. After another minute she said: "The world's still there."

"Come on," he said.

"In a minute."

He wondered if he could carry her if he had to, and how far. She was breathing regularly. He could see her chest going up and down inside her plastic raincoat. Should he make her get up? Make her walk? But after another minute she stirred.

"You said something to those boys."

For a moment he didn't know what she meant—or rather, thought she somehow meant one of the graves around them.

"You were defending me," she said. "You were defending my honor."

She meant of course the boys at the ball. Was she making fun of him? Of his having ridden to her rescue?

"They were just kids," he said because he felt he had to say something.

"Just kids . . ." she repeated in a faraway voice and she smiled again. And then in the same dreamy voice she said, "You're the most beautiful man I've ever known."

He didn't know what to say to that, so he didn't say anything. She had this calm little smile on her face, her hands folded across her stomach, legs out straight, hair in a swirl on the grass. He wondered what time it was. Five or so? He had to be at the Casino at nine o'clock.

"Confident of awakening into eternal life, here reposeth Alice du Pont."

Another car went past on the road.

"The Plastics Princess."

"Come on," he said, and he leaned over her, slipped his hands under her arms, under her raincoat, and started to lift her up. But she made herself deadweight, the smile broadening, and he had to do it for real, get his legs under him and lift her onto her feet. At the last moment she staggered, and then—how exactly had this happened?—she was in his arms, pressing herself into him, her good palm against his chest, the side of her face on his shoulder. He had dropped his hands almost instantly, but then—whether out of reflex or because not to do so would have been too insulting—put his hands on her shoulders, but he did so lightly, tapping her like hey, okay, that's enough, let's go. But she kept herself pressed into him. A few awful moments passed, and then she spoke into his chest.

"Sometimes I'd give anything to have a man hold me."

This, of course, was what he had been fearing ever since he'd met her. That a wrong signal would be sent, that something would get out of hand, that he'd have to hurt her, that without ever intending to he'd have to add himself to the list of hurt the girl had sustained.

"Let's go," he said softly, as gently as he could.

"Kiss me first."

She had pulled back a little, was looking up at him.

"Kiss me," she said again. "It doesn't mean anything. I know that. But kiss me."

He could think of nothing to say, could do nothing but look down at her. Had he not told Aisha that she was pretty? In a nervous, edgy, hopeless sort of way? But it didn't matter, couldn't matter.

"It won't count," she was saying. "We've stepped outside the world. You can kiss me. I won't hold you to it."

He tried to smile down at her, down at her upturned face, but couldn't quite pull it off. And then—horribly!—he found himself leaning over and kissing the top of her head. Kissing the part in her light-colored hair as if she were a child.

She went stiff in his arms. "Oh!" she said and she shut her eyes. And then she was pushing back, away from him, out of his arms. He took a step after her, but she said "No!" and walked away as quickly as she could manage, over the wet turf, between the gravestones, away.

"Alice!" he called. But she kept on—blindly, drunkenly—and he knew there was no going after her, no making it better, that the sexual gulf between them had been exposed and there was no undoing that. There was nothing for him to do but watch her go—her poor, hitching gait: electrocuted!—watch her work her way farther uphill, farther into the cemetery, farther away from him, until the taller gravestones began to hide her, and then the fog.

He sat back on one of the old grave markers. On the ground there was her deerstalker hat still.

❧ 1896 ❧

When finally Franklin wheeled Mrs. Newcombe's bicycle into the semi-circular drive that led up to Marble House, he was tired and sweaty and thirsty and in a foul mood. The bronze front doors (they were reputed to weigh one and a half tons apiece, the weight of an elephant, Mrs. Belmont had told him)—the front doors were wide open and one of the footmen came out to greet him and to take the bicycle from him. He let it be known that it was Mrs. Newcombe's bicycle, to which the footman replied, "So I understand, sir." (Was he, then, an object of derision among the staff? He would fix that when he was Mr. Newcombe—; that is, when *she* was Mrs. Drexel. Good lord!)

He took a moment to straighten up in the mirror under the massive staircase and then walked through the enormous hall—marble every-where!—to the doors that opened out onto the acres of greensward that fronted the ocean. There were children with their nannies and govern-esses playing a game of croquet on the lawn, and in the distance the bright red Chinese teahouse Mrs. Belmont had absurdly built when she was still Mrs. Vanderbilt. It sat with its roofline like a vizier's helmet and its drag-ons and griffins and lord-knows-what anchored to the rocks overlooking the surf. He could see guests milling about on the pagoda-like veranda. He slowed down as he crossed the grass. He prepared a smile, summoned his jovial self, and called out a hearty "Give it a good thwack!" to the children.

And just as he did, one of the women he had taken for a governess turned to him. It was Mrs. Newcombe. She had changed out of her bicy-cling outfit. Her children, of course, were part of the game. "Mr. Drexel," she said and he found himself begging her pardon, though for what he couldn't have said.

"I hope you didn't find your ride too trying," she said with a moue over Mrs. Belmont's behavior that she seemed to think they would both understand.

"I flew like Hermes!" he said and smiled.

Odd how unattractive she was. There was not, after all, anything hideous about her—she did not have hair sprouting out of her chin—but her parts did not coordinate. Her nose did not quite make it all the way up to her forehead, the corners of her mouth resisted her smile, her hair seemed to want to escape from off her scalp. And her expensive clothes—the simple day dress she had changed into was quite exquisite for its type—instead of helping hide her lack of grace, seemed rather to draw attention to it. She had at least, he acknowledged, fine manners, studied though they might be.

"Is that your boy then?" he said, following her eyes out to the children. The boy looked to be six or seven, dressed in a wide-collared, bottle-green Fauntleroy outfit. Some of the other children were so small as to need the help of a nurse in swinging the heavy mallets. "He's a well-made lad."

"*Ah!*" she murmured.

He turned with what he intended to be an indulgent smile at her maternal pride, but he was struck by the expression on her face. She had turned on him a look of—of what?—of gratitude, he supposed, as if his praise of her child had meant something beyond simple courtesy. She was even now trying to conceal her reaction by pointing out her daughter—a girl of four toddling in the grass with her nurse—but he was left with the impression that he had glimpsed something of her private self, something she had prematurely exposed.

And then it came to him that his was not the only campaign Mrs. Belmont was waging. That for every tête-à-tête he had had with her about marriageable women, Mrs. Newcombe had had one about marriageable men. He had, in short, been *described* to Mrs. Newcombe. The handsome gentleman from the Baltimore Drexels. The amateur watercolorist. The *witty* gentleman. The gentleman with the beautiful manners. He had—it gave him a strange shiver—been in Mrs. Newcombe's thoughts without his realizing it. And one of her thoughts had evidently been what would the gentleman with the beautiful manners think of her children. The gentleman who was a bachelor and several years her junior. The gentleman was not, it amused him to realize, the only one coloring the gray in his hair.

They had begun to stroll. And whatever awkwardness had come between them was dispelled by the sight of Mrs. Belmont's tea train starting its trek across the lawn. For Mrs. Belmont, in building her teahouse with all its architectural flair, had neglected to include any facilities for actually making tea, and had then remedied this oversight by installing a miniature railroad that carried the tea things from the main kitchens out to the teahouse. TOWN TOPICS had been merciless in its description. And to see the white-gloved footmen seated one to a car, each holding a silver tray with its paraphernalia, eyes forward, back straight while the toy engine chuffed along on its rails, was a sight indeed. "Poor souls," Franklin couldn't help remarking to Mrs. Newcombe, "for I suppose even a footman has his dignity. And the smoke must get in their eyes." When the little train had finished its hundred-yard jaunt and blown its whistle, applause burst from the teahouse.

"You missed, I think, Mrs. Lydig's last party," Mrs. Newcombe said. He understood her to be taking up his remark. The Lydigs had thrown a party in which actors and actresses had been hired to impersonate royalty—one could dance with a string of duchesses, Franklin understood, or have a cigar with the crown prince. His own name had not been included on the guest list. "I wonder sometimes what we are about," she added with a glance up at him.

He marked the "we."

"We are about the pursuit of pleasure," he said. "According to the papers. We are the standard for the world."

"I shouldn't mind that," she returned, "if there were in this pursuit of pleasure some actual . . . well, *pleasure*."

They walked in silence for a few moments.

"Do you not take pleasure in your life, Mrs. Newcombe?" he finally ventured. She thought longer than what he considered the question warranted.

"I take pleasure in my children," she said, pausing and looking back at the croquet. "And I love Windermere. And I love my gardens—you must come see the maze we are just encouraging. And I love my bicycle," she said with a little laugh that was almost charming. "But Mrs. Belmont's tea train? Or dancing with the *faux* Prince of Wales?" And she eyed him to see how he took her doubts.

"As to that," he said—some response was demanded—"Mrs. Belmont is a paradox, is she not? On the one hand, we have her absurd teahouse and her even more absurd train. And we have her moving heaven and earth to get poor Consuelo married to the Duke of Marlborough. And yet she has taken up the suffragettes' cause—serves tea to them, if I'm not mistaken, in that very teahouse—and supports them financially. And she is a force behind the Political Equality League. And she has turned the scandal of her divorce into a rally for women's liberty, indeed for liberty in all our social relations. Why, she has even made me a minor skirmish in her campaign."

He had meant his presence among them despite his lack of fortune and he assumed she understood this. But when she spoke, she said something quite different.

"Do you mean because she wishes to include artists and other worthies in society?"

It took him aback. He was not an artist. He occupied himself in making aquarelles and ink drawings, but he was not an artist. Her remark gave him another glimpse of how Mrs. Belmont had "sold" him.

"I mean," he responded, "she intends to renovate society as thoroughly as she is renovating Belcourt." And then, because he felt obscurely unethical not denying it: "I am not an artist."

"Ah, but I have seen your work, Mr. Drexel! A lovely watercolor of the Bethesda Fountain in the snow! Mrs. Belmont has it in her boudoir."

He was not—thank god!—privy to Mrs. Belmont's boudoir, but he well remembered the picture. He had had the good sense to let the white of the paper predominate so that the angel on the fountain appeared to hover in a snowstorm. A whirling snowstorm in the midst of Central Park in the midst of Manhattan was the feeling the picture gave. It was quite beyond what he was usually capable of. He had given it to Mrs. Belmont just when news of her impending divorce had become general. He had meant it to appear as a token of his support. The frame had cost him dearly.

There was another scream of the train whistle, followed by a startled cry from the teahouse, and then laughter.

"Mrs. Belmont says she treasures it."

He made a little bow of his head, acknowledging the compliment. He wondered sourly whether Mrs. Belmont treasured it as much as her Titian but thought better of asking. Instead he contented himself with letting his impish look come over him and saying: "I am relieved that you find me so capable an artist, Mrs. Newcombe, because then you will not mind learning how *in*capable a cyclist I am." He let the change of register affect her. "Completely incapable as it turns out. I had to walk your machine here."

"What?" she cried.

"It quite defeated me."

"You *walked* it here?" she said, mock-horrified and shaking her head at him. He was dimly aware that this was all rather charming of him, that he was her servant and all that.

"Don't tell Mrs. Belmont," he continued. "I will take steps to rectify my shortcoming and then she need never know. I will be able to present myself to her on the matter of bicycle riding with impunity. I must say, at one point in my walk an athletic young man came pedaling past me and I found myself quite regretting not being able to follow after him." *Down, boy!* he thought, and wound up more safely: "He seemed so free."

"Ah, *free!*" she said. "Think what it means for us women. Miss Anthony calls the bicycle the Freedom Machine." And she simultaneously frowned and laughed at the epithet. "But if you are worried about Mrs. Belmont learning of your imperfection, I would be glad to teach you the skill before she has occasion to find out." And she hurried on so as to cover the implication of the offer. "It's quite simple once you get the hang of it. And it *is* fun."

"So *that's* where pleasure resides," he took up and smiled at her. "Well, henceforth I shall consider myself your pupil. We shall pursue bicycling together and prove to the world how modern we are!"

"Agreed," she said and extended her hand to him. He shook it, aware that they were being observed from the teahouse; to spend any more time together would make them a subject. "Now I must collect my children and you must get your tea."

"You're not going?"

"Yes," she said. "But only over there." And she pointed toward the trees. "You have never seen Windermere? That's it there. Or its roofs anyway. We are quite in the habit of crossing the intervening lawns. My James likes a good hike."

He could see up the coast above the treetops the top floor of a cottage with its green tiles and gables and seven ornate chimneys. *Ah!* he thought, and again he felt the prickle of sweat breaking out on his ankles.

"Good-bye, Mr. Drexel," she said.

"Good-bye, Mrs. Newcombe."

She turned in her lovely blue dress and began walking back toward the croquet game. As Franklin watched her go, it occurred to him that she might actually be a fine woman. And what a shame that would be.

～ 1863 ～

~For a break from my spying—and because after my intercourse with Miss Taylor and her young brother I now consider the Ocean closed to me—I went yesterday with Sarge out to La Farge's studio, spent the morning looking over some watercolors and the afternoon walking out to Paradise Rocks. In the evening there was to be a lecture on the history of the Jews of Newport at the Athenaeum and I proposed to go with Sarge, but he afterwards was tired from our hike ("To tarnation with the Jews of Newport!" he said) and took himself homeward. When I returned home myself I discovered that Father, who I knew was a friend of the lecturing Professor and had planned on being in attendance, had been waylaid in his study by a Swedenborgian Angel eager to discuss the question of Divine Love, and so could not. William was nowhere to be found. Alice said *she* would go with me, but I told her she was too young, and went out by myself.

And in the manner of novels, Miss Taylor was there. Quite out of place, I thought, for lectures at the Athenaeum were not the sort of thing the resort people attended. But I having trespassed on *her* world, she evidently would now trespass on *mine*.

She was sitting toward the front of the room and did not see me as I entered. I confess to experiencing a momentary impulse to retreat, but the dramatic interest of the situation got the better of me and I stayed. I sat at the back where I could occasionally catch a glimpse, between the seated shoulders, of the feathered hat she was wearing. The Professor's lecture was of some interest, detailing as it did the generations of Jewish inhabitants of Newport, their escape from the Portuguese Inquisition to the islands and plantations of the West Indies, their eventual presence and mercantile importance in Newport before the Revolution. He told the story of several such families, one being the very rich Isaac Da Silva, whose house and warehouses still stood (and at the end of whose wharf I had listened to the absurd steam organ concert). I began to sketch in my head (and take the occasional note; my indefatigable hand!), for I thought there might be a subject in this history for a story of some antiquarian interest. I was standing at the back of the Athenaeum giving Da Silva a lovely young ward who might be a subject of interest to a gallant French officer during the Comte de Rochambeau's occupation when I became aware of Miss Taylor bearing down upon me with what novelists are pleased to call a "quizzical" smile.

"More local color, Mr. James?" she asked.

"And for you too, Miss Taylor?"

There was then an awkward moment, for I was expecting someone, her mother, a hotel acquaintance, the aunt I had invented, someone at any rate who had accompanied her, to come up to us. But there was no one.

"You have ventured out alone?" I found myself asking.

"I have indeed," she responded.

I gestured toward where the lecturer was surrounded by admiring auditors. "Would you like to be introduced to the Professor? He is a friend of my father's." I was at something of a loss.

"Thank you. I think not."

"Then," I said (what else was left me?), "then would you allow me to escort you back to your hotel?"

She hesitated, and I thought I had overstepped. But when she spoke she said that she had thought of going to see the Synagogue of which the Professor had spoken. He had roused her interest in it, for it seemed a thing of some wonder, did it not?

"And it has the virtue," she said with a mordant smile, "of not being on the hotel's list of Newport sights. Do you know it?"

I said I did. It was a venerable building, over a hundred years old. If it were not growing dark, I said, I would gladly walk with her and show it to her.

"Oh," she said, "it is not so *very* dark. I would be obliged to you."

Which I made a mental note of, a note on the evident freedom of the young ladies of Waterbury.

We walked westerly down Bellevue, the lavender sunset behind the housetops and in the trees. There were carriages returning to the hotels and people still about. We talked as we went, the darkening air filled with birdsong and the thud of hooves on the earthen avenue. Every now and then a spot of reddish sunlight would bloom on some expanse of grass, or dapple the wall of a building we were passing, or appear in an upper-story windowpane.

I wanted to compliment my companion on her hat as we walked. It was a most striking raiment, made of pheasant feathers and black netting and held quite closely to her fair hair. But I did not dare, for I must be careful that she does not mistake my intentions. She must understand, without my actually saying it, that my intentions are not what is common in such relations, not what the world, observing us, would suppose them to be.

(Although *why* my attentions are not what the world would suppose is a question I find myself more and more at a loss to understand. But that is not for this notebook.)

After ten minutes we reached the Synagogue on its plot of earth, shuttered and gloomy, for as the Professor had told us, there are no longer Jews in the city. We remarked on the building being canted away from the street, the effect of its being oriented toward Jerusalem, and on its overall classical look, not unlike some of the grander houses in town, yet for all the similarity, still inexplicably *different*. The building's face had in the gloaming a sad aspect, and there was about it a sense of history, of lives lived, lives now vanished and unknown. We stood for some time in meditative silence. Finally I remarked that I was put in mind of the feel, the *tone*, of the Point.

"Have you had a tour of the Point?" I asked.

She said she had not, that—alas!—she was quite en-dungeoned in her hotel. I smiled, and told her she must visit the Point for the quaintness of its houses all huddled together, the small, queer lanes, and the tiny-paned windows behind which one might catch an aged Quaker face gazing out as if from another century. It was the oldest part of the town, I told her, and quite charming.

On our way back up Bellevue we stopped outside the Jewish cemetery and peered in. It was quiet and still and the evening darkness seemed to fall and pool about the gravestones. After a moment I asked Miss Taylor did she know the poem Longfellow had written about the cemetery. I had the first quatrain memorized and recited it to her.

> How strange it seems! These Hebrews in their graves,
> Close by the street of this fair seaport town,
> Silent beside the never-silent waves,
> At rest in all this moving up and down!

She asked me to recite it again, saying it was hard to catch the meaning on the wing, and when I had finished, repeated the last line.

"Is that not us?" she said. "All this moving up and down? The quick, the alive?"

I gazed at her and said I supposed it was. She seemed in some inchoate way touched by this.

"Can we go in?" she asked. She went up under the great granite portal with its wings overhead and looked between the iron rails of the gate. I turned to see if anyone was observing us.

"We should not."

She swung open one of the heavy gates and peered in. I hung back. After a moment she turned to me.

"Will you not come?" she whispered. "We needn't scruple, I think. Did not the Professor say there are no Jews left in Newport?" She urged me with a little gesture of her head, and then when I did not move, forsaking the furtive fraternity of her whisper, said: "Ah! I see I mistake you. You are worried about my reputation." And something like a mocking smile spread across her features, though gently. "But it is *you* who live here," she said, "you who will have to salvage your reputation, not I!" And with that she turned and walked in, leaving the gate ajar behind her. I forbore looking around a second time (I wished to appear craven even less than I did scandalous) and instead followed her.

She made her way slowly through the unmown grass, between the imposing obelisks and the more humble grave markers, some of which were nearly covered with vegetation. I hung a little ways back and watched her. In the deepening dusk and under the canopy of trees and with the theater of the graveyard around us, the movement of her white dress with its muslin furbelows seemed like that of a specter. She stopped from time to time, read an inscription if it was in English, or let herself marvel at the enigma of the Hebrew letters, which she would caress with her fingers. Once she gazed back at me and I thought I saw a dark fervor move across her face. We did not speak, but let the melancholy of the place, its rich suggestiveness, take hold of us.

"*Esther,*" she murmured once, running her fingertip over the beveled incision of an inscription.

At the rear of the cemetery we stopped and for a time simply stood in the gray air with the somber gravestones about us, and the dark tree limbs arching over us, and about our ankles the eddying mystery of it all. My companion said something once, which I could not quite catch. And then, perhaps because she knew I hadn't heard, she said it again. "*I have had this feeling before,*" she said. But when I turned to her, somewhat mystified, she did not explain. Her face was in shadow, but I could see there some evidence of emotion working on her, and yet not an emotion of dismay or withdrawal occasioned by the gloomy place we found ourselves in, but rather something like elation, or perhaps rather exaltation. Whatever it was, I did not dare trespass. Through the trees and houses we could hear someone calling a dog home.

"It's as if we have stepped out of the world," she whispered after a time.

"Yes," I murmured, so as not to be discordant with her mood.

She closed her eyes, and I thought I could see move through her some psychic vibration, as if she were what I understand Father to be, subject to the incursion of spirits and currents from some other world.

"All this moving up and down," she said in her low voice, still with her eyes closed. And then: "We are but the temporary inhabitants of our bodies."

I did not understand her and so kept silent. I watched her breathing, the fabric of her lovely gown moving silently, slowly, in and out.

"Others will come and take over," she said.

And did I not marvel at her? Her speech had some of the mystical import that I find in Father's writing. And which is so unlike me that I am at a loss whenever I encounter it. She turned then, and opened her eyes, and fixed them on me. And though they were but pools of shadow, I had the sensation all the same of their color melting and re-forming.

"Have you not had that sensation?" she asked after a moment. "That your life has already been lived? That everyone's life has already been lived?"

"Ah!" I intoned, for I felt I had to say something, and I did not want to go too far with her. "All except in the details."

At which she inclined her head, as if allowing the exception. "Yes, the details are different," she said. "You're a gentleman, I'm a lady. You have dark hair, I have light. These Jews no doubt had dark, but *the thing itself—*" she said with intensity, and she left off. And then she tried again: "Life," she said.

I held back. There was the call of a whippoorwill. We stayed some minutes in silence.

"It's the graveyard that has made you susceptible," I said softly, as if to recall her. She turned her face toward me and I thought I detected a look of disappointment. "But," I quickly went on for I did not wish to be found wanting, "I understand you."

"Do you?"

"Yes," I said, because I believed I at last did. "I take you to mean that we have all strived to live, we have all strived to be worthy, to love and be loved, to live lives that will not be found wanting. You and I. These Jews. In that sense the details do not matter. One's religion, one's class, one's manner of loving. Whether one—" and here I took a leap, "whether one stammers or not. In that sense—" And I left off, hoping I had come close to her mark. She seemed to soften where she stood.

"Yes," she said, and something like the fervor of her thought seemed to exhale from her. And then she said, curiously: "Thank you."

We listened to the night sounds. There was distant music from one of the hotels. The colorful feathers of her hat had turned gray.

"Though perhaps, after all," she mused when another minute had passed, "perhaps all we know are details. Perhaps details *are* the thing itself."

She smiled at me as if to beg my forgiveness, and then she did something that would have disconcerted me earlier but which, in the circumstances of the cemetery and the spell it had cast over us, seemed natural. She put her hand in my arm and with her other hand pressed me upon the wrist, and together we made our way back to the cemetery gate. When we reached the street, she removed her hand.

On the veranda of the Ocean with its oil lamps brightly lit, color and gaiety all around and the sound of a waltz from the Germanians within, I told her I would enjoy being her docent to the *real* Newport if she would have me. I told her that I had a young sister who was but a few years older than her brother; perhaps together they could act as our *dame de compagnie,* our chaperone, I added, for I was unsure of her French. My sister was sickly and could do with getting out in the air.

"Her name is Alice, too," I said, beaming.

~ 1778 ~

Apr 7

Am returned from my northern Reconnaissance and have finished the Draft of my report. I have given it to Col° Wharton for his Approval before handing it to Gen¹ Pigot.

The days preceding my Departure had been filled with the rumor that Burgoyne would embark for England from Newport. And now that I am returned I discover that Gentleman Johnny is indeed amongst us. He comes from Cambridge where he has left the remnants of the Convention Army, and is attended by an Aide de Camp to the American Gen¹ Heath, who after the Saratoga surrender is placed in charge of the Convention Army. With them is a Rebel Commissary who is charged with making arrangements for supplying the surrendered troops. We have not enough Provisions for the Newport garrison, but now we are to feed a dis-armed Army as well.

Burgoyne is to embark in a few days upon *The Grampus*, storeship.

The billeted Officers had yet another discussion as to whether Gentleman Johnny is disgraced. Rumor says he is impatient to Embark and that once returned to England will demand a Court-Martial that he may defend himself against the many Calumniations of his conduct in the late Battle. Smithson expresses the opinion that a General's duty is to win at battle, but if he cannot, if he is surrounded by superior Forces as Burgoyne was at Saratoga, then to seek the best Terms he can and that Burgoyne has done that, and that the Freedom of the Convention Army as well as his own person to return to England on their Parole is the proof of that. To which I expressed the opinion that a General's duty is to not get his Army surrounded in the first place. There was a general Agreement that the true danger of the Action was that it would embolden France, for the French will see that these Colonials are perhaps not the Bumpkins they are thought. We might find our Action after all.

The Weather has turned fine. Spent an hour walking the Meadow to see if the Birds are returned and had a moment of exquisite feeling standing alone atop a rise with the Warmth of the breeze on my face, and the smell of the Waking earth in my nostrils, and not caring about anything.

Apr 8

We are to have an Assembly in Genl Burgoyne's honor. He is said to have attempted to dissuade the organizers, for in Cambridge a similar occasion was a great Failure, the Ladies of Boston being unwilling to come out, but here in Newport they are determined to right that Wrong. As an Officer of Genl Pigot's staff I am invited.

Have had an Interview with Phyllis in which I acquainted her with my Design. I was blunt with her, for I fancy the life of a Slave quickly cures one of being a Fool, and she is none. I will risk her informing Da Silva of my intentions. I think she will not. It is in her interest to work my Purse instead. Indeed, it struck me that there was some Desire in her to see her Mistress played.

So I have instructed her to send me word when her Master quits his house, so that I may appear to call upon him, and not finding him at home may have Occasion to be entertained by Judith. A simple move, but a promising one.

Should she need to send a Boy, we have a Signal for him to use so that he will not be an Ear to our Duplicity.

Apr 9

Sailed into the Harbour some days ago the *Isis* from New York carrying letters that had lately arrived by the February packet from England and they are finally distributed. I have received five, one from Father, one from William, and three from Mother. Mother frets that William is as yet un-married and wonders how I am to marry being at the ends of the Earth. She writes no further of my Melancholia. The future Lord Stevens for his part is only interested in his dogs. The second page of his letter is devoted to the most astute Analysis of the abilities of Hecate who he was sure I would remember was of Persephone's litter just before I left England. It would seem Hecate has a sixth-sense for foxes. Brava, Hecate.

Father maintains he is working to get me Preferred so that I may return to London. He fancies I might be attached to Lord Hazlitt's staff, but this, of course, will cost money, my Commission having already set back the Family's Fortune £6000, he writes in case I had forgotten.

Mother writes of Elizabeth, would have me imagine the girl sits under the Oaks & Ashes of Crosswell and pines for me.

Apr 10

Genl Burgoyne has had his Assembly and the Ladies of Newport did indeed turn out. There were 40 of them, another 60 of the men, and perhaps 60 British officers. There was punch and dainty Victuals and a violin band to play. A receiving line was run past the General, who looked weary tho' I could see traces of the Courtliness that has given him his Nick-Name.

The gathering was held in a public building of some Pretension which the townspeople call The Colony House, and whose ground floor is given over to a Great Room rather like those of our Guild Halls. I went out of a desire for Amusement, but as well because I knew Da Silva would be there with Judith. I arrived before they did, paid my respects to the General, and then stood about with some of the Officers remarking on the women who took the occasion, in these times so rare, to come out in their Finery. Some of the local servants seemed to be on loan, for I saw Hannibal amongst others acting as Footmen & Servers. I was struck again at the sight of Africans in such fine livery. 'Tis something you see on occasion in London, tho' more as Piquant decoration whereas here it is the common thing. The punch was not bad, the Musicians a little out of the habit of making social Music, but all things considered, not too dreadful. Tho' only April, it was warm, and the great doors to the outside were kept open, as were some of the Windows.

When Da Silva arrived I broke from my group and went to him and after inquiring after his and Miss Da Silva's health, asked whether I might not present him to Gen¹ Burgoyne. Judith was dressed in a most stunning green Brocade. I could feel upon her the eyes of the Officers I had lately quitted, for her hair was most becomingly done and her Charms resplendently displayed. Whether the General and the others considered it fitting for a Jew to be presented I did not concern myself with. Was not the corset of Convention loosened in time of War? I so managed the thing that Da Silva seemed a necessary Accompaniment to Judith's Beauty. Indeed, I told the General that she was considered the Rose of Newport, to which he responded in his most Gallant manner that she seemed rather an exotic Orchid. But he clearly did not mind being in her Presence, for she was Radiant in the candlelight, and a little overwhelmed in a most Bewitching way.

There is a Mister Kent in Newport who is accounted something of a Dancing Master and it was given to him to organize the Dancing. He, I think, wanted to show his Students off and so had the musicians begin with a French Allemande and a Cotillion, but with their complicated steps they were not a Success. We settled instead into simpler dances, had a Minuet and a Rigadoon and a Scottish Reel. I danced the longways dances, and some Diversions, and when once I was partnered with Judith gave her hand a squeeze the meaning of which she could not help understand.

I drank perhaps too much of the Rum punch. For I began to have the feeling that I sometimes have and which was a Prelude to the Incident with Mrs. Winter in Cambridge. I danced and was danced with. I felt the women under my fingertips, felt the Silk of their waists and their arms, felt their Smiles turned upon my face. I was as handsome and as Favoured as any man there, and yet I felt that Feeling again, that overwhelming Sensation I have at these moments of Exclusion. I do not know how to say it. It is as if I am standing outside the World and looking in, as if I am on the Edge of the world's Orchard and I can see the Fruit hanging on the trees but am denied them. Or again, as if I am forbidden to hunt on the Grounds on which I stand, and yet the Grounds are somehow *my* grounds. It is not just Exclusion, but Exclusion from that which is Mine, that which I have a Right to. I know not how much of it was the rum and how much of it was the antic Disposition that at times besets me, but I felt a deep Anger at being Debarred, as if Judith's Beauty were a direct taunt to me, as if the display of her Charms were as an Article in a shop window with a Price beyond my means. And yet that is not it either. For it was not just dancing with Judith and then having to relinquish her. That is but mere Impatience. It is that and yet not that, is instead, or in addition to—how to say it?—it is somewhat like the feeling Lucifer experiences when he stands outside Eden and sees the Beauty and Innocence of Paradise and feels himself forever Divorced from it. It is the Awareness of Goodness and Vitality residing outside oneself which one can never Possess and so must Destroy. And so it happened that I, under the Influence of the rum and of this Sensation that I can only characterize as a State of mental Aberration, that I heard a Major Browning of the Engineers make a remark about the Jewess's physical Attributes (this was toward the end of the evening when Da Silva and Judith and several others were leaving), some remark he would never have made about an Englishwoman and I found myself accosting the man and slapping him.

There ensued a Consternation over the Insult, a simultaneous attempt at Appeasement and a drawing up of sides. I watched it all as if I were not only Debarred from the world but from my own self. Yet so ingrained is the practice of being a Gentleman that I said the things I needed to say, struck the Pose I needed to strike. There was talk of Seconds and at the same time the Urging that this was no Cause for a Hostility. Had we not Enemy enough? It was just an idle Remark, &c.

I said the Major need only enquire as to where I was Billeted if he wished Satisfaction, and turned to leave. But I was quickly surrounded by those Officers of the Fusiliers who were in attendance, the Engineers rallying to Major Browning. There were further calls on both sides for Harmony & Forbearance, but I struck off, walking out onto the Parade Ground toward Thames Street, shrugging off those who would accompany me.

And all the time, I still felt it. The twin urgings. One, the dim mystical Apprehension that I was excluded from the Orchard; and the other, the clear, hot, manly Resolution that I would eat of the fruit of that Orchard, violently if that was what it took.

It was something like this, some Eruption against Goodness and Beauty and Innocence—against Life itself!—that was in me when I stood in front of my mirror, my shirt undone, my razor in my hand . . .

Apr 11

I had barely time this morning to address myself to Smithson on the matter of his being my Second when there came to the house a Major Jensen of the Engineers with words to the effect that Major Browning hoped Major Ballard would understand that his Remark the previous night was merely an Expression of a Soldier's Frustration, and were not the Lot of us the worse for lacking the Company & Solace of the inferior Sex?

I offered him a chair and the last of Bradshaw's coffee, which we drank while a newly returned Warbler in the Forsythia bush outside the breakfast window did its best to record the Terms of Surrender.

No sign today of last night's Fit, or rather it remains as the distant thunder of a departing Storm. With each passing hour I regain some of my accustomed Confidence. Will soon move my Rooks onto an open File.

Apr 12

Went out this morning to find myself with the absurd Renown of being a defender of the Reputation of a young lady. Indeed of all young ladies, for it is allowed the One in question could not be of import to me, and that for defending a poor Jewess on behalf of all the Innocent Ladies I am accounted the Noblest of Knights. Bradshaw says he personally knows of a young lady or two back in Somerset that require defending, could I not embark with Gentleman Johnny and attend to them? There are other such Quips and Cranks, but behind all the Raillery is, I sense, some new respect, poorly earned, I allow, but useful nonetheless. A hasty order from Genl Pigot that he will not tolerate Dueling amongst his Subordinates has only served to brighten the buttons on my uniform.

And now the Morsel most choice! For Phyllis came this evening with a letter from Judith. She gave it me with a smile at our Conspiracy. I allowed myself a Private moment with her and when she was gone, read the Letter. I will reproduce it here and then leave the Artifact within these pages so that years hence it may amuse me.

Dear Major Ballard,

    I have been apprised of your Behavior in Defence of my Person the night of the Assembly. The World keeps the exact Circumstances from me out of Concern for what it considers a young woman's Innocence, but I am led to believe that you acted as my Protector and at great personal Risk. You cannot know how deep is my Gratitude, nor how Relieved I am that the Fineness of your Spirit has not brought with it a Cost to your Person. That you would risk your Life for my Honor appears to me the Greatest Proof I might have of your Friendship. I have taken the Liberty of writing to you that you may be assured of the Esteem in which I hold you. 'Tis perhaps a Brazen Act for a girl of Sixteen, but how could I comport myself under the Cowardliness of Social Stricture when you have shown yourself so publicly Courageous? I am forever in your Debt.

Judith Da Silva

I have just finished composing my own Letter in which I tell the Jewess how much I treasure her Note and the Sensibility it communicates. And I tell her in turn of my own Esteem, of my Admiration for her person, and of how she occupies my thoughts, and of how I would willingly do her any Service, &c., and of how my Imagination dreams of being with her alone that we might have freedom to converse without the Strictures of Society, for I believe (I wrote) that we both understood how the Differences in our outer selves, our varying Stations in life, even the Religions in which we were reared, were unimportant, that the Heart has its own Truth, sees with its own Superior eye, and that Love would o'erleap any barrier, &c.

I will let the Letter tread water overnight and in the morning, if I think it not too Bold a move, will have Phyllis deliver it.

Apr 15

Burgoyne has sailed aboard *The Grampus*. There were a number of us come down to the wharves to watch. These several days past it has been a question whether there would be a Salute as the ship left the Harbour. Bradshaw and I have half-a-crown on the question. There was none.

Coming back, I passed the tavern Da Silva mentioned in his story about the Tidewaiter. And indeed there are about the dirty place water Rats enough that I fancy a handful of Guineas could find one to do a Deed if a Deed needed doing.

And let me put down now what I forbore to put down the night of the Assembly, so addled was I then by the events. And it is this: that after I left the Colony House I was in such a State that I could not return to my Room, but instead walked along Thames Street and Franklin Street, past those same Taverns and low Inns. My mind was afire, yet not so much with the recent Altercation and the prospect of a Duel, but with the physical beauty of the Jewess. It was some Combination of the prolonged Months of my Attention to her, and of the sight of her that night in her green Brocade, and the touch of her as we danced, and the Damned mental Fit that I know not how to explain, but I felt as tho' I had swallowed her like a Poison, for she worked in me so that I was Aroused beyond all Sanity. How she was one minute the Fruit of an Orchard from which I was forbidden, and the next a Poison in my Veins, I know not, but it was so. I went down amongst the wharves where there were Whores about, went in and out of the Taverns thinking I might blunt the Passion with one of them, yet I could not. In time my feet carried me to Da Silva's. I stood in the shadows across the way and looked at the broad face of the House. I do not know, even now, what I intended to do. There was no light in any of the rooms, neither in the Kitchen toward the rear, nor on the third floor where Phyllis and the other servants had their Chambers. I went up to the door and tried the latch. I think I had the idea that I would enter, would go upstairs and have—ah!— have Phyllis if nothing else. But of course the door was barred. I walked then to the farthest point of the Wharf, to where we had all watched the Sun set that evening a Fortnight past, and stood there with the lights of the Fleet twinkling against the darkness, and there I unbuttoned my Flies and closed my eyes and spilled my Seed into the Harbour water.

～ 1692 ～

1st Day

After Meeting, John Peele approach'd me and ask'd if he might not come to the House on a Visit later that day. I waited for him, and again I had a fore-knowledge of what he might say. We sat in the Parlour, me with my coif on and a clean Apron and he with his black Hat in his lap. He said he brought with him the news of a propos'd Match. He said the Match was with a Member of our Society and did I consent to hear it. I told him I did.

It is with Edward Swift whose wife Mary died these two years past. Her grave marker is but a rod from Mother's. He has two boys about my age, and Sarah who I was at School with. He is accounted a hard-working man, with several of the Trades. I believe the two trivets we have are iron wrought by him.

Oh, I have not the Skill to record the flagging of my Spirit at this proposal. I had not thought such a thing would work upon me so. I tried in my Thoughts to be fair and generous, and mindful of my own and Dorcas's fate, and yet I wished to push it all from me, as one might push away a meal for which one has no Appetite.

In time I was able to answer, and instructed John Peele to tell Edward Swift that I would consider his Offer and would Pray over it, but could not say when I might be clear in the Matter, that he would have to wait. He nodded gravely, and as I thought, Sensible of some misgiving. I told him I would keep Silence about the Proposal, thinking that that might be what clouded his mind. But the look of Conscience did not abate.

Perhaps he is Sensible of having gone from asking me a Month ago did

I not wish to return to School, to asking me would I consent to be married. And to a man Father's age.

I was left with the Evening falling, and the Parlour fire turning to Embers.

4th Day

We have had a great, blasting Storm. Dorcas does not remember Snow from last Winter. She would go to the Kitchen window and look out at the Dooryard, and then toddle to the Parlour Window to see if it was snowing as well at the Carters'. It seem'd as a Miracle to her.

Edward Swift sent his two boys over. I believe their names are Edward and James. They clear'd the Snow off the Woodpile and set about making a kind of lean-to over the pile that it might be kept dry. I watch'd them from the Kitchen with Jupiter curl'd up in my lap. They did not ask did we want such an Improvement, but they were handy at the job.

6th Day

Are not men ugly? Jane Beecher ask'd me today. We were at her house doing our laundry together. I have not yet told her of Edward Swift. With their Beards and their coarseness, she said, were not men ugly? I said I suppos'd they were, that I might fall into her Humour. And she went on in a like Vein, saying a woman was so much more handsome, for we are soft and smooth of skin. She said she was sure any woman would prefer a smooth Face to kiss than a prickly one. Was it not a Pity that women could not marry women? She laugh'd at this and I laugh'd, for it took me out of myself and was Sport as I might have had with Hannah and Martha. And then she made more Sport of men and of their Courting, mimicking them in their walk and showing her Muscles as if she were one such. She made to embrace me in Mockery and kiss me. We were in a Fit by then and the water in the Washtub slopp'd between us. *Thy lips, O my spouse,* she said, *drop as the honeycomb,* and she embrac'd me again as a man might. And then she did kiss me, holding me behind my head, but I push'd her away. I was laughing for I thought we were still in the Riot of her mood, but when I look'd again, her face was strain'd and of a Passion I know not wherefrom.

Perhaps she is more afraid than I allow. Perhaps she feels a need to strut and contend, or otherwise it were to show Weakness, and that by showing it she would become it.

We are both of us lost, I suppose, and unsure how to find our way.

7th Day

I have had a Dream. We were all together and it was warm, and there was a Light over all and over all was a Warmth that was not of the world alone, but seem'd to come from the Hearts and out of the Eyes of Mother and Father and Dorcas, and out of their Prudy too, as if we were each other's Light and Comfort. I know not how to describe it, but we seem'd to swim in an Air and a Light that was warm and was of the Air, and yet was of us too.

How horrible it was to wake into the cold and the dark and the Knowledge that it was not so! So overcome with Griefe was I that I could not help myself and cried. I went then and stood over Dorcas's trundle-bed and I felt a deep Wound at the sight of her, for I could not give her my Warmth and she could not give me hers.

That we might have the Light always! That we might understand! But we move in Darknesse, as it seems to me. We do not know who we are. We do not know who others are. We do not know how they work on us.

5th Day

I have rais'd up the courage (I know not why I should need courage, but I did) to tell Jane of Edward Swift. Her face grew hard at the Knowledge and she said that she expected something of the like was about. She had a great Sorrow for me, and then a Despair that I should be so forc'd. We were in her keeping-room and it was not yet dusk tho' the room was dark and Wintry. She took my hand and held it in a way that was like an older sister to me and I felt greatly moved by her Care of me.

We talk'd and talk'd, and it grew darker in the room, and the darker it grew, the more her Fancy seem'd loos'd, so that she spoke of how she sometimes dreams of going away, of leaving Newport and all the town behind. Even her children, she said in this Fancy. She dreams of going into the Wildernesse and living alone in a house by herself as a Pilgrim, or as I suppose, a Hermit.

Other times, she said, she imagines going with her children, and at still others, with other women, that they might make a Household away from the World and become Quaker Separatists, as we hear they have in England.

Other times, she said, she feels the Leaning is God's, that he is calling her to make a Testimony elsewhere than Newport. That a new Life of Women separate from Men might be to live even more clearly in the Light. For if we have our Meetings separated by Sex, she says, then might not we have our households, yea, our whole Lives so separated? If it is right for the One, why is it not even more right for the All? She pos'd this Question to me, and I must admit it had a great Force of Logic, altho' I cannot conceive of life with Women only, nor believe the Lord intends such Separation. Perhaps she means only to point out the Unfairness of our separated Meetings, and our separated Schools, for if being a Friend is to treat all as Equal, and not to honour a Magistrate above a fishwife, why are we then so apart?

However she meant it, she seem'd greatly inflam'd with her Conception.

7th Day

The Snow is melted and it is turn'd so warm that Dorcas and I went out without our cloaks. I fashion'd a Purpose to walk past Edward Swift's house that I might see it and appraise it and try to imagine myself its Mistress. Young Edward was at the Forge and he stopped his hammering long enough to watch me go past. He is much bigger than I am. And I would be his Mother!

I may confess here that I do find myself sometimes when I am a lazy Slow-worm thinking of John Pettibone and of his lovely unruly hair, and of his laugh which leaps out of him as if it were a Jack-in-a-box, and of the fun he and Hannah and Henry Whitlow and I used to have playing skipjack down along the breakwater. Oh, that those times might return, and everything else vanish as if a Dream!

3rd Day

The Lord grant that someday I may show these Pages to someone who has a love of me. That he might understand me, and know who I am in my inmost Self.

5th Day

This evening I had a most beautiful sad Colloquy with Jane. We had done our work and were sitting in the Kitchen as the sun went down. We did not rise to light a candle, but sat in the Dark with the Fire low and talk'd. We talk'd of our old Selves, and Jane said it was as if they had been set adrift and lost over the Horizon. This Picture work'd on me greatly, as I think it did her. Our old Selves as if in a Tub, set upon the Waters and drifting vanishingly away even as we watch'd from the Shore.

O! to what unknown Countries, and to what Centuries hence?

II

Substance and Shadow

≁ 2011 ≁

The Monday after the Champions Ball Sandy brought the deerstalker hat with him to the Casino. He would give it back to Alice as a way of acknowledging what had happened without either of them having to say anything about it. He would give it to her with a softness—a gentle smile, a rueful look: something anyway—so she would understand he was sorry. Understand that he was still her friend, that they could still talk, go for rides and stuff, hey? But she didn't stop by as she usually did. Not after Margo's individual lesson, or the next day after her doubles league. When he asked Margo about it ("Hey, where's Alice these days?"), she made cuckoo circles around the side of her head and said the girl was going off the deep end again. And when he pressed her about it—what did she mean? not, like, *seriously* the deep end?—she grimaced, shrugged like she'd had enough of Alice.

"I'm not my sister-in-law's keeper," she said.

So after a couple more days he took a deep breath and set out for the Redwood Library—was this a good idea?—walked the couple of blocks from the Casino down to the elegant eighteenth-century building with its wide lawn and stately trees, and went up to the main entrance. But as soon as he put his hand on the door he was suddenly sure that no, this was *not* a good idea. The deerstalker hat in his hand, the little speech he'd been writing in his head the past several days, his bare arms and legs (he was still in his tennis whites)—none of it was a good idea. So he had turned around and left, and on the walk back to the Casino gave himself a talking to. Wasn't this just another type of killer instinct he lacked? He didn't want to hurt people—he didn't want to hurt *her*—but maybe sometimes you had to. There was no helping it. There was nothing short of kissing her, making love to her—*loving* her—that would make it all right. And he didn't see how that was going to happen.

Back at the Casino, he grabbed a hopper of balls and went out onto one of the grass courts and hit serve after serve—slice, kick, twist, down the T—until a little crowd gathered. It was something to see, a pro doing what he could do.

And then it rained for three days. His lessons were off, and Aisha was down in Brooklyn minding her interns, so there was nothing to do but stay in the condo, stare out at the rain, make recipes from the owners' diet cookbooks. He got so bored he read *Daisy Miller* again, struck this time with how clear it was that the girl wanted Winterbourne to kiss her. And what a dud Winterbourne was.

By the time he heard from Aisha—could he pick her up at the Amtrak station in Providence?—he had determined that he had to tell her what had happened. He hadn't mentioned it to her yet, hadn't in fact even seen her since the foggy night, hadn't brought it up when they'd last talked on the phone because he had been still imagining Alice in a *stupid-me* frame of mind and not in a *seriously deep-end* frame of mind. But now somebody had to know, didn't they? And he couldn't see himself telling Margo—that felt too much like betrayal—and Tom he didn't know well enough. It was Aisha who was her best friend.

But back in his condo after the motorcycle ride down from Providence, after they'd caught up, made love, started in on some truffles Aisha had brought back from Brooklyn, he got all messed up in the right and the wrong of it. Wouldn't this just be a further trespass on the poor girl's heart? You didn't go around broadcasting someone's failed gesture toward love, did you? But at the same time the thought of the girl harming herself, if that *really* were to happen . . . Couldn't he tell Aisha what had happened without Alice ever knowing?

So he made some decaf to go with the last of the truffles and they sat on the sofa looking out at the shipyard, Sandy in his boxers and Aisha just out of the shower. She had a towel turbaned around her hair in that way women had, and she had on the silver necklace she'd been wearing earlier, a scimitar-shaped thing that cut from collarbone to collarbone. It was just dusk; they had the lights off, and out the big window the harbor was beginning to sparkle.

"Listen," Sandy said finally. "This thing happened."

And he did his best to tell her about it. About the ball, about the fog and the walk through the Point, about Alice drunk and the graveyard and what happened there. She listened quietly, thoughtfully, pursed her lips when he got to the kissing part, imagining—he supposed—her friend's humiliation. And then he told her what Margo had said, and that he was worried about her, and that he thought she—Aisha—should know so that, you know, she could keep an eye out for things, for how Alice was acting and stuff.

He waited for her to say something, waited for her to give him a sorry look, to sigh *Oh, boy!* with a grimace for her friend. Instead she sipped her coffee and looked placidly out the window at the harbor lights, at the sparkling water and the grid of hotel rooms out on Goat Island. She spent a minute just sitting and thinking, running her fingertips up and down the length of the mermaid tattoo on her arm, and then turned back to him.

"You could've just kissed her," she said quietly.

He wasn't ready for that. "Kissed her?" he repeated and he made a face. He had upbraided himself for everything else: for not nixing the whole thing from the start, for not insisting on getting her a cab, for agreeing to be her date to the ball in the first place. But he had never once thought that he should have kissed her, kissed her and thereby—was this what Aisha was saying?—evaded the moment of humiliation, gotten through that night at whatever the cost, and then the next day have had something ready to say, some excuse, evasion, something to help her save face.

"You have to give things to Alice. Give the right amount and she won't expect more. She understands things."

He wondered at her. What was the "right amount"? How did you kiss Alice the right amount?

"I'm not sure I can do that."

"Sure you can," she said, turning to him. "You've made love to women you didn't love before, haven't you?"

She'd said "made love" with a little smile at him. For it was one of the

Southern Gentleman things he said, like "geez" or "cripes." He could never say "have sex." She kept her eyes fixed on him a moment longer and then undid the turban from around her head, began pressing each individual dread dry. "With Alice you have to give what she'll be grateful for," she said. "Attention. Sympathy. You have to find the point where you've given her enough. And then she won't expect more. And she'll keep her side of the bargain."

He struggled to maintain an even expression. He remembered Aisha more than once saying that she loved Alice. Was this her idea of love?

"Is that what you do?" he asked.

She stopped drying her hair, checked his face. "I haven't made any secret of my dependence on her," she said, and then as if challenging him to say otherwise: "I'm sure in certain quarters I'm seen as using her, as exploiting our friendship. I'm sure there are those who see me as a kind of remittance man," she said with a little laugh, looking to see if he knew the term. "But it's a fair exchange. I give as much as I get."

"I know," he said, though he wasn't sure he did. Or if he did, he didn't like the implication. "But I don't need to keep Alice satisfied," he went on a little stiffly. "It's not a question of kissing her or not kissing her. Or kissing her 'the right amount,'" he added, and he felt a little thrill at spurning her terms. "I'm not indebted to her. I only brought this up because I was worried about her. I thought someone should know."

"Because you think she might injure herself."

He fixed her with a look. "It might be the last straw," he said. "You should know that better than anyone."

She inclined her head as if acknowledging his point, then said carefully: "I wasn't asking you to keep her 'satisfied.' I was asking you to be kind to her, to give her something. It helps her."

Again he shook his head no. "That's too dangerous," he said, and he marveled at her. Did she really think that you could make love to Alice and that Alice would understand it wasn't real love, that it was just "having sex," and so would be okay with it? Did she think that Alice was like Margo that way, like—he had to admit to himself—like her, Aisha?

"I can't do that."

"Okay."

"I *like* her," he found himself saying. "I think she's funny and—" and what?—"and I think she's got a good heart, a *deep* heart," he said. "If things were different—" And what did he mean by that? if he wasn't sleeping with Aisha? with Margo? if she didn't have cerebral palsy? wasn't bipolar? "I just want to be her friend," he wound up lamely.

"Okay."

Except she said it like she was resigning herself to a shortcoming of his. Like he was too simple of mind, too simple of heart, to understand what she was saying. Were they—were all of them, Alice too?—so sophisticated, so counterfeit in their emotions, that they operated one or two steps removed from the substance of things?

"Just look in on her," he said. "Make sure she's okay."

She clutched her shirt around her. "I've been doing that for ten years," she said with a thin smile, and she went in search of the rest of her clothes. He watched, feeling like there was more to say, but what?

"Poor you," she said when she was ready to go. She raised herself on her toes and kissed him lightly on the lips. "All the girls fall in love with you."

At which he tried to smile.

When she was gone, he stood at the big window looking out at the night harbor with the breeze coming in and for the first time acknowledged to himself how things were. He was sleeping with two women, neither of whom loved him. And then he immediately felt stupid—*quaint*—for thinking that. He might better ask himself, did *he* love *them*? Surely not Margo, but Aisha? Well, he had been waiting to see—a consequence of his rootlessness, of the shape he was in—waiting to see if something good might happen, if having sex might turn into making love. He had contented himself with thinking that things were just tentative with Aisha, that the constraints of silence and secrecy that had been imposed on them from the start were stunting the natural course of things. But that in simpler circumstances—and could not such circumstances come about once out of Newport?—they would be more free to find one another. And so he had held off scrutiny, kept at bay the misgivings that grew from the apparent ease she had at sharing him, the way she seemed able—and he said this out loud to himself, standing there gazing at the dark harbor, at the thicket of masts in the moonlight—the way she could take or leave him. She seemed to have no quotient of jealousy or possession. A good thing, right? But maybe not when you *wanted* to be possessed, when you wanted someone to smile and slip her arm in yours and whisper, *"You're mine!"*

And how strangely passionless she was! He didn't mean during lovemaking—that was a different kind of passion. But she was always on such an even keel. Nothing ruffled her. Even just now, what he'd told her about Alice, how calm she'd been! For all her far-out jewelry, and her mermaid, and her dreadlocks, she seemed to approach the world more like an MBA than an artist. It was as though upon meeting him she had wondered how he might be of use to her, and having figured that out, she was keeping him around for some motive that was not visible to him, but which was there all the same. Maybe he was just being snarky, paranoid, hurt, but he always felt that she was two steps ahead of him. That she was never just *with* him, but always weighing how this or that might play out. She was ambitious, he knew—she readily admitted it—but he could not see how he figured into her ambition. Or maybe he had hold of that by the wrong end of the stick. Maybe he *didn't* figure into her ambition and that was the problem. She wasn't going to saddle herself with someone who was so distinctly not going anywhere. Which meant she was not so far from Margo as he had thought.

"They're using you, douchebag," he said to the reflection of his face in front of him. "They're *having sex* with you," he said, and the reflection had no answer to that.

→ 1896 ←

"She has shown it to me, my dear boy, your gift!—she has it hanging in the library at Windermere. You prove yourself quite the tactician."

Mrs. Belmont was speaking of the aquarelle Franklin had made for Mrs. Newcombe—"Ellen" to him now—or more precisely, she was speaking of what the aquarelle indicated: his genius for the business of wooing, the little gifts and asides, the doting touch, the planted detail. Or to put it another way: his talent for deceit, for duplicity, the treachery of his smiles and—lately—of his kisses. But he chose to misunderstand her.

"You are too flattering of my watercolors," he said and he inclined his head in a little bow, as if accepting Mrs. Belmont's flattery all the same. "They are poor things. Though genuine expressions of my affections."

"Ah!" said Mrs. Belmont knowingly.

He had spent the last month learning to ride a bicycle. The accompanying humiliation—how he had smiled the whole time!—had been for him the figure of his surrender, the compact to which he affixed his name, the covenant (oh, he could go on!) by which he sold his life as the Free Young Man, and put on the Uxorious Harness. The whole time he had kept up a cheerful dim-wittedness (it was, after all, her dead husband's bicycle he was learning to ride: there was an indecent metaphor somewhere there, by god!), had even apologized profusely to Mrs. Newcombe's footman—poor Hobbes!—who had had to run alongside him those first few days, steadying him as he pedaled, Hobbes with his stiff collars knocked awry and his beautifully polished shoes scuffed. They had kept at first to the walkways of Windermere, then when that grew tame had ventured out onto Bellevue and Ochre Point, until finally as his *chef d'oeuvre* they had bicycled out to Ocean Drive in the buffeting wind, lunch-basket strapped to Mrs.

Newcombe's machine, the two of them in their bicycling outfits, seagulls laughing overhead, the occasional carriage or trap passing, everyone hooting hello to everyone.

The aquarelle he had made of that day—and which was now hanging in the library at Windermere—had been of the breakwater where they had had their lunch. He had used a good deal of yellow ochre that the day might appear golden, the breakwater jutting into the sun-spangled water, and two figures—a man and a woman—out at the very end of the jetty, seated facing away from the viewer, the silver surf threatening to souse them, the distance and their postures making it impossible for the casual viewer to identify them—they were merely an emblematic couple—but that of course was the beauty of the gesture: *she* knew who it was who sat there in intimacy, in the exquisite gold of the moment. (The damned bicycles he couldn't help putting in—like the devil in a medieval panel—an infernal suggestion in the lower left.)

"You should not minimize your achievement in painting," Mrs. Belmont went on to say. They had stopped at a little gazebo that sat quaintly on the grounds of Belcourt.

"My achievement?" he said with a wry look. He merely painted charming scenes, he said, gave them round to friends.

But the remark was but a prelude, for she went on to wonder (all the time appearing to be spontaneous, to be thinking out loud): Could he not collect together fifteen or twenty of his pictures—she would lend him her own *Angel in a Snowstorm*, as would (she was sure) Mrs. Newcombe her *Lovers upon the Jetty*—and could they not persuade the Athenaeum to mount a show of his work? Did not Mrs. Newcombe sit on the board of directors? Ah: there was an idea! They could get up a fund-raiser for the Redwood Library, a charity event, champagne and cakes to be served, all proceeds benefiting etc. Better make it twenty pictures.

He saw what she was after, the tentacled Monster. He was, as he had said that first day to Ellen, a flanking action in Mrs. Belmont's war, and this show of his paintings would be yet a further advance. How the woman worked! Miss Alva Smith of Mobile, Alabama! (He called her that from time to time, when he was being the dear bad boy.) When she had first married into the Vanderbilts, they and their dirty railroads were not in-cluded among the Four Hundred. Yet she had worked it so, induced her husband to build a fabulous mansion on Fifth Avenue (Franklin had twice been inside), and then let it be known that she would be giving a masquer-ade ball that would surpass any other such affair. She had planted delight-ful rumors, little anxieties, and when expectation had reached a frenzy had said, alas, she could not invite Mrs. William Astor's daughter since Mrs. William Astor had yet to call on her in her new home. And that had been that. Mrs. Astor had come like the Pope to Napoleon, and Napoleon had lifted the crown off Mrs. Astor's head and lowered it onto her own. Now with her divorce and her remarriage to O. H. P. Belmont (who was forever away riding his horses and sailing his yachts and shooting his guns), she meant to destroy the world of the Four Hundred. Or at least to so remake it in her own image—season it with suffragettes and artists and the Political Equality League (with the occasional moneyed divorcée sprinkled in)—that it would be unrecognizable to Old New York. Was not the twentieth century just around the corner?

Well! he did not mind! If he was a profiteer in this war, if she promoted him for her own reasons—Franklin Drexel with his looks and his charm and his watercolors—that suited him. If it meant he must assemble his ink drawings and his aquarelles—she was already telling him to make a list of those to whom he had given pictures: she would prevail upon them—then so be it. Such a public show (it was unclear to him whether it was for the benefit of the Redwood Library or the Athenaeum: what the devil was the difference anyway?), such a show would have the double-barreled virtue of assigning him an identity as both artist and as a member of the benefactor caste. It would be yet another golden light in which to allow Mrs. New-combe to see the fineness of his features.

Mrs. Belmont asked him now whether he would be at the pavilion ball ten days hence. They had started down the long drive toward the gilt-tipped gates that opened onto Ledge Road. He was, he supposed, being dismissed.

"Mrs. Newcombe will be going, I know," he temporized.

"Then you must be of my party. There will be a passel of us. Strength in numbers."

He inclined his head, acknowledging her generosity, accepting. "I believe," he said after a minute, "her father will be there."

"Mr. Ryckman?"

"He's coming up from New York."

At which she raised her brow. "To meet you?"

He equivocated. "I'm told it has been the old gentleman's custom to spend some time each summer at Windermere with his daughter. And of course, his grandchildren."

"He's coming to meet you," she said in her blunt way. "Depend upon it."

He let that pass, said instead that he believed there were, in these matters, always fathers with which to contend.

"He may not," he pointedly intoned, "be coming to affix his signature to the deal."

She waved him away. "Mrs. Newcombe is a grown woman. She has two children. She is not a debutante. She does not need her father's approval."

For once—in his manner, in his speech, in his thought—he was the sober one. "He is the kind of man, I'm led to believe, who will have made inquiries."

She turned a clouded face to him. What was he saying?

"He will no doubt have discovered that I am—" he let the possibilities hang dangerously, deliciously, in the air—"that I am not of your . . . of Mrs. Newcombe's set. That I am—" he wielded the term like a bludgeon—"what is commonly referred to as a 'remittance man.'"

"You are an artist."

"Is Mr. Ryckman such a great lover of art?"

She pursed her lips as if she saw how that line led to an unpleasant check. "Let me work on him. Mrs. Auld and I. And I believe he is an acquaintance of Mrs. Lydig's husband."

"Ah!" he intoned with a grateful bow of his head. "But let me first find out which way the wind blows. Let me meet Mr. Ryckman, see if he is immune to my particular charm." And he smiled at her, clicked his heels like a Prussian officer. "I shall report back."

"If you think so," she said.

"I would prefer—" and he paused, as if thinking through a delicate point—"I would prefer that Mrs. Newcombe believe that she has won me on her own. That it is a matter between the two of us. A matter exclusively of the heart. If that's not possible, there will be time for you to bring up the horses and cannon."

They had come to the gates. She stopped and extended her hand to him, and when he shook it, held on to him meaningfully. She turned her pugilist's face up to him.

"I must say, my dear boy, I did have my doubts about you."

"How so?" he charmingly wondered.

She had not been convinced, she said, of his determination, of his ability to set his shoulder to the work that must be done. She lifted her face, seemed to smell the breeze as if it were the smell of one of her successes.

"In short," she said, "I was not sure you possessed the instinct to—" and she paused as if in search of a word, or perhaps to judge him one last time—"the instinct to go in for the kill."

⇥ 1863 ⇤

~We have had to postpone our excursion to the Point, for the weather has turned inclement. Instead I accompanied Miss Taylor and her mother to the Redwood Library, where we viewed the pictures. Such Old Testament grandees and patriarchs were these ancient Puritans and Quakers! We had a laugh and a wonder that such grim men and women walked the very streets where now we walk, and where the *beau monde* takes its pleasures in the Newport sun without a thought to the salvation of its soul. I was engaged in making just such amusing remarks to Miss Taylor when, upon exiting the gallery, I saw my brother and Sarge Perry sitting in the Reading Room, evidently having just lowered their newspapers at the sight of me. They gazed from me to Miss Taylor, back to me and then back to Miss Taylor, each with the look of a stunned fish. And then as we moved toward the door and Miss Taylor took my arm (with Mrs. Taylor behind us like the duenna in a Spanish tale), they must collapse in mirth.

And now, of course, I have had to endure an afternoon of being called Lothario and Lochinvar and Don Juan, endure William and Sarge remarking upon Miss Taylor's physical beauty and asking had I attempted any familiarity with her, and would I like some advice on how to do so, and what *they* would do if given half the chance. It was all, I suppose, meant good-naturedly. School-boy stuff as I had often heard in Geneva (there was that Heinrich who would go on so about Madame Beauvoir's bosom!). It is not that that has disconcerted me, but rather *why* I do not wish the things of which they speak. Nor is it the first time I have so wondered about myself. For to hear the boys I have grown up with—William and Sarge and oh! how Will Temple used to speak of Missy Gardiner!—the hold that female beauty has over them is absolute. They live as willing slaves to the female form. So why is it not the same with me? For I must confess that I have never felt what they evidently feel—neither for a woman nor I hope (as I have most horribly heard of) for a *man*. And Miss Taylor? She whose beauty is beyond dispute, and whose intelligence and gay satiric temperament are to me so fresh and beguiling. What is it that is wrong with me that I do not wish what other men wish?

And yet I *do* want very much to be in Miss Taylor's company. To surround myself with her rich femininity, with her beauty and grace and wit. But in the privacy of this notebook I will confide that that desire grows not from these other natural wants, but rather out of the desire to watch her, to observe her, to make of her a presence in my consciousness, that I may later call on her, know her, *use* her.

~I have, in a state I can only call disturbed, reread the above. There is so much more I could add, but for now will remark only this: that it was Mr. Hawthorne and his curious tales that first caused me to think of the eye as a moral faculty, and to consider that watching, observing, marking, had an ethical dimension. How chilling is his depiction of the soul who watches without sympathy! Wherever it takes me, this incessant looking, this watching without doing: it must not take me there.

~We have now had our outing to the Point with its quaint houses with their backs bent and their shoulders rounded with age. We went up and down the straggling streets, past the little cent shop and the gingerbread shop, past a cabinetmaker's with his double doors thrown open and the smell of fresh-sawn wood, and farther on a stonecutter's yard with a bank of blank slate gravestones awaiting purchase and the engraving of a name. Alice (for she and young Harry accompanied us, as did Mrs. Taylor) was much taken with the latter. She worried over them in her queer way. Which would she choose for herself? she wondered. Which suited her? Which was most like? When Mrs. Taylor attempted to draw her away, telling her there were yet "years and years and years" before she need fret over a marker for her grave, the dear thing cast a fond, longing gaze at the row of stones and said she certainly hoped not.

Curious, I'll remark again: Miss Alice Taylor with a Harry for a brother; and Mr. Harry James with an Alice for a sister. Though the mirroring ends there: one cannot imagine more unlike families than the Jameses late of Union Square, Paris, Geneva, and god-knows-where-else, and the Taylors of Waterbury. The "Brass Valley," she says they call the region. They are all gears and bearings and clockworks, and we are all books and idealism and importuning spirits.

(By the by, I have righted myself and put behind me—indeed, have even crossed out—the questions I worried over in the entry above. For *need* these matters enter into my relations with Miss Taylor? Can I not simply be her friend? As I am of Minnie and Kitty Temple?)

Back at the Ocean we had an ice on the long third-floor veranda. We were delightfully tired from our tramp and had a lovely desultory conversation. Down below, the thoroughfare was being watered to keep the dust down and there was the sound of horses trotting past with the jingle of harness bells (for the hotels "get up" the poor creatures in the most elaborate ways, with braided manes and combed tails, and their noble heads adorned with colorful ribbons and plumes). We had the rooftops of Newport all before us, and the bright blue harbor with its myriad sails and water sparkling in the sun. We spoke of the upcoming *Soirée Dansante* and then of Dan Rice's Circus (notices for which were pasted up and down the Avenue) and then considered where we might venture next, for our first excursion had been such a success. Miss Taylor proclaimed that she would not go to the beach, for she had been once and had been appalled to see the manner in which it was overrun by carriages and ladies on horseback and bathers drowning themselves in white trousers and red frocks. Was there not some part of the ocean unpolluted by society? she wondered with her characteristic satire. I suggested several alternatives, recalled how when we lived in Newport before the war one could take a ten-minute sail from Bannister's Wharf to Fort Adams, where one might walk about the ramparts with a lovely view of the town and the harbor and the bay, but that I believed the fort was now closed to the general public, serving as it did as the Naval Academy.

"But if you are in the mood for indiscriminate democracy," I said with what I hoped was my own satirical hue, "the island is studded with wild footpaths that Alice and I and our brothers are in the habit of following where they may lead. We might make it out to Lily Pond, or Doubling Point, or even as far afield as Purgatory Bluff. Would such a trek suit?"

And more of the like. It was most free and delightful. Yet all the time we talked and bantered I was listening to the conversation of those at the table next to us, for I felt in what I overheard the stirrings of a subject which (to return this Notebook to its proper purpose) I will record here.

The conversation was between two men. Their wives were present but they did not partake. They were medical men, as I made out. They were comparing notes as it were, speaking of medicaments and febrifuges administered and of seeing patients in their surgeries. But what struck me was how one of them laughingly confessed to intensely disliking one of his regular patients (he described the man's brows and his ill-humor) and how it was all he could do to set aside his dislike and tend professionally to the man. Indeed he said he sometimes amused himself (and here one of the wives interjected her disapproval), amused himself with the ways in which he might, in the guise of giving physic to the man, instead undermine his health. The two doctors found a good deal of mirth in the conceit.

But here is my story. For it so happened that as I listened I was following with my eyes on the avenue below, in the near distance, a group of wounded soldiers the like of which are sometimes to be witnessed about Newport, having come down from the convalescing hospital at Portsmouth Grove. And the confluence of these two unlike apprehensions (and I suppose the lovely presence of Miss Taylor) has impregnated me with a subject.

Might not a most intriguing moral dilemma be explored in this? To wit: before the present war a young man and a somewhat older doctor are (unknown to the young man) rivals for the affection of the local belle. The young man's hopes as regards the young lady are no secret to their respective families and to the town itself, whereas the doctor's attentions, whilst never overstepping the boundaries of propriety, are unknown to all but the doctor and the belle herself. (And even she, perhaps, in her innocence, in her unworldliness, does not fully apprehend what underlies the doctor's friendship.) At the outbreak of war the young man goes off with a regiment raised of the town, the scene rendered with the shrill piping of fifes and colorful banners unfurled, and of course the young man handsome and heroic in his uniform. Whilst he is away, the doctor continues to visit the belle and her family. He must bear the reading of the young man's letters, and the general swoon of the small town over his courage, etc. Finally there comes word of a disastrous battle in which the local regiment is rumored to have partaken, followed by the roll of casualties in the local paper, and finally the young man coming home horribly wounded, yet expected to mend under the diligent care of the doctor.

And there, of course, is the doctor's dilemma (a good title?). Does he take care of the young man or only *appear* to do so? Appear to work assiduously for the young man's recovery all the while ensuring his continued deterioration, that he might claim his prize when the boy is gone. One might even end the story *before* the doctor makes his decision, for that is where the essence of the subject lies: the moment when the conscience vibrates against the urgings of the heart. And what that reveals of the doctor's moral being.

Might that not make a story? If well-imagined and fully-colored?

One more thing of this day: at some point I found myself apologizing to Miss Taylor for my habit of substituting French words for English words I found difficult. I said I would try not to do that. And from that I mused on something I have often thought, perhaps because of Father's wooden leg, the reality of which was such a wonderment to me as a very young boy. Each of us, I told her, is maimed in some way, though to the world the evidence may not be visible (or audible, I said with a smile at my own infirmity). She said then with that delightful impertinence she sometimes has that she understood how *I* might be considered crippled, but in what way was *she*? And she looked brightly at me, as if she had set a challenge for me and wondered how I might meet it. I told her she was perhaps crippled by innocence. By innocence? she exclaimed. And I said yes, that one might be impertinent, and satirical, and sick of ladies on horseback at the beach, and still be impaired by innocence.

By the by, allow me to add here that I have completely lost my sense of

Miss Taylor as a dressmaker. What a too melodramatic conceit! A beginner's error. Indeed, I cannot fancy her "after" a husband at all, and I take solace (and relief!) in that. She is altogether too original, she with her splendid shifting sensibility and her way of gracing one with a light, postponing laugh. I must not smutch her with melodrama but reserve her for some fine tragedy!

1778

Apr 16

And now how the Farce unfolds! For I have had the most extraordinary Interview with Smithson! He has gone from being my Second to being on the Verge of needing his own Second. For it is his Opinion that I have engineered the late Contretemps with the Engineer for my advantage, that I insulted Major Browning and risked a duel knowing the news would reach Miss Da Silva and that this would position me in her Favour. He said he would un-mask me if I persisted. I laughed and asked him did he think I had such control over the damned Engineer as to prevail upon him to insult Miss Da Silva in my hearing that I might rise Gallantly to her Defence? He says no, but he understands me to have taken Advantage of the Opportunity that presented itself knowing it would cast me in an Heroic light. To which I responded, did he account me such a Tactician that in the heat of the moment I was Calculating how to best turn my face so that Miss Da Silva might see the fineness of my Features? And more of the same, *viz.* did he account me such a Chess-Player that I would risk my life to prove to a young Lady I had her interests at heart as a means of stealing that Heart? To which he responded that indeed he did consider me such a Chess-Player. In all this he was quite hot, and I was laughing and trying to show the man his Lunacy all the while Marveling at how fit his Accusation was, even if I had had no such original Intent as he laid to me. Surely the man could not know of the girl's letter!

He then brought up the Cambridge incident, saying it was one thing to lay a Trap for a married woman, that the married women of the World might know better and be on their own Lookout, but a Colonial girl, however blessed by Nature with Wit & Grace, was no fair opponent. And that I should mark him in this. He would not let me make a Sport of the girl. He would inform Da

Silva that I was not a man to be trusted, would tell Judith of the incident with Mrs. Winter and withal of my true Nature if I persisted in my attentions. Mark me, Ballard, he said and left me. Upon my word, I was quite speechless.

Even now, writing this near Midnight, I am still amazed. The damned fellow! Does he not see that it is against the Jew I move my Pieces, and that his Daughter is but the Spoil?

But I must rally and think this through, for I now have action on the Flank and it threatens the whole Campaign. What Forces to divert, what Ploy to devise to counter it? I must find a line that leads to Checkmate. For whatever comes, Smithson must be silenced.

Apr 17

To clear my mind I today stole away to try some Bird-hunting. I walked out the two or three miles to Doubling Point where the land turns waste and no Troops are quartered. I write waste, yet the point offers a fair if rude Prospect, something like Cornwall I think with its Cliff walls that rise from the water and the hurley of low Vegetation (the wood-cutting Detachments having raped the land of anything larger). It felt good to have a Rural ground underfoot. I tried to keep inland so as to pretend I was back in Dartmoor, tho' on this Island one can never get very far from the Sea and the damned Nautical men. I have had enough of spunyarn, lines, and worming.

I managed to shoot some Doves and what I take to be an American Woodcock, scrawny things but perhaps fit for a soup. I put them in my bag and hiked into the hilly Interior. There were spring flowers about, Columbine, and something that looked a type of Quinquefolia.

But for the wind and the cries of the gulls overhead the land was empty, with only some sheep and an occasional Farmhouse to which I gave a wide berth.

If one needed to do a Mischief to a man, one might do it out there.

Apr 18

News today of a Deserter of the 54th who was missed at his post last night and was pursued by a Serjeant's party. He was discovered at daybreak on the extremity of Commonfence Neck where he had fired his piece as a signal to a Rebel boat to come and take him off. He was hailed by the pursuing party but turned and fired upon them. He then threw himself in the water and made to swim to the Rebel boat, but several shots were fired at him and he was drowned.

This Apprehension is rare, for most who Desert are never heard from again, so easy is it to pass from Briton to Colonial.

Perhaps one of the Rebel maids had flashed her eyes at him and he could no longer bear it.

Apr 21

Went this morning to Da Silva's to see if I might learn whether the Waters have been disturbed, but he was Gracious and welcomed me so that I was reassured that Smithson had yet to play his Cards. Judith was not there. She has lately joined the Loyalist women of the city who sew and mend and write Letters for the Common soldiers, and is of late helping at the Hospital which has been made of their Synagoge. Da Silva expressed the hope that by her Presence and Service there she might help dissuade any further harm to that treasured building. Had I heard of the ill-use of the Redwood Library and the looting of its volumes?

I asked was he not concerned about Miss Da Silva's physical Well-being? An occupying army was not a Pleasure-Party, I said. To which he answered that Phyllis accompanied his daughter everywhere she went, and he believed he still had some teeth about the Town, and after all she did not go about like a bona rosa in a flaunting dress. What was my pleasure, Sherry or Chess?

Half an hour later the door opened and Judith swept in with Phyllis behind, stooping to kiss her father on the forehead. She was dressed in the most Ordinary gown, something of Phyllis's perhaps, so as not, I supposed, to unduly arouse my sick countrymen (tho' such is the Figure of the girl that even Homespun might not disguise it). When she turned and asked how I fared, there passed between us a look I could not mistake. She had my Letter, and she knew what it meant. I had hers, and she trusted I knew what *it* meant. There was a dark Boldness in her eye and a Shadow about her lips, as if she meant for me to know that she understood us to be in league together, come what may. That we were beyond the Curbs of common life.

She spoke for some time of the Manner of her Assistance at the Hospital, how she read to the sick and wrote letters for them to their Mothers and Wives, how they particularly liked it when she brought with her one of the Rebel papers that were to be had about the town. For they liked to laugh at the Opinions therein. Woven into her Account was, I thought, a thread of how I might waylay her. For she walked on Tuesday and Friday afternoons in the company of Phyllis to the Synagoge at two, she said. She was quite alone, she said, except for Phyllis.

When I left Da Silva I had to walk about the muddy, darkening, damned City to calm myself. Jove, I did!

Apr 22

I forgot to write last night that in parting I asked Da Silva had he heard that the Province was reputed to be raising a Negroe Reg^t to send to Washington's Army. We had a laugh over that, and I told him he would have to keep Hannibal under lock and key or before long the black Bastard would be crossing the Alps on an Elephant.

❧ 1692 ❧

4th Day

Last First Day as I was leaving Meeting I was waylaid most unexpectedly. The African joiner Charles Spearmint bore down on me as tho' to speak to me, and then thinking better of it (as we were still in sight of the Friends) tack'd and instead follow'd me at some Distance as I walk'd homeward toward the Point. I did not think he meant me any Mischief and so when I turn'd down Chestnut Street, I stopp'd and waited for him to reach me. He thank'd me, begg'd my pardon, call'd me Miss Selwyn, said he wish'd to speak with me on an important Matter, and might he have permission to Call on me at a Time convenient to us both.

I have often noted him sitting amongst the African men at Meeting. He is accounted a fine Joiner and an honest man. Father I know treated with him to make the Clothes press in his and Mother's room, and the Settle in the kitchen is I believe his handiwork. He was brought up in his Trade by Philip Sumner, who when he died, being without Issue, left him his Workshop, which action I remember Father saying did raise some Brows in the city. As a freeman he named himself Charles (after the King that was then, I believe), but most do still call him Spearmint.

And now we have had our Interview, and what an extraordinary Interview it was!

He came as we had appointed. It was snowing, and he wore no hat, and the Snowflakes were all about his Negroe hair. And as we sat in the Parlour, the snow would melt and trickle down his forehead and neck and he was forever wiping himself.

He seem'd surpriz'd that I bid him into the Parlour, that we did not stay in the Kitchen. But he is a Freeman, is he not?

He spoke in a most grave manner and treated with me as an Adult. This made me uneasy, and at first I could not understand him, for tho' he speaks as we do and not in the language of the Islands (as does Ashes when she wishes to annoy!), yet he would circle round and round so that I had some Difficulty following him. He spoke of a most involv'd Plan, and did go on so, and did not give me a moment to approach what he meant so that I felt beleaguer'd and forc'd to halt him that I might ask questions. I realize now that his circling was a Consequence of his own Anxiousness, coming to me on a Subject so important to him, and so much and for so long in his thoughts. Yet at the time I was so whelm'd by the News and his manner, and the feel of the world, already so chang'd! yet changing more.

But this is the Case: It seems he did come to Father six months past and presented him with the very same offer he describ'd to me today. I am most amaz'd at it! For he wishes to sell himself back into Slavery that he might purchase Ashes as his Wife! He did not say it in these Words, yet that is what it comes to. I am to understand that he had from Father a Price for Ashes, and since he has not that Price, he laid out a Plan by which he would Indenture himself to Father for seven Years, giving to Father some percentage of his Wages from his Trade, that at the end of the Term, he would have paid the Price and Ashes would be a free woman and they might marry. Or rather, if I understood rightly, they would have already married, as servants, been married those seven years, but they would at the end of the Term be the both of them free. Oh, I am in a mix, and cannot write clearly.

Seven years, as did Jacob for love of Rachel!

What to think? How to act? Might this not solve the Difficulty Dorcas and I find ourselves in? Would not that seven years of Income help keep us? Spearmint holds that Father, before he embark'd on this last voyage to the Islands, did tell him that he would think on his Offer and give him an Answer when he return'd. Yet the African said this in such a Manner that I wonder'd was it the Truth? And had not Father turn'd him down firstly? This may be unfair of me, for Spearmint is accounted a most upright man. And he is a Friend, tho' African. Yet I could not help but feel that he came to me to renew a Suit that had already been refus'd. He sees that Circumstances have chang'd and has suppos'd that I know nothing of the Matter and that I am in a Strait and he may expect a better answer.

But what of that? Must I abide by Father's decision? Am I bound to keep the house as it was, as I hear some do keep a token of their dead undisturb'd? Would Father not rather want me to look about myself, to judge the World as it goes westerly, and set a Course the most favourable to me and mine?

6th Day

From the window in Mother and Father's room I can see down to the Harbor, and sometimes I can make out John Pettibone on his father's wharf moving some lading about, rolling a cask, or going up the gang with a wheel-barrow. He has this last six-month grown lanky and strong, I think. And though I upbraid myself for spending my time so, and scold myself that I must go to the window each day—and aye, sometimes more than once!—yet it seems I cannot help myself. At the sight of him, I feel a most warm Desolation. Aye, that is the feeling, both Desolate and Warm.

5th Day, 1 x mo.

I cannot help but look at Ashes now with new eyes. That she has inspir'd such love! She with her scarr'd face!

I am left to wonder how Spearmint and Ashes have been meeting one another. For I cannot believe this love of his has generated itself by merely seeing Ashes once a week across the Meeting Room! I lay in bed last night and my Thoughts would whirl so! I thought of little times when she was out on an Errand and seem'd to take too long. It is but a five minute walk to his joiner's Shop where it sits north of the Point. How often has she gone there?

All day today Ashes went about as she has always done. She did not speak or sign in any way that she knows I have been approach'd. Is she so practic'd in double dealing?

I have pictures in my head of them meeting. Of their intent Countenances. Their low Speech. Their hands press'd together.

How they have baked together this Sugar work of a Future!

7th Day

I had a new thought (much to my Shame as I will record!) that it was possible Ashes did not know either of Spearmint's offer or of his Affections for her. That he had come to buy her without her knowing, without her Consent, as those of the slave trade do. And once he had bought her he would have her, will she or no. Would that not explain what appeared to be her Deceitfulness? For it was none such, if this were so.

All morning I tried to ask her. We were about our work in the kitchen, cleaning the Lisbon ware, and Dorcas was there on the floor, and I kept looking at Ashes as if she might supply me the wanted Courage. But I scrupled to ask such a question. It seem'd too (I know not what!), too great a Trespass even if I am her Mistress. And I thought too that before I spoke to her of the Matter I should have my Answer settl'd as to Spearmint's Offer, for the case may be that she does know of it, and desires it.

In the afternoon, I retir'd and pray'd that I might labor toward Wisdom, but I felt no Light. I had only my own Confusion, and not only about this present Matter, but of my own Life. I sat at the Window in my room and look'd through the diamond Panes out at the Yard, and at Jane Beecher's, and I long'd to go to her and seek Comfort from her. For I felt most alone and overwhelm'd and she is so strong. She has said she would be as a Man to me and I had need then of such a one. But I did not go. I sat in the cold with a blanket about me and tho' I yearn'd for Light yet all I saw was Darknesse. Still, I weigh'd things as I knew Father would have me do, and slowly I determin'd that if I could not ask Ashes what was the Truth, yet I might go to Spearmint and ask him. He had come to me with a Business offer and I might wish to clarify certain Terms or Prospects. And this planned Course of Action, even just the having of it, did somewhat set my mind at ease.

So I charg'd myself with going the next morning. Yet hardly was I back downstairs than I found myself putting on my Cloak and strapping on my Pattens. For I determin'd I would go then and there and know the Issue.

I made my way northward through the Point toward where I knew his joiner's Shop to be. The door was open'd by an African boy (I had not consider'd that there might be Apprentices), and I was bid enter. Inside I took off my cloak and pattens. Spearmint betray'd some Agitation at the sudden sight of me, but he master'd himself and ask'd did I wish to step into the room next over for I had come to the Shop itself with its Benches and Tools and the floor cover'd in curly Shavings. I said no, we could speak here. There was a set of six Chairs with ladder-backs that were evidently his current work and he drew one across the floor and set it behind me and placed a short Plank across the seat which still lack'd its woven rush. He did this with something of a smile, I thought, as if it were a droll thing. He told the boys (for there were two of them) that they might retire as it was growing dusky. One of them, the one who had open'd the door, was about my age. I believe I have seen him at Meeting.

I began by saying I had not yet come to a Decision, for I did not want him to labor under an Anxiety during the whole of our Interview. I ask'd him again what Father had said to him, expressing to him that it was not like Father to put off a Decision. He repeated (I thought with some Pique at what he must have consider'd my Disbelief of him) that Father had set a figure for Ashes and had listen'd to his Suit with respectful Deliberation, and had said he would think on it, but that this close Voyage to the Islands would prevent him Answering until his Return. I thank'd him and answer'd that that was what I had understood him to say the other day. This was but Dancing on my part for I wanted to Veil my reasons for coming. We had more of the like. He return'd each of my questions with Consideration and Patience. Finally I ask'd had he discuss'd the Matter with Ashes? Was he in the habit of seeing her? He ask'd then, in return, what did I mean, which fluster'd me somewhat as I thought the Question clear. I ask'd yet more plainly, did Ashes wish to be his Wife? He said then that he believ'd Ashes return'd his Affections, that they saw one another on First Day, and elsewhere when they could. I thought there might yet be some

Evasion in that, so I ask'd did she favor this Plan of his, that he should sell himself that her Freedom might be bought.

It was then that the first Cloud cross'd his Countenance. No, she did not, he said plainly. Ah, I said, then she does not wish to marry. He look'd at me then as if he marvel'd at what I could mean. It was not that she did not wish to marry, he explain'd, but that she did not wish the State of Servitude on him. He had been a Slave once and having had those Fetters once untied, she would not have him resume them. And then as I was silent, he said he believ'd it was a Testament to her Love toward him that she would not have him back in Bondage.

I continued with questions: oh, I know not what, about where he imagin'd he would live, how could his Apprentices have an indentur'd Master, and the like. But I was just Acting. For I felt a Confusion and a Shame running through me and I thought my Face redden'd even as I sat there. I stumbl'd through to the end of the Interview, telling him I had been in a Mix the other day, so surpriz'd was I by his coming, and thanking him for this further Talk which would allow me to think on the Matter more clearly. I must have look'd a Fool, for when I left, tho' I threw on my Cloak yet I neglected to put on my pattens, something I realiz'd the Instant I was back out in the muddy thoroughfare, but I could not turn back, and set off through the streets, my thoughts sinking downward.

For it seem'd to me that I had exercis'd a kind of Meanness toward Charles Spearmint, or at best a shameful lack of Charity. For who was it, I ask'd myself, who conceiv'd such a doubling Scheme as his getting a Wife by buying one who did not wish it? Whose scheming mind was that? Aye, it was Prudy Selwyn's mind! Evil be to him who thinks evil, as Father has so often said. For was not my Judgment reveal'd then as a deceitful Balance as we hear some cheating Merchants use? And he an African and I a New Englander for the further Shame of it!

I did not return home then, but rather walk'd down to the Wharves in the gloaming that I might sink further into the Dark. I look'd out at the bobbing masts, and the gray and cold Ocean beyond, and I wonder'd whether I was a Friend at all, for so scarce was God's Light in me. I had always felt it a shameful Secret that I did not experience, or so rarely experienc'd, the Goodness and Clarity I did hear about in Meeting. Yet I accounted it my Youth, and that in time God would grant me an Influx of Light that would reside in me and not go out in the next Instant as it seem'd always to do. But now in this dark Humour I batter'd myself with Questions. Why was God so stinting of His Light to me when He gave it so readily to others? Why did He not help me see the Good? Why, when it was left to itself, had my Mind entertain'd such base Suspicions? What could it be but that God did not watch over me, that He did not Love me, that He did not see me worthy of His Love and of His Light? Oh, I spent an Hour in the most abas'd State!

Now, writing in my room, I am somewhat recover'd. Yet there is this with which I must reckon: Ashes is belov'd of Charles Spearmint, and Charles Spearmint is belov'd of Ashes, and Each nobly looks to save the Other.

✦ 2011 ✦

At the Casino over the next few days Sandy kept his head down. He had done the right thing, had told Aisha about Alice and could now—couldn't he?—move on. He called some of his buddies in Florida, texted Todd Martin, checked in with Saddlebrook, where he'd coached the previous winter. He saw Aisha once and she acted as if nothing had happened. (Maybe nothing *had* happened.) They went out for clam rolls and a beer, and he defaulted to sleeping with her, but it wasn't the same. He couldn't help but let a certain distance—an irony almost—come into his touch, into his way of being with her. If she noticed, she didn't say anything.

And then he got a call from his rental agent with the news he'd been dreading all summer. The condo owners wanted their place back. They weren't getting divorced after all and since he was renting week to week—that's why the condo was so affordable in the first place, the agent reminded him—she was afraid he would have to leave on short notice. She offered to help him find another rental if he could afford a little more.

A little more turned out to be a lot more. It was summer, it was Newport, no one else was getting a divorce. The only other option was to forgo looking at the summer rentals and search instead for what the agent called "townies." But she was afraid she didn't handle those. He could check the classifieds, maybe Craigslist.

So he spent Wednesday, his day off, looking. But all the apartments, even the small furnished ones, wanted a year's lease. He followed up on a Roommate Wanted ad he'd found in a candy shop, tore off one of the tags with a phone number, but the apartment turned out to be some stoners' place—mattresses on the floor, Bob Marley on the stereo—and he'd never felt his quads so out of place. He ended up in a rooming house—a big old renovated run-down Victorian thing with asbestos shingling—being shown a high-ceilinged room with violet walls and the reek of cigarette smoke and a shared bathroom down the hall. It was a hundred fifty a week.

Back on the Indian, pissed off—was he really going to live in such a dump?—he took off through town, out past the Burial Ground, out to the naval base and then circling around to the string of beaches on the east side of the island. From the start he had told himself not to be fooled and yet it had happened anyway. He had let the condo with its chichi sculpture and thick draperies and its view of fifty million dollars worth of sailboats in the harbor lull him into thinking he was part of this world, as if there were an equation sign between some millionaire's yacht and Sandy Alison on his antique racing-red motorcycle. The sun, the women in their slingbacks, the expensive cars parked all over town (U-WISH one of the license plates had read): maybe the bozo had been right about him after all.

Back in town he got the light at Memorial and was coming up on the Casino when he realized the figure he'd just seen at the side of the road—back there, across the street from the Athenaeum—the woman sitting at the trolley stop, had been Alice. He gunned the Indian as if to say screw you and your house, and then felt stupid, let up, turned down Berkeley and onto Freebody Street, where he pulled over to the side of the road.

Was that how she was getting around, he wondered, riding the little trolley buses that ran up and down Bellevue for the tourists?

Geez, he had to see her *some*time, didn't he?

When he came around again she pretended not to notice him, even when he stopped in front of her—big as life—and let the Indian idle at the curb. "Hey," he said, but she didn't answer, kept her head turned from him, gazing off like there was something of interest in the other direction. He took heart: she was ignoring him in an actressy way, a funny-Alice sort of way. He maneuvered the Indian up the curb, shut the engine off, and put it up on its kickstand.

When he crossed to her, helmet in hand, she leaned over and spread her things out on the bench. "Sorry," she said, "no room."

He stood over her, and there were his quads again.

"I got kicked out of my condo," he said. He had to say something.

"Morals charge?" she asked, turning her face to him. She was dressed in a denim skirt and a cowgirl shirt with flowered embroidery, and her hair was in braided pigtails like she was the sweetheart of the rodeo. She didn't *look* depressed at least. He bent over, picked her things up—her laptop and her photocopies and stuff; couldn't the girl afford a briefcase?—and stacked them beside her so he could sit down.

"The divorcing couple isn't divorcing anymore."

"Good for them, bad for you," she said.

He pulled back at that, waited a minute, waited for her to say she was sorry or something. But she didn't.

"I went up to the library to look for you once," he tried. She had her lips pursed, wouldn't look at him. "But I chickened out." Still she didn't look at him. "I was worried about you."

"Because of these?" she said, and she pulled back her cowgirl sleeves and thrust her upturned wrists at him with their pale scars exposed. And she fixed him with a look that was so angry he thought, good god, what had he done? And then she seemed to recoil at her own behavior, pulled the cuffs of her sleeves back down, and dropped her hands in her lap. She turned her head away from him. This time there was nothing actressy about it. He had the good sense not to say anything.

"I'm not in love with you, you know," she said after a time. "I just wanted someone to hold me. I was drunk. And you were there."

"Okay," he said.

"It could've been anybody. These things come over me."

"Okay," he repeated.

"Oh, shut up," she said. She picked up her papers and her laptop and squared them on her lap, sat there all tight to herself as if to minimize points of contact with the world. She had her head turned from him in such a way that he could only see the side of her face, her cheekbone, and a blinking eyelid. He couldn't tell if she was crying, but he didn't think so. After a couple of minutes the little trolley came, its sides plastered with images of the Breakers and the Chinese teahouse, and the tourists inside looking over their heads at the Old Stone Mill behind them. The driver gave Sandy a quizzical look until Sandy waved him on.

"Can I give you a ride home?" he asked when another minute had passed.

"I'm waiting for the trolley."

Which was maybe supposed to be funny. So he stayed where he was, quiet, waiting, looking past her at the traffic, the light turning and the cars starting up, turning again and the cars stopping. A couple of blocks away the green pennant advertising the International Tennis Hall of Fame flapped over the entryway to the Casino. The air was warm.

"You lied to me," he heard after a good five minutes had passed. He returned his gaze to her, let his mind roam over that night: what was she talking about?

"No," he said.

"Yes. You did."

He frowned to himself, looked at where her hair parted at the back of her head, the two cowgirl braids that fell down the fronts of her shoulders onto her chest.

"About Margo," she said.

Ah, he thought. And then temporized with, "And you know this how?"

She didn't bite. "I know."

He quickly considered, and then just as quickly discarded, denying it. "It wasn't a lie," he said. "I mean it wasn't directed at you. I couldn't very well tell you the truth, could I?"

"It doesn't matter," she said. "You can sleep with whomever you want."

He thought of telling her that—as it turned out—he *couldn't* sleep with whomever he wanted: there was his job, his getting kicked out of his condo, his owing his old traveling coach eight thousand dollars, but he didn't. Instead he asked if it had been Margo who had told her. She shook her head no.

"Surely not Tom."

She didn't laugh, crossed her legs at her ankles. "No, it was Aisha."

He supposed he kept his face composed, but he felt like he had been slapped.

"Aisha?" was all he could say.

"I think she was trying to help by making you out to be a creep. Not worthy of my affections."

"Aisha told you about me and Margo?"

She nodded, self-conscious enough not to pick up on his tone of voice. She was looking down at the stack of stuff on her lap. "That horrible night," she said. "I was upset and when I got back to the house I woke her up and told her everything." And she laughed an awful laugh and put her hand to her mouth. "Like a teenager!"

He tried to keep his voice even. "You told her about that night? In the cemetery?"

"Not to worry," she said. "It reflects well on you."

He stared at her. Aisha knew. The other night when he had so carefully broached the subject of Alice and the cemetery, she had already known. Why hadn't she stopped him? The pretending, the pensive look, the not letting on, the charade of it all.

"Does you credit," Alice was saying. "Very gentlemanly of you. Not taking advantage of the feebleminded and all."

"Not guilty of—" what had she called it?—"*abus de faiblesse?*" he said a little sharply. "Is that it?"

She looked at him as though he had cut her, then recovered: "Exactly so." Then colder: "Well put."

He would leave, he thought. Forget moving out of the condo into that rooming house. He would just up and leave. The Casino could manage without him. There was a whole Eastern Seaboard of friends who would be glad to see him, who'd put him up for a couple of days—people he still knew at Duke, friends at resorts on the Outer Banks. Saddlebrook would be glad to have him back. Okay, he wasn't James Blake or even Robby Ginepri, but he was a former top fifty player. They didn't grow on trees.

He shifted his helmet from one hand to the other, shifted it back. He looked down at her lap, at her hand with its strained ligaments, that taut, tense, yellow, waxy look it had. Another five minutes went by.

"I'm sorry," he found himself saying finally. He could see, a block away, another trolley coming. "It just started. Last year. When it didn't matter."

"It always matters," she said, standing up, papers and laptop clutched to her chest.

What had he said to himself that night with Aisha?—he was the only one among them who wasn't counterfeit in his heart. And he had felt the truth of it, he really had, and yet it was *he* who was sleeping with two women at the same time. And keeping it secret from everyone.

"I don't think you understand my situation," he said, standing himself. "I don't have a place to live. In another two months I won't have a job. And I owe people money." *And you and your ten-million-dollar mansion!* he wanted to shout at her.

"Nobody understands anyone's situation," she said and started across the sidewalk to where the trolley had pulled up. When the door opened, she made it up onto the step in her halting way and then turned back to him. "I'm sorry I wrecked things between us," she said. And then she tucked her face in, began to turn so he almost didn't hear her say: "But I have the right to feel things too."

And she made her way down the aisle. The driver waited until she was seated and then pulled away.

Back at the condo he opened the bottle of bourbon the condo owners had left behind and which he'd been denying himself all summer. And he used his copy of *Daisy Miller* to make one last fire in the fireplace. He tore the pages out one by one.

Two days later he called a taxi, gave the cabbie a twenty to help him pile everything he owned into the cab, and sitting in the passenger seat with a brave front saying "Let's roll!" moved into the asbestos nightmare. When Margo came by, she couldn't stop laughing. "Oh, dear!" she kept saying, sitting on the edge of his bed in her tank top and miniskirt, patting her lips as if she were going to burp. Making love, he gathered, was out of the question so they ended up walking over to the White Horse Tavern and having roasted clams and gin-soaked lemonade in the bar, Sandy wondering out loud where on earth they could go if *her* place was out and now *his* place . . . letting the ellipses hang pointedly in the dark, woody ambience of the tavern. Maybe they should quit while they were ahead, he ventured.

"Who's ahead?" Margo asked.

"Your ad," Sandy smilingly replied, hoping he sounded subtle or suggestive, though he didn't know what exactly he was being subtle or suggestive *about*.

"You want to quit?" Margo pressed.

This was uh-oh territory, he knew. Even if Margo wanted to quit, she wouldn't want *him* to want to. She preferred the score to be forty-love, her favor.

"I was just taking the opportunity to give you an out if you wanted one," he said, and then in his best Southern Gentleman voice: "It must be difficult for you." And when that didn't work, feeling some heat come into the tips of his ears: "Of course I don't want to quit."

At which she fixed him with a look, then popped the last clam in her mouth and got out her credit card.

A day or two later he was wandering down Thames Street with the skateboarders and the teenage girls in their summer tops and he had entered All That Glitters, the chic shop that carried Aisha's jewelry. He had stood in front of the display case that held her stuff—*Goldwork Variations* by Aisha DuMaurier—as if interrogating the mermaids and serpents would tell him something about her. But what it told him (DuMaurier was not her real last name), he already knew.

So he had turned away, browsed through the other stuff—bird's-eye puzzle boxes, ceramics, Japanese tea servings—and then picked up this beautiful leather briefcase with the sudden bright idea—hey!—that he would buy it for Alice. For about fifteen minutes—while he survived the shock of the price, got out his credit card, let the shopgirl compliment his taste—it seemed perfect, just the way to say he was sorry. But as he walked back toward his room it began to eat at him, what he'd just done. With each street he felt stupider and stupider. Surely the girl already had a briefcase! Maybe she hated briefcases! When he got back to his room he threw the leather thing onto a chair and lay down on his bed, closed his eyes. In a day or two he would see if the shop would take it back.

He was avoiding Aisha and yet he knew he had to see her. More than that, he had to call her out. So he texted her, told her he'd be playing basketball in Storer Park the way he did some nights. Their secret meeting place, ha! When she showed up, he looked for signs that Alice had told her of the trolley stop. How would she maneuver, how would she explain? But she seemed as always—the bare summer ankles, the sheen of her brown skin, the self-possession with which she handled herself. If this was how she always looked, he wondered—now, when he *knew* she was hiding something—had she been hiding something all along?

The black guys messed with her in the way they had, called her "sister," called her "bitch." She should try a brother, enough of this Larry shit! None of it fazed her.

They went out onto Da Silva's Wharf. The Terrace was full but they were able to get seated inside the main house in a room that had four carved cherubs in the overmantel, one of them missing its nose. The windows were open to the wharf and there was a nice breeze. Aisha ordered a bottle of wine, said it was her treat.

He had been trying the last couple of days to think himself into a place that was cool and disengaged, some place where he might make use of the fact that he knew something about her that she didn't know he knew. There was a kind of power in that, wasn't there? But now that the moment had come, he found he no longer cared. What would the power be *for*? he wondered, except more falseness, duplicity, deception. More moral *infirmity*. Out the window he could see the terrace where he and Alice had sat the evening of the breakwater. He could see their table, could almost—like he was watching a film—see the two of them, Alice in her biker-babe outfit telling him about Jacqueline Bouvier, about getting drunk and walking through the town at night and imagining stuff. And he remembered something from *Daisy Miller*, a moment at the end of the story when the Italian count guy says to Winterbourne after Daisy has died: "She is the one whose esteem one would have liked to have had." It was a moment he was literate enough to know turned the whole story on its head. And it made him—sitting there looking down at a phantom Alice while Aisha poured him some more wine—it made him detest himself for the falseness he'd let come into his life.

They were halfway through the bottle when he heard himself saying—with no prelude, no excuse, no telltale expression—just his voice calm and disengaged: "Alice knows about me and Margo."

She cocked her head, managed not to give herself away. He watched her try to read him: did he know?

"She says you told her."

Her lips thinned. "When did you see her?"

"A couple of days ago." He wasn't going to say more. She took a stagy breath, tried to let a softness come over her, then peered at him as if to ask could he take this?

"I had to tell her."

"Why?"

"It was a tactical move."

At which he raised his brow. "A tactical move," he repeated.

"To help her fall out of love with you."

He was used to her confounding his expectations. She was always more sanguine, more on top of things, more—he didn't know what— more *prepared* than he thought she would be. But each time his expectations were overturned he was surprised all the same.

"Tactical," he repeated.

"To protect her," Aisha pursued. "She was hurting. I was worried about her. I told her so she'd be able to begin to—" She paused as if waiting for him to finish the thought, but he was still ungiving. "So that she'd see you as someone she shouldn't—" and she searched for the words—"someone she shouldn't care for."

"Someone not worthy of her affections." Hadn't Alice said that herself? "Is that it?"

"Something like that." And then with a soft, girlfriend look, reaching out and touching his hand: "I'm sorry."

It all sounded sensible, the kind of thing a friend might do. But—and here he didn't know if he wasn't simply burned by too much secrecy and double-dealing—but he didn't believe her.

"Is that how you think of things?" he found himself saying. "Tactics? Strategy? We talk about this stuff all the time in tennis, but in real life?"

"It was just a way of saying it."

"Of saying what?" he asked with a pointed look, but she didn't respond. "What's the difference anyway?"

"What?" she said like he'd lost her.

"Between tactics and strategy," he said.

She had her tongue between her teeth, her face dark with trying to figure him out. "Okay," she said—as if whatever he was after, whatever the game was, she would acquiesce, she was not his enemy. "Isn't it that strategy is an overall plan and tactics are the individual parts of the plan?"

"Ah," he intoned, smiling as if so *that's* it. "So, the one time I played Federer my strategy was not to get bageled. My tactics were—" he spread his hands in a gesture of surrender—"well, there were no tactics. He was Federer."

She laughed, smiled as if maybe things were okay between them. He smiled too, but the smile felt cold on his face.

"So what's the strategy?" he said.

She drew back as if he'd ambushed her.

"Strategy for what?" she asked, and when he didn't answer: "Whose strategy?" And when he still didn't answer: "I don't know what you're getting at, Sandy. I don't have anything to gain in this. I was just trying to help her. She was in a state."

"Didn't you think telling her might make her even worse off? If she was in love with me, as you say, telling her I was a cheat? Telling her I was cheating with her sister-in-law?"

She pulled back. "I didn't tell her you were a cheat."

"Yes, you did."

She turned her hands palm out as if to say, okay if that's how you want to see it.

"And that night after I picked you up in Providence. You let me go on about it. Me and Alice, the whole story. And you already knew all about it."

She kept her lips pressed together.

"You knew all about that night in the cemetery. She came to *get* you after it happened. Why didn't you say so?"

"You don't understand."

"What don't I understand?"

She had a look now of injured merit. "You don't understand that I have divided loyalties. She was so distraught. That night. I was afraid for her."

"But afterwards—you could have let me know."

She shook her head. "I'd promised Alice not to tell anyone. Not

promised—it was *understood*. These things are understood between us."
And when that didn't seem enough: "If I'd told you, and she'd found out . . .
it would have been a further—" and again she searched for the right
word—"a further *flaying*. She's so *naked*. I couldn't."

He was making and unmaking a fist. It was an old nervous locker room
habit. "And if she ever found out about *us*?"

She closed her eyes, shook her head.

"If she ever found out that all this time while you were being her best
friend, and I was being . . . if she were to find out we'd been sleeping together? Lovers? And keeping it from her? What would that do to her?"

"Don't," she said.

And there seemed suddenly between them a palpable sense of what had
brought them together in the first place. They were each in this world by
someone else's sufferance, issued a kind of backstage pass that could be revoked at any moment. In those first weeks they had been mates that way,
comrades-in-arms, the need for secrecy—the assignations, the retreats into
motel rooms, even the Storer Park basketball court—casting over them a
delicious confederacy. ("Larry, your chick's here!" the guy he'd been guarding had said. *His chick!*) But now he saw—surely he had known all along—
that Aisha was not going to choose him over even a tenuous hold on
Windermere. Her loyalties were not really all that divided.

"She can't ever find out," Aisha was saying now, pulling her face out
from behind her hands. They looked at each other, and there was, he
thought, an acknowledgment between them: whatever it was they'd had,
it was over. "You're with me on this, yes?"

"Yes."

"Because if she ever found out—" And then as if she were trying to
pledge him to something: "You understand?"

"Yes."

"Okay," she said. She lifted her wineglass, reached across the table, and
clinked his where it sat. "To us," she said with a wry look, with a sorry look,
with an ironic look, but with no sadness or regret that he could detect.

It was only afterwards as he walked back to his room and ran the whole
thing through his mind that he wondered how it was that—if she'd been

so concerned for Alice that awful night—how it was that Aisha had felt free to leave for Brooklyn the next day. He counted back the days and, yes, it had been the very day after the Champions Ball. Alice had come to her at six in the morning in a state, enough of a state that Aisha had felt compelled to tell her that the man she loved had been sleeping with her sister-in-law, and then had up and left. It made him stop walking—half a bottle of wine in him and no food—stop walking and stare at the gaslight above his head. Everything he'd ever heard from Aisha about Alice—and he'd heard a lot: college, Venice, the suicide attempts, Alice coming into her bed in the middle of the night just to be near her—everything had always cast her, Aisha, as a kind of savior, the one person who could talk Alice down off the ledge of her own personality. But here was this instance, the only one Sandy had direct experience of, where if ever the girl was going to need a friend's bed to crawl into this was it, and yet the friend had up and left, stayed away for a week. He gazed at the gaslight above him, then at the recession of gaslights down the narrow street. What did he think it gained Aisha by leaving Alice that morning? And what would Aisha have gained if Alice *had* harmed herself? Wouldn't that merely have revoked her backstage pass? And yet he couldn't escape the feeling that he had caught her out. That he had seen something she hadn't meant him to see.

On impulse he stopped in the library and took out a copy of *Daisy Miller* and back in his room made himself three peanut butter and jelly sandwiches and read the last few pages looking for the part where Giovanelli tells Winterbourne that he would have liked to have had Daisy's esteem. He had determined that he would give the briefcase to Alice after all—that that would be the first step in cleansing himself—and that he would copy out the passage about Daisy's esteem and put it inside by way of apology. Only it turned out he had misremembered and it wasn't Giovanelli who said that of Daisy, but rather Daisy of Winterbourne. He had to read the passage several times—mouth stuck together with peanut butter—to get it: Daisy, it's reported after her death, would have appreciated Winterbourne's esteem. He blinked over the ill-lit page. It somehow made everything worse.

~ 1896 ~

The prattle in TOWN TOPICS was all of the Masked Ball to be held at Berger's Open Air Pavilion the coming week. It was a most unusual event, the editors opined (Mrs. Auld was reading the article aloud to them), for the regular *habitués* of the Pavilion were the vacationing masses who stayed in the lesser hotels and not the names engraved in the Register with their ocean houses and their mansions up and down Bellevue Avenue. But this one night of the season the *beau monde* descended in their carriages upon the "slums" of Newport. Ah! What a majestic diversion to witness the Charge of the Four Hundred into the Valley of Death! Had they not the previous year had the affliction of having to dance on rose petals strewn across the pavilion floor! Surely it would only be their masks that would keep them from dying of shame, the noble Four Hundred!

"Ours not to reason why," said Franklin Drexel, playing a jack of spades. "Ours but to dance and die!"

They were in the gallery at the Dovecote, Mrs. Auld's brownstone pile out on Ochre Point, and the conversation—prior to Mrs. Auld's attempted diversion—had been of the scandal sheets and could not something be done? For that morning it had been rumored one of their number (there were knowing looks) had had anonymously delivered upon the butler's silver server a note that demanded that some activity or other (again, the looks) must cease or it would be bruited about in the sheets. There were backstairs spies, everyone knew. And poison-pen letters flying about. And there were those of the papers who offered bribes for information, for salacious tidbits, for who was visiting whom and at what hours. And there was most heinously the rumor that the sheets had taken to blackmailing those unfortunate enough to find themselves under scrutiny. For there was more to be made, it turned out, from not publishing a story than from publishing it.

And all during this discomfiting topic—just how competent *were* the hairless imps of his fate?—Franklin had felt, from two tables over, the eyes of Mr. Ryckman upon him.

They had met earlier that day. Mrs. Newcombe had sent him a note (would he not stop by? she needed his opinion on some plantings) and he had been coming up Bellevue on his (that is, on the deceased Mr. New-combe's) bicycle when he was passed by Mrs. Newcombe's carriage going the other way (*sans* Mrs. Newcombe). He recognized its cranberry-colored sides, and its driver, and surmised who it was the equipage was being sent to fetch. An hour later he was outside with Mrs. Newcombe when a man—evidently freshly changed—appeared on the broad front porch, gave a "halloo" to the children, and made his way across the sloping lawn.

He was short, and getting old, and inside his trousers Franklin sus-pected him of having spindly legs. But there was a bluff of a chest, and one of those noses that gets bigger and more ugly with age, and whiskers dating from the seventies, and a history of making men knuckle under in the manufactory of—well, Franklin didn't know what, of mercerized thread, he believed. Mrs. Newcombe and he had been standing (of all places!) in the maze when Mr. Ryckman had come down, and the children had squealed and charged at the sight of him. Franklin and Mrs. New-combe had begun making their way out of the labyrinth (only two years in the ground), but Mr. Ryckman had leapt the Lilliputian walls as if he meant to show them—show this upstart Drexel!—that if there were paths in the moral waste that needed to be blazed, by God he was the man to blaze them!

Now as they played cards at Mrs. Auld's with that morning's scandal like a dark undertow in the room, the talk turned to the Masked Ball: what would everyone be wearing? what would be the great success? had they sent to New York for their costumes? Someone asked Mr. Ryckman if he had heard about the mysterious Blue Domino from the previous year—no? did he not read the society pages?—and what did everyone think: would there be any such game this year? The Blue Domino, various voices explained to Mr. Ryckman (who sat amongst them, Franklin thought, as though he were Odysseus tied to his mast), had been the outrage of the previous year: a beautiful woman dressed in a blue gown and a blue mask, with a black-and-white die embroidered upon her bosom as if she were the very symbol of a treacherous fate, or at least an invitation to gamble your heart away. She had been a beautiful, bewitching enigma—"*La Belle Dame Sans Merci*," one of the papers had said—and there wasn't a man there that night who hadn't fallen under her spell. Oh, the rumors that followed! She was the illegitimate daughter of the Comte de Vichy, she was an actress hired by Coddington, she was the Thayers' French governess (who the next day had disappeared)!

"If it's men's hearts she bewitched," said Franklin (even while some voice in his head told him: *Don't say it, dear boy. Too much, too much!*), "then I believe the Blue Domino must have been Mrs. Newcombe."

At which the room tittered, smiled at the gallantry, for they knew, they knew! And some shot a look at Mr. Ryckman, still tied to his mast and not looking at all bewitched.

That evening back at Windermere there had been the manly after-dinner cigar smoking scene, obligatory (Franklin knew) to all melodramas of the drawing-room caste. Mrs. Thorpe and Mrs. Thayer—it being a weeknight, their husbands were still in New York—had withdrawn with Mrs. Newcombe, leaving Franklin and Mr. Ryckman alone at the dining table. Hobbes had brought cigars, and while the humidor was held open for Franklin, Ryckman—like a tomcat marking his territory—let it be known that he always kept a supply at his daughter's house, had that very morning had his tobacconist send up a box.

"A good Havana," he said, taking one of the obscene things himself and admiring it at arm's length. "Eh, Drexel?"

"Indeed, sir," said Franklin, inclining his head so that Hobbes could light him. Under ordinary circumstances he might have declined the pleasure—the damned things tended to make him ill—but he was getting to know the lay of the land, as he'd told Mrs. Belmont, and acquiescence in such matters—he was wearing unimpeachable evening clothes—seemed a tactical prerequisite.

To Ryckman's questions he trotted out the unexceptionable—if unexceptional—members of his family. His father a banker in Baltimore, his mother of the Louisville Nesbits, his sister married into a Main Line family. He himself had a quiet place down below Union Square (he didn't say just how far below), though every year it seemed another old family quit the tiny streets and moved up the wide avenue, and another building was hung about with bohemians. Still, it suited him, a good bachelor's flat, he said, drawing on his cigar. Ryckman kept a steady gaze on him.

"Ellen tells me you're a Princeton man. The classical languages, was it?"

"Ah, Princeton!" he said with a smile for the memory of his dear old alma mater and his own undercooked self. He had a soft spot for Princeton, he said. Princeton would have made him a man, he supposed (with a laugh: because, of course, here he was a man, smoking a cigar, by god! surrounded by dark wood and glinting silver and leather seats, and about to marry your daughter, eh?), Princeton would have made him a man if he'd stayed. But in his third year he'd had the opportunity to travel and he had taken it. Had visited all the great cities of Europe, had spent afternoon after afternoon in the museums (he enumerated them like a list of references: the Louvre, the Alte Pinakothek, the Rijksmuseum, the Uffizi). It had been a great education in itself, he wouldn't trade it for any number of Princeton degrees. For travel was a great educator, didn't Mr. Ryckman agree? Indeed it had taught Franklin that he was no artist! Ah, it had indeed! He might have continued on at Princeton, or at the Pennsylvania Academy, and never—until it was too late—discovered he had not the dark, honest soul of Rembrandt, nor the daring of Titian, the fury of Turner. And then there was his discovery of the Parisian dealers! Oh, what they were showing in their shops! The color, the light, the splendor of life! It was still a scandal what was going on in Paris! But he had loved it, even while he had felt himself diminished. Diminished and enlarged at the same time, that was the thing! For travel was the natural enemy of small-mindedness, of prejudice and intolerance and vanity, didn't Mr. Ryckman find it so? Ah, he had always intended to return to Princeton, to finish his studies—*non scholae sed vitae discimus*—but he had not been able to see his way to it. Not after Europe. Not after the experiences he had had there.

"And Ellen—" he said and caught himself. Should he go back? C̶o̶
it to Mrs. Newcombe? Or let the intimacy hang like a challenge between
them? "Ellen speaks very warmly of the tour she had of the great European cities after Miss Porter's. She was—what, twenty? That was very generous of you. And wise if I may say so."

At which Ryckman eyed him, sending his tongue behind his teeth as if
some food remained there and letting his gums make little sucking sounds.
Franklin kept his smile on his face, the smile that charmed the world,
waiting for Ryckman to speak, to pick up the conversational thread and
get knitting with it. But the man didn't—pointedly—and Franklin found
himself a little nonplussed, casting about for something further to say.

"Looking back," he went on, and he allowed a quizzical, amused look
to come over him, splashing the ash off his cigar, "I suppose it was fortunate that I didn't go over to the Academy as I had planned." He had never
planned any such thing. "This was ten or twelve years ago, just shortly
before the scandal with Mr. Eakins." And he looked for a response. "Perhaps you don't recall the incident? It was in all the papers. It got Eakins
dismissed from his post." And now the pause was to call attention to his
interlocutor's ignorance. "Well, picture this. It appears that one day in the
drawing studio Eakins had removed the loincloth of one of the male mod-
els. And this while there were female students present, you understand.
And it wasn't the first time such a thing had happened. I had it from some
painter friends of mine that when one of the female students had inquired
about the movement of the pelvis, Eakins had taken her into his office and
stripped to show her! How's that for education!"

And again he looked for some reaction from the man. A look of dismay
at least. But there was only the appraising gaze. Franklin felt a queer,
prickly heat about his collar, and a smile going stale on his face. And still
Ryckman kept his eyes impassively on him.

"There's a rumor about," the man said finally—he drew fatly on his cigar,
threw his head back, let out a great cloud of smoke, and then returned to appraising Franklin—"a rumor that you've set your sights on my daughter."

Franklin had obscurely known that something of the sort was coming
and so managed to keep the small slight smile on his face from vacating its

..e I have 'sights,' as you say," he responded after a mo-
..waved away the objection.

..tend to propose to her," he corrected all the same.

..me to value Mrs. Newcombe's friendship extremely. She
seems .. .. n altogether fine woman."

"D'you not find her remarkably homely?"

At which Franklin felt himself visibly start. Was this the tactic then? To discomfit him, to rattle him in hope of shaking something loose?

"That's an odd thing for a father to say," he responded coolly.

"You do not deny that you are courting my daughter?"

Still he equivocated. "I have been keeping company with her."

"As a prelude to marrying her?"

At which he kept silence, though that silence felt like an acquiescence all the same. Yet why should he not acquiesce? It was just the man's damned manner that was objectionable.

"It's not illegal, I hope?" he said finally. Ryckman knocked his ash off, all the time keeping his gaze fixed upon Franklin.

"You will recognize my right to inquire after your finances."

"Your right?" Franklin repeated. "Is not Mrs.—" with an emphasis on *Mrs.*—"is not Mrs. Newcombe of age?" he said with a meaningful smile. "At any rate, I have yet to ask for the honor of her hand. Perhaps you could wait until I do."

"I don't wait," Ryckman replied. "I haven't the habit."

You'd better damn well acquire the habit, Franklin wanted to say, but he held off. "I have a small income," he allowed. "Enough to keep me in a gentleman's ways."

"Enough to keep a wife as well?"

"That would depend on the wife," Franklin said, and then—there was no point to this coy parrying; it was just the damned fellow's manner: "Mrs. Newcombe, I understand, is quite capable of keeping herself."

"Aye, that's the game, isn't it?"

"I beg your pardon!" Franklin heard himself saying. It had been an outright insult. Ryckman had finally a smile on his face. They fronted each other for a good half minute, and then Ryckman gestured with his hand.

"Your cigar's gone out, man."

Before he could tell himself not to, Franklin turned the thing around and looked at its gray tip, and then stupidly drew on it. There was nothing. And Hobbes had vanished.

"I knew there'd be someone," Ryckman was saying. "After James—after Mr. Newcombe died. I knew there'd be someone. I just didn't know it'd be someone like you."

"Someone like me?" Franklin found himself repeating.

"Aye."

"Meaning what, sir?" What did the ogre know?

"'They toil not, neither do they spin,'" Ryckman said, narrowing his eyes.

But ah! if it was just Franklin's lack of a profession! If that was all! He summoned back his smile, let it mingle with the candlelight and the glinting silver, and then said handsomely: "They only require a good tailor." And then, pushing back his chair: "Now, if you've finished insulting me—"

And he let the words hang between them. For he had seen the way forward. He would refuse to engage. There clearly would be no winning the man over, but he might let his beautiful—infuriating!—manners forever put Ryckman in the wrong and he, Franklin, in the right. For only that would matter to Ellen.

"If you've *quite* finished insulting me," he repeated, still with his handsome smile but now standing up, "shall we join the ladies?"

⤖ 1863 ⤖

~We selected Fort Adams, and if we proved to have the strength, the break-water beyond, for our next outing. Alice (my Alice, that is) and the other Alice's brother Harry, and Mrs. Taylor, once again rounded out the party. We had a basket with sandwiches made up from the Ocean's kitchen. I doubted Mrs. Taylor would make it to the breakwater, but I kept my reservations to myself and we sallied forth.

In Geneva I used to think of New England as gray and solemn, lugubri-ous even. For at that distance I overlaid Mr. Hawthorne's somber tales of the Puritans upon my own memories. But the walk southwest with the land falling away to the sail-studded and sun-spangled water was most bright and pleasant. One of the steam ferries was coming in, hooting its brassy horn, and some of the passengers at the rail hailed us. We kept to the grassy path, Miss Taylor and myself in the front, followed by Alice chirruping at young Harry, and then Mrs. Taylor.

As the land veered southward we paused to look back over the harbor at that notable prospect of the town the point affords. At the sight of the dozens of pleasure craft in the harbor, I mentioned the steam organ con-cert of a week past, said that I had seen Miss Taylor there on the wharf, and wondered did she think it was fit, all this seeking of pleasure in the midst of war. She cast a wistful gaze out over the patchwork of masts and sails, the breeze blowing a strand of hair into her face, so that she drew it back from her lips with her fingertips.

"People will have their frivolity, I suppose," she answered, "even in these terrible times."

Mrs. Taylor seemed to hear a criticism in my remark, perhaps of their partaking of the frivolity of Newport, and asked did the war not affect me more than it seemed, did I not intend to enlist? She did not say this like an accusation exactly, but still there was a meaning to her tone.

So I told them (we had begun walking again) the history of how William and I had wanted to "join up" in the first heady fervency of the war, but had been prevented by Father, who in those days held that Mr. Lincoln was no better than a slave-driver that he did not free the slaves instantly. But as was characteristic of Father, I hastened to add, within the year he had changed his mind about Mr. Lincoln, but by then I had injured my back while helping with a fire pump, an injury that persisted, even now.

"But my two younger brothers have enlisted," I said by way of covering what must have seemed an excuse to malinger; and then like a *coup d'éclat*: "Our Wilky is adjutant to Colonel Robert Gould Shaw of the 54th Massachusetts."

"The Negro regiment?" Miss Taylor asked in surprise.

And so as we walked, and the great stone battlements of the fort hove into view, I found myself telling them (dear pixilated Alice must have wondered at me, for I spoke more that afternoon than she'd heard me speak the past month!), narrating how Wilky and Bob, since our return from Europe, had been students at the Sanborn School in Concord and had breathed in the air of Transcendentalism along with the odes of Horace. Mr. Emerson's children had been sent there, I told them, and the poor orphaned daughters of John Brown. They had all imbibed Abolitionism there and when the daring scheme to raise a Negro regiment and put at its head the best sons of Boston was bruited, Wilky had volunteered to serve in that regiment though he was but seventeen at the time. I described to them my visit to the regiment's encampment at Readville, and what a sight it was, all the Negro men in their uniforms, and their white officers.

"They are now down in South Carolina. We've had a letter from Wilky. There is a grand action in the offing, but he could not say what."

"We are greatly afraid for him," Alice put in. "All we do is sit in the garden and wait to hear something horrible."

"But you must be very proud," said Miss Taylor. "There was such a ruckus in the papers about the morality of a Negro regiment."

We went on in like manner, talking of the war as we walked along the great broad face of the fort wall, inside of which were those functions of the Naval Academy that had not been moved to the Atlantic House. Miss Taylor's older brother was with a Connecticut artillery regiment, but thankfully (Mrs. Taylor said) he was stationed along the Potomac, guarding the capital, though he wrote them there was a great deal of disease in camp. We had our sandwiches on the grounds of the commanding officer's house, and so fortified, began the traipse across the neck for the breakwater. It was a lengthy hike and we soon fell into that pleasant silence that can be part of a good walk among friends (though every now and then Alice would pipe up with one of her extraordinary remarks).

I tried to judge the paths correctly, for though I have been all over the island with William and Wilky, with dear Sarge, and with cousin Minnie and pretty Kitty, yet the island is crisscrossed with the most wild, rambling footpaths. From time to time we would hear the sound of the surf when the breeze came from the south, and now and again, when we were climbing some hillock in the interior, we would catch sight of the great blue blaze of the Atlantic to the east. At one of these blessed sightings I looked at Miss Taylor and she smiled most beautifully at me. Above us the clouds scudded like music.

"When *I* get tired or ill," we heard Alice say behind us to some complaint of young Harry's, "I simply abandon my body. Let it suffer as it will. I myself pass on."

And a little farther along: "I find one must choose between muscular sanity, and mental. Don't you?"

Behind them Mrs. Taylor paused now and then to wipe her brow, but she was proving herself a true Yankee matron, a matriarch of the Brass Valley, no mere resort dweller.

At last the vegetation grew more sparse, and the ground underfoot took on a more sandy character, and when we came up over a ridge we saw the great violent imaginary seam where bay met ocean. We grew revived at the sight of it, and with the fresh strong wind blowing straight into our faces, hurried down to the little bluff that fronts Brenton Point. Below us the granite breakwater was like the spine of a great Saurian lurking underwater. The waves from the Atlantic broke against it and sent spray up its side.

Alice declared that she believed the boulders would be too much for her and that she would wait for us, and that we shouldn't hurry on her account. Mrs. Taylor said she would keep Alice company and allow the breeze on the bluff to refresh her. So Miss Taylor and her brother and I made our way down the escarpment and up onto the first stones of the breakwater. Young Harry went ahead of us. We told him to be careful and followed more slowly, Miss Taylor holding on to my arm as we maneuvered from rock to rock. There is not much to write: it was all in the impression of the moment. The breeze and the bright sun, the booming surf, the schooner-rigged boat in the middle distance placed there by some divine compositor, and of course the company of a pretty and intelligent young person, the wind blowing her hair where it escaped her bonnet and pressing her dress against her. We did not speak except to caution against this or that rock, the slippery surface, the little pools of stranded water. But there was between us, I felt, a fellowship silently acknowledged, and which did not partake of romance but rather of a yet rarer quality: the colloquy of two souls who recognized one another, who found themselves in the ordinary world to be obscurely trapped, yet in each other's presence (for the moment, come to the end of the breakwater with the sea spreading perilously before them, and the careless clouds forming and re-forming in the blue overhead) to be free.

⤙ 1778 ⤚

Apr 23

What does the girl imagine? I have for so long occupied myself with how I might Fortify my positions, throw up a Redoubt, engineer a Breakwater, take possession of a forward Position, that I have hardly thought of what the Jewess is about when she is alone with her Thoughts. What pictures does she paint herself? What does she make of my Confession of love? What Future does she see? She must think my Intentions honourable (for she is not a slattern about the Taverns), but how does she explain to herself the Secrecy of our looks? Does she think I adopt this Duplicitous pose because I understand that her Father would never countenance a Gentile? And that the Ruse itself, which must be abhorrent to one of my principled Nature, is yet perversely a Testament to my passion that I am willing to so compromise my Virtue? Well enough. Plausible. But what then? Does the girl imagine life as a Noblewoman back in Devonshire! Lots of nigger servants about, and a Stallion out of the Studbook upon which to canter through the Vale at dusk! In short, does she think that I would marry a Colonial girl (a Jewess!), bring her home to my father Lord Stevens, and have her sit in the same room drinking tea with my Mother & Sisters? Can she be so innocent of the world, and of the Restrictions placed upon the Public behavior of someone of my Station? And of her own station of being a Jew?

Or does she fancy herself an Adventuress in a French novel? And our Passion an illicit yet chaste relation painted in oils by Fragonard!

But damn her and her eyes!

We are never alone and I have no opportunity to deploy the Feints & Ploys of the Book of Seduction. Her beauty! my inflamed Passions! And oh, my captured Heart!

(The island is lousy with 8000 troops. One may not piss without a Dozen eyes upon one! How to effect the final Assault?)

Apr 24

This day being Friday I endeavored to be free of any Duty in the afternoon so that I might station myself on lower Jews Street (and with such a fluttering heart: am I a girl?), where I thought she must surely pass on her way to the Synagoge from her house on the Wharf. And indeed in time I espied her, and with Phyllis accompanying. The hub-bub of the town is such all Sights are to be seen, yet I had some Trepidation, for I did not know how we could go about together, given her youth and beauty (however disguised!) and that business at Burgoyne's Assembly linking our names. I made it so I was rounding a corner that it might appear we met by Chance. I even said something of the like, that we might keep a Pretense, even to ourselves. But she did not fall in, neither did she Scruple or play the coy Maiden, but rather looked me honestly in the eye, as if she meant to affix the Sanction of her will to whatever was to come.

We could not stay in the street, so she took me within, and made to show me about the Temple and how it served as a Hospital. We had then, with Phyllis attending, at least the Semblance of some especial Employment as I made it appear that I had been sent over on some Inspection business or other. The sick (for there were no injured) rallied at the sight of her, lifting their heads as best they could (for they are bedded inside the box Pews as if in rehearsal for their Coffins). Judith said to each she would attend them in time. She would continue with the next chapter of *Humphry Clinker* presently, but they must be patient while she showed the Major about. And could Phyllis get them anything? Again, I was struck by her Equanimity and altogether the Composure of her person, for she acted more the Matron than she did the Virgin. There was one Chasseur under the onslaught of fever, yet who roused himself in her presence and tried to pull his body upright on his tick. Not the only thing the German bastard wished upright, I'll vow.

The whole time, of course, I was mad with the Desire to have her alone, and with the Impossibility of any such Opportunity. And mad further, for now I believed, as I had never allowed myself to believe before, that the girl wanted the same thing. The closeness of her, the little Accidental brushing of arm to arm, the rustling of her Skirts against my side, the fertile looks, the odor of the Essential oil I do believe she perfumes herself with, it was all almost more than I could stand. Truly, I think I have never felt (no, not in all such Exploits!) so overcome with the sheer, surging, violent, whelming Desire to have a woman. Even when the damned Surgeon-Major discovered me and of course must come over, I was trembling as if I would leap from inside my skin.

He dismissed Judith and had at me, honored and gratified he said that the General had sent someone from his Staff, had heeded his Pleas, and more of the like. He was a drunk Peacock and I could barely countenance his alternate Braggery and Sycophancy, his importuning for support, and Tonics, and divers other ingredients to make his especial Febrifuge. Jove, it was as tho' I had stumbled unawares onto the stage of a damned Drury Lane farce!

When finally I rid myself of the fellow, telling him to write down everything he'd imparted to me and have a Courier deliver it, I went back through the Temple, making noise as I went that the girl might discover me, but she was nowhere about. Vexed to a Fury, I departed the front entrance, and oh! the clever thing was waiting for me under the Portico! We could do nothing but keep a Public pose, yet the look I had from her eyes and the brief touch of her hand! She asked did I want to meet her? Would I come to the Jewish Cemetery some night at dusk? It was the only place! she said. She would send word to me on a likely night. I told her I died for her.

The cemetery, damn my eyes! Perhaps the girl is a practiced Libertine!

Apr 25

I have had it out with Smithson. Or rather, he has had it out with me. He says he has learned that I am still calling on Da Silva and that I have been seen in the street with Judith. Says he has warned me against my continued Attentions to the Jewess. (Miss Da Silva, he calls her.) Says if he is not satisfied he will go to the Jew and tell him of me and my Character. Will go to Pigot and remind him of the Cambridge incident.

My Character, the presumptuous fellow!

I kept a rein on myself. Told him that he misunderstood me. That yes, the Jewess was a remarkable Beauty, what man could not see that, what man would not enjoy sitting in her presence (did the Jewess not have the most Magnificent bosom? I asked just to goad him while appearing to appease), but she was a mere child, a Colonial, unschooled, &c., and even the duplicitous, black-souled, cloven-hoofed Major Ballard would not stoop to that. It's this damn inaction that sets us on edge, I told him, retreating a Knight. Be a good fellow, I told him, and I'll break out a bottle I had from Da Silva. (Where does the damned smuggling Fellow get the stuff? I asked.) He turned me aside, said he did not believe me, said I was making light of it, that the Others may be, but that he was not my Dupe, &c., that he wanted me to swear upon my being a Gentleman, and upon my father's Title (my father's Title!), swear in the presence of the rest of the damned Officers quartered in this damned Quaker house that I would not Attempt the girl. No matter what Fit might come upon me, he said. At which I nearly blundered a Rook and told the damned Dwarf that I would do no such thing. That he had my word, and that would have to satisfy him.

No matter what Fit, the Fellow says! Does he intend then to use my Weakness against me, my Confiding in him?

But now, let me record this: I have had for this fortnight, ever since the Absurdity with the Engineer, the stirrings of a plan regarding Smithson. Yet I did not let myself fully entertain it for I account it an Extremity. I have only considered of it in the Hypothetical. That if one needed to, one might do this, and one might do that. So I have coldly thought it. Yet here's the Insolent fellow! I will not have my Desires interfered with. Not when it comes to the Jewess! Nor will I have Smithson's peasant's mind be the Measure of what I may and may not do.

'Tis this: I was much taken by the story Da Silva told me of the Tidewaiter. How he brought the offending man into one of the low places that dot the Wharves, bought him a Rum, and mused about how did not the Tidewaiter think any one of these wharf Rats would do a foul deed for a few pounds, a handful of Doubloons?

Could not a British officer, in this time of War, go in amongst these colonial Rats and take a likely one aside and treat with him? Did not the War itself provide a Mask? Might it not be used to provide a False scent?

Doubling Point is a likely place. So was half my intention in hiking out there the other day. Could I not get Smithson, under the labor of an Apology on my part, to accompany me on a Shoot? Just he and I, good friends again. And the Rat waiting out there in the Wastes for us. It could not be more credibly done. And what a Garnish to walk up to Smithson when he lay Mortally wounded and say to the man: Check & Mate!

And as a kind of douceur: to be rid of the one Soul who knows of the damned Incident with the Razor!

Question: to dispose of the Rat afterwards? As a defensive move?

And my story: We were bird-hunting and we happened upon a Rebel party. There were shots exchanged, &c. I gave chase, but there was a boat, &c. And brave Smithson, &c.

Apr 28

Damn me to hell! I have had word from Judith but it is not the word I have been awaiting! Rather she is gone with her father into the Interior. 'Tis a Visit they have long been meaning to make, she writes, and no result of the Love (she uses the word!) between us being discovered. But she must visit her Step-Mother and her young Siblings. It will be ten days or a fortnight, she writes. Can I wait? she writes.

I do not know if Phyllis is gone with her, or who delivered the note. Or if Smithson knows.

May 4

The days pass and no word. I am in the foulest State. And a kind of Madness is come over me. I have taken to passing the Jewish Cemetery, twice, thrice a day, and at night going in amongst the slate stones as if I might find her there, waiting, undressed, ready for me. And in my Rage, I find some Wife's stone, some Miriam or Esther or Rachel, and I undo my flies and work myself up and Defile the face of it, the name, the Hebrew writing! What is it in me?

The pages of this Volume are at an end. I will pack it up, along with its Brother, and send both tomorrow aboard the *Lark* back to England.

And with it, pray, all such Madness!

☆ 1692 ☆

2nd Day

I was searching through Genesis early this morning when one of Charles Spearmint's apprentice boys came to the house to return my pattens. He was very polite.

And now I have found the text I was looking for and will copy it out here.

And Jacob loved Rachel; and said, I will serve thee seven years for Rachel thy younger daughter. And Jacob served seven years for Rachel; and they seemed unto him but a few days, for the love he had to her.

And yet how deceiv'd was Jacob, to be so trick'd that after his Servitude he must have Leah!

I watch Ashes from out the corner of my eye, and I am fill'd with wonder at her dark skin and her dark eyes and her pock-mocked face. And O! the love she has engender'd!

3rd Day

In the afternoon I was coming out of Samuel Judah's shop just as Edward Swift was going in. We were each of us affrighted and confus'd and we could do nothing but stand and speak most awkward to one another! We could neither address what was between us, nor simply say a good day as we might have before. Finally he ask'd might he not come to speak to me later that Afternoon. I said he might.

And now he is just gone. It was a most awkward Interview. I kept

Dorcas in the room with us, and had Ashes stay about the kitchen. After some fitful topics, and his mentioning of Father, and the great sorrowful loss of my Mother, he said how much he Admir'd me, that in my Loss and Sorrow I had shown myself an Able young woman. And more of the like. He was most stiff as he spoke, rather as if he were reciting something conn'd and not of the Heart, tho' it may be uncharitable of me to say so, for one may be awkward tho' one goes feelingly. He said he had wanted to come to me before, but he was Advis'd against it, and truly he did not wish to press me in this difficult time. He only wish'd me to know that he Awaited me.

I did my best to answer him. I told him I was but fifteen years of age and did not know whether I was prepared to take on what he would have me take on. I told him I was not yet convinc'd that Father would not return. I told him I awaited Light on the matter, that I could only wait further.

As he rose to leave he ask'd did I want anything? Did the house need any repair that he might send over one of his sons?

He is a good man. I do heartily believe that. Yes, as Jane Beecher says, he may see my house and land and my Chattels and think it a wise action to unite those to his, but what of that? Would not Father think alike were he in Edward Swift's place?

As indeed he is, if he be still alive.

Oh, *must* my Life go this way?

4th Day

I have finally work'd up the nerve and have ask'd Ashes about Charles Spearmint. She says she knows of his proposal. She says she has told him he may try to earn her if he so wishes, but that she cannot Promise herself to him, for she believes one night she will be taken back to Africa and will return to Newport no more. He will find himself Indentur'd and no wife, she says.

She cannot truly believe this. It is but more of her ill will.

5th Day

Yesterday I felt so cast down, and the World seem'd so gray, and there being nothing but want of Hope, I threw everything down and went out of the house. I knew not where I was going, at first toward Mother's grave, then toward Spearmint's to settle with him, then without intending it onto Spring Street where John Pettibone's family has their house. And was not that the most foolish Fool thing to do? He is but fifteen years himself, and he has a Mother and Father and no need of me tho' I know he did like me once. Oh, I pray he did not see me! Passing his house in the falling Dusk like a Wraith!

But my Heart would not be still, and my thoughts would not rest. So I then went out Jews Street and further until I had gone past the boundaries of the town and come upon the new Ropewalks. They are such low-slung, long, worm-like buildings! Yet the workers were quit for the day so I went out amongst them, and then through the snow to the land beyond where I had never before gone, where there are no houses or paths. And there I stopp'd. And I remember'd Jane Beecher's fancy of going away, of living alone in the Wildernesse where no one might have her. How I understood her then! and chaf'd and long'd to have the wings of a Dove, as it says in the Psalms, that I might fly away!

Yet I am back now, for there is nowhere to go. Neither inland (belike into the hands of Indians). Nor seaward to the strange Islands, nor beyond to far-away England. There is no place but the place I find myself in.

3rd Day

Before I spent any more of my Heart upon this matter of Ashes and Spearmint, I thought it wise to go to see John Peele. He is accounted a kind of Magistrate among the Friends, and it would be he who I would have draw up the Articles with Spearmint, should it go that way. I wanted to understand what laws of our Province might bear upon what Spearmint proposes. For setting the unusual Circumstances aside, do I even have the lawful right to sell Ashes?

We sat in his front Parlour with its fine paneling and brass Betty lamps and I acquainted him with Spearmint's proposal, laying it before him as clearly and simply as I could. He was much taken aback by it, more than I had entertain'd he would be. At first I thought he merely wish'd not to entertain the Notion of a Friend, a member of our Meeting, selling himself into such Bondage, and that may indeed be a good part of what disturb'd him. But it struck me too, and strikes me so now as I write, that he found it unnatural that one African might own another. For that, he pointed out firstly, is what Spearmint propos'd. Once the seven years was up, he ask'd, would Spearmint not own Ashes, even tho' she be made his Wife in that time? I had to say that I had not consider'd of the question in that way. To which he responded, as if discovering the matter at its root, that with his Indentures the joiner was buying the servant. He would have paid for her and would own her.

To this I said that I could not believe that that was Spearmint's Intention. And if it were not, would he not agree to an Article in the Contract that would make it out as such? I meant to say, could we not so write the Articles that they would make it binding upon both Parties that the weekly Payments were to be put toward the purchase of Ashes' Freedom, not her further Bondage, and that at the end of the seven years' term, both she and Spearmint would be free?

Mr. Peele then rose from where he was sitting and with a thoughtful air went and stood at the window. After a time of Reflection he said without turning back to me that he understood the great Difficulty I found myself in, and that he was perhaps remiss in not taking that into consideration. He then said in the kindly Manner I know him for, that we would put our heads together and think this through, and he came back and sat beside me again.

So we talk'd a good deal, first of how such an Arrangement might be made, whether it were necessary that Spearmint live in the house, what Benefits there might be to me in his doing so. There were also Matters I had only dimly thought on, such as the unusual status of Spearmint's apprentices being Freemen apprentic'd to an indentur'd Servant, and then, delicately, the question of a child. For if Ashes and Spearmint were to have issue, by the laws of the Colony, Mr. Peele pointed out, the child would be a slave and would belong to me. For all of these matters, we thought Articles could be written into the Covenant to satisfy the parties. There was also the matter of Freedom dues. For it seems in Articles of Indenture there is a giving of land and other goods to the Servant at the fulfillment of his Term. I had not known of this and said there could be no question of any such. That Spearmint had already a Trade and a place of business. The Articles were solely for the purchase of Ashes' freedom, that Ashes was to be his Freedom dues. To which John Peele smil'd and call'd me a good man of business. That he would mind in future any Transaction he might have with me.

As I was about to leave he ask'd had I thought any further on Edward Swift's offer. I paus'd at this and then told him how, at the beginning of the winter when he first came to me with Mr. Swift's proposal, I had not been able to fancy myself a Wife. But that now, tho' only a few months had pass'd, I had grown in my own thought and in my own heart in ways that made me think I could be married. Married, I said with what I hope was a not unkind smile, but not to Edward Swift. That I had not told Mr. Swift so with any such baldness, but that I believ'd he understood all the same.

He ask'd then did Dorcas and I have enough in store, and did we have enough money to get through the rest of the Winter. I told him that there was yet a little Specie in our Bible box, to which he ask'd was that but our everyday money, and had not Father a hidden place where there might be a more substantial amount? I said I did not know of any such.

2011

He was in the maze and damn him if he wasn't lost! He had the briefcase with him, had come out to Windermere to give it to Alice—a last gesture before he washed his hands of them all—and had been met at the door by one of the Salve Regina girls who lived on the third floor and helped with the running of the house. She'd told him Alice was in the maze. Reading, she'd said. So he had gone in, had even done what the college girl had told him to do, to always keep his right hand to the hedge wall as he went, but somehow he'd gotten off, thought he'd be clever and avoid this or that cul-de-sac and now he was messed up, lost, certain he'd passed that bit of dead growth before. He would have turned around and left if he could have—he was nervous enough as it was, worried again that the briefcase was a stupid idea—but he no longer knew whether he was going in or coming out. He had several times the impulse to call out, to call "Alice!," to laugh and ask her to say something so he could follow her voice. But no, that wasn't any good either.

And then suddenly he was there. The narrow path opened onto a little trapezoid of lawn where there was a chaise longue and an iron café table. But there was no one there. He did a three-sixty but there was just the monotonous green of the hedge. He hefted the briefcase from one hand to the other and, just as he did, noticed on the glass top of the iron table a little ring of water like that left by the sweating of a summer drink. He touched a fingertip to it. It was cold.

He straightened up, listened as if the still air had something to tell him. She had been there. She had heard him coming and had avoided him by going out of the maze while he came in, stepped into this or that dead end as he'd gone past. It gave him an eerie sensation. As if he'd been unwittingly observed.

Well, he would leave the briefcase all the same, place it on the chaise longue with its quote from *Daisy Miller* and leave it there for her to find. She could accept it or not, but he would have at least made the gesture.

Back out on the lawn he couldn't shake the feeling that he was being watched from somewhere. He looked along the veranda, at the banks of windows on the second floor, shot a glance at the Orangery. Down along the Cliff Walk there were the usual tourists on the other side of the fence. When he climbed onto the Indian he had the sense that he was done. He had made a break; he was done with them all.

It only remained to tell Margo. And he did that two days later. He didn't know what he'd expected from her, some imperious scene perhaps, but she took it way better than he'd thought she would, even stopped him with a smile and a shush when he started overcomplimenting her, telling her how great it'd been. She seemed more amused than anything, and he had the thought that he'd simply anticipated her. The summer had begun to turn anyway. It had the curious effect of freeing them to talk a little. She asked him what his plans were, managed to let him know (this was the only thing she said that had a little edge to it) that he probably wouldn't be coming back to the Casino next summer, but by then he'd have a proper position, a college job—right?—and to that end she'd be glad to use her board of directors stationery to write him a recommendation, a *character* recommendation she meant, not a tennis one. He'd be fine, she said. He'd land on his feet.

That evening he put an ad on Craigslist to sell the Indian—the Holy Grail of Cruisers, he called it—then went and played basketball with the Storer Park crew. When it got too dark they walked over to the Brick Alley for pitchers of beer. It was the first time he'd ever been out with them. They talked nothing but sports. It was his new life.

When he checked his phone he had three calls about the Indian. Back at his place he went down the driveway to the side of the garage where he kept the motorcycle. Before he could call anyone back he needed a gut check about whether he was serious. He let his eyes run over the sleek antique thing with its chrome and valanced fenders. It was dark and so it took a moment for him to realize that there was a piece of paper—a note—tucked behind the throttle cable. It hadn't been there earlier when he'd taken pictures to upload with the ad. He pulled the note out and brought it over to the light. It said simply, *Thank you.* He eyed it, eyed the grammar-school cursive. He didn't need to wonder who had put it there. Margo or Aisha thanking him for the time they'd had together? Not likely! It seemed to put a final bit of punctuation to everything. She had accepted his apology—not just the briefcase but the *Daisy Miller* note he'd put inside—but she was not about to see him again or take up where they'd left off. She was still hurt, and although she seemed to understand that that hurt had not been his doing—not his *intentional* doing—she still felt it.

That, at any rate, was his reading of the note—its clandestine appearance, its reticence. So he wasn't prepared the next day when he found a second note. Same paper, same handwriting, this time tucked into the Indian in its parking place at the Casino. *She would have reciprocated one's affection,* it said. He looked around as if she were there somewhere, watching him, seeing how he reacted.

She would have reciprocated one's affection. It was from *Daisy Miller,* of course. He'd check when he got home but he was pretty sure Winterbourne says this, realizes it, at the end of the book. Was she simply repeating the valedictory, regretful tone of *his* note—standing over the grave of her affection for him, throwing in flowers? Or did she mean to reopen things between them? Whatever it was, he wasn't going to respond. Indeed, there was no *way* to respond. He wasn't about to write notes back.

The next morning when he went out there was another. He stared at it a moment and then plucked it from behind the throttle cable.

Half the time she doesn't know what she's saying.

Okay, so maybe what she was doing was supposed to be funny, self-cuttingly funny, but funny nonetheless. It was Alice in Aliceland, as Aisha used to say. He could take that. He understood that.

But the next morning he came out and found, *It was evident that Daisy was dangerously ill.* Which didn't seem so funny, seemed in fact something like a threat.

And even less funny was the note he found out at the Casino when he was done for the day: *Her grave was in the little Protestant cemetery.*

What on earth was the girl up to? He had meant his note to say simply—what? Well, what it said! That he would have appreciated her esteem. Meaning, that he respected her, that he liked her, and that he would have appreciated a reciprocal respect. It was meant to acknowledge—to apologize for and yet to *continue to maintain*—the distance between them, and that though he could not kiss her he would have liked her friendship nonetheless, and that he was prepared to give his in return. But this! She was taking bits and pieces of the story and rearranging them so she could act the part—wittily? cuttingly? manipulatively? ominously?—of a deceased Daisy Miller.

The next note was: *Through the thick gloom . . .*

And then: *It's so plaguy dark.*

He looked each and every one up. None of these originally—in the book itself—pertained to Daisy's death. She was appropriating them, taking the elements of one story and shuffling them into another. Was this creepy or was it funny? Was it dangerous or was it paradoxically—Daisy speaking from beyond the grave, ha-ha—a sign of health even in her hurt? He didn't know what to do, whether *doing* something was even called for. Two days went by with no notes. Then:

He seemed to wish to say something.

And two days after that, after he *hadn't* said anything:

It had ceased to be a matter of serious regret to him.

He got the damn book out, the library's copy he hadn't yet returned, and read through the final scenes, keeping an eye out for something susceptible to a double meaning. But he did not, as she'd once told him, view things sufficiently metaphorically and he had to settle for *her mystifying manners . . .* , copying it onto a piece of scrap paper and tucking it under the throttle cable. When he came out the next morning it had been turned over and on the other side he found:

. . . may be viewed this evening, at seven, in the maze. Casual dress. No gifts.

Meaning her mystifying manners might be viewed. If one cared to. Which one didn't.

But of course he couldn't just let her sit there alone, the sun going down, slowly realizing he wasn't coming. So when the time came he climbed on the Indian and roared down Bellevue. He found her just as she must have been that other day, seated on the chaise longue at the center of the maze, a summer drink on the iron table beside her. She was wearing a bowling team shirt. White and starchy looking, too big for her, with HARRY embroidered in red above the breast pocket and NAPA AUTO PARTS on the back. And she had on pedal pushers, tight around her calves with little bows of yarn lacing up the side vents. He expected some clever remark, some retooled *Daisy Miller* quote, and failing that some bipolar moment, but she just put her book down, smiled, and said simply: "Hi, sailor."

She made no mention of the briefcase or the notes, treated it all as if it hadn't happened, or rather as if it had been a kind of secret handshake, acknowledged at the time but not afterwards referred to. Instead she launched herself into being "the perfect hostess," seizing the maze as the nearest topic and telling him about her grandmother—the non–du Pont grandmother who had bought Windermere in the fifties when the great Gilded Age properties were going for fire-sale prices—her grandmother who had replanted the maze based on old photographs and now it was the thing Windermere was known for. Had he come to Champagne at Windermere last Labor Day weekend? she asked with her hostess face. There'd been so many people in the maze you could barely make it through! she said with a laugh and he realized with something of a shock that she was nervous, like a girl on a first date.

(Although as they walked back out of the maze he noticed that the book she'd been reading—like a stage property, like an elbow to the ribs—was *The Wings of the Dove*.)

For the next half hour they strolled along the sloping lawn, going from place to place as he'd done that first day with Aisha. There were the tourists down along the Cliff Walk, the red teahouse a quarter mile away, the Adirondack chairs, the flowerbeds. Every now and then they would turn and catch sight of the magnificent house with its chimneys and richly weathered shingles, its long veranda and countless windows. The whole thing was like a parody of that day with Aisha when he had felt so overwhelmed by the beauty of the place: the ocean, the sky, the lime rickeys. Only Alice couldn't know about that, right? The parody, the *palimpsest* to use one of her words—the overlay of one day on the other and the felt connections—they were all his.

Once when he held back and she went a little ahead of him, he noticed that the logo on the back of her bowling shirt had been markered so that NAPA read NADA.

She took him inside the Orangery and he had to pretend he had never seen the place before, the mandrels and rows of hammers, the little anvils and casting equipment. There was the big green tank of oxygen he'd helped Aisha move that first day, and the little narrow cot. She showed him the pieces Aisha had made that summer, holding each necklace draped over her forearm or up to her neck for him to admire. He looked for signs that she was setting him up, that she knew about Aisha and was checking to see whether he'd lie about her as he had about Margo. But there was nothing he could see in her manner or her voice. Rather, she seemed intent on putting him at ease.

Back outside they strolled along the curving pebble path that led up toward the house. He wondered whether it was intentional or just reflexive that she kept to his left as they went, so that her bad side—the hitching foot and the hand like a shepherd's crook—was away from him. Up at the house he saw that someone had come out on the veranda. For a second he thought it was Margo, but no, it was the caretaker's wife. Mary, he thought her name was. She was cook and housekeeper, supervised the Salve Regina girls. Alice gave her a little wave and the woman went back inside.

"Oh, dear!" she said when they reached the porch steps. She was looking down at her pedal pushers. One of the bows had come undone. For a moment he didn't get it. And then he realized she couldn't tie it, couldn't— he shockingly realized—probably even tie her own shoes.

"Here," he said and he knelt down, took up the two wayward ends.

He tied the bow quickly, and then had the strange sensation that this was the moment—in his normal life, in the normal course of things— when he would have touched the woman for the first time, touched her bare calf—lightly, meaningfully—and then waited for the reciprocating feel of her fingers in his hair. He made a show of tugging each of the bows in turn—like a parent! there!—and then stood back up.

She fixed him with her strange light-colored eyes. "Thank you," she said simply, and she started up the stairs. She took them one at a time.

On the porch they turned to look at the view. There was the green slope of the lawn and the tumble of salt-spray rose that grew around the Cliff Walk fence and in the distance where it was sunny still the sparkling water dotted with white sails. He remembered Aisha that first day saying how it was like you owned the summer itself. Now it was growing dusky and there were swallows diving through the air, and a racket of birdsong from the boxwood hedge of the maze. Alice strolled down to one end of the veranda, stayed there a few minutes, and then came back and stood beside him.

"Can I quit now?" she said. He turned and gazed down at her, at the blondish wisps of hair at her temples.

"Quit what?" he asked.

"Quit reassuring you that I'm not the Mad Heiress." She looked at him with a grim smile.

"Has it been so hard?"

She hiked herself onto the knee wall, crossed her arms, didn't say anything.

"A real stretch?" he prodded.

She smiled, not at him exactly, but a smile anyway. Behind them one of the French doors that gave onto the dining room opened and Mary came out with an open bottle of wine and two glasses. She set them on one of the little tables that dotted the veranda and without looking at them— without looking at Sandy—went back inside.

"You know what's wrong with this place?" Alice asked, still looking away, not acknowledging the wine but aware, he thought, of his questioning eyes on her. "No kids," she said.

He let that pass.

"I've got a lot of things to hold against Margo, but that's the biggest one. If you've got all this—" and she gestured at the veranda, at the lawn—"and you don't want kids. It's immoral."

"I can't fancy Margo a mother," he said a little stiffly. She turned her face to him, suddenly fierce.

"If it was me I'd have twenty kids! They'd be falling down the stairs and tumbling out the windows and getting lost on the third floor. But they'd be *here*! They'd be *loved*! They'd be living in all this beauty and I'd make damn sure they knew it!"

He just looked at her, nonplussed.

"Now you have to stay for dinner," she said. She gestured at the wine bottle and glasses as if they were evidence of his staying. "I was supposed to ask you earlier, but I didn't have the nerve. Mary's made something special, and it'll be super embarrassing if you don't stay. And yes, this is very manipulative of me."

He pursed his lips, didn't say anything. She went over to the wine bottle and with her good hand poured a glass, poured another, and held the rich red liquid out to him. He felt the need for a show of some kind of resistance.

"And Margo and Tom?"

"They've gone up to Fenway. We have the place to ourselves."

He held out a moment longer—long enough for her to understand whatever it was he needed her to understand—and then took the glass from her.

Inside they sat in the window seats in the hall with its rich wood, its chandelier, and the wide stairway opening onto the second floor. He found himself telling her—he had to get it out of the way—telling her that he'd broken it off with Margo, that he should've never let it go on for so long, but now it was over, done.

"Why tell me?" she asked when he'd finished.

"Because," he said; and when that didn't seem enough: "Because I lied to you about it, and because I'm not proud of it, and because one discovers, after all, that one would appreciate your esteem."

He expected some sort of smile at that—it was the first time either of them had gestured toward the notes—but she kept a sober look, sipped from her wine. "She'll be lying in wait for you," she said after a minute. He held his hands palm out in a no-foul gesture.

"She said she'd write me a recommendation."

At which a string of laughter spilled out of her. "I'd pass on that if I were you!" she said, cocking her head at him and smiling as if—once again—marveling at his innocence. *"Honi soit qui mal y pense,"* she went on, and then: "You don't see it because it's not inside you and so you don't recognize it in others."

He stiffened. "What's the 'it'?" he asked.

She worked her way off the window seat and stood up. "You don't even know what the 'it' is."

He held back. And then he knew what she was telling him, what she meant. "Enough with the killer instinct," he said.

She crossed to him with that electrocuted grace she had, stood in front of him, and with the back of her hand—her *bad* hand—with her knuckles, brushed him daringly across the cheek.

"That's a *good* thing," she said. "Maybe not in sports. But in life. Don't let anyone tell you it isn't."

"And you," he said, still resisting her. "Have you got the killer instinct?"

She turned her face to his and for the first time he had the impression that her eyes had a way of changing color, as if there were some molten substance inside her onto which her eyes gave that was dissolving and remaking itself.

"Only toward myself," she said.

And something of the old wound, the impulse to self-hatred he'd seen when he first met her, resurfaced. She kept her face turned to his and for some moments she did not try to hide the emotion there, seemed even fiercely to want him to see that she loved him, that she was his if he would just take her. He was aware of a certain peril in the moment, of trespassing onto ground upon which he should not tread, and still he felt moved to take her hand, gently as he had done that very first night in Margo's SUV. He held it softly a moment, and then with his other hand touched the scar on her wrist, placed his palm over it as if he meant to press the life back into her. She dropped her eyes, seemed to shudder inside her clothes.

From down the hall came Mary's voice saying dinner was ready when they were.

⇀ 1896 ↽

They made a bathing party out to Bailey's Beach, Mrs. Newcombe and her children, Mr. Ryckman with his eyes on Franklin, Mr. and Mrs. Robert Garrett and their children, and some of Franklin's friends—Parrish and Briggs and that whoremonger Hobson who had managed to smuggle in a couple of Smith girls. They had taken three carriages out—Mrs. Newcombe's and the Garretts' and Briggs's mother's—but having determined they would afterwards join the hoi polloi and return to Windermere along the Cliff Walk, had sent two back. The third would carry back the children and their governesses.

He had apprised Ellen of his conversation with her father. She had inquired anxiously, hopefully, and he had managed to say, without disclosing just how objectionable the interview had been, that it was his, Franklin's, opinion that her father did not relish the idea of Franklin as—and he let the phrase *as his future son-in-law* hang a moment between them—and then said instead "as a regular dinner guest at Windermere." He tried then to ameliorate her dismay. He would kill her father with kindness! he exclaimed. He would continue to be his light, airy self. Had not one of the society columns called him the Ariel of Newport? Oh, he would treat her father with all the civility and charm and delight at his disposal, not—and of course he did not say *this* to her—not because civility and charm and delight would win the man over, but because they would win *her* over.

So it was that upon alighting at the pavilion at Bailey's Beach, he had played the kindly seigneur with the governesses, helping them carry the children's things out onto the beach. Neither too patrician, nor too plebeian, he hoped, just a touch of genteel condescension authorized by the democracy of bathing. He was charming and considerate to all, was Franklin Drexel.

Those who thought they might bathe took to the bathhouses to change. Franklin helped the more stolid faction set up the canvas chairs, remarking how he wouldn't be caught in his coffin wearing—here straightening up with his hands on his hips and gazing down at the bathers standing in the surf—those absurd striped "pullovers" and the accompanying shorts that assaulted the world with one's spindly legs. Even a straw boater, he said—with here a charming smile toward Mr. Ryckman and his boater—would make him lose all self-respect. Consequently here he was in his top hat. And he gave the silk thing a pat.

At which the Smith girls laughed.

His top hat was, of course, quite absurd for the beach. It was the sort of thing that would end up in TOWN TOPICS. *Mr. Franklin Drexel, the gay gadabout, was seen at exclusive Bailey's Beach,* etc. But it furnished forth its own evidence, did it not? For what man, so absurdly dressed, could be suspected of lying in wait for—could be suspected of having in his "sights"—a wealthy widow? He almost wanted to point it out to Ryckman. The cleverness, the finesse, the tactical *coup de maître.* The man was never going to see it on his own.

They fell into a desultory mood with the sun and the sand and the sounds of the ocean. Briggs had brought the *Times* with him, and happening upon an article on the Newport season, began reading to them selected tidbits. In another corner of the conversation the Smith girls were full of the *tableaux vivants* they had all seen the previous evening at the Casino and were speaking to the Garretts about them. The children—James and Sarah, and the three Garrett progeny—were down along the water's edge with the governesses in their wool bathing dresses. In the distance there were sails and overhead the sky was blue and cloudless.

Hobson had begun musing on the name of Mrs. Newcombe's estate. Wasn't that writer fellow, that playwright, the English one who was tried last year for—oh, what did they call it?—for "acts of gross indecency." Wasn't one of his plays about a Lady Windermere? What *were* acts of gross indecency anyway? Eh, Drexel?

"Irish," Franklin corrected, unperturbed, pouring a lemonade for Mrs. Newcombe. "Not English." And before Hobson had a chance at a rejoinder: "And now: Miss Gould, Miss Stanton—" turning to the Smith girls—"I overheard you speaking of last night's *tableaux vivants*. Which did you find most charming?"

It was Miss Gould and Miss Stanton's opinion that the Fragonard had been the evening's greatest success. *"The Stolen Kiss!"* they cried with a sweeping look around the group. The beautiful young lady had been Miss Stoughton surely! But who, they wondered, had been the young man behind the drapery reaching out and taking hold of her?

"I believe it was Bobby Hobson," one of them said, pointedly not looking at Hobson. "That boy has as many hands as the Buddha!"

"Not the Buddha, dear! Surely!" said the other.

"Vishnu," put in that pedant Briggs, not looking up from his paper.

Franklin had been there. He had escorted Mrs. Newcombe to the Casino because her father had earlier expressed a distaste for such displays (although in the end he had accompanied them all the same). They had had their own table out on the ballroom's parquet floor, as did others of society, while in the gallery the denizens of the hotels who had paid five dollars for entry stood and looked on. On the stage there was a raised platform, and off to the side an artist's easel upon which a placard was placed with the title of each tableau. The stage would go dark, there would be a rustle of movement, then expectant quiet, and then the electric lights would come up to a collective "Oh!" from the audience and then applause. They had had Rembrandt and Gérôme and Delacroix. Part of what Franklin supposed was the evening's fun was trying to identify who partook, who among the Four Hundred had put on a servant's garb, a soldier's armor, a toga or chiton. Most delightfully, there had been the half scandal of a Velázquez depicting a black handmaiden (whose servant was she?) pouring a jug of wine.

One of the Smith girls politely asked Mr. Ryckman what had been his favorite, to which the industrialist responded that though the electric lights had impressed him, he preferred more invigorating diversion such as the races, or a polo match, or even the lawn tennis. These tableaux of the night before, he said, were too dilettantish for his taste.

"You're a painter, Drexel," Hobson had to put in. "What did you think?"

Drexel took a sip of his lemonade and said that he thought perhaps he agreed with Mr. Ryckman, that the tableaux tried to mix art and life in a way that trivialized both.

"But do you know what I was thinking?" he went on, turning to the girls with his handsome smile. "Last night, while I watched? I was thinking that the finest thing would be to try to live one's life as if it were a work of art! What do you think of that?"

What a beautiful idea! the girls cried.

"And I was thinking," Franklin went on, taking his top hat off and putting it on one of the girl's heads as if to show he was just having a lark, "is it not possible that God has made the world as a great work of art and that we disappoint Him when we go about blindly as some people do in a museum? And that it is our moral duty to look about us and try to *see* the world. And in turn to try to add ourselves—to add our lives—to the great museum. How will *you*, Miss Stanton, Miss Gould, make of your life a thing of beauty? You cannot do it with paint and line and volume, so with what?"

They looked for a moment blankly at him, and then Miss Gould—or was it Miss Stanton?—was saying she was quite hopeless as an artist! Why, she couldn't even draw a straight line, and was forever dripping watercolor on her crinoline!

"But you would not be drawing or painting," Franklin felt called upon to point out. "You would be *living*. You would be living your life as if it were an endless, ongoing painting!"

The girls were silent at that, and then they were wondering what painting they would live their endless lives in if they could choose. "*Salome!*" one of them screamed and they were off laughing. Hobson reached out and took hold of the top hat and placed it back on Franklin's head as if it were a dunce's cap.

But an hour later up on the Cliff Walk, Mr. Ryckman picked the idea up. They were walking in twos and threes, in single file when the path narrowed, the cliff on their right falling away to the ocean. The Smith girls had their parasols deployed.

"This business about living one's life as if it were a work of art,"

Ryckman called from the back of the group. Franklin could hear him swatting the grass with his cane. "I'm afraid I don't understand that. Surrounding oneself with beauty, with paintings and sculpture, with gardens or a fine home, I appreciate that. But to live as if you were yourself a painting, Mr. Drexel? What good does that do anyone?"

But Mr. Drexel did not take him up. To the east a racing yacht heeled and unfurled a spinnaker.

"In order for your life to be beautiful," Ryckman went on, "d'you not need to align yourself in some way with the good? D'you not need to make the world a better place?"

"Drexel makes the world a better place simply by being Drexel," Hobson called back. "Just ask TOWN TOPICS."

"But surely in order for an action to be considered beautiful, it must improve people's lives."

"Oh, Daddy, we are all too delightfully tired."

"Eh, Drexel?"

They had come to a little opening in the path and had slowed and turned to face one another. Franklin said he had just been spinning out an idle thought, that it was just a way of seeing things. But to fold into his idle thought Mr. Ryckman's belief that the beautiful must be in some way ethical—which he understood Mr. Ryckman to be saying; perhaps in reference to Mr. Keats's ode?—he supposed that instead of paint and line and volume, one might live with love and compassion and generosity. Perhaps moral qualities along those lines might make up the materials of a life lived as a work of art.

"But even so," Ryckman pressed, "how would any of that benefit society?"

"It would benefit those of us in the museum, those of us who are looking at the artworks, who care about beauty and truth and style," Franklin said, and then: "It would benefit me."

"Exactly, sir!"

"I think," Ellen interrupted, stepping back from where she had been at the head of the party and giving her father a dark look, "that what Mr. Drexel means is that the cultivation of a personal view based upon an appreciation of that which is beautiful and truthful is in and of itself a way of living ethically. That to cultivate oneself along the lines of love and compassion and generosity is to add strength to the fabric of society. And that having thus cultivated such a personal view, one may then act upon it."

"I think we all understand Drexel to be acting upon his personal view," Hobson put in.

"Mr. Drexel," she said with a look at Hobson that came near to knocking him off the cliff, "is even now engaged with me in raising money to help the poor of Newport. We go this Wednesday to the Point in the company of a wagonload of groceries. And he is also engaged in mounting a show of his watercolors for the benefit of the Redwood Library. Those are both, I believe, beneficent actions that grow out of his personal view. Do you have any such to match, Mr. Hobson?"

At which the Smith girls laughed and wagged their fingers scoldingly at Hobson.

"Now, Miss Gould and Miss Stanton—" she said, adopting a tone that signaled the subject closed; Franklin was not used to women coming to his rescue and it quite took his breath away—"has anyone recounted to you the horrors attendant upon public access to the Cliff Walk?"

Goodness, the girls said, spinning their parasols, no one had!

So she related to them—all the while with her father walking in a glower behind her—how the walk was protected by law as a public right of way, yet the owners of the cottages believed it represented an unwarranted intrusion upon their privacy. *An unwarranted intrusion*, she repeated. One of the papers had joked that Mrs. Vanderbilt had once sat down to her morning peaches at the Breakers and found herself being stared at by an insurance man from Hartford! Indeed, she (Mrs. Newcombe) had had all sorts strolling across her lawn, going in and out of her gardens. She wouldn't stand for that sort of intrusion, she said. There was talk now of putting up a wire fence the three-mile length of the walk, something at least to demarcate the private from the public.

"Which I hope," she said with a glance back at her father, "will not be necessary."

Oh, the Smith girls said, they could understand how vexing it all was.

Yet it was so pleasant, was it not, to be able to stroll along such a dramatic cliff, with the frightening ocean below and the wide, beautiful lawns and the distant mansions?

"Does ownership of the lawn," Ryckman pointedly asked, poking his cane into the turf, "entail ownership of the view?"

"Ah!" cried Franklin, for he could feel Ellen rise beside him. "Here's something I haven't thought of in years!" And he took her by the arm and related to them all how when he had first visited Newport he had made the faux pas of going upon the Cliff Walk on a Sunday afternoon and finding himself in the company of butlers and maids on their day off.

"Fortunately, I look rather like a butler myself. Don't you think, Miss Gould?" he said to one of the college girls, both of whom broke out laughing.

"*I'm* Miss Gould. *She's* Miss Stanton."

"And a poor butler at that!" said Franklin with his beautiful smile.

⤛ 1863 ⤜

~Today a colored "hall boy" from the Ocean came to the house with a note. Mother has just delivered it to me. She begs my pardon, says the envelope was addressed to Mr. Henry James, and that they had assumed it was meant for Mr. Henry James, *Senior*, but they could make neither "heads nor tails" of who had written it and what it proposed so had understood their error. She left hanging in the air an opportunity for me to explain myself, but I adopted an air of *mystery* and merely took the note from her.

It is from Mrs. Taylor, who writes that a party from the hotel will be taking the ferry to the war hospital at Portsmouth Grove. That she and her daughter, having wavered in their resolve of going the last time a party visited, have determined that this time they will do their duty to bring what comfort they may to the sick and wounded. Knowing that the James family is so intimately involved with the prosecution of the war, she asks whether I would like to accompany them. The party is for this Thursday. After which, it is expected Mr. Taylor will be joining them from Waterbury. She adds that the trip would not be suitable for young Harry and young Alice.

One must take care that one's life does not begin to resemble the plot of a novel.

~We have had a letter from Wilky in his encampment somewhere in the Carolinas. How these letters upbraid me with their exploits! He eats hardtack and drinks coffee out of a tin dipper!

Is it possible for a man to discover himself in war? For Wilky, who was forever (and *l'ingénieux petit* Bob even more so!) in the shadow of his older brothers, has cohered as a young soldier, has effortlessly taken on qualities which were most certainly not learned at Geneva or at Father's supper table, but were perhaps always there, cocooned within him and only awaiting this apt (if terrible!) moment of metamorphosis.

When I visited him this past spring at Camp Meigs in Readville, how struck I was at seeing the soft companion of my childhood hardened into a supple manhood and so at ease with the fellowship of soldiering! It was a bright breezy day, quite luminous and beautiful and radiant with the laughing, welcoming vivacity of the sunburnt young men. Whether it was a true revelation of their inner selves or a façade of handsome carelessness I know not, but they treated their circumstances almost as a frolic, with so little apparent consciousness of the desperate, momentous occasion that brought them together, and of the great test they were about to embark upon and which was the very cause, the impregnating origin as it were, of their brotherhood. I remember too my sense of exclusion, for I was reduced to watching, envying, applauding, and finally pitying (as I am now, reading again Wilky's letter) all from the security of my Newport life, my Chateaubriand, the quiet insects here in our garden, and the golden sunshine.

A great action is expected for the Negro regiment. It is in all the papers, a *cause célèbre*, and the James family is paralyzed with worry.

~In my idleness I have reread my earlier entry detailing our hike to the breakwater, and I find that last impression of myself and Miss Taylor standing at the end of the jetty gazing out over the surging sea has acquired a radiance in my imagination. For I feel almost as if we are still there, as if (striking conceit!) we had been imprisoned there in our freedom by some unknown painter (La Farge on one of his *plein air* excursions!), painted and so forever caught, and even though we have still our free selves (Harry James here in his room and Miss Taylor on the veranda of the Ocean), yet are we forever unfree, varnished into a painting which the world will view and sigh: *Young Love upon the Jetty.*

So lovely is this vision of life as art (or rather the manner in which art traduces life!) that I hesitate to spoil it by recounting the conversation Miss

Taylor and I had on our return hike. We were by then all very tired, and Miss Taylor was carrying her bonnet in her hand, and her face was flushed and her hair a little disheveled. I looked to amuse her and so told her I had a confession to make, namely that I had been engaged in duplicity as regards her person, for I had been surreptitiously observing her and taking notes on her behavior that I might use her—had she never guessed?—as a character in a story. But now that I knew her, now that she was my friend, I supposed I must give that over. But, I wondered aloud, if she was not to be used as a subject in a novel, what was I to do with her?

"Do?" she responded. "Do you need to *do* something with me?"

"Which would you prefer?" I gaily asked. "A light comedy? Or should I employ you in a fine tragedy?"

At this she let a mordant smile come upon her lips, but kept her face turned to the watery horizon. "Well, if you must *do* something with me," she said finally with that light satiric air she has, "then I suppose you must marry me."

"Marry you, my dear Miss Taylor?" I replied, trying to match her tone, but feeling the first adumbration of alarm.

"I believe," she went on, "that is typically what young American gentlemen *do* to young American ladies."

"Ah!"

"I'm led to believe it is something of a custom of the country," she added.

"Ah!" I stupidly repeated, and then hurrying on: "But I expect you are already much besieged with talented, acclaimed, accomplished, marriageable young men back in Waterbury."

She let loose then her lovely, renouncing laugh. "The talents of the marriageable young men of Waterbury are all inclined toward lathes and milling machines and the brass foundry. They can bat up a storm when the topic of discussion is bevel gears and escapement wheels." And she let those terms lie between us a moment and then said in a voice more taut: "They do not interest me."

"What does interest you?" I felt called upon to ask.

"Oh!" she said, as if this indeed were a question. But she did not at first go on, and we walked in silence for a time.

"I feel quite trapped there," she said eventually.

I could think of nothing to say to this, so kept quiet.

"What interests me," she took up finally, and there was now no touch of her characteristic satire, "is a life in which I am engaged in *discovering* what interests me. Not just now, as a young woman, but when I am a wife, and when I have children, and beyond. A life of imagination, and experience, and engagement, and commitment to something beyond myself."

"And can you find none of those in the Brass Valley?" I asked.

"I do not know, perhaps I can," she said, and then, turning back to where young Harry and Alice tramped behind us that she might cloak what she was about to say: "But I've found them *here!*"

Ah, my dear Miss Taylor, I beg of you: Do not attempt to remove the varnish from our painting. Do not take it down from off its wall and set its figures moving amidst the hurly-burly of the world. Do not mistake Art for Life!

⇥ 1778 ⇤

May 5

I begin a new Volume of these my War Journals. I must recover some of the Equanimity I know myself to possess.

Sought out Smithson, and as a Feint that my further Actions may be guised, apologized for this our late falling out, told him I had felt myself upon the Precipice of one of my Antic fits, but that thankfully it had passed. I told him he was a good fellow and that I valued his friendship. We went out into the yard and had a Smoke together.

Two of my Spaniels returned last night from being about the Rebel towns and they report great Rejoicing all over the country on account of the Alliance with France. I spent the afternoon in my Interrogation of these returned Spies, to get from them what I might, and I have made my Report. Afterwards I had some Rum with one of them and questioned him how he manages to pass amongst the Colonials for it is a Subject that interests me, what Feints & Gambits might be employed. He says one must wear homespun, murder the King's English, and fart a lot.

I wait, I wait, and no word.

May 6

The *Gibraltar* of 64 Guns, Capt Vandeput, anchored this morning in the Harbour. She brings letters and amongst them I have one from His Lordship telling me that he has reason to believe that I will soon be attached to Lord Hazlitt's Staff in Whitehall. He and I and William shall soon be dining at Burton's, he writes.

This business is but a waiting business. It does not alter how the Pieces are arrayed. The end will be played out. I will enjoy the Jewess, will let Da

Silva know she has been enjoyed, and will sail for London where my tales of War and my Adjutant's uniform will dazzle the young Virgins of Mayfair.

May 8

News finally that the Jew is back. I had both Rumor of this and, feigning business at the Waterside, saw him standing instructingly with one of his Draymen. He had a roll of Maps or Charts under his arm. No Judith, but her Note cannot be long coming.

It is always a Delight to first discover how a woman is in the act of Love. The little Sighs & Cries & Gasps she gives, particular to her. And then the Collapse, the Surrender, the Possession, the Domination!

May 12

Four days and she does not write! Has she had time to bethink herself or has something Miscarried?

I took myself to the Synagoge and asked after her, affecting a Disdain. Is the young Jewess I spoke to the other day about? I asked, stiff in my uniform. She was not, I was told. She was gone out of the city. But has she not return'd? I asked. They looked at me with Wonder, as well they might. I affected a great Distance, as if what I was about was beyond them, was a matter for the General's Staff, one of the urgent Affairs of War. I felt a deuced fool!

To knock upon Da Silva's door as if I am still his Chess-playing, Sherry-drinking friend seems impossible now. Too much has passed, even if it is only in the Orb of my thoughts. Yet what other Course of action is there? Hang me, is the girl come back or not?

May 15

At last, at last! Some colonial Fellow who is come to the city from the Massachusetts, from Taunton which he says is where she is, has brought me a Letter. He was eager to be away, for I surmize he is not one of the Loyalists, but I importuned him to tell me of her, how she looked, what she said to him. But he could not Satisfy me. He is not Acquainted with the young

Lady, he said. Rather she sought him out. How she knew he was bound for
Newport he could not say, but she begged him deliver the present Letter.
She paid him, and said the British Officer to whom he was to deliver the
Letter would pay him the Sum yet again. This, I understood, as a way of
insuring the Missive would be delivered. She is no fool, my Jewess.

How my heart beat when I had unsealed the Envelope and beheld her
hand! The Ecstasy I felt and yet hard upon the Despair! I could barely calm
myself to read the note, for my Eye would fall down the page looking for
something, some Sign, some Word, that would make things right. I had
finally to sit down, press my fingers to my Temples, and commence to read.

We are betrayed, she writes. Her Father has learned of our Love and
has used the Ruse of a Visit to his Wife & Children as a means of spiriting
her away. She did not understand this until it was too late, until she was
already some days in her Step-Mother's abode. It is not Phyllis who has
betrayed us, she is sure. Perhaps Hannibal. Or who knows, for her Father
has Spies about the City, about the Island. She says she has been Tortured
by the thought that I must hold her now in such Contempt. That I must
think her a shallow & inconstant Girl. But she is none such, she says. She is
true & constant, she says. She has been most Bitterly tricked, she says. And
now there is no way back. A Wilderness separates us. And a War. She begs
me to remember her.

Aye, how he must have enjoyed it! The Jew! The feint, the dissembling
Face of the man! It all comes clear to me now, enacts itself like a Play.
Smithson bent upon his righteous Errand. The Jew listening to tales of
Perfidy. My friend excusing his Betrayal of a fellow Officer as the necessary
duty of a Gentleman to the well-being of a Maiden. And Judith distraught
at going away, yet Innocently writing to me it was but a Delay, could I wait
for her? And after some several days, the Shock of learning she was not to
return with her Father. That Major Ballard was not to be trusted. That he
was a Man who enjoyed setting Snares for Women. Well, here was a Snare
set for *him*. Aye, I comprehend it all!

'Tis Midnight now, and I have only just returned. For I wrote myself a
Pass that I might be out past Curfew, and have walked all over the city. Oh,
how I walked! From the Point to the Fort, out to the Ropewalks which are

being taken down for firewood, and through the Cemeteries, through check Points and Sentries and finally back down along the Wharves. There were the Engineers' fires out on Goat Island, and further out on Torpedo Island fires like the Devil was encamped there, and the dim-lit Masts of the Fleet in the Harbour, and the sailing Clouds across the dark-visaged Moon. And all of it, the darkness and the Ghostly lights and the hissing lap of the water, were the very Picture of my Thoughts.

May 18

I feel something like my Fit lurking at the back of my Mind. Like a Straggler following me at a neat Distance who, when I turn to confront him, slips behind a tree. He is there and not there simultaneously.

I go about like an Automaton. I note the weather. I note what ships come in. I note Smithson in his daily duties.

I am placed in charge of Spies, send them out, reel them in. I ask them Questions, write down Answers, distill a Summary for Genl Pigot. All the time there is another me, observing, waiting, mocking.

No word of my Appointment to Hazlitt's staff. Perhaps my Shadow is preferred.

❧ 1692 ❧

4th Day

This matter that John Peele rais'd of Father's having a secret place worked in me so that I spent the entirety of this morning looking through the house that I might discover a hiding place. I found none such but the most queer thing. In a space where a Purlin had pull'd away from a Rafter in the Attic I found hidden some shells and some other much broken worthless things, and also something like a Doll, though none such as I have seen here in Newport. I set these things before me, in my room, and ponder'd upon them. I could not think that either Father or Mother had hidden these things, and I knew I had not, and surely not Dorcas, so there could be none other than Ashes. I wonder'd at them, and then in the next instant felt it as a Stake driven through me.

Of the many things we have heard tided of the late troubles in Salem Village was there talk of a Servant woman of the Islands who had been found to have little Dolls made up in the guise of Townspeople that she might conjure a Mischief to them. Had I most horribly discover'd another such Evidence? And Mother so lately ill! And Father lost!

I went about the rest of the day in a Daze. I could fancy Ashes in a pique, angry with us, spiteful, but I could not fancy her to be in league with the Devil against us. Had she not laugh'd with us, had she not presents from us, had Mother not treated her kindly, work'd alongside her whatever the Chore? Had we not play'd hull-gull how-many when we were younger? Yet here were these queer shells and this terrible Doll. There is now much talk of the townspeople of Salem having seen Evil where there was none, and that by seeing that which was not they had done their own Evil. I would have no such fabricating Blindnesse about me. But is there not as well a Blindnesse in not seeing Evil when it lives with one, yea, even in one's own Breast?

After supper while Ashes clean'd up I quietly laid the Items on the Kitchen table that she might turn around and see them and I might register her Feeling at their sight. She did so and it was as I dreaded. For she did verily start, looking from the things to me with a most awful shock. Her look was as a Confession to me, and I felt stir in me the most awful Rage that she had kill'd Mother, driven Father's ship upon the Shoals.

But yet I controll'd myself, demanded of her what these things were, would she explain herself. She did answer then, and neither in our language nor the language of the Islands, but the language of Africa which we had but rarely heard her speak. It came out of her as in a Downpour, having no sense to my ears, yet with such a great Feeling behind it! In time she made me to understand that these things she had with her from her home, that she had had them with her when she was taken, and that she had carried them with her across the Ocean to the Islands and from Barbados to Newport with Father these eleven years ago. That the shells were accounted good omens in Africa, that there was a feather of a bird we have not here, and other things now unrecognizable, and that the Doll was her Doll that her Mother had made for her. She said these things in a state of such Emotion, in a Passion of, oh, I know not how to say it! of Despair and Torment and Anger and a Fear that they might be taken from her. Yet I could not at first credit her, and press'd her upon the matter of Witchcraft, for my mind was still taken by that Notion. She seem'd not to understand me, and her face grew yet more Miserable, and yet defiant of me, at which I felt my Suspicions leak out of me as from a wallow'd bung, and I relented. And in truth the Doll look'd nothing like Mother or Father. Indeed it look'd rather like a draggled Ashes.

I did try then to mend things by saying might we not give the Doll to Dorcas that it might prove again a pleasure to a Child. But at that she snatch'd the things up from where they lay on the table and held them to her. Her face did work again with a most Mysterious emotion. And then with a Wail I have never heard come from a Human throat, she pitch'd the things into the fireplace! I was, I may say, now in a shock myself. Yet I cross'd to the fireplace and pick'd up the Doll which had landed in the ash, and brushing the hot stuff off, gave it her. She ripp'd it from me, and then ran out of the room, upstairs, and I have not seen her since.

I am writing this in the dark. I have set my little table over against the small window of my room, where the Moonlight shines in, and the light from off the Snow. For I am fill'd with something I wish to explain, yet feel I cannot.

Who was it who brought Ashes to New England? Who was it who took her and her Father and carried them away across the ocean? I used to think, when I was little, when I first came to understand that Ashes was not of us, that she came from so very far away, I used to lie in bed and imagine being so stolen. I would imagine someone coming into my room at night and carrying me off to Africa and how horrible that would be. It seem'd surely more horrible than it was for Ashes, for in my childish mind Africa was a place of Darknesse and Evil, and Newport was a place of Goodness and Light. I say in my childish mind, but do I not still think so? For Ashes was taken from a Heathen country and brought to a Christian. And tho' I understand she must miss her Mother and her Sister, and wonder where her Father is, yet she is brought into the Light and may gain her Salvation and is that not worth a great deal?

But O! if I could have Mother and Father restor'd to me would I not give up my Salvation? How wrong a thing to say! And yet it is true, so weak and feeling a girl am I! To have Mother back from out of the cold ground, and Father about the house, and Dorcas untroubl'd. Tho' Ashes speaks of Christ and of the Light and comes with us to Meeting, I think I know that inside her it is the same. She would pitch us all as into the fire if she could return home, dark tho' her home may be. How that strikes me in the Heart! For it is not God or Nature who has robb'd Ashes of her family, but us, we the people of Newport and our like. Is there not a sin in that?

⤙ 2011 ⤚

Half an hour later Sandy and Alice were seated at one end of the big dining room table with a Blue Onion tureen between them. They were a little drunk by then, and there was around them—to be resisted! Sandy kept trying to remind himself—the urging beauty of the room itself, the rich wood, the wall sconces with their gentle light, and the long-waisted French doors that looked out onto the veranda and the darkening lawn. He didn't quite know how he got started, but Sandy found himself talking about tennis, not so much about the woe-is-me stuff, but the good stuff, the stuff that had brought him out onto the court ever since he was eight years old. How he had loved just hitting the ball! He could do that for hours on end, never mind the points themselves. Right from the start the thing that had motivated him (why did she look so lovely? what had happened to her?), even as a little kid, he said, was he wanted to make beautiful shots. Sure, he wanted to win—who didn't?—but more than that, what he wanted was to be beautiful on the court. Not he himself beautiful, he hastened to add. Not Sandy Alison the man do-you-want-to-sleep-with-me beautiful. (At which she rolled her eyes.) But the thing he was doing. The sound of the ball coming off his strings, the arc of the shot, the spin, the angle, the heat rising off the court, the white lines, the hush of the crowd watching: he wanted it all to be beautiful. It didn't even matter who won the point. It just mattered that the point itself, the play, the interconnectedness of it all, that it be beautiful and right.

And that had made her talk of the beauty of Windermere—how deeply she loved the place. How her grandmother and then her mother had worked to bring it back—he should see the photos of what the place had looked like in the fifties! the fluorescent lights someone had hung in the hall!—and how now she, Alice, felt a duty toward it, toward its beauty and its perfection and toward her grandmother and her mother who had loved it too. Not just the house and the grounds, she said, but the history of the place. From when it was called Doubling Point, and the little farmhouse that had stood here during the Revolution with its rude dooryard and cowbells and sheep grazing out on the rocky point, and then the Gilded Age tearing everything down and putting up mansions all along the coast, and the tragedy of the original owners who had no sooner had the house built than the husband had died and left the wife with their two young children and a just-planted boxwood maze. They were in the house still, she said; could he feel them? And then they were back to that drunken night on the Point when he had been so dense (she said) and she so charming (she said) trying to get him to see and hear and smell the seventeenth century in the crooked streets and the little Quaker houses. But he could see now, couldn't he? He could hear and smell and feel now, couldn't he?

"I would love to give it to someone," she said, reaching over and stabbing a mushroom off a platter. The sun had gone down and the wall sconces made the room—the silver on the sideboard, the china and the silk tapestry on the wall—glitter. "Windermere," she said. "I would love to be able to give it to someone—I mean the *experience* of it. I think to bring kids up here, in the history and the beauty, in the idyll of the place, that would be everything to me. It would be—" and here she fixed him with a look; did he understand?—"a moral act, an *aesthetic* act."

He cocked his head, hoped he looked thoughtful.

"Because being rich," she went on, "is an inherently immoral act." And again she looked to see if he followed. "You can do one of three things. You can just say to hell with the world and enjoy yourself, what we'll call the Margo option. Or you can give it all away, which we'll call the not-bloody-likely option. Or you can try to ameliorate the immorality by doing charitable work, sitting on nonprofits, raising money for the Redwood Library or whatever, which is how most people square their consciences, but really you're only buying yourself a slightly higher circle, aren't you?"

He shrugged, smiled: he wouldn't know about being rich.

"It's been a dissonance in my head for as long as I can remember. *Two* dissonances really, childish questions you can't help but have: why me, why am I a cripple? And why me, why am I rich? There was a time, during college mostly, when I ducked the question by seeing one as paying for the other. Not just being rich as a compensation for the cerebral palsy. But the CP as a kind of punishment for being rich. They factored out. I was quit with the world. I could enjoy being rich because I was paying for it."

He had an impression, again, of the range of her selves: bowling shirt, I'm-already-brain-damaged, seventeenth-century Quakers, her research, her suicides. She was always ahead of him, ready with her wit, with her irony, with her—what else to call it?—with her *depth*. Sometimes he felt quite lost in her presence.

"This is the place I call home," she was saying, warmly, looking at him with meaning. "I can't help it if it's privileged. It's my home. It's where I was born. It's where my mother used to comb my hair to calm me after we'd done my stretching exercises and I was crying. It's where she died. It's what I am."

And yet, in one thing he had been ahead of her, had been ahead of them all. For he had inadvertently passed the test of the Heiress's Dilemma, hadn't he? He hadn't intended to, wasn't even aware he was taking the test, but he had passed. She could not suspect him of being after her money. He had rejected her right from the start, had turned her aside, had caused her to slide into one of her depressions. She had placed herself in his path and he had treated her—almost cruelly, he saw now—as a kind of mascot of the world he found himself in: the Casino, Windermere, cars with U-WISH license plates. The result of which was that now—he could never have planned it so!—now he was perfectly positioned to make his shot if he wanted to. He had opened up the court; there was all that green into which to hit the ball. If he wanted to.

"Because this is the thing," she was saying. She had one elbow on the table, her chin resting on the crook of her bad hand. "The privilege is part of the beauty," she said and leaned toward him. "It took me a while to see that. The guilt and the self-consciousness, the whispers at Miss Porter's and college. It took me a while to realize that it isn't just the warm brick and the seven chimneys and the leaded windows. It's the air of privilege and leisure and fulfillment, of being there, of not struggling toward wholeness but already having it—that's what's beautiful. You can't subtract the privilege from a place like Windermere without lessening its beauty, without injuring it."

He nodded, like okay, he got that.

"That's the paradox. If you love the place. I mean if you love the place *aesthetically*, you have to accept the privilege. You can't put out the back of your hand and deny it. It's part of the beauty. That's why I want twenty kids."

At which he raised his brow. She smiled, closed her eyes, let her head sway as if to admit she was a little drunk.

"That's why Tom and Margo should be expelled from the garden. *Will* be expelled if I ever get married and have twenty kids. Aunt Margo and Uncle Tom will be allowed a three-day visit over the Fourth of July and that's it."

And she held her hand out as if to forestall his objections.

"What we're talking about is a kind of high-level tourism," she picked up after a minute. She opened her eyes and fixed him with a look. "Not the tourism of ogling the Eiffel Tower, but a tourism where you're on the *inside*. Where the outside world, the *literal* world, is only a sign, an avenue, to an internal world. Like when you watch a movie or read a novel," she said, seizing on the idea. "You're a tourist, but if you're reading right you're a tourist simultaneously on the outside *and* the inside. You're simultaneously yourself and someone else. Nineteenth-century Vevey, let's say. The Dollar Princess and her exquisite clothes. Common enough when you read a novel or watch a movie. But what about life itself? Could you live your life while at the same time keeping an eye out for signs and symbols, for meaning, patterns, connections?" She sat back, smiled drunkenly at him. "To *live* your life and *read* it simultaneously. That's what I would try to give my children if I had them. Not just Windermere here in the twenty-first century, but Windermere during the Great War and the Gilded Age. Even Windermere before it was Windermere, when John La Farge used to hike across Doubling Point looking for flowers to paint. Imagination. Empathy. *That's* the moral act," she wound up. "Not to live too simply, as if there was only this."

And with that last word she gestured at the room around them, only this time she didn't seem to mean Windermere and all it meant to her, but rather the literal world and all it *didn't* mean. He smiled and slid his empty wineglass over to hers and clinked it where it sat.

"Show me those photos," he found himself saying. "The house in the fifties. Your grandmother."

At which she smiled, leaned back in her seat, and closed her eyes. And then with a funny grimace at how sated she was—food, wine, the presence of Mr. Winterbourne—she made a show of the dicey business of standing up.

Out in the wide hall he was struck by how large and dark and empty the house felt now with the sun going down. Even with Mary there somewhere, and up on the third floor presumably the Salve Regina girls. And who knew? Maybe Aisha was in for the night, being discreet in the bedroom that wasn't quite hers. And yet it was so deathly quiet, and big, the ceiling so high the light from the wall sconces seemed to lose its way. He found himself strangely affected by the thought of Alice in the house all alone as she must sometimes be. What did she do with herself? Even when she wasn't alone, what did she do? The house was simultaneously the emblem of privilege—of "being there" as she'd said—and a kind of mausoleum against which she fought with her bowling shirt and her sweetheart-of-the-rodeo clothes. Tom, Margo? One was utterly unlike her, the other actively disliked her. Even Aisha—who claimed to love her, and who he had come to see as using her—would one day leave Alice when the right opportunity presented itself.

It had, of course, been staring him in the face all along. It wasn't like he hadn't seen it: the obvious solution, the simple answer. And yet he had never considered it, had never even picked it up, turned it this way and that. He had been too . . . what, too much of a gentleman? too used to better— Well, he was about to say to better women, but what did that mean? Prettier, sexier, more athletic, okay, but better? He gazed down at her there in the dark library, at her body quick and intent beside him. She was showing him the house in the twenties, thirties, the house reclaimed by her grandmother in the fifties and sixties, her mother in these wide-cuffed dungarees surrounded by workmen. No, it was impossible. It ran too counter to the idea he had of himself. He lacked the killer instinct, after all, had documented proof of that. And yet, why not? He was a little drunk himself, he'd admit, but really: why not? She was within the circle. Their bodies touched—were they both not aware of it? Each time she reached over to turn a page of the album, or leaned forward to point out her eight-year-old self in this or that photo, she made it so that her shoulder touched his upper arm or her elbow brushed against him. Could he not turn to her, pull her fragile body into him? Make her feel what it would be like? Feel *himself* what it would be like?

He stole a glance at her—her sun-lightened hair, the nervous tautness of her face, the strange vitality she had in spite of her broken body. She was showing him a photo of her grandmother helping to lay out the maze with stakes and mason's twine and someone manning a surveyor's transit, then a photo of the hedge two feet tall, four feet tall, six feet and topped with snow. As if to camouflage his thoughts, he joined in, pointed out in the upper corner of one of the photos a 1978 Mercedes in the shadows under the porte cochere. But all the time he was feeling her beside him, allowing himself to fall under the allure of her body—her long hair, her thin arms!—the two of them alone in the dark library with its walls of books and leather chairs, and around the library the big house with its twenty-eight rooms, its banks of windows and ornate chimneys, and around the house the dusky grounds, the massive trees with their circles of bare earth surrounding the hundred-year-old trunks, and around the grounds the black wrought-iron fence tipped with gilding that told you this wasn't yours, you weren't invited.

Could he bend himself to it? Could he say "love"—could he *feel* love—not just once in the eccentricity of the moment—Alice du Pont and Sandy Alison!—but again in the light of day, and then the next day, and the next? Because there would be no "trying out" Alice as a girlfriend. That was a wrong within the other wrong that would be beyond him, fatal. The divide, once crossed, had to remain crossed. Did he understand that? Did he grasp that? There would be no going back, no return to the Florida camps, to the resorts on the Outer Banks, to the girls who showed up at the courts in their summer shorts with their bare backs and their hair dyed blond.

Or was he just playing, a little drunk, holding his hand out over the fire?

She had reached the end of the photo album and was now showing him the blank pages at the rear of the book. The blank pages on which were pasted photos of her kids, she said—here was young James trying to learn how to stand on his head, and Sarah with a croquet mallet too big for her, Judith playing in a mountain of Christmas wrappings. And look! here he was—Sandy Alison—in shorts and a tight T-shirt, reclining in one of the Adirondack chairs, a gin daisy held gingerly out over the lawn as if the naked baby tucked into the crook of his arm had just reached for it. And here he was again smiling through his sunglasses at the lovely—he could take her word for it—at the lovely photographer.

In the library window he could see their grayed-out reflection, the two of them standing before the heavy oak table with its glass-shaded lamp and the big photo album spread out before them, and at the same time, behind them the south lawn sloping darkly down to the maze, still faintly visible. He closed his eyes and breathed deeply the still, silent air. There was the sound of the front door opening, closing.

In a moment, he knew, he would kiss her. In a moment, he would turn her slender body into him, enclose her, and kiss her on the lips.

→ 1896 ←

A GAY WEEK AT NEWPORT
Season at Its Height
BALL AT PAVILION A SUCCESS
COON BAND APPEALS TO "DEPRAVED TASTES"

NEWPORT, R.I. JULY 25—The season is fully at its height and is being made the most of not only by society, but by that class of well-to-do people who are now thronging hotels and private boarding houses and registering at the Casino. Though it is remarked that the great difference between cottage life and hotel life, even at those hotels considered *de luxe*, is that a hotel may not discriminate against those deemed undesirable, still there is a great admixture of types, and we can report that not only has the high-water mark been reached for the present summer, but for any summer preceding it.

The highlight of the week was the Masked Ball at Berger's Pavilion. Though there was no reappearance of the Blue Domino who had so bewitched the ball last year, yet the costumes and the decorations were all declared a great success. The pavilion was transformed with red bunting and crimson tapestry divided by pillars of blue and white hydrangeas. The ceiling was festooned with silver maple and in among the branches small electric lights flashed, the globes being covered with red gauze. In these branches, too, were colorful birds whose wings had been clipped so as to prevent their taking flight.

Notable were the floral decorations upon the supper tables, which formed aquatic scenes with garlands of lotuses and lilies cascading to the floor.

As to the Four Hundred, they had vanished, and in their place came Cleopatra and Julius Caesar, Marie Antoinette and Casanova! The costumes were a marvel, as were the coiffures and wigs and headdress deployed. The Baird Brothers Dance Orchestra provided a most appealing accompaniment to the festivities.

But the highlight—dare we say the lowlight?—of the evening was the appearance of Tiger Terry's Sewanee Coon Band! Tiger Terry himself was there, fresh from his talking machine recordings that are become so popular among the lower classes. But what a shock to the Four Hundred! For at the opening strains of "The Darkies Awakening," there were cries of horror and a general exodus from the dance floor. Seeing that the evening was in jeopardy, the organizers of the ball (take a bow, Mrs. Lydig and Mrs. Auld, if you dare!) attempted to dance to the jungle rhythms of "All Coons Look Alike to Me." But it was not a success and the whole evening seemed on the verge of collapsing when Mr. Franklin Drexel led Mrs. Ellen Newcombe onto the dance floor, and along with her others of the young and daring and those desirous of being considered "up-to-date." So it was that the Ariel of Newport—will he henceforth be known as the Caliban of Newport?—rescued the ball by showing the Four Hundred how to "cakewalk" and "coon dance."

Still, it was overheard among the older, more refined members of society, those who felt it their duty to uphold civilization (were they not Cardinal Richelieu? were they not Queen Elizabeth?) that such music had only "low-life" appeal, that it was not a boon to the Terpsichorean art, and that the banjo was an instrument only the infirm of mind could approve. The decision to foist such sounds upon the attendees of the ball by the organizers was deemed regrettable. Such immoral music, Joan of Arc was heard to opine, had no place in Newport. Indeed, we might remark, *après* "Carve Dat Possum," could the deluge be far behind?

Wherever one stood on the controversy, it could not be denied that the bringing of the new fad of "slumming" to the cottagers of Newport was a *succès de scandale* that next year's organizers will be hard-pressed to surpass.

~ 1863 ~

~I have spent the last several days considering whether I must give over my friendship with Miss Taylor. I was even twice on the verge of writing a note begging off accompanying her and her mother to the war hospital at Portsmouth Grove, but in the end I did not do so. Whether this is because I selfishly cannot deprive myself of the pleasure of her company, or because I have come around to thinking our colloquy on the hike back from the breakwater was but more of her satiric disposition, or whether there is something after all a little malign in me—that I would *see* where things led, though I would not lead them myself—I do not know. But I set my scruples aside and accompanied them on the expedition to the hospital. Now, returned, and seated at my writing desk, and taking up the notes I made this afternoon, I believe I have not erred.

The party from the Ocean numbered two dozen in all, ladies mostly (the men perhaps feeling in any such outing a latent accusation). I was relieved to see that Miss Taylor and her mother had the good sense not to dress as if they were members of a boating party, for some of the others from the hotel were arrayed in colors and frills that would surely strike a discordant note when we were among the sick and wounded. We each paid our quarter-dollar and boarded the *Perry* and took seats on the open deck under the morning sun.

I know I sometimes fall into the writing of a diary, and not the Writer's Notebook I intend. Yet I find I cannot merely transcribe my notes without supplying them with the atmosphere that accompanied their making. And too: how can I know what detail, what undone button, what soiled cuff, altogether what glimpse of life as it is lived around me, may not unfurl a story? So I remake the world more fully here: the sparkle of the sun on the water as we made our way up the bay, the scream of the steam-whistle, the small clapboard houses along the shore each with its circle of life, unknown, unrecorded, unfathomable. Yet I must add too the tissue of my own life, and of Miss Taylor's, for what is ordinary among us becomes fabulous when read by those distant from us in place and time. What wonders my breakfast (toast, Mother's jam, a carved peach, and the kitchen table with its black ring where someone had once put down a hot pan) would hold for a reader in Moscou, or in centuries hence!

The war hospital is sited at Portsmouth Grove at the northern tip of Aquidneck Island, next to the small islands with the old Puritan names Prudence, Patience, and Hope. It was low tide when we drew near the wharf, so our first sight of the hospital's patients was of those convalescents who were able-bodied enough to be employed down in the mudflats "clamming" with their trouser legs rolled up. They stopped to look at the ferry and watch us disembark. They looked a sorry lot, though they were likely the best we would see.

Word having been sent ahead, we were greeted by the Chaplain and one of the nurses. There were also those called sutlers who attempted to sell us goods and little *cadeaux* that we might present to the invalids within. I had understood from Father (who had delivered a lecture at the hospital this past winter) that gifts would be appreciated, so I had come with a small satchel of pamphlets and newspapers and some books (including an inscribed copy of his own *Substance and Shadow*, just printed, the giving away of which I hoped would relieve me of the duty of reading).

I must confess I did feel some inward discomfort as we were shown about, for it was very much as if we were sightseeing, Baedeker in hand, though the sights were human misery and suffering and sacrifice. The buildings all bore the mark (except the main administration building which had formerly been a resort hotel) of having been hastily thrown up, with no foundations to speak of, whitewashed so that the rough wood yet showed through. There were fourteen "pavilions" in all, our guide said, and they could hold as many as 2,400 wounded. Pointed out as well were the support buildings, the mess hall, the guard barracks, the stables, a laundry, bakery, blacksmith's, etc. And there was a chapel where the convalescents might seek refuge and spiritual comfort, attached to which was a library where I left, discreetly I hope, Father's book.

Notable as we walked were the condition of the guards themselves, each of whom had suffered wounding or amputation, though now recovered. They called themselves the Cripple Brigade, one of the soldiers ruefully informed us.

The Chaplain left us with the encouragement to go amongst the patients in their beds for, he said, they were always pleased to see visitors and to talk and to hear stories, and to receive our little gifts. Yet what a paralysis I felt! I, who have enough trouble speaking to the members of my own family, to be there amongst strangers, all of whom were so needing of comfort and I having no means to supply that comfort, and no words for them. The sutlers had followed us down into the great compound, knowing, I am sure, that we would want their wares now if we hadn't before. And what misery we saw, and what disfigurement and bodily destitution! There were the most horrific wounds—limbs amputated, faces shot away, bodies luminescent with fever, wasted by bowel disorders. To those who were not so bad, or who were more along the road to healing, we spoke, and here I must say that Miss Taylor showed herself a most capable and forward nurse, for she gave to each invalid her most beautiful smile, and sat beside them and inquired of their names, and what town they were from, and how they had been wounded, and how they were getting on, and was there anything she could do for them. These were the most natural and simple of questions, yet how impossible I found it to ask them! And with what gracious ease did she do so! One soldier asked her if she might read a letter to him and from the condition of the letter we understood it had been read to him many times. It was from his mother, and Miss Taylor read it in a most lovely, calm voice, asking him when she was done about the various people mentioned by name and so giving the soldier, who was disfigured by a scar running from his temple to his Adam's apple, the opportunity to talk of those whom he loved and missed.

For my eyes alone I will record here that while I moved amongst those several acres of men (some of them younger than I!) who had had their lives so wretchedly altered, I bethought my and William's earlier enthusiasm for

enlisting in the war effort and realized as deeply as I have ever realized anything how thankful I was that that had not come to pass. For no decision I
ever make in life could be as wrong and against my being as would be the
decision to go to war. I do not mean only that I recognized at that moment
that I am no soldier, and could never be one, and that so inept would I be
that surely my fate would have been as these around me, or worse. I mean
rather that as I stood there and saw so many destroyed bodies, so much
amputated life, I knew in the deepest part of my being that there was no
cause, no country's existence, no slave's freedom that was worth my life,
worth the mutilation of my consciousness and the extinguishment of my
senses. Yes, how horrible to admit this of myself, and yet how true! I cannot, in my own presence, deny it! And what awe and wonder I felt for these
men (and Wilky and Bob!) who had so selflessly given of themselves. Did
they *know* and still give?

I am not proud of this—I will not call it cowardliness, rather egotism.
(The bosom serpent!) But I *will* see clearly. Even to my own failings.

In one of the pavilions there was a quarter given over to cots on which
lay soldiers of the Confederacy. They were attended to, so the Chaplain
had said, without distinction. Whether that is true in practice I do not
know, but they seemed no different than the Union troops, though there
were none of the visitors about them. Maugre my dismal shyness, I had
grown a little more at ease with the wounded, and with Miss Taylor's deportment as my model had begun to ask the invalids little questions, and
even came across one who hailed from Cambridge and so was able to
speak some of his home. Another I sat beside because I saw Emerson's *Rep-
resentative Men* on his cot and so asked him about it. He said that though he
read it he did not understand it, that at times it was just words to him, and
he did not know whether this was the fault of his injuries or of Mr. Emerson. I in turn did not know whether he meant this humorously or not, so
fell to explaining what I thought were the intention of the essays, getting
quite stuck on Napoleon. I am afraid I left him in a worse state than I
found him.

It was only then, upon standing up, that I became aware that Miss Taylor had crossed to the Confederate cots, was going from one to the next as

she had been doing with the others. There was something of a stir in the room, I thought, something of disapproval. But those amongst the Confederate soldiers who could do so raised themselves in their cots, smiled at her coming, and thanked her. When she came to one who could not raise himself and who bore the signs of a dreadful fever, she sat beside him and spoke to him, and then (most boldly! most beautifully!) she took from her reticule a comb and, first wiping the fever-sweats from the boy's face, began to comb his hair as we had seen one of the nurses do. The boy seemed only half-aware of her, yet I think he did calm at her touch. When she was done she straightened his bedclothes, and with a gentle caress of his feverish cheek rose and moved on.

"A very different excursion," she said to me when we had regained the outdoors. I took her to mean different from our last to the breakwater.

"And which do you prefer?" I asked that I might fall in with her. She kept her gaze from me, and looked rather at the horizon.

"Both," she said, inhaling so her chest swelled, as if it were life itself she breathed. She exhaled, and then let a weary look fall upon me, saying: "But I think I have had enough of this for now."

We rejoined her mother, and then not knowing where else we might go, walked back to the wharf area, though it was still an hour before the steamboat returned from Providence. There were no benches there, but as we were tired and the day itself had broken decorum, we lowered ourselves and sat on a spot of turf under the spreading branches of an oak tree. We were shortly joined by some others who had as well had their fill. There was conversation of what we had seen and heard, and protestations over the inhumanity of the war and the evil of the South and its seceding. I stupidly found myself saying that though the South was surely evil, that evil was not due to its seceding, which I believed (and *do* believe) it had the right to do. Some of the others took me up on this (was I a sympathizer? etc.) and I found I had to defend myself, first marshaling much of Father's rhetoric and lofty fire against slavery, but then more boldly explaining my belief that, slavery aside, any region of any country has the right to secede from that country. That to hold against their will those who wish to leave any union is itself an evil, the imposing by force of one will upon another.

"Which is," I rather magnificently wound up, "the essence of slavery, is it not?"

There was much consternation over this, but I did not retreat, and went even further, maintaining that each person's consciousness was a country unto itself, accountable to its own laws and truths. (To which someone said surely, I meant *conscience*, didn't I? I did not.) And if those truths brought the solitary consciousness to seceding from the values and structures of the society it found itself in, then it must do so. For fidelity to the truth one found within oneself was, to me, the highest good.

To which Mrs. Taylor asked surely I did not mean that every union was frangible? Were not a husband and wife indissoluble? Were they not united until death did them part? And united to their family? And that family to other families? Where did one draw the line?

One drew the line, I answered her, always and forever, at the individual self.

On the ferry back we sat quietly in deck chairs, for the day had been exhausting. And in the declining sun I experienced again as I had on the breakwater a sense of Miss Taylor's fineness, and how that fineness seemed to spread over me, and include me, and seep into the world so that the air was infused with a lucid charm, and the hour it took for us to glide back to Newport seemed, by some wondrous secret, to know itself marked and charged and unforgettable.

(Details I have not managed to work into the above narrative but which may someday prove useful: the stench of the latrines and outhouses; the bloody dressings; remnants of hardtack and salted beef; buttons used for checkers; bromine, quinine; one of the guards court-martialed for being "corned"; the railroad spur to the east with its solitary red boxcar; the cemetery; roll call for the able-bodied soldiers; the horses in the stables swishing their tails against the summer flies.)

⇀ 1778 ↽

May 20

I have been to the Jew. I went without ever making the Decision to go, but
let my feet carry me there and my hand pull back the Doorknocker. It was
clear from the outset he did not wish to see me. I managed a solicitous
Calm all the same, asked after his recent Journey inland, expressed my
Hope that he found his Wife and little ones well. Only then did I mention
Judith, inquiring was she not come home. To which he responded that
Miss Da Silva would for the time being continue to abide at Taunton, that
the recent Entry of France into the War had given him pause as to his
Daughter's Safety, as it was now much more of a Surety that the English
Fleet would be engaged and that Newport would suffer. Allowing her to
stay behind in the city had perhaps been an unwise Decision all along, he
said, but Judith had herself wished it so. The girl was game for the Privations of War, he said with something like Pride, yet was she now safely
away, out of Harm's way, he said pointedly, and she would remain so. I expressed my Sympathy and my understanding, adding in my best Courtly
manner how impoverished the city was become without her young
Beauty about, but such indeed were our own Privations. To which he
bowed his head, seeming to accept the Compliment. Yet then it was that
he looked across at me, and with his hard Jew's eye (as if he were treating
with some Merchant outside his Tribe whom he was about to Fleece), said
there was also the matter of his hearing from a reliable Informant that a
Major of the Royal Welch Fusiliers who was a frequent guest in his house
had been engaged in the attempted Seduction of his Daughter.

How to relate what then happened? I do not mean what happened in
Da Silva's sitting room (with its four carved and gilded Cherubs watching

us! and which I will recount below), but what happened to Major Ballard. For I found my Voice speaking on its own, and my hands gesturing, and my face working up expressions of Alarm & Entreaty. It was as if I had become translated, as if my Shadow or this Straggler of whom I have written above had exchanged places with me, so that I watched myself as from a distance, heard my Voice, saw my Face, applauded this or that Ploy, this or that impromptu Stratagem, but all from a vantage Point outside the room, as if I had been Stolen from myself.

Yet what a Tactician this Straggler proved to be! For he did not affect Outrage, or protest the Calumny, or work up an injured Merit. Rather he confessed to the Charge! He was, he said, in love with Miss Da Silva! It had not started so, he admitted, for he had at first been merely amusing himself. So far from home, in this Miserable war, he had allowed himself to be distracted by her Beauty and her Charm. But O! how he had come to see what great Worth was at home in the young lady! How Nature had found fit to match physical Beauty with Beauty of Spirit! He had grown to have the greatest Respect for the young lady, and to value her opinion, and the Measure of her intelligence. All through the Winter he found his thoughts taken over by her until it had become a Struggle to keep away from the house. He had had to Ration his visits! he said with a rueful laugh. Did his Interlocutor not know that? And how he had scolded himself, censured himself, upbraided himself for the Futility of the Attachment. He knew the circumstances to be impossible, the Barriers many and insuperable. There was, forgive him, the difference in their Stations, and yes, the difference in their Race. Who could not see these? No wonder Da Silva's informant, whoever he was (he was Lieutenant Smithson, wasn't he? now, wasn't he? the good fellow!), had mistook his intentions. He had thought himself a young man of Reason, and of balanced Comportment, yet his friendship with Miss Da Silva had made him realize he was also a man of Passion and of deep feeling! Impossible his Love might be, but he did not apologize for it. Nor like Peter at the Cockcrow would he deny it!

The Jew demanded then what did I mean? Did I mean to offer Marriage to his daughter? he scoffed. I should get myself under Control, he said. If I had come to explain an immoral Behavior, and to explain it by confessing to a Weakness of the Heart, very well. Though he disapproved of both, the one was a greater Evil and he could understand my wishing to clear my name of it. But I had myself enumerated the many Objections, nay, the utter Impossibility, of any acceptable Union between myself and his Daughter. And still I dared speak of his Daughter in the words, and yea, with the Warmth of a Suitor!

Gravely, I answered that I meant no Disrespect toward either him or his daughter, nor had I acted with any such Disregard. That I was a man caught in a Whirlwind. That I could not deny what I viewed as a noble Affection. And then, seeing an opportunity to move a Rook onto the seventh Rank, said that I believed his Daughter returned my Affections. That the world was filled with those who had turned aside from such natural Attachments to their great and lasting Injury. Did he wish that for his Daughter?

And did he not then swear an Oath at me! I had never heard such from him before! O! Was I not enjoying myself! Even while I hid behind my tree and let the Straggler probe & feint & goad, I was in a rage of Pleasure. I said that it was quite impossible for me to convert, but that it seemed not so as regards the young Lady. Indeed, she had confessed to me once that she would do so if it meant we might Marry, meant she would be welcome across the ocean at Clereford Hall. Such Conversions and subsequent Alliances were not unheard of, I believed. Yes, surely, my family would be greatly Astonished by such an action on my part, but we were forward-thinking people. Indeed my brother the future Lord Stevens was regarded as something of a Freethinker and would welcome, I was sure, a converted Jew as a Sister.

He stood then and I thought the Man must burst of an Apoplexy. He said I was no longer welcome in his house and that there was an end to our Interview. But hardly had I stood with expressions of Surprize, than he launched himself on a Tirade of Justification. Did I think, Sir, that his family had withstood two Centuries of Ignominy & Deceit, his uncle forced to Recant on his knees at the Aveiro Cathedral, his parents forced to leave behind all their worldly Riches and flee their home like Criminals, and he himself made to navigate the ignoble Duplicity of being named Sebastiao, so that once free of Intolerance & Cant & Bigotry, their Descendants might take the first opportunity to add their names to the roll at Trinity Church? He would not Countenance any such talk from me or from anyone! He would not have any such talk in this his house! He was no longer Sebastiao, he was Isaac Da Silva. He was a Jew and those who were his were Jews. And any who did not like it could be damned! Good day! he said.

At which I smiled, bowed, and with my mind a Riot, went out.

↜ 1692 ↝

7th Day

Today I have been a most wondrous slow-worm and lazy-bones! There was work to be done, yet I would not do it. It was snowing, a most beautiful, silent, slow, calming snow. I sat in the parlour with the last of Father's cider and gaz'd in a Dream out the window. I told Ashes she might go out for the afternoon. I can at least give to Charles Spearmint that much.

Oh, I dream'd of a great many things. Some, it is true, of the troubles I am in, but not so terribly much as to cast me down. Rather there was such a beauty in the world, the snow falling, and a hush over all, and the warm fire, and John Pettibone in my thoughts, and Mother's blanket over me, and out the window the green spruce trees made indistinct as if by a snow fog. So lost was I in a Meditation, so under the spell of the falling dusk and the goodness of Father's cider and the beauty of the world, that I wonder'd most Philosophically of things! I wonder'd from whence the feeling of Beauty came and was the world beautiful in itself, infus'd as it was with God, or did we paint it with our own Beauty? I write this not as richly as I felt it (such is always the way of my writing), but what I mean is this: Do we feelingly paint a world that has not feeling itself? Or when we apprehend Beauty, has it always been there, but in our Darknesse we do not see it? For I was struck so powerfully with the beauty of the falling snow that it seem'd itself a moment of Revelation, almost as if each flake was as a Piece of God's love falling upon the world. Oh, the most odd conceit came to me! To wit, that each snowflake was the undergarment of an angel! That the tiny angels of heaven disported themselves and in their play let loose their white undergarments that they might float slowly and silently and spinningly down to us! Just so does Heaven bless the world below.

In this warm and dreamy mood I heard Ashes come in the kitchen door and such was the strange state of my mind that I found myself blessing her, and blessing Charles Spearmint. Oh, that he might have the wife he desired, and that Ashes might be free, and Dorcas her mother restor'd to her, and all the wounds of the world heal'd by God's love!

I felt it deep in my heart, and staring at the red and yellow embers in the fireplace whilst Ashes put her cloak away, I wish'd it could be so, and yet knew it could not.

3rd Day

I have spent the day at Jane Beecher's, for she had several Hams which wanted smoking, one of which she will give to us when it is done, and as the day was cold and gray I did not mind being in her Kitchen with the slow fire. I had a moment of Strangeness with her which I will write of here. I do not know what to think of it, or even if it be at all, and not just my Fancy.

As I am small still she had me climb the kitchen ladder and bring down two skepfuls of Cobs from where she stores them under the Eaves. They are good for a light smoking fire and give any meat an agreeable Flavor. With what we did not first use, Dorcas and Sarah and Ruth built a cob house and play'd, and then when we must needs take parts of their house to feed the fire, play'd at hull-gull how-many.

While the Hams smok'd, Jane and I found we might rest and talk. We had not broach'd Edward Swift's proposal since the day we had huddl'd together in the cold dark and had such a lovely long Converse. That was the day she spoke so feelingly of her leaving, of her living in the Wildernesse, of how she might make a fit Life if she could be but alone. She said she had been before too chary of my Wants to ask whether I had accepted him, but that she had not heard any such News when she went out into the Town. Had I then turn'd him down?

I told her of what had pass'd. That I had not turn'd him down but had not encourag'd him. And that I did not think I could bring myself to Accept him, as long as Dorcas and Ashes and I had enough to eat, and Wood enough. Tho' I might bring my mind to Sense, yet I could not bring my Heart, and so would hold out until I could no more.

She said she was greatly reliev'd to hear me speak so. That she had been in a Fright that I would be forc'd into such an unsuitable and uncomely Marriage. That a maid like myself would be quickly ruin'd. That she would help me hold out. And more of the like, her face growing flush as she spoke, and little laughs spilling out of her as if a string of Beads had broken and she could not gather them up and stop them falling. From down on the floor little Ruth and Sarah look'd up at their Mother in wonder at such an unwonted Fit. For she was giddy as with a Deliverance, which Agitation was most unlike her.

But that is not the Strangeness. I pass'd on to telling her of Charles Spearmint. I do not think I wanted her Advice, but rather just to tell her, and perhaps to marvel with her, and know from her: Was there such Love in the world? That a man might sell himself to have a Wife as Jacob had done? But as I told her of my two Interviews with Spearmint, and as I set out the Terms he offer'd, and the History with Father as I understood it, and my talk with John Peele, she grew more and more (how shall I say it?) more Dark in her Thought. The giddiness that was formerly in her left her as if Flush'd out a drain. I tried to rouse her and bring her back. Was this not good news? I ask'd her. Was this not a way I might tread water until (I did not say until John Pettibone grew up!) until I was old enough? I might after all have Ashes's help for the whole of the seven years. Toward the end of which I might marry more fit, and so have made my way through this Vale of Tears.

She did not speak for a time, and when she did said that she did not Advise me to it. Had I not said that I thought Father would be against it? Did I want him to return and find I had acted so rashly, lessening our Estate when there was no need to? And did I really want to bind myself to such Articles? For having escap'd the frying-pan of Edward Swift, did I want to fall into Charles Spearmint's fire? But in all she said I could not rid myself of Misgiving. For she seem'd to make her Argument not as an Address to my Wants, but to her Own! I know not why I thought this, for how could my selling Ashes be a Hurt to her? How could my signing such Articles with Charles Spearmint injure her and hers? Yet I felt it, a Mistrust I know not how to explain.

Oh, it is good there is no Pillory for what one thinks. For would I not be stood in it expos'd for such ungenerous thoughts, so ungrateful a Heart?

5th Day

O! just so! Unhasp the Pillory and stand Prudy Selwyn in it!

For how wrong and stinting have I been! This Mistrust I have had of Jane Beecher, how it is reveal'd now as a painting I have made with the colors of my own spiteful Spirit.

For she has laid before me a plan that will help Dorcas and Ashes and me through these coldest months. She has done so at some Bother to her and her own. For she proposes that Dorcas and I close up the house and move in with her for these next two months. The firewood is low, and it is most dreadful cold. Why keep two houses with fires in their fireplaces? she says. Why heat water for two laundries? Why keep two stoves simmering soup? It is easier to make porridge for a single household of six than to make it for two households of three, she says. Why can we not, the six of us women, she says, live together until the warm weather comes? We will split the cost, and we will both of us have savings. It will be a trial for my Separatist nation, says Jane. We will be like the Amazons, she says.

Hers is a house smaller than our own, not big enough for six, tho' there are those about the town who live with more under less roof. Still, there are no men, so privacy is no matter.

We spent the afternoon going through the house, and she pointed out how things might be. We would bring over Dorcas's trundle-bed that she might sleep in the same room with Sarah and little Ruth. Ashes may have the closet off the Kitchen, and Jane and I may share the great bed. The plan has a sense to it. We will unite our Troubles and our work so that our lives and our suffering may be lighten'd. We will use one-half the firewood we would otherwise. And when the Spring comes we may disband our Amazon nation, Jane says, and we may look about us then, husband and Father unreturn'd if that be the case, and we may then plot and devise our way forward.

I have thought on this for a full day now, and I think it is good and right. For I have not been able to come to a clear thinking on this matter of

Ashes and Spearmint. And tho' that may prove to be the only way out of this Wildernesse I find myself in, I cannot yet take that path. Perhaps in the Spring, if my Heart finally lets go of Father.

7th Day

I have told Ashes that she may inform Charles Spearmint that he must wait for his Answer. That it is yet too hard upon Father's disappearance. But that he will hear from me a definite Answer, in the Spring, let us say when the Planting is done.

We have moved everything into Jane's house, our winter clothing and goods, Dorcas's bed, what victuals we had, and I am come back into the house under pretense of bringing over some favour'd cookware. But I am here in the dying warmth of this my home instead to write what will be my last entry in this my Spiritual journal.

For it has been a Failure, this attempt to find Light. It appears there is very little spiritual about Prudence Selwyn! I had made to record what movements of light I found within me that I might have a poetry of my Spiritual life, but what I have written is a prose (nay! an account-book!) of my Physical life instead. So little exercise of Grace do I find recorded here, so little the clarity of gift, but rather the Labyrinth of my fears and petty desires. It has been a Vanity I must give over. Let me say good-bye to my young Self, and close these pages.

He couldn't help wondering what the others thought, Margo and Aisha, the realization dawning on them that he wasn't just hanging about, and Tom, who was down in New York and didn't know anything about it—what would he think when he came back, found his sister lying on the couch drinking a margarita, sighing *"abus de faiblesse"* from time to time like a punch line and watching a movie with her head on the lap of that tennis guy?

At the Casino, having her group doubles lesson, Margo just gave him a you-can't-be-serious look, punched a volley right at him.

Those first few days he wondered whether he shouldn't just come right out and tell Alice about Aisha, say that it was all part of this mixed-up summer, part of his homelessness, and let the chips fall where they may. But he couldn't bring himself to do it. He didn't want to hurt her, didn't want to add himself to her personal injury list. In a drunken moment, in a hurt, diminished moment in his life, he had taken custody of Alice du Pont's broken body and her breakable heart and he would do everything he could not to manhandle them.

And anyway only Aisha knew about Aisha, and she had her own reasons for keeping that under wraps, didn't she? And the whole Heiress's Dilemma thing? Well, there would have to be some new testimony introduced to change that. He would have to be revealed as some talented schemer thinking several moves ahead so that the original renunciation was a way of building credibility, of laying the groundwork for future maneuvers. And honestly, did anyone think that he, Sandy Alison—he who lacked (didn't everyone know it?) the killer instinct—did anyone see him as capable of that sort of strategy, that sort of chess playing? What new development could possibly make it appear as though he had the wits to manipulate the Heiress's Dilemma until—brilliant tactic, if he could only claim it!—until it became evidence in his favor?

In the meantime, there was Alice: funny, weird, electrocuted Alice! He still had to show up at the Casino every day, put in his time, but afterwards they went about the island like teenagers looking for places to make love. His place was too grotty, and Windermere was off-limits whenever Margo or Aisha—and now Tom—was around. (And motels were too Margo-ish, Alice said.) So it was off to the Norman Bird Sanctuary, to Rose Island, the grounds of St. George's (the darn mosquitoes!), and once like a return to Where It All Started out at the breakwater at midnight with the land and the lights behind them, an occasional car motoring past, and nothing but the black ocean in front of them and the black breeze blowing against their bare limbs. And how in these moments—really, he'd never seen anything like it—how she gave her body away! Gave it away as if it wasn't hers, this thing that had fought her her whole life, gave it away without reservation, as if in his arms her body could stop fighting, could stop trying to be something it wasn't but could just *be*—cerebral palsy and all: loved, possessed, thrilled.

One thing he did was, as a kind of apology, he texted her to be outside her house one night—two a.m., he said—and he had come by on the Indian (no need to sell it, after all), come by and swept her up, and with her holding on for dear life had brought her down to the Point, where he'd pulled out a pint of bourbon just as she'd done that awful night, and started walking her through the squirrely streets under the gaslights, calling her Watson and pointing stuff out, asking her out on the Elm Street Pier if she could hear the tolling of the Rose Island bell, dismantled in 1912, hey?

He didn't get everything right ("I believe, Sherlock, it's *that* house where the Vicomte de Noailles lived"), but he did his best, pointed out the street where all the Newport cabinetmakers had had their shops, the houses where the British officers had been billeted during the Revolution, the Creole witch's house, the house of the Quaker girl whose household account book was one of the Redwood Library's prized possessions. She played beautifully along, pretended to be Sandy Alison the local dolt. It was dark and cool and deathly quiet.

In the North Burial Grounds—after they had looked over the slaves' tombstones, read the Quaker inscriptions by moonlight—they lay down in the dewy grass and with a mourning dove moaning in a nearby tree did with each other—"I say! Holmes!"—what you were supposed to do when you were young, in the summer, in the playground of the rich.

She took his education in hand, said if he was going to join the land-holding class of Newport (she was always saying stuff like that, those first couple of weeks, as if she were daring him), if he was going to join the local nobility, then he would have to acquire at least the patina of noblesse oblige, that and some V-necked sweaters, she said.

She took him to the Coggeshall House and the Hunter House, to the King's Arms Tavern, where the lowlifes hung out during the Revolution. He had to survive quizzes on wainscot and carved shells, follow her point-ing finger through a slanting rain and name a gambrel roof, a hip roof, a fanlight. True or false: The whale oil chandeliers in the Touro Synagogue were financed from profits in the slave trade. True or false: The cowrie shells uncovered during the restoration of the Selwyn-Lyman House were of a type found not in New England but in Senegal. True or false: Sandifer was a dim bulb.

(She had taken to calling him Sandifer, having asked once whether Sandy was a nickname, was it short for something? Sanford? Sandifer? Sandcrab? Surely his parents hadn't been so *déclassé* as to name him just plain *Sandy*! Again, if he was going to join the moneyed class, he would have to have a highborn name. Sandstone? Sandpiper? Sandweasel?)

One of the places she took him for his education was a funeral home on Spring Street where Henry James had lived as a teenager. They had gone inside and when the funeral director approached them with his clasped funeral director's hands she had lit into him for having removed the mag-nificent stairway that had once led to the second floor. Did he have no sense of history? she asked the bewildered man. This was Henry *James*'s house, *William* James's house.

Back outside, she told him Henry James had had a sister named Alice, and that William James had married an Alice. Which made for *two* Alice Jameses in the same family.

"Which," she wound up, "is too many damn Alices."

She was, she said, a Manic-Depressive, jg. ("Junior Grade," she explained. "That's military talk, son.") Bipolar disorder nowadays, though she preferred the whiff of the antiquarian, the name Robert Lowell and Sylvia Plath and Anne Sexton knew their illness by. She had at various times over the last twelve years taken lithium, Stavzor, Depakote, alprazolam, Abilify (great name, eh, son?), and for the last eighteen months Symbyax. Sometimes she took her meds and sometimes she didn't, she said.

And indeed she still had moments when the Mad Heiress peeked out. They might be in the dark of the White Horse Tavern or leaning against a ferry railing or sitting on Da Silva's Terrace, sunlight on the bobbing masts, pennants flapping in the wind, and her spirits growing more and more elated until some point was passed and a kind of hysteria crept in. And then it would all collapse on itself—the giddiness, the fun, the blending of their moods—and she would start to watch him as if from a distance, as if she were looking out a back window at some trespasser on the edge of her territory, moving from tree to bush to gate. She would grow quiet, and her hair would fall about her face in that way she had, and the old, reckless, lacerating tone would emerge. She would throw her hair aside and make some cutting remark—What did he think he was doing? Amusing himself with the Plastics Princess? Did he think she didn't know?—as if she wanted him to hit back, to hurt her, as if the dissonance between what he professed her to be and what she knew herself to be was too much for her to bear up under.

He would try in these moments to keep steady, to reassure her, to talk her down off what she had once called the ledge of self-hatred. Or not even talk really, but just *be* there, big and male, Sandy Alison with his sun-bleached hair and the muscles in his forearms, those absurd quads emerging out of his shorts. Let the shrapnel hit him. It wouldn't hurt. It wouldn't do damage. Show her that he wasn't going away, that, hey, he was still there, until the second collapse came—the little volleys of viciousness spent, the fight in her drained away—and she would let him hold her, half crying, half laughing, kissing him, calling him her Clutch Cargo.

Winterbourne, Sandifer, Clutch Cargo: okay, he could be whoever she needed.

(Though sometimes when he was alone, back in his asphalt-shingled, cigarette-smelling, bathroom-down-the-hall boardinghouse, he found that the shrapnel *had* hit. *Was* he serious? Did he mean to go through with it? Margo as his sister-in-law? Aisha with her knowing looks? The world with *its* knowing looks? Was he just proving to himself that he had the killer instinct after all? Or had he—almost while he wasn't looking—actually fallen in love with the strange creature?)

~ 1896 ~

Franklin and Mrs. Newcombe had just come from the little crooked houses of the Point, where they had—with other members of the Ladies' Anti-Indigent League—distributed a wagonload of groceries to the poor, going from house to house with their smiles and their kind words. Franklin had never before walked about the Point and he was struck by how mean and close the houses were. In some earlier century they might have been charming, he supposed, filled with plain-dressed Quakers and Puritans forever sweeping their floors, but now they were given over to hordes of Irish children with their smutched faces. It was all Franklin could do to stand politely in the front room while the wagon driver and his boy carried boxes around to the kitchen.

Afterwards they had taken tea at Baylor's Coffee House, and then, when the children and their governess arrived, had walked down to the wharves, for there could be no trip to town without James wanting to see the ships and the railroad cars. Ellen had her parasol up, and Franklin his cane, and as they went there was a consciousness between them, Franklin thought, of how like a family they were. James led them onto Long Wharf and then alongside the railroad yard, only prevented by the governess from running to the roundhouse with its turntable, behind which was the chuffing stack of a waiting engine. Out past the roundhouse one of the New York steamers was docking, the wharf filled with hacks and carriages awaiting the disembarking passengers.

He had survived Mr. Ryckman. Whatever the man thought of him, whatever final interview had occurred between him and his daughter—Franklin liked to think that Ryckman had had to listen to Ellen enumerate Franklin's many fine qualities—he had not managed to persuade her to abandon the path she was on, or even to retreat. Indeed, if anything, she looked at Franklin now, spoke to him now, as if they had come through some trial together, as if her father's opinion of him had only served to strengthen her purpose. She was not, after all, a shrinking woman. She had her own money and her own station, which was now, frankly, above that of her father's. Perhaps the man cared only to deliver himself of an imprecation and, having done so, had withdrawn with his hands washed. If that indeed were the state of things, then was not the last impediment removed, and did not the way to Windermere truly lie before him?

He took in the woman strolling beside him. Strange and unexpected thing! For he found he rather liked her. She with her homely face, and her fierce love for her children, and her simple honesty. Just the day before, as if she had been laboring under some scruple, she had felt compelled to explain to him why she had undertaken the planting of the maze. It was a last gesture toward her late husband, she had said with a nervous glance at him. For the maze had had its genesis during their honeymoon in England. She and her husband had been so taken with Hampton Court that they had vowed they would re-create its maze on the Newport property that had been a wedding gift from her father. But oh! children and architects, and setting up house in New York, and then the work of building Windermere itself (there was the old Doubling Point cottage that had first to be pulled down) had delayed them. And then her dear husband had sickened! It was, she said—she meant the planting of the maze; she had turned to look wistfully at it, for they were strolling upon the lawn at Windermere—a living monument to him, *in memoriam*, she meant. She hoped he did not mind.

He had told her he found it charming, *charming*! And her loyalty to her late husband—how well it spoke of her!

Now, walking beside her along the wharf, he wondered: Did it make it better that he actually liked her? Or worse? Would it—the thing he did; the life that loomed—would it, after all, be more easily accomplished, more easily *endured* if the woman were unlikable—vain, foolish, inconsiderate, a receptacle for his contempt?

Not for the first time he entertained an idea: Was what he was doing—well, he wouldn't use the word "evil" with its antique reek and its cloven creatures—but all the same, would not the world consider what he was doing *immoral*? Not his marrying for money, of course—people did that every day—but the other thing, the one great, deep lie, the duplicity with which he cloaked himself and which she would find out about only when it was too late. For had he not masked his true self with polish just as he did his graying hair? All his charm and his doting asides, his taking her hand, the chaste kisses. She would soon enough learn—dear God, that first night!—that they were not the prelude she thought they were.

And was that evil? He supposed it was. The sheer amount of deception the thing entailed, the designing, the fabrication, the spinning of the web. And still he knew he would go through with it. He had never for a second wavered, was not wavering now. If the world had no place for him as he was, if it must call him the most vile names and force him into falseness and deception merely to exist, then did he not have the right to use that deception, that falseness, in the prosecution of his life—in short, to turn the rules of the game to his favor? And after all he was not planning on enslaving the poor woman. She would be quite free to live her life as she wished. She could continue with her reform movements, her gardening, her children. She could entertain, and visit, and drink her tea with milk as she did. And he would be there by her side when required, attentive, well-dressed, with always a charming smile for her and her guests. And who knew? He had heard that some women did not care for the bedroom, that the passions of their husbands were something they tolerated but did not encourage. He would hold on to that happy possibility.

"It's the *Puritan*," he heard beside him. They had come down past the chandlers' and the shipwrights' buildings and were now where they could see the steamer at its moorings. He had booked passage on the *Puritan*'s sister ship, the *Pilgrim*, for the following day.

"I won't be gone long," he said.

"But a week," she said with a pout she sometimes used and which did not suit her. "Does it need to be so long? The season's passing."

They stood and gazed softly at each other. Little Sarah was holding her mother's hand and asking could they not have an ice. Franklin let a thoughtful expression come over him, and then gazed away across the harbor waters down to the leadworks with its great octagonal shot tower.

"It's not just New York," he said finally. "I must go to Baltimore. There is a matter of some importance about which I must speak to my father."

He let it hang between them, yet another filament. It was quite bracing, the discovery that one was capable of such spinning.

✦ 1863 ✦

~I have been remembering something from childhood that might make a story, a story of Innocence and its benighted perception. I have had to consult Mother so as to know that what I remember was real and not some apparition of memory. For I had a playmate in our old Union Square days who was a colored boy named Davy. He and his mother were the servants of a Kentucky family who moved in next door to us and who spoke with the most outlandish accents, and who made sausages on their back porch. One day Davy and Aunt Silvie (for so was his mother known) simply vanished, and there was a great consternation over their vanishing, and only now do I realize, and Mother confirms, that they were slaves and that they had taken the opportunity of being in the North to run away.

But ten years later how it lives still! The charming lilt of Davy's voice, and the too big trousers he wore, and how little Alice asked him if his skin tasted like chocolate, and how he used to say "dog" as if it had two syllables.

Imagine if one could record every thought, every occurrence, every person, every object, all the atmosphere of one's consciousness—record everything one has ever thought or experienced and record it perfectly, in the fullness of its impression: the time of day, the feel of the breeze, the cat peering from under the porch, the rattle of carriage wheels on the cobbles! That one might make of one's life a picture in words, so many thousand—nay, millions!—of pages long and so have one's life preserved, its every instant varnished and immutable, like a work of art!

In the meantime I have begun my story of the Doctor's Dilemma. I keep to my room and hide the sheets when I finish. How difficult to extract an Eve from one's rib!

◇ ◇ ◇

~Dear queer Alice has set up a court in the garden. She says to me that I have studied the law, have I not, shall I not be the Prosecutor? Father is to be Judge, Mother the Plaintiff's attorney; for Jury we have the Temple sisters and William and Sarge and Colleen. The crime (we are evidently all accused of it) is *abus de faiblesse*.

William remarks it is a curious court in which the attorneys, judge, jury, are also the defendants.

Alice says the whole world is the defendant, that we are only the world's local representatives, and that we may now begin questioning her, for the *charmante jeune fille* is to be the sole witness.

~Father believes that in this dreadful war spirit will prevail over shot and ball, that the one side has a spiritual good at its core and so cannot fail of success. I cannot help but think of how in his stories Mr. Hawthorne has shown us just how evil may be the victor in a fallen world! Which makes me, once again, wonder at how little my mind and my mode of thought resemble Father's. We have the same name, and are bookish alike, and though the penetration of his intellect and his moral passion, and still more the verve of his speech, have been the schoolroom in which I have been educated, still I am at times as unlike to him as hawk to handsaw. How I find myself more like to sit under the shade of Chateaubriand, he who seems to suggest that there is no meaning resident in the world, but that we export meaning from within ourselves and so live in a world colored by the paintbox of our hearts and minds.

But Father would have us all be Swedenborgian Quakers awaiting an infusion of spiritual light. For him the self is the generator of delusion. He considers anything that has its birth in the individual self to be the offspring of evil, removed as it must be from universal truth. Even the physical world (though he seems enamored of it, does he not? the delight he takes in our garden and its bedewed spiderwebs) he says is but a pasteboard mask of a higher reality, a mere shadow of true spiritual substance.

Yet how his son loves the real world, the beautiful, sunlit, myriad-voiced real world! If it is shadow, then for me shadow *is* substance. For I would live in large measure by my eyes, to look and to evaluate and to understand, and not have truth delivered by means of some metaphysical corridor to things beyond. Give me the rich tint of Miss Taylor's hair, for that is all the experience of divinity poor Harry James needs! And though I would not disagree that action based upon the promptings of selfhood is the root of evil, yet I would differ with Father and the Swedenborgians in this: May we not combat such delusions by the moral engine that is our eyes? May we not look and apprehend and tell honestly what we see and so, in time, rid ourselves of delusion and gain clear sight? And there is this: Is not the world in all its rich progress a paradise of interest? Who would willingly live in a world where the peaches hang year-round in perfect ripeness upon their perfect boughs? It is in the gradations of behavior, in the shades of our motivations, in their inversions and variations, in the slow ripening and the quicker rotting, where lie education and insight, and a kind of artistic delight.

~Miss Taylor has been spending her mornings sitting for her portrait at Mr. Hunt's. She is doing so upon my recommendation to her mother, for I have told them of my sorry apprenticeship in his studio, and of how much I admire Hunt's skill in capturing not just the likeness but something of the inner atmosphere of his subjects. This morning, to occupy myself during this dreadful wait for news of Wilky, I visited the studio and afterwards walked Miss Taylor back to her hotel. Of the remarkable revelations of that walk I will tell in due course.

But how strange it was to be back in Hunt's atelier! For over the years his studio has taken on for me something of the coloring of a sacred place. The canvases strewn about, the paints in their pots, the smells, this or that decorative *accessoire* cast aside or awaiting its place. How I once swooned over it all! What I had seen hanging on Parisian walls, and in Geneva and London, *this* was its source! That first year I hung about the studio so much Hunt took to calling me the Mooncalf. Yet how disappointing were my own attempts at drawing, how inferior to William's, how Hunt's attempts at encouragement fell limply onto the floor between us, until that last day when Gus Barker posed (dear Gus! dead!) and I simply could not create on paper the beautiful life I beheld before me. So has the studio become for me a place of initiation and of rejection (and so, of *awareness*; therein lies its sacredness!), and to be there again, with Miss Taylor (who was most beauteously arrayed for her portrait in a voluminous rose-colored gown), with this notebook the beginning of my own studio: ah, in those first few moments how disconcerted was I! I could scarcely attend to the pleasure of being once again in Miss Taylor's presence.

Hunt of course must take it upon himself to play the devil. For when I had seated myself he directed at me a string of questions regarding Miss Taylor's face and figure. How did I think her beauty might best be caught? he wondered. Did I think he had it right? How was the light upon her cheekbone? And what would I say were the qualities of her beauty, he meant (he said) the moral qualities of her face and her dress, for he had heard from La Farge that I was setting out to be a writer (indeed he had read my theater review in the *Daily Traveler*), and therefore he wondered: what qualities of thought and character would I ascribe to her physical attributes? In short, how might a young belletrist paint his subject in words?

It was Miss Taylor herself who came to my rescue (for I was blushing and stammering some answer) by saying surely Mr. Hunt did not believe that a person's outward self was a representation of her inner life. Did all beautiful people possess beautiful spirits, and the homely ugly ones? Indeed why was it, she wondered, that painters were forever painting heroes and heroines as if they were gods and goddesses? Napoleon was, she believed, a short little man, was he not? Might not Joan of Arc or Cleopatra been squint-eyed? For herself, she said with a glance at me, she hoped she would be blessed with family and friends who did not mistake the fragrance for the essence, the shadow for its substance. If she was beautiful as Mr. Hunt seemed to think, and she did not for a moment believe him, then she would renounce her beauty if it meant her true self would be opaque to the world's lazy gaze. She had to confess she had not thought Mr. Hunt such a shallow soul.

The shallow soul was laughing the whole while. It was all true! he said whilst continuing to paint and looking up from time to time at his beautiful subject, but it was not just painters who so belied the world.

"For Harry," he said, "did not your father's great friend write that Nature always wears the colors of the spirit? What is that sentiment but a way of saying that the natural world is the physical emblem of spiritual qualities? Don't blame us poor painters, Miss Taylor, if great philosophers also mistake the rind for the core. And you *are* beautiful. Is she not, Harry?"

I said she was, for we had slipped into a badinage that might serve as a *camouflage* for such an admission. But I wondered at Hunt that he, a forty-year-old man of the world, might speak so to a young lady. Indeed, much of what he said, though it was addressed to me, he seemed rather to say to her *through* me.

A short while after this flirtatious exchange, Miss Taylor wondered whether Mr. Hunt might not emancipate a poor slave of a sitter so that she might have an escort back to her hotel. She felt like such a fool walking in an evening dress through the noontime streets, she said. At least if Mr. James accompanied her, he might divert some of the public's ridicule. Hunt smiled and bowed and said he would not stand in the way of young love.

Outside we walked in silence for several streets, during which time I could feel Miss Taylor gathering herself beside me, as if she had some subject she meant to embark upon. I did not speak, but instead waited for her. She had on the same pheasant hat she'd worn the night of the Athenaeum lecture.

"Your Mr. Hunt tried to kiss me the other day," she said finally. She turned her face to me to see how I "took" this.

"The blackguard," I said, as if I were a character in a dime novel.

"Or rather, he *did* kiss me," she said, with something like a look of contrition, though whether at her mischaracterization or the kiss itself I couldn't tell. "I had never been kissed before," she went on. "I allowed it as an experiment."

I wondered at her, for she seemed to be saying these things with nothing like indignation.

"Have you ever kissed a young lady, Mr. James?" she asked when I did not respond.

"I have not."

"Oh," she said and she laughed, "don't let your collar get all stiff! You have quite a way of getting stiff, you know."

I inclined my head, in acknowledgment, in acceptance, but I did not speak. We walked for a time in silence. The Jewish cemetery lay just ahead of us.

"He's quite a talker, your Mr. Hunt," she took up when a minute or two had passed. And then she raised her voice, for a drayman's cart was passing noisily alongside us: "He quite lay siege to my maidenhood."

"Miss Taylor!"

"He attempted familiarities with me. I believe that's how the novelists have it."

"Have you told your mother any of this?"

She merely looked at me with a broad amusement, and yet there was something sharp, precipitous, in her look.

"Shall we go in?" she asked, for we had come to the portal that led into the cemetery. I balked, shook my head no.

"My father will be coming from Waterbury soon," she said against my demurral. "I think you and I will not be seeing much more of one another. Indeed this may be our last time together." She reached out and swung the gate back. "And I have more to say to you."

I felt a dim apprehension—although over what, I wasn't sure—but all the same followed her in. We walked in a pantomime of that first night to the deepest part of the graveyard where we had spoken so intimately. Someone had recently scythed the grass. It lay in yellowing drifts upon the ground. Miss Taylor leaned against one of the gravestones, the bright rose of her brocade striking against the muted greens of the cemetery. She took off her hat and stroked one of its long feathers thoughtfully.

"Do you remember that day we spoke of marriage?" she said after a time. "Coming back from the breakwater, that marvelous day?"

"I do," I said.

"What I didn't say that day, and what I have been thinking since, is that I should like to be saved in marriage, and in turn, to save someone."

"Save?" I repeated.

"Yes. Do you not think that we all need to be saved?"

"Saved from what?" I hazarded.

"From—" and she seemed a moment to wonder at my not understanding her, and then indicated the gravestones around us, and then the world itself—"from emptiness," she said. "From isolation and sterility, from the slavery of the conventional, from that which is not genuine, and from loneliness."

I gazed intently at her, but kept my silence.

"There is a fineness about you, Mr. James," she went on. "A fineness of intellect and character. And a seriousness of purpose, and a responsiveness to the world, and for all your doubting of yourself, an ambition that I admire." She paused a moment to let me take her words in, and then resumed with something of her old satiric tone. "And though you are short, and you stammer, and your hair already shows signs of your being as bald as your father—really you are altogether quite ridiculous!—still I find that it is you—" and here she peered intently at me and her mockery fell from her—"you above any other whose esteem I would wish to have."

With a sensation of something like the earth giving way under me, I assured her that she did have my esteem.

"Ah! That is the very ridiculousness of which I complain!" she said, and then, pushing off the gravestone and coming toward me with the full force of her beauty: "I'm asking you to marry me, Harry."

I could only stand as I was, stricken, my throat swelling.

"It will be our first step away from convention, the wife proposing to the husband." And she smiled and then, shocking to me, reached out and touched my cheek. "Your spirit is alive, Harry. Do you not wish your flesh to be as well?"

I could feel a deep flush overspreading my face.

"For *that* is how I can save you!"

And she peered at me with an intensity I do not believe I have ever seen in a woman. She searched my face for some sign, for something to read.

"Will you not hold me?" she asked. "Will you not kiss me?"

One of my legs was trembling inside my trousers, and I grew dizzy so I had to steady myself against a gravestone.

"Will you not say yes? Not just to me, but to life! To *life*, Harry!"

At which I cast my eyes down so that I must have looked like a shamed child. I wanted to speak, to answer her, to defend myself, but my mind was a tangle of guilt and terror and mortification, and I could not. Even now, writing, I have not the words. After a minute she let her hand drop, and I felt her pull back from me. Out on the street a carriage rolled past, the horses' hooves pounding the earth.

"Ah! I see!" she said when at last I lifted my eyes to her. Onto her face there pitched a smile more bitter than mocking: "It is not a light comedy, but a tragedy in which you have cast me!" And then, drawing herself up, she added pointedly: "In which you have cast *yourself*!"

And she turned from me and began making her way out of the cemetery. I had not the power to follow her, nor the will. On the grass amongst the gravestones—like a stage property—lay her pheasant hat.

☞ 1778 ☜

June 15

I have not written for these several Weeks for I have not been myself. What Wildness have I been possessed by! I have been as Lord Kittredge's tiger, pacing from one end of the Cage of this damned city to the other, neglecting my Duties, or falsifying them so that I might go up the Neck, through the Sentries and the Fortifications to test how this country held me, and how I might break through. Though what I would break through to I do not know: what Fit, what Voyage into Ruin? For I have allowed myself to dream of that which I taunted the Jew with, that I might capture the Jewess, convert her, marry her, bring her as mine and Damn the world! I have been so afire with this Conception and yet with its Impossibility that I thought I must break in twain. So Estranged am I from the self I know to be me, and haunted by this new self who knows not how the Pieces move, and tries to jump his Bishop as if it were a Knight, who tries to add to the board Squares that do not exist, who does not seem to know that it is he who is Checkmated, however he might like to Strut & Insult. Yet when I feel myself coming out of the Fever, when I talk to Major Ballard as if he might heed Sense & Sanity, yet hard upon comes the thought of the Jewess and her dark Eyes and the Rustle of her skirts and the soft mass of her hair with its Jewels of Light, and then am I undone, and consumed by the idea of going to her, of fleeing with her, and with Fancies of how we might to Ireland or Italy or the coast of Bohemia, damn me!

But I am come back to myself. The Fever is broke. If the Jew has beaten me, yet is his Victory like that of Pyrrhus at Asculum, for I have seeded in him Doubts that will eat at the Foundation of his house. Still and yet, I do not like to lose. Nor will I allow myself to acquire a habit of it. Aye, for there is another who has Betrayed me, a Serpent in my Bosom who has shown himself a Traitor and a false friend. It is the thought of Smithson and the Retribution that must be mine, that has helped restore me, brought me back from the Wilderness of my Loss & Madness. I must Retire into myself and think on this, and no more of the Fury & the Rage, but think on it with that Coldness & Precision I know to be mine. And then I must act.

June 18

Played Chess today. Am in the process of devising new moves, new ways to punish Incursions into my Territory. I find, after all, there are Squares off the board. Dark places onto which to move my Pieces.

I have been down to the Taverns along the Waterside, have met up with some who must be Reckoned amongst the most unusual of His Majesty's subjects. I went dressed as my Spies do, in the coarse linen Twill of the Colonials and for a lark affected their Speech. I went to stir the Dregs to see if I might learn something even here within our Fortifications. The War has been hard on these fellows, for their livelihoods are disappeared, the Distilleries & Ropewalks & the Shipping, so that they know not which way to turn, and lurk about the Wharves like Ghouls, ill-clad & unshaven. They would go to sea if they could, but with the presence of the Fleet and the closing of the Harbour, the city's Commerce is curtailed. I did what I could, bought those I spoke with some Rum, tried to cheer them with some Hope of the future, all the while reflecting on what the sutler Da Silva said to me once. What would these men not do for a Purse with some weight to it?

Came in a Wherry this Evening with six or seven Colonials. They come and they go in this War and we do not know who is a Combatant and who is not. It is not a war of Rank & Insignia, not a war of Equals. Yet a Gentleman might find a way to turn his language and his looks to his Purpose, to make, as it were, a Disguise of the Ordinary.

June 20
My Appointment does not come.

June 24
Tomorrow Smithson and I steal away to do some shooting out on Doubling Point. I affected a Bonhomie and painted for him the Pleasures we might have, how good it would be to be off and away and pretend we are back in Dartmoor. Carefree young friends, the greenery of Summer all about, Woodcock & Partridge, and afterwards some sherry and a girl in the Village.

⊰ 1692 ⊱

7th Day

It is six weeks and Ashes and Dorcas and I are now back home. And I find I must needs take up my Journal pages again, for a most dreadful thing has happen'd, so dreadful and wrong and black in my thoughts that I cannot tell anyone of it. I cannot even write of it here, and yet must write of it, if only Sideways that I may deliver myself of it.

Is it not enough that Mother and Father are taken from me, but that my great Protector and friend must be proved—ah! I cannot write it!

The Lord has treated me as Job. I know not why. He afflicts and chastens me but I can find naught in my heart nor in my mind to understand why. Job's faith did not waver. But I am not Job. I search myself for the stains that have occasioned the rod of the Lord, but I can find none. Mayhap it is this very Blindnesse, this Failing to see the inky blots set upon me for which I am punished. If that is so, then I pray for the Light by which I may see.

But Jane Beecher! Can there be some so blasted with Iniquity and Godlessness, yet who go about in a Disguise of Goodness and Strength through which the coiled Snake must spring forth? And yet so sorrowfully! For afterwards what Despair was upon her! How moved and troubl'd and sorrowful was she, that she could not stop talking to me, begging of me, even as I would not listen! How her heart aches and into what Despair is she thrown! With what Turmoil and Horror of herself!

I cannot, ever! speak to her again. I would not even let her help me carry our things back from her house, would not let her touch them, but must do it alone with Ashes.

We did hear of such things, Martha and Hannah and me, but we understood not. There was that talk of things out at the Stoughton farm, but we understood not.

4th Day

Yesterday morning I tramp'd through the mud over to Ruth Dodson's to borrow again some of the old books that I might remove my Thoughts, and I have been reading in Sandys's *Metamorphoses*. And also I have read again of the Choice of Heracles and the story of Theseus and the Minotaur. Oh! for an Ariadne who might lead me out of this Labyrinth!

6th Day

I do not eat and I turn my hand to my work with no joy. At night I lift Dorcas out of her trundle-bed and carry her to my bed that I may have some-one beside me.

I have seen Spearmint at Meeting and about the town, but cannot meet his eye.

I am gone like the Shadow when it declineth.

4th Day

This morning, pricked by the thaw, I went out of doors that the Spring-like feel of the Air might lighten my Spirit. I took Dorcas to visit Mother's grave, for it has been a long time, and I felt as tho' we had abandon'd her. When we came back to the house I had still in me the urge to walk, to be about, to be away from home and from our neighbor, so I gave over Dorcas to Ashes and set off by myself, without my pattens, wearing instead the shoes I had ruin'd that day after visiting Spearmint.

I went north up the coast. I ought to have been cheer'd by the weather and the feel of the world, for the melt ran in little Rivulets and the Sun sparkl'd off the wet, and there was about the air the sound of Birdsong and of life returning, but it seem'd I alone was still in Winter. The long brown grass lay matted from the winter's snowfall, and there was here and there in the Shadows a patch of blue snow. The Robins were about, and a family of Waxwings fluttering about a mulberry bush. I look'd upon these things as if I had been divided into two people. There was the old Prudy who noted them and did wish them well, and felt herself one of them, and all of us part of the glorious sailing Ship of God's natural world. And at the same time there was the new Prudy who saw them as through a Glass darkly, where the blue sky was gray'd, and the bird breasts were dun, and the patches of Snow but dirty rags upon the Ground, and the birdsong and the tinkle of the melt muted and as if heard from underwater.

I walk'd a good ways northward and only stopp'd when I espied a family down among the rocks (for it was low tide) who appear'd to be gathering Mussels. I stopped then and retreated a few rods until I was out of sight. I sat upon a Bluff that overlook'd the water, for I did not yet feel right enough to return home. I sat but could not think, and only star'd down at the gray water. I do not want to write too strongly what I felt then, for I think it was but the swelling of a Mood, but I did feel the strongest allurement of that water, of its depth and its Motion. Goodwife Pemberton it is said did purposely throw herself into the Bay two winters ago, she who had been for years given to Fits, and spells where she could not work, and yet who had a Husband and children. I was never about to do so, yet what strange dreamlike Power had that water, as if it knew my name, was my old friend, and call'd to me to come.

When I was able again to think, this is the thought I had: that I have been remov'd from out of life. It is as Mother once did with a cup that had gotten a bad chip, which she had taken off the table board and put up high and in the rear of the cupboard. It was not so broken as to be thrown out altogether, yet neither was it any longer good for use.

5th Day

In my Despondency the other day (a Sadness and a Darknesse that lingers still) I did meditate some on this matter of Spearmint and Ashes. I have prayed for Guidance in this, to be shown the right and good thing to do. Yet the more I pray and the more I think on it (and not just now but these months past), the more I feel Ashes's very life a reproach to mine own, as tho' she were a finger pointing at me in Accusation! For having taken her from her mother and father, do we not now keep her from yet another she loves? Aye, I have a worldly, civil right to do so, but what natural right have I?

If I must be remov'd from life, if I may not be happy, might I not at least give another Happiness?

But this proposal of Spearmint's, how ill it sits the more I think on it. To sell yourself back into Bondage! Is there no other way? What is it, after all, but a Debt? Ashes owes my family a certain sum of money. Might it not be paid as any other debt, without recourse to Articles of Indenture?

Were she a man I might find her work outside our house, caulking at the Shipyard as do other Africans who then turn their Wages over to their Masters. Still, might that not serve as a Type of an Agreement? Might Ashes work in the household and workshop of Charles Spearmint and pay Dorcas and me some portion of her wages over the seven years until the debt is paid off? These wages would be a type of smiling Duplicity between us, for she would be Spearmint's Wife and not earning any such. But the money would come to Dorcas and me all the same. There would be no Signatures, but rather a handshake between us.

I would be burdened with all the work in our household, and the raising of Dorcas. But what of it? If Jane Beecher can do it, can not I? Tho' it be untimely, am I not become a woman?

6th Day
If there is no one to take me down from the Cupboard, then I must take myself. But how? I must do, but what?

~ 2011 ~

He began helping Alice with her CP exercises. This had been one of Aisha's jobs, he knew, and before Aisha, her mother's. She would lie on a roll-up mat in her bedroom and close her eyes and concentrate while Sandy flexed her leg, stretched her wrist forward and back, provided resistance for this or that muscle. He would touch her as gently as he could, trying his best to do a good job, keep a buoyant manner even though he knew he was hurting her. There was something about it, something about the touching and the trust and the pain and the vulnerability of it all, that was more intimate than the other intimacy.

She showed him what she called her "retard bicycle," which was this adult tricycle that was supposed to be part of her exercise program back when she was a teenager. She'd ridden it exactly once, she said, and it had sat in the carriage house ever since. Sandy had wheeled it out into the daylight, and over her protests—it was just too uncool, she said, it was a fat lady's bike—hosed it down and set it in the sun to dry. And then he went back into the carriage house and got out Tom's old racer, oiled the chains and derailleurs: hey?

At first she'd only ride up and down the driveway, but in time he coaxed her out onto the sidewalk along Bellevue, and then down Coggeshall. She had a hitching way of pedaling—good leg, bad leg—and went so slowly Sandy had to keep circling back to her. All the same they made it down to the Forty Steps once, once to the Redwood Library, and then, for her chef d'oeuvre, the three miles out to the Brenton Point breakwater, where they had a picnic on the lawn with the ocean in the distance, the salt smell of the air and the screaming gulls, and a dozen colorful kites overhead like fireworks.

On their way back he told her that he loved her. It had just come out of him, unbidden, unplanned. He had been circling back to her on his bike, swooping around behind her tricycle, and there they were, the astonishing words. He circled back again, and then again, and each time he said it—"I love you!"—she had this little smile on her face like "Well, of course you do!" After the third time he took off down Bellevue as fast as he could go, feeling the burn in his muscles, the wind in his face—amazed at himself, and stupidly happy, and stunned all at once.

It was a few days afterwards that something happened, or rather, something was *revealed*. Something Sandy wasn't quite sure how to take. They had gone—the three of them, Aisha too—to Cardines Field for a baseball game, sitting in the old wooden grandstand under the lights with the sun going down, and the bush-league loudspeaker, and the moths, and the swallows dive-bombing the outfield, and the players' girlfriends down along the first row. Sometime around the fifth inning Sandy went to the men's room and when he came out Aisha was there. She made it look like she was coming out of the bathroom herself, but she wasn't. She stood before him in that pose former lovers have: arms folded across the chest, head cocked in a question, body there but no longer available. "I see you're developing a killer instinct after all," she said, and she gave him this sardonic, meaningful smile.

"Whatever you think it is," he found himself answering, "it isn't."

"Good" was all she said.

"I love her."

"Good," she said again. "That will make things easier." And before he could respond she turned and began walking toward the exit. "Enjoy yourself," she called over her shoulder.

But that wasn't the thing that happened, the thing that was revealed. That was back in the grandstand after another inning or two. He and Alice had barely spoken, just a kind of summery contentment between them, the sky over the third-base line darkening to purple. Aisha had left her sweater for Alice and Alice put it on now against the chill, tried to pull the cuffs down, made a wry face at Sandy over its being too small for her.

"She's such a shrimp," she said and, when Sandy merely smiled in response, cocked her head a little as if debating something with herself, and then added: "She's my heir, you know."

He allowed himself a little quizzical look, but inside he felt a stirring, as though something that had been vague and uncertain before, something he had only barely been aware of, was on the verge of announcing itself.

"What?" he said.

She turned back to the field, watched a batter strike out, and then started in on how she had a list of things she had to do at least once every summer. Every summer she had to tell the docents at Touro Synagogue they were immoral for never mentioning the slave trade, and she had to go to the Historical Society to see the cowrie shells that had been found in the Selwyn-Lyman House, and have dinner with the cherubs in Da Silva's sitting room, and sit quietly in the Quaker Meetinghouse, and go into Henry James's Funeral Home, and out at the Burial Ground say a prayer over the slave gravestones. And every summer she had to thank Aisha for saving her life.

"Those are the coordinates of my being," she said. "You might want to know them."

Still he kept a guarded smile. He was trying to figure out his own reaction. Why so struck? Why did he feel as if some suspicion had been confirmed?

"Does she know that?" he asked finally.

"Does she know about the coordinates of my being?"

"Does she know she's your heir?"

She kept looking straight ahead, watching the game, enjoying the drama. "Yes," she said finally.

"You told her?"

"Yes."

"Does Margo know?"

At that, she turned to him, looked him over. "No," she said. "Nor Tom." And then, as if she meant to lay out the ground between them: "I've got bequests for a lot of things. The Redwood Library, the Whitehorne Museum, Vassar, the Restoration Foundation. But as long as I'm single and childless, the house, and a trust to keep it up—that goes to Aisha."

He pursed his lips, nodded. Was he being imprudent? Was he open to misapprehension?

"She saved my life," he heard her say again. "Twice. At college and then that night. Me and Isolde and our Liebestod."

At which he had enough sense to take her hand, hold it in his lap, and when the seventh-inning stretch came put his arm around her while the crowd sang "Take Me Out to the Ballgame."

But afterwards—after he'd brought Alice home, kissed her under the porte cochere—he couldn't escape the suspicion that he had caught Aisha out, that a curtain had been pulled aside and he'd seen something he hadn't been meant to see. It had left him with an impression, something that made him so restless that when he got back to the asphalt-shingled nightmare he couldn't settle and so had headed off down Thames Street to where the people were.

Okay, Aisha was Alice's heir, but so what? How was that anything more than just another extravagance of Alice's, another grand gesture? Yes, Aisha had seen fit to withhold the information from him, but what was she supposed to say? Hey, I'm in line to inherit a ten-million-dollar house? It was no business of his. Bad form, really, if she had let him know. Evil to him who thinks evil, Sandifer.

And yet, and yet. He remembered something Aisha had told him about that night, the night of the suicide attempt. This was when she was telling him the whole story, how she'd heard the music, come out of her room, found Alice. Tom had been in New York, she said, but Margo had been home. And here was the thing, she had said with a penetrating look: Tom and Margo's bedroom was closer to the alcove, and yet it had been she, Aisha, on the other side of the house, who had awoken and wondered what the heck? and had gone out, down the hall, and around the corner and found Alice on the wicker couch, blood everywhere. Was Margo *that* heavy a sleeper? she'd asked Sandy, and she let the implication hang in the air between them.

And now, as long as he was thinking evil, he might turn that implication back on Aisha. That night—morning, really—after the Champions Ball when Alice had come to her and told her what had happened in the cemetery, why had she up and left for Brooklyn a couple of hours later? Knowing what she knew about Alice, did she think it was safe to leave her alone? No worry of an encore performance of *Tristan*?

Single and childless, Alice had said. And he understood suddenly something that had happened a couple of days ago. They had gone out to Bailey's Beach—the three of them plus Margo, Aisha, Tom, and a couple of Tom's clients—had spent the afternoon there, and afterwards walked back to Windermere along the Cliff Walk. Tom had been sort of needling Sandy the whole afternoon. Didn't Sandy really belong on Reject's Beach? he'd asked with his smile, Reject's being the public beach adjacent to exclusive Bailey's. When there was more of the same up on the Cliff Walk—this time Tom telling his clients the story of the heiress Doris Duke running the car over her upstart chauffeur, name of Sandy, he believed—Alice had stopped walking, turned a withering look on her brother, and then, in front of everybody, had asked Sandy did he have a condom? Margo had rolled her eyes, said something about Alice being off her medication, eh?

"I believe the well-appointed gentleman always has a condom about his person," Alice had said. "Wallet?"

It was one of her drama queen moments. There was nothing for it but to play along. So Sandy had fished out a condom and Alice had taken it with her good hand and frisbeed it out over the cliff down toward the water, as if to say to them all: Get it?

He hadn't gotten it, but now he saw what she had meant. She was staking a claim. A claim to him, to Windermere, to the future, to this new world of Mr. and Mrs. Sandy Alison and their twenty kids. And what did Tom and Margo think of that? And Aisha, in line for Windermere and its trust fund if Alice remained single and childless—what did *she* think of that?

III

The Maze at Windermere

June 25

I have just returned from the Synagoge where I have delivered the body of Lieu^t Smithson. I have made my report to Genl Waring and am back in my Quarters now but in too Antic a state to sleep, and so will recount what I told to Genl Waring, so that I may Marvel at myself.

We had set off this morning as we had planned and I affected a goodly Pleasure at our being away from the War, if but for a day, that we might step out of the tight Garment of our Posting. Smithson fell in with my Mood and agreed that the lack of Action and the close Quarters of this little seaport town had worn on us all. We walked down the Peninsula until we gained the rough Meadows that lay south of the city and there we divided so that we might serve as each other's Beater. From time to time we would halloo that we might not stray from one another. I took note of where the Cliff gave way and where I might later report having seen a Skiff or Cockboat or some such that was pulled up onto the Shore, but which at the time (I would tell Genl Waring) I did not think of any import. We went on, shooting, giving a berth to the occasional Farmhouse, and all the while I was in a kind of Fever of Anticipation.

Toward the early Afternoon I heard a distant shout and then a Piece discharged that I understood at once was not Smithson's. I waited a minute or two and then clambered through the Brush & low Greenery until I came upon Smithson lying wounded in a marshy swale. He had his eyes upon me, and his mouth worked tho' it gave no sound. I pretended to give chase toward where I heard a receding movement, acting my Part even unto the discharge of my Piece tho' I had only dust-shot. I waited then some several more Minutes, that the Life might run out of Smithson, for I did not Wish any more of the look of his eyes.

When I returned to him he was lifeless.

Too unkind! I told the General, to leave Smithson alone in that marshy land! Yet to carry a Corpse for any distance, even such a one as dear Smithson (whom we did lovingly call the Dwarf, I said with a sad smile), is no Task for any but the strongest man. And so I marked where Smithson lay by breaking the top of a tall Sapling so the lighter green of its upturned leaves would be as a Pennant, and set out toward where we had last passed a Farmhouse. After an hour or so, and having to Circle back on myself, I came upon one such, a sorry white-washed, low-roofed Hovel with chickens and dirty children about the Dooryard. I approached and was met by a Man, and behind him his Wife. I told them as briefly as I might what had transpired, and asked them did they have a Horse & Wagon with which I might carry my dead Friend back. They said they had no horse, but that they had a Mule. I gave the man a guinea, and told him where he might collect his Mule the following day.

When I was finished my tale, Gen¹ Waring asked did I think it worth the while to dispatch a Party that we might flush out these Rebels, these cowardly Murderers, he said. But I told him that I was of the opinion that they were long gone, that the Skiff I noted was surely theirs and that it betokened the Impermanence of their Presence, and having worked their Mischief they had no Doubt fled. He regretfully agreed, and touching my shoulder in a fatherly fashion said he was sorry for my Ordeal, and that I had done all I could. And that the Rebels were making Bold, and that he supposed there was an end to any such Excursions for his Officers. I requested that when Gen¹ Pigot wrote to Lieuᵗ Smithson's parents, that I be allowed to include a Missive of my own, attesting to their son's Valor and my Friendship and the apt Execution of his Duty.

And now I am returned to my garret upon the Point. And there is no Smithson, and there will never be again. He is a taken Piece, and has been removed from the Board.

~These last several days after my extraordinary interview with Miss Taylor in the Hebrew cemetery, I have kept to myself, indeed kept to my small room, so mortified, chagrined, lost am I! I am forever beginning a letter to Miss Taylor in which I try to explain myself, and when it proves a cul-de-sac, begin another in which I beg her forgiveness and tell her that I would, indeed, be honored to be her husband. And then I stand up and pace about the room, pick up Chateaubriand, put him down, pick up Mrs. Eliot, then my law book, then reread these miserable pages that seem now so fraught with misapprehension, culpability, blindness.

There is one thing I have fastened upon, for I am struck by what I wrote when I visited Wilky at Camp Meigs, the portrait I painted of the sunburned young men bathing in each other's attention, as if they had submerged their individual selves in a pool of manhood. How beautiful I thought them! And yet, though I might admire and yearn, feel the exclusion of my observing self from their camaraderie and ease, yet I would not be *of* them. And not just because I am no soldier, but because *I would not lose myself*, would above all keep the sovereignty of my mind, even if in order to do so I must doom my body to being unloved, untouched. Is that not a horrible thing to realize?

How the future opens before me with all its appalling infinitude! For this proposal of Miss Taylor's comes to me with the certitude that if I do not accept her, if I do not act now and stride down the well-trodden avenue onto which face the homes of the happy, that I sentence myself to being forever alone, forever *removed*, taking notes *upon* life but never *living* it. And yet what have I begun to understand this summer if not that I cannot engage myself with the ordinary scrum of life? It is not just that I do not feel what other men feel—that is a texture of my make-up about which I can think no further—but that the artist's life upon which I have embarked requires the very withdrawal which so terrifies me. And yet if I am to do what I have set out to do, become what I have set out to become, do I not need to be above the roil of the world, to be un-implicated as it were, watching from outside the chalk lines that I may take the game I observe— life!—and shape it into a thing whose beauty and meaning are *mine*?

But to do so, to live so, to remove oneself so! Is it not a kind of monastic cell to which I doom myself?

2nd Day

I am in a most downcast and hopeless State. For who did the Lord put in my way today but John Pettibone. All Winter I had seen him each first day at Meeting, and sometimes down a cross-street or along the wharves, tho' we never talk'd or even dared look at one another. But today as I was coming out of Samuel Judah's shop where I had just purchas'd some Thread to do a bit of work Esther Pennington has charitably given me, I did nearly run straight into him. We each of us gave a start. He has grown the way boys do. His nose is bigger, like his Father's, and he is near a half-foot taller than me. He did seem most discompos'd to see me and was at a loss for what to say. Perhaps I was no better, but I did manage to say hello and to ask after his family. Gone, it seems, is the free teasing of our Childhood. He would not look at me, almost rudely I thought, and hasten'd to say something of how he was about an Errand and must be gone. He turn'd his back to me and went into the Shop.

That was some time ago and I have been most downcast since. The wild thoughts I have had! And the Despising of myself that I used to spy on him from Mother's window, and that I did once think, that I did once hold some hope that he might be a path out of the Wildernesse I am in. All my foolish, girlish hopes! And I thought how he had not come to me all Fall and all Winter, never even to offer his Sympathy, and I came to see with a new and sudden clearness, and said to myself that he is embarrass'd at our old childish Friendship and sees that it can be no more without becoming the other, which he does not want. He does not want it! I said to myself aloud, over and over, until I realiz'd Ashes must hear me. And then instead I wrote it over and over, which I have now cross'd out, and broken my

Quill doing so. And now I don't know what to write. I have sat here these five minutes recutting my Quill, but there is nothing to write.

And then the thing that had always been there, the thing Sandy had been obscurely waiting for, half expecting, happened. Or rather *seemed* to happen, for that was part of it: he didn't know for sure.

He and Alice had spent the last week of August on final preparations for Champagne at Windermere, which would come off the Saturday of Labor Day weekend. There was the readying of the grounds to be overseen, arrangements with the company that would provide security, the rental tent erected, phone calls to be sure that the plates and champagne flutes were lined up, and finally the first-floor rooms—which would be open to the public—cleared of everything personal. Sandy did what he could, mostly moral support while Alice bustled and phoned and directed the Salve Regina girls and a handful of volunteers from the library. Tom was back in New York. Margo seemed always to be smoking a cigar on the veranda. Afterwards, after it happened, Sandy would think back to those days—how busy Alice had been, how *abilified*, and yet wired, anxious, a little wild-eyed, not sleeping. Had it all been a kind of manic buildup? Should he have seen what was coming?

How it started was simple enough. Alice didn't answer his text. He didn't think much of it at first. They were in the habit of texting stupid stuff to each other, and maybe she was too busy, maybe she was lining this or that up, didn't have her phone with her. So the first day went by and it was no big deal. But then an e-mail went unanswered, and when he called her cell he got shunted to her message box. He backed off a bit, let another day go by. One of the things he'd learned in relationships was to slice the backhand when your testosterone was telling you to rip it crosscourt. At the Casino he looked quizzingly at Margo on the other side of the net, but there was nothing forthcoming from that quarter. He let another day pass, checked his phone every half hour, but there was nothing.

Right from the start he had been a little chary of seeing her too often. Maybe it was just an Heiress's Dilemma tactic, but he had decided early on to let the thing develop at Alice's pace. He was scrupulous about never just showing up at the house, tried his best to keep a low profile around Margo and Aisha, not to mention Tom. It wasn't always easy to do. Alice seemed to want to flaunt him, was always coming over to the Casino, calling him, texting him, taking his arm when the others were around, teasing him into taking her somewhere, throwing condoms into the ocean.

And now this. A sudden and absolute silence. Something had happened, but what?

Well, he would go out to the house. If she'd found out about him and Aisha, okay, so be it, but he couldn't just wait. And maybe that wasn't it. Maybe she really was a Mad Heiress. But he would find her, talk to her, learn what had happened—or at least get a *sense* of what had happened— and then back off if that was what she wanted. If it was all over—if there were to be no V-neck sweaters in his future—then fine. Well, not fine—he would miss her, he knew, he could feel already the beginning of a hole in his life where she used to be—but he would have to live with that. He would go back to his old life, or his *new* old life, but first he needed to know.

It was one of the Salve Regina girls—not the one who'd told him about the maze that day, the homely one, but the other one, Rachel—who answered the door.

"Good day, sir," she said with a look that was halfway between prim maid and snarky punk. "I'm afraid Miss du Pont is not at home."

Whatever he had expected—and he'd imagined all sorts of things—it wasn't this. Like he'd been expected, like someone had written a line for the girl to say. He made a face at her, as if to get her to drop the theater-major thing. But the girl didn't bite. So he tried again, asked did she know where Alice was? But she would have none of it.

"I'm afraid Miss du Pont is not at home to you."

He noted the "to you."

"Did someone tell you to say that?" he asked, but she didn't answer, kept up the front of the disinterested maid.

"Come on," he said, working up a smile like they were comrades-in-arms, both on the outside looking in. "Did Alice tell you to say that?"

"That's how it was done in the Gilded Age," the girl said, still sounding like she was reading from a script. "With the social climbers, I mean. One could find oneself quite destroyed." And Christ! if she didn't start to close the door right in his face! He reached out to stop it, pushed back with a little too much force so the big oak door swung inward with a shudder. For a second the girl looked frightened, but then she resumed her act.

"I'm afraid Miss du Pont—" and she paused queerly, as if gathering strength for the truth, but then said simply— "is not at home to you."

~ And now: how all the confused striving above has been put to rout! For yesterday as I was attempting to write to Miss Taylor, I heard Mother suddenly call from downstairs, and then Father as though he were struck like Saul, and O! how then did Life intrude upon me!

For the horror we have been dreading all summer is upon us! There are in the papers notices of a most terrible battle involving the 54th Massachusetts. They caution that the news comes from telegraph summaries of what is being written in the Rebel newspapers and so may not be accurate. But it seems the Negro Regiment has been engaged in a most bloody battle and is greatly decimated. I pray the reports are exaggerated, or if true that Wilky is one of those who has come through. We can do no work but stare in front of ourselves and wait, all except Mother, who cleans the kitchen with Colleen, and then cleans it again.

My letter to Miss Taylor, my vows, my cloistered life: how the world elbows its way in, plumps itself down on the divan, and will not budge!

And now we have the accounts in the *Times* and the *Tribune* and the *Traveler* before us. And indeed Wilky is severely injured. One paper lists him as "Adj James (ankle and side)" and another as "Adj G. W. James (severe)." And young Robert Gould Shaw is killed. Father accounts Shaw's parents as his friends and has taken himself off to write to them. And I am here writing because I don't know what else to do. Mother is as a ghost, except when she scolds Alice for her morbidity.

Minnie and Kitty have called, but even their beautiful spirits are dimmed. The news confirms the worst of the rebel sources. There was a great bombardment of Fort Wagner, which guards the city of Charleston. There were gun- and mortar-boats and five iron-clads, and two siege-batteries. This dreadful fire rained down upon the poor souls within the fort for a full day until it was deemed (by whom? Mother wants to know) that they were ready for the taking and so the order was given for the New York and New England regiments to advance. They advanced in columns, all but the 54th, which the papers make a point of saying was awarded the honor of leading the attack. It is just this that we had so feared, that the notoriety of the 54th, the great moral weight given it for being the first colored regiment, would cause it to be ordered into some gallant action so as to serve as an example to the world. And so it has turned out, for the papers are filled with lofty praise of the Negroes, of their courage in the face of what appears to have been a most horrific slaughter. Mother says the Union makes its metaphysical point upon the physical grave of her son. That a symbol has killed her son. But he is not yet dead. Ankle and side, it is not head and heart! Mr. Russell departs tomorrow to go in search of his son, Cabot, who it is hoped is in one of the hospitals upon the coastal islands, at Hilton Head or at Beaufort. He will look as well, he says, for our Wilky.

Fort Wagner, Battery Bee, Folly and Morris Islands: why is it that these names (mere words!) call up for me the smell and sound of war? Siege guns, rifle pits, the glacis, and the ditch! Canister, grape, and musketry: they hold a most awful poetry, redolent with battle, with courage and horror, in ways the battle itself does not. The list of killed, wounded, and missing, one of the papers says, foots up at fifteen hundred and thirty. Yet it is not the fifteen hundred and thirty that I mark, but the phrase "foots up."

I have set aside my letter to Miss Taylor.

Franklin had spent the early part of the evening—his first night back in New York!—simply walking the city. It was a way both of draping himself in freedom and of tormenting himself, for he had passed all his haunts, all the places where he had his friends, and took his pleasures, and kept his real self, passed them without going in as if to deny himself so that later the giving in would be all the more delicious. He had gone from his flat on West Fourth through the Washington Square Mews, and then up to Fourteenth Street, where he had promenaded with his cane and his red tie, always ready with a sisterly smile for the streetwalkers. He had paid his respects to the Sharon, to Manilla Hall and the Orchid, then as the sun began to set circled around to the Bowery with its theaters and saloons open to the street, its dance halls and dime museums and its host of what the *Herald* in one of its exposés was pleased to call "fairy resorts"—the Artistic Club and the Parésis and Little Bucks. From time to time he would pass someone he recognized—not someone from uptown, for whom he always had a story at the ready, but someone he knew from the Slide or the Black Rabbit. Once from down a side street a voice called his name—well, not his name, but the name he used down here—but he merely waved his cane, smiled, gestured he had somewhere to be. The whole time he felt the layers of deception that had accrued in Newport, the rind of his other self, the dried-on lineaments of his many smiles melting away. All that charming and gadding about and encouraging a chorus line of *bons mots*. It tired one so! In another block or two—he was well down in the Bowery now with its rumbling Elevated, the fire escapes dotted with immigrant families having their supper in the fresh air, and on the upper stories of the buildings advertisements for hats and cigars and Equitable Life Assurance—yes, in another block or two, he would have regained himself. And then he could begin.

He had been summoned by Mrs. Belmont just before he had left, and, sitting with her in the breakfast loggia of Marble House with its soft air and clouds of gilding, had delivered himself of a report. And as she nodded her approval, pressed him on this or that point, he had for the first time a glimpse of how she would withdraw from him when the time came. In a month or two, after the engagement was announced, after the wedding, after the world had gotten used to the idea of a Mr. and Mrs. Franklin Drexel of East Sixty-Second Street, Mr. and Mrs. Franklin Drexel of Windermere, Alva Belmont would cease to bother with him. It was not that her house would no longer be open to him—no, he and Ellen would simply be united on her secretary's list—but he would no longer be one of her projects, and so would cease to be of interest to her.

Which, he supposed, turning onto Chrystie Street, would be yet another benefit of marriage.

For the hundredth time he ran through how he would manage it, the Clubs he would join, the this-or-that League, the Artists Association. He would have his charities and duties outside the home, so there would always be a reason to go out. Not every night, of course—he would continue with his attention to the children, with his smiles and his public affection, with dinners and cigars and his evening clothes—but once or twice a week, surely that would be possible! And if so, if he had always the safety valve of the Bowery and the Village and the Sharon Hotel (and afterwards a swift hack ride back uptown), then would not his life be the best he could hope for? The best he could hope for in this, the world as it was?

He had circled back to Bleecker Street. The sun had fully fallen now and the air had darkened but for the faint yellow of the gaslights touching the brick house fronts. He passed a few couples out for the night, a newsboy hawking the last of his evening papers, a trio of sailors traipsing arm through arm. He looked in at the dancing at the Black Rabbit, stopped and gazed up at the soft-lit windows on the upper floors of the Lavender Inn, and finally ceased his walking outside the door to the Slide. There was the familiar sound of Black Andy's Orchestra, the cries and laughter, the hooting. He closed his eyes, felt fall away the last scales of his second skin. He had only the week—he was certainly not going to Baltimore!—only the one week so he must be sure to have his luxurious fill.

3rd Day

Oh! I believe I might murder Ashes! For yesterday as I was about my Room so low-spirited as I have written above, I heard a knock upon the downstairs door and then Ashes saying I was not at home. I rushed to the window and who was below but John Pettibone! It was but a few hours since we had seen one another outside Samuel Judah's. I was at first mortally shocked, but I recover'd myself and hurried downstairs, and with a furious look at Ashes threw about myself a Cloak and went out of doors.

He was but a little gone from the door and turned at the sound of my coming out. It seemed to me that he was in a state, as if he had girded himself to some Task. And so he had, for he stood there in the muddy Dooryard and deliver'd himself of a Speech as tho' he had conn'd it word for word. He said he had come to Apologize for his behavior earlier that afternoon. He said that for six months now he had held himself in Despisal. He said that when Mother died he had wanted to come to me as a friend ought, to say how sorry he was. And that as the weeks went by and the Town people began to talk of Father having been lost, he did want to come then as well, but that he did not. He was not good at Speaking, he said, he was clumsy with words, he said, but that was not an Excuse for not coming. He scorn'd himself, he said, and accounted himself a Coward, and that the sight of me was like a Reproach to him. The World had been terrible to me, he said, my Losses were many and so very hard. And that I had not deserv'd such Treatment. It was almost beyond Reckoning, what had happen'd to me, he said, and he felt it most sorely, and sorely too that he had nothing he could offer that might help me, and had felt the unmanly lack, and yet none of that should have stopp'd him from coming to me, if just to say he was sorry for me. For which Behavior he could not forgive himself, he said.

It was deliver'd, as I say, all of a piece, and when he was finish'd he made to leave, as if he meant to remove himself from my sight. But I reach'd out to stay him, and thank'd him for his Kindness. I said that it had indeed bother'd me that he seem'd no longer to take a Notice of me, that I had accounted our friendship a Brightness in my life, but that sometimes the Heart is too full to act upon its Fullness, and that his coming today was surely a Proof that he was no coward, and other suchlike with which I hoped to quell his Embarrassment. I said I hoped we could continue as friends, tho' we were no longer children, and things had chang'd, yet we might find one another from time to time. He thank'd me then for treating him so charitably, and wonder'd whether he might not help me from time to time, which phrase I had just used, and his using it so hard upon seem'd to embarrass him anew that he was clumsy of Speech, but he brav'd on and said if there were a thing about the house a man could do, would I not call him? I need only ask, he said with something like to his old smile.

Back inside Ashes was speaking Island speak as if she meant to flood the whole of the downstairs with Demons.

~A colored hall boy came this morning with a note from Mrs. Taylor. Alice waylaid him and asked what he thought of this great action of the 54th. Was he not proud of his race? So many shadows sent to Hades! she says.

Mrs. Taylor writes that her family has heard the dreadful news and that their thoughts and prayers are with us. She adds that they miss my company and says if it would help take my mind off the waiting for further news, she is sure Alice would welcome another visit at Hunt's studio some morning, for her daughter finds sitting tedious. (She cannot possibly *know*!) She says her husband will be joining them any day now, and would, she is sure, enjoy making my acquaintance. She prays for Wilky, she says, and hopes we will soon be reunited with him.

I have written her briefly, but cordially, I hope, thanking her for her kindness. I ask her to give my regards to Alice and to little Harry. I will walk the note over to the Ocean in due time. But I cannot, of course, call on her.

Miss Taylor's pheasant hat sits like a reproach on my writing table.

June 27

This morning we commended the body of Lieu^t Smithson to this Alien ground. The Fusiliers turned out in their Scarlet and were a sight to behold, arrayed about the open grave (for we had helped ourselves to a Plot at one of the local Cemeteries, and what Damned rocky soil it was, I heard a Soldier say). It was a beautiful day, sunny and blue and with a gentle Sea breeze, as if the world had no Care toward our Sufferings, or to the Loss of a young man. The Chaplain read the Burial-service, and then several of us stepped forward to praise the Deceased. There was much employment of the word Honorable. Bradshaw became so caught up in his Portrait of the man that he broke down and had to give over. I spoke of Smithson's good Humor, and told a story of our time in Cambridge which made all smile and remember. We then each of us let fall a handful of Earth on the canvas bag, after which, in twos & threes, we drifted away.

But the work of War must go on, and so I spent the afternoon in Consultation with some others of the General's Staff. We have reports of the Rebels having erected a Beacon upon the high ground overlooking Howland's Ferry and having hung a pitch Kettle out at the top in order to give a speedy Alarm to the Country. Expected daily is the appearance of a Squadron of French Ships of War off the coast of New England ('tis said they consist of 12 Sail of the Line and 4 Frigates, under the command of Count D'Estaing), and we may presume they will find their way to Newport Harbour. All this has served to heighten expectation of Engagement and the Staff was at some pains to work up an answering Strategy. I was looked to for recommendations in my especial Sphere, and did so, suggesting that we be more Numerous & Assiduous in our spying parties, and that we better and more frequently reach our Informants & Agents in the countryside. I would accompany a party myself, I said, as I have done in the past, that I might get a direct Intelligence.

I have in some Measure regained myself, felt that Puissance which formerly thrilled my limbs to again inhabit me. I perform my Duties with a brisk Vigor. I show a precise Demeanor and a calculating Spirit befitting a counseling Adjutant. Yet the whole while I am watching myself, noting myself, appraising, approving, goading, as if I am become *dédoublement*, as if I have my own Sebastiao, only one not for the Public world, but to face me in Private. What was once a dark Decoration of mood or the shadow-side of Volition has taken up a facing Residence, planted itself on the other side of me, and will not decamp. Even in writing these Entries I hear a voice suggesting words and means, and a taunting that I do not *do*.

Through it all, like a first Motion, is the thought of her. How she flows in my Blood and arches over my thoughts as the sky completes the World! I can hardly call to mind that time in the Winter when she was but a girl I was toying with, so changed am I toward her, and so changed is the Presence of her now she is gone. In bed at night I summon the Image of her, draw her down to me, torture myself with the slow removal of her Garments, the slow exposure of her Flesh, let her fingers run in my hair, let her Lips brush my skin. And for a moment or two, eyes closed, world banished, I am reunited with myself.

Am I become a man who dreams & moons & satisfies himself with nocturnal Fancy?

There is only some forty miles of Village & Country between us. What stops me?

~We have had at last a telegram from Mr. Russell. He has found Wilky and is making preparations for bringing him north by boat. Ankle grievous, he says. Almost as an afterthought he adds that his own son, Cabot, is lost.

We wait as in a nightmare. I have been trying to distract myself by reading Mérimée and de Musset and Chateaubriand. Their stories enthralled me in Geneva, but now they seem silly stuff.

And I have been unkind to Alice, for in a foul mood I told her that if she wants to put the world on trial for the abuse of the frail, then she might do so on Wilky's behalf, and on his Negro brothers', not her own. That it was a world of slave-mongers and butchers. Even here in Newport the shot tower is run day and night.

I have got at least this out of Chateaubriand: *One inhabits, with a full heart, an empty world.*

He texted Alice asking flat out what was wrong, what had happened? Told her he missed her. Would she not see him? And each time, with each text, with each e-mail, there was no answer. The silence was so pronounced, so outside ordinary behavior as to seem cruel, sadistic even.

He found himself alternating between two possibilities. One, that she had fallen into a depression so deep that to text him some response out of the paralyzing gloom—Aisha had once described to him how her eyes went dead—was simply beyond her. And the other: that it was some game of hers. The woman—hadn't he told himself a hundred times?—was beyond him, subject to subterranean currents (the Rose Island bell!) that he could not hear, could not see. Perhaps all along the whole thing had been some scripted game, utterly beyond him, twisted, vengeful, self-destructive.

Or was that crazy? Had he not seen love in her eyes, felt love in her touch? Had he not himself said "I love you," felt that love rich and improbable in his heart? Seen it in her too? Surely that had not been a game!

He wrote a long e-mail to Aisha. Said he was worried. Whatever had happened, would she not help him see Alice? For the sake of their old friendship? But there was no answer.

He called Newport Hospital, asked for a patient named Alice du Pont. Then Butler Hospital in Providence, Eleanor Slater, McLean just outside of Boston.

At the Redwood Library he pretended to happen upon the director, asked nonchalantly after Alice, but the director said he hadn't talked to Ms. du Pont in days and, strange to say, now that he thought of it, she hadn't returned his call. But he expected to see her on Saturday for Champagne at Windermere. Would Sandy be there?

In the end he e-mailed her one last time. He was coming out to the house that afternoon, he said. He loved her, he said. Whatever had happened, would she not let him try to help? Wouldn't she please come out and see him, please talk to him, if only to explain. Five o'clock, he said. He would wait for her in the maze. Casual dress, no gifts, he tried to write with a wan smile. It would break his heart, but he would leave her alone afterwards if that was what she wanted. He just needed to *know*, he said. He needed to know that she was all right.

So at four forty—with the same feeling in his stomach he used to have just before walking out on court—he rode the Indian up Bellevue, left the motorcycle a side street away so its roar wouldn't announce him, and walked down to Windermere. He used the key code to open the gate, headed up the drive, passed the house (again with that feeling of eyes on him!), and went into the maze. When he got to the center, she was not there, nor was there any evidence of her having been there. But he was five minutes early. There was still a chance. He sat down on the chaise longue to wait, sat there with his palms on his thighs like a patient in a waiting room. In time he thought he heard someone coming and then again that he hadn't. More than five minutes passed. And then there was a sound on the other side of the hedge, a rustle, a footfall. He stood up, held his breath, listened.

But it was the Salve Regina girl, the one with the attitude. She came around the corner of the hedge with this look on her face—amused, mocking, he didn't know what, but he was aware he had just the moment before called out "Alice!" She was wearing a bare-midriff thing. It took him a moment to realize she had something, a piece of paper, in her hand.

"You," he said; then: "Where's Alice?"

She lifted the piece of paper, a servant executing a commission, and read from it aloud.

"'She with her necromantic glances and strange intuitions is retired to a Sisterhood where she is deeply immured and quite lost to the world.'"

"What?" he said.

She read it again, in the same flat, ungiving, dutiful voice. He reached out for the piece of paper and, when she pulled back, took her by the wrist, twisted it until with a cry she let the paper go.

She with her necromantic glances and strange intuitions is retired to a Sisterhood where she is deeply immured and quite lost to the world.

He turned the paper over, turned it back. There was nothing else. But it was the same grammar-school cursive of the *Daisy Miller* notes.

"What's this supposed to mean?" he said.

"Just what it says."

"Which would be what?" he nearly shouted at her.

She blanched, took a step back, then regained herself. "'She with her necromantic glances—'" she began.

He felt like hitting her. "What's it mean?" he said and stepped toward her. "Where'd you get it?"

The girl stopped, blinked at him.

"Did Alice give it to you? Is it from Henry James?"

"What?" she asked, and then, as if she knew she'd broken character, composed herself and started her recitation again.

He felt such a sudden stinging anger run him through that he grabbed hold of the girl, pulled her into him so that she had to go up onto her toes.

"Hey!"

"I'm not fooling around! Where is she? What's happened? What're you people doing?"

"You're hurting me!"

"What's happened? Where is she?"

"She isn't anywhere! She's fucking crazy! Let go of me!"

He gave her a shake, almost pushed her down, then let go and took a step back. His chest was burning and his knees had gone weak.

Could they be seen? he wondered suddenly, and he shot his eyes along the crest of the hedge. The tops of their heads anyway? From the second floor of the house? From the third?

"What do you think?" the girl was saying. She was rubbing her wrists where he had held her, petulant and yet with an air of triumph. She had stopped acting. "What's a guy like you doing with someone like her? Except for the money. What do you think!"

He tried to calm himself, fixed her with his eyes. One of his knees wouldn't quit shaking. "I'm not a guy like me," he heard himself say.

July 1

Fog last night. A most unnerving sight, like a Bank of porous Stone looming just off the shore. Like a gray Fate or a slow-moving Premonition.

The pump was primed, the arrow nocked, the hammer cocked—oh, Franklin was swimming in poetry! He would have to see to it that the occasion, the setting, the sough of the breeze and the birdsong accorded and supplied their effect. Moonlight? The sound of the sea? A pity the breakwater was so distant.

He was returning down Bellevue to his hotel room, having attended a garden party at the Dovecote, where he had seen Ellen for the first time since his return. He had spoken with her, entertained with stories of his time in New York, managed to send her a look or two that decried the existence of these others! The whole time there had been between them the weighty presence of his having gone to see his family, of having spoken to his father, and now how much there was to say! That it could not be said here, in public, had only served to heighten the lovely, heady intoxication. At the same time he could see that the moment had come. It would not do to further temporize. When next they met, he must appear to be incapable of withholding himself, so overcome with admiration and impatience and—well, not passion, but sentiment, sympathy, hope. He would lay before her his heart and she would claim it as her own.

He was no sooner back in his room at the Massasoit (ah: next season, there would be no Massasoit; there would be rather Mr. Drexel of the wide halls and leaded glass and seven chimneys of Windermere—delightful name!), no sooner back in his room than there was a knock at the door. He had a flashing thought that it was Ellen, Ellen flush with the irrepressible passion of a dime novel, but when he opened the door he found a boy from one of the other hotels, the Ocean by the look of his uniform. He had an envelope in his hand. Franklin, who had been undoing his tie at the knock, continued for a moment to undress, unbuttoned his shirt on the off chance that there might be some reaction, some quickened look?

The note was from Ryckman. He felt a little stab of panic at the sight of the signature. Did the man intend to challenge him to a duel? He was evidently back in Newport, but staying at the Ocean, not at his daughter's. He requested a meeting with Franklin, wished to discuss a matter of mutual importance, wrote that unless he heard otherwise—he would tell the hall boy to await a reply—he would expect Franklin at two the following afternoon in the dining hall of the Ocean House. He had then evidently bethought himself to add a postscript: *Please do not inform Mrs. Newcombe of my presence in Newport, though you may do so after we meet.*

What the devil?

He lifted his eyes to the waiting boy, then dropped them back to the note. He read it again, and this time it dawned on him what it was about. The man had come to buy him off! Whatever persuasion or pressure he had worked on his daughter—he was evidently not as disinterested as his departure two weeks ago had made Franklin think—whatever arguments he had marshaled had proved inadequate. She was intent on her purposes. She would have her Franklin! And so now Ryckman was reduced to this last stratagem. He would offer Franklin a sum of money—and no small sum, one had to presume!—and in a single stroke hoped to both rid himself of Franklin and prove to his daughter that her lover was a blackguard after all.

What was that novel? The story of the homely Washington Square heiress whose rich father knows her suitor is only after her money and goes about proving it to her by unmasking the fortune-hunter. Only the poor girl knew all along, was willing to be used if only for the semblance of being loved.

Ah! but Franklin would not be so easily set aside. Twenty thousand? Fifty thousand? Whatever Ryckman intended to offer would not equal the house on Sixty-Second Street, would not equal Windermere. Not to mention the permanent rescue from his circumstances. Not to mention (at last!) a manservant. Not to mention how Mrs. Belmont would close her house to him forever—and all the houses of the Four Hundred—were he to withdraw now. The fellow was operating with an insufficient understanding of the battle lines.

Well, he thought, sitting down to write a response, he would look forward to a *tête-à-tête*. It would prove most amusing. He would protest at each escalation of price. Declare his love. Did not Mr. Ryckman understand the deeper recesses of the human heart? Ah: so! Well, they would never speak of this unfortunate interview again. Time would prove to his future father-in-law, etc. He rose, smiled at the hall boy, gave him a quarter-dollar along with his reply.

Did he not hold all the cards?

$$\rightarrow\ \leftarrow$$

2nd Day

Jane Beecher has accosted me and tried to explain herself to me. At first I would not listen. But she begg'd me and I relented and listen'd without speaking a word myself. She says it is but a Fit that came over her. That she is destitute of Heart with her Husband lost. That she is used to a loving touch and deeply feels the want of it. That my being in her Husband's place did send her Wits out of her. That she lov'd me and honor'd me and would not have me despise her.

I told her that I understood, that I saw how lost and sore of Heart she was, and that we would speak no more of it.

All the world, it seems to me, is lost and sore of Heart. And there is no balm.

~Mr. Russell has returned and he has brought our Wilky on a stretcher. He is feverish and we are not sure he knows where he is. We did not dare carry him upstairs and so he lies in the downstairs hall beside our beautiful staircase. A canister ball a full inch and a half has been removed from his ankle.

So overtaken by emotion was I that I had to leave the hall. As I went I took up the blanket Wilky had come wrapped in. I meant to throw it out that I might be of some use, but on the back stoop I instead sat in the dark with the commotion all behind me. I put the blanket to my face and at the smell of tobacco I remembered that day at Readville when I visited Wilky and the regiment and was welcomed by their youthful forms, stripped to the waist they were and smoking their pipes. How young and joyous and beautiful and of the summery world they were! And how many of them— I know not their names!—are now mutilated, dead, buried (as we read they were) in that ditch along with their colored brethren!

How I wish I might speak of this—and of so much else!—to Miss Taylor. But I feel myself marooned on the island of my self. And how horribly I see that that is just what she wished to save me from!

He looked up "necromantic," then he looked up "immured." Then he Googled *she with her necromantic glances and strange intuitions* and, sure enough, there it was: Henry James, from something called "The Author of *Beltraffio*." His heart gave a little leap. Was this, then, more play? Deeper, sicker, more hurtful, but still a game of communication, connection, a gesture toward him?

He found the story and read it, pencil in hand, marking sentences that might be pressed into duty. If she was hitting him a serve, he would try to return it. But the whole time it felt off, wrong, not the dance of *Daisy Miller* but some darker game. Were they not past this? When he went back through the story trying to pick the best of his selections—the most inferential, the most susceptible to double meanings—he was struck by a sentence he had heavily underlined: *She was a singular, self-conscious, artificial creature, and I never more than half penetrated her motives and mysteries.*

But he sent off a quote anyway, and when there was no response, with the palpable sense that he was trying to prolong a game beyond when others had quit playing, sent another, and when again there was nothing, a third. But no balls came back across the net. Whatever she had meant by staging that last theatrical communion she seemed now to be gazing at him—*sending a necromantic glance at him*—from some place beyond the world. The strangeness called to mind this recurring dream he used to have, a dream where in the middle of a match the tennis court—the rectilinear sanity of baseline, service line, doubles alleys—began to unfold irrational spaces, as if the court were turning itself inside out, extending a finger into some other dimension, all of which he had to cover against some malignant, unseen opponent.

The image he couldn't rid himself of—where had it come from? from *immured*? from *lost to the world*?—was of Alice standing in the embrasure of one of the third-floor windows, looking out at him, down at him in the maze, her breath barely stirring the gauze of the curtain that enshrouded her.

July 3

This morning the most alarming news. I am to be brought before a Board of Interrogation, the notice delivered by an adjutant of Gen[l] Waring. He could not answer my Queries, he said. Was only come to ask if I would submit myself tomorrow morning to some Questions of the General's Staff regarding the late incident on Doubling Point. There were some Matters of Confusion that wanted clearing up. I smiled and said I would.

Something is gone awry. Someone has been speaking in someone's ear. Or my wharf Rat has been mouthing about the taverns. Damn me, I should have dispatched the man instead of letting him stand grinning over his Deed!

What can they know? Did Smithson himself speak beforehand to the men? Let his intentions be known as regards my Conduct? Confide whatever misgivings he had? Yet there have been no looks of Suspicion or Insinuation from those around me, none at the Burial service, none now. Would it not be just like Smithson to not tell anyone he was about the blunting of a fellow Officer? The damned honourable Fool! No, whatever intelligence has come it does not come from the Regiment. From Da Silva then? If so, I will have to brazen it out, act the insulted Aristocrat: are they going to take the word of a damned Jew? And if they have my man, then I will deny, put out a Screening fog. How do we know this is not the very Rebel who came ashore and, happening upon Smithson, did the deed? And now, caught out, tries to enlarge his Perfidy by claiming yet another of the King's men? I know how to handle myself.

But still, this change in the Wind is not good. I must prepare an avenue of Retreat. If it comes to that.

~Mr. Russell tells us that one of the stretcher-bearers who helped rescue Wilky was shot dead while doing so, and is now himself immured in the alien soil of the South. The grotesque symmetry of this has put me in mind of Mr. Emerson's poem in which (do I remember this aright?) a soldier kills another soldier and in doing so mystically kills himself. Father too sees such transcendental affinities. We are all, he says, sourced from the same great tap-root. But are we not, his son wants to demur, in that sameness, most unfathomably different? As in the famous Panopticon in Geneva, the mirror maze where one is oneself and at the same time variants of oneself: inversions, deviants, distortions recessing unto the Horizon, regressing into the Infinite!

Alice has taken to repeating my Chateaubriand. It matters not what anyone says to her, the response is always: "One inhabits, with a full heart, an empty world."

2nd Day

This morning I saw John Pettibone on Thames Street. He was in the company of Henry Whitlow and some of the others, and so we could not stop to speak, but he did send to me when the other boys could not notice the most lovely smile and it has warmed me like the Sun. Indeed it made me disregard the Errand I was upon, and so light was my step become that I kept walking as in a Dream until I had passed out of town and into the rough land out toward Doubling Point. And there I wasted the afternoon amongst the Warblers which are returned from the South and the Titmice and the soft green moss like a Prodigal spendthrift!

And oh! how this spendthrift's Thoughts ran wild, and how many times did she give Ashes her freedom, and Charles Spearmint his love, whilst she kissed John Pettibone over and over!

July 4

I am just returned from my Interrogation. As I thought, it is Da Silva himself who has informed on me. My Interrogators did not say this, yet such were their Questions, such the Doubt & Mistrust expressed, that I believe it can only be he who, having learned of Smithson's death, and of my being in Smithson's company at the time, has come forward with his Suspicions and his Story-telling.

Gen[l] Waring, and Colonels Peech and DeVere were those present, and some damned Recorder with his quill and ink cup. Was this a Tribunal? I laughingly asked when I entered the room. It was a hot day and the windows were open and we could hear the faint booming of Cannon from up the Bay where the Rebels were celebrating the Anniversary of what they are pleased to call their Independence. Genl Waring was Solicitous toward me, apologizing, thanking me for coming, saying that to question a fellow Officer under such Circumstances was most odious, yet some Irregularities had come to their attention that they thought I might explain. Very well, I told them, I was at their service, and then at a new Discharge of cannon, and wishing to appear at my Ease, remarked how we would cause these damn Rebels to regret the waste of their Powder, would we not?

They began by asking how I would characterize my relationship with Lieu^t Smithson, to which I wondered aloud what could they mean. The Lieutenant was my friend, I told them. They went about the bush a bit more, and then finally asked was there not some recent Ill-feeling between the Lieutenant and myself. How so? I inquired, affecting some Perplexity. It had come to their attention, they said, that Lieu^t Smithson had taken Issue with some activities of mine, and that there might have been ill blood between us. Ill blood? I repeated. Why on earth would we have gone off shooting together if there were ill blood? Nonetheless, they persisted, they had a report of some Disagreement between us. I asked them then, what was this Disagreement, and that they need not be so Dainty as to what they wished to ask.

Col^o Peech then enquired about what he called the Cambridge incident of six months past. Had not Lieu^t Smithson expressed his Disapproval of my—and here he smiled and said he would not be dainty—of my bedding Mr. Winter's Wife and the Consternation this caused. If he did, I laughed, it was because he wished to bed her himself! At which Peech did not smile, asked instead had Smithson not considered my behaviour a Black mark upon the Regiment? I answered I had never heard him say so, but they might enquire of the Reg^t if they liked, perhaps he had expressed such an Opinion to the others. They said they would enquire in due time. They asked then could I tell them of the Incident on the night of the Assembly for Genl Burgoyne, which had subsequently caused Genl Pigot to issue an order against Duels and such Challenges, had not that Altercation been over my Attentions to a young Lady? Indeed it had not! I answered with some Fervour. It was over a damned Engineer speaking rudely within my hearing of a young Lady of my acquaintance. Yes, they allowed, but was not the

young Lady one upon whom I had showered my Attentions? I did not know
that I would say that I had showered my Attentions on her, but yes, she was
a young Lady I held in great Esteem. I considered myself as having acted as
any Gentleman ought to act. And that far from being a Black mark upon
the Reg^t, I believed my Courage, and the Engineer's subsequent Apology,
was regarded as a feather in the Regiment's cap. Indeed, was I not cele-
brated in the Reg^t for my action, Genl Pigot's subsequent order notwithstanding? Damn my eyes! but how would they have had me respond? Oh,
they hastened to say, they had no doubt I had acted as a Gentleman.

Through it all, of course, I saw Da Silva's hand, that the Jew had come
to them with the news of Smithson's Perfidy (becostumed as Honour, I
doubt not!). Yet I saw as well that they had no Certainty in the matter, that
they had not the wharf Rat as Witness and proof. But yet under this guise
of casual Enquiry were they determined to try me, to see whether they
might rouse me to an Admission, to a Blundering. But I had my Pieces
well-arrayed. Had not Smithson been my Companion in every step of this
damned War? I asked. Had we not quartered together in Cambridge, yea,
shared a bed? Were we not to be seen always in one another's Company?
Indeed was he not my Second in this very Contretemps the night of Burgoyne's Assembly to which they had alluded? I did account it yet a further
Injury that I had not only to weather the foul Murder of my friend, but
now an Imputation from this Board. And more of the like.

And all the while I felt warmed by the Flame of what I had done. Even
while I was yet endangered, even so! That I had been crossed, affronted,
and that I had responded with a force that the Common might say was not
of a Proportion to my Grievance, but which action I view with Pride and a
warmth at its Execution. I almost wished to tell them, my insolent Interrogators, and with them the Reg^t and withal the fools I play with! That
they might take the Measure of who I am.

And yet still I wonder how far Da Silva's fingers reach. Into the Taverns
& Whorehouses along the wharves surely! And if so, might he not yet
learn something? Might he not goad himself to Pursue and not to merely
Receive? Even returned to Quarters as I am, can I presume myself safe
from further Suspicion? I must be sure to keep these pages close to my

Bosom that they may not grow Legs and find their way to Col⁰ Peech's
breakfast table.

   Next time, do away with the damned wharf Rat!

   If my Appointment comes, I will be away.

Something was afoot. Franklin had come into the Ocean at the time appointed for the interview, had readied his smile and his conciliatory remarks,
and had made his way down the wide hallway to the dining room only to
find Ryckman seated at a table with another man. A man whose loud
checked suit and whose bowler—which to Franklin's astonishment he continued to wear, even while indoors, seated, and dining—a man, in short,
who even the déclassé clientele of the Ocean must have looked at askance.

   "I will beg your pardon, sir," the man had said when Franklin was seated.
He spoke in some accent, not quite Scottish, perhaps Yorkshire. He kept his
knife aloft as he spoke and barely looked at Franklin. "But I've just had a long
train ride and I do not much care for the fare they hawk on the platforms."

   And he went back to his beef-steak. Franklin attempted a smile at
Ryckman, but Ryckman was having none of it. He sat with his hands
clasped before him and with a sharp eye for Franklin. That he had neither
introduced the man in the checked suit to Franklin nor Franklin to the
man seemed not to bother him in the least.

   "Will you take something?" Ryckman asked, making to signal for a
waiter.

   "Thank you, no," said Franklin.

   "As you wish," said Ryckman; and then, still playing some part, though
Franklin could not yet discern what: "You have, I believe, just returned
from a spell in the city. Is that right? Did you enjoy yourself?"

   "I had some business to attend to."

   At which Ryckman nodded. "Ah, business. Well, as you say . . ."

   What the deuce! thought Franklin. The man in the checked suit took a
drink of cider, went back to his dinner. He seemed barely aware of the
other two.

"And Ellen tells me you went to visit your parents in Baltimore as well? How did you find them?"

"They are very well," Franklin temporized. "I thank you."

Had he been caught out? But it was impossible! He let his eyes roam over Ryckman's face for some clue, vowed he would be silent, wait the old man out. The other—by god, he had all the marks of a tradesman!—kept at his meal. The room was but half full.

"You wished to see me?" Franklin finally couldn't keep himself from saying.

"Indeed," said Ryckman, "but . . ." And he indicated the man with the checked suit. The devil if Franklin wasn't supposed to wait until he had finished! Aware he was holding things up, the man lifted a finger as if to signal he was nearly done.

"That'll do. That'll do," he said finally, balling up his napkin and tossing it to the side of his plate. "That's a good meal. None better!"

"Can I have them bring you a sweet?" Ryckman asked.

"Ah, no. Thank you, sir."

"Very well, then."

And they sat for a moment in silence. Something was up. Of course something was up, but what? Franklin gave a quick tug at his collars, crossed his legs at the knees, and gazed about the dining room at the ladies in their white dresses, the men in their sport clothes. He would have to wait, trust to his native resources. Surely he could handle Ryckman and this rube!

"Now to the matter before us," Ryckman said after a time. He made a little preacher's tent with his fingers. "Let us begin—" and he paused as if deliberating on just how to proceed, "—well, what d'you say we begin with the circumstances under which you withdrew from the college at Princeton."

He felt brought up short. Was that it? To whom had they been speaking?

"How do you mean?" Franklin asked, inclining his head as if he didn't understand.

"I mean," said Ryckman, his voice growing a little more pointed, "the circumstances under which you withdrew—were *asked* to withdraw—from Princeton."

Franklin made a gesture of innocence. "Why, I believe I've already told you all that," he said; and then, patient, the soul of reason: "I had got it into my head to be trained as a painter, and unable to do that while following a course of study at—it was called the College of New Jersey in my day—I had determined, after my year abroad, not to return to Princeton but rather to enroll at the Pennsylvania Academy. But there was the Eakins scandal. As I say, I've already told you this. There was no *asking* me to withdraw," he wound up with his own pointed tone.

"I don't believe that is quite accurate, sir," the man in the checked suit said to the remains of his beef-steak.

"I beg your pardon," Franklin said, turning his face full to the man, "but we have not been introduced."

"Ah! Apologies!" Ryckman exclaimed. "Mr. Crowder, this is Mr. Drexel. Mr. Drexel, this is my friend Mr. Crowder." And then he added: "Mr. Crowder of the Crowder Detective Agency."

Detective agency? Franklin thought. What the deuce was a detective agency?

"Well, Mr. Crowder of the Crowder Detective Agency," he said with his smile, "it is customary, I believe, to remove one's hat indoors."

"Of course it is, sir," the man said, reaching hurriedly and taking off his bowler, "of course it is. I'll again beg your pardon."

Was the man a half-wit? Or was this all part of some act the two had ginned up?

"As to this matter of your de-matriculating"—he enunciated the syllables as if he had practiced them—"from the college at Princeton, there was, I believe, an unfortunate incident with a Mr. Alewife. A Mr. Richard Alewife, who, as it turns out, de-matriculated at the same time, and is now of Charlottesville, Virginia. Your family wished, in the parlance, to hush the matter up by sending you—again, in the parlance—on the Grand Tour."

"Did my family tell you that?" Franklin found himself asking. "In the parlance?" He could not help smiling.

"No, sir."

"Who, then?"

Mr. Crowder removed from inside his coat a small notebook of the sort sold at a stationer's, flipped through a few pages. But when he spoke, he said: "I'm afraid it is the policy of the Crowder Detective Agency, sir, not to reveal our sources. Unless it becomes necessary to do so," he added with nothing like a threat, though it was threatening all the same.

"Well, your sources are evidently addled," said Franklin. "You do well to keep them under wraps."

And he turned a look on Ryckman as if to say that he would face the man down on this matter. That if that was all he had, then he had nothing. It was twelve years ago. A misunderstanding. He could turn it this way and that way, and Ellen would believe him.

"They seem to hold," Mr. Crowder continued, "at the college—a certain housemother does—that something untoward occurred between you and Mr. Alewife."

Franklin merely gazed at him, ungiving.

"Would you care to tell us what?"

Still, he did not speak.

"Ah, I suppose it was a long time ago," the detective conceded.

"Indeed," said Franklin icily.

The detective let a little disappointed look come over him—was the fellow an actor?—and went back to consulting his notebook.

"Was it, I wonder," he said after some time had passed; he spoke tentatively, as if he were trying out a hypothesis, "was it—this incident, I mean—" the fellow flipped a page, then another—"was it of the nature of your activities this past week?"

Franklin could feel Ryckman's eyes on him. Under the table he crossed and uncrossed his legs.

"This past week when you were pleased to return to New York?"

"To attend to some business?" Ryckman put in.

"Whatever are you talking about?" said Franklin with too loud a laugh. "This is absurd!"

And for the first time the man looked straight across at him. "I have only facts to report, sir. Whether those facts are to be characterized as absurd or something else, I leave to others."

"*Do* report your facts, Mr. Crowder," said Ryckman. "I believe Mr. Drexel enjoys being the subject of a story."

"Very well, sir." And then—what the deuce!—the detective put aside his notebook and began reciting—evidently from memory—the itinerary of Franklin's wanderings that first night. The Orchid, the Paresis, Little Bucks, his ending up at the Slide. He ticked them off, the street names, the time of the evening, whether Franklin had stepped in or not.

"And would you now, Mr. Crowder," Ryckman said when the detective had come to the end of his recitation, "would you characterize for us the nature of these establishments? And of this last mentioned in particular?"

"They are outposts of what I believe the newspapers call the demimonde. I hope I have that word correct," the detective said to Franklin, and he paused as if for confirmation. "They are places of licentiousness and depravity, known gathering spots for degenerates of all sorts. And by degenerates—please excuse my language, Mr. Ryckman—I mean to indicate sodomites, pederasts, drink mollies, nancies, fairies, and every other type of pervert. The Slide, which Mr. Drexel entered and where he spent a good deal of time, in particular is infamous as an establishment where one may see men dressed as women, rouged as women, where they call one another by women's names, Princess This and Lady So-and-So, Michelle and Rebecca and Deborah. There is dancing, mincing, and the singing in falsetto of ditties. Mr. Drexel is himself, evidently, a great lover of dancing."

Franklin laughed—what could he do? he had to brazen his way through—laughed and adopted a look of pity for the poor, benighted fellow. Did he not understand? Why, this was the new fad of slumming! he told them. Those men were his friends from uptown. Young men of good families—the best!—with whom he sometimes went into this demimonde, as Mr. Crowder called it. Why, it was better than the zoo! And the dancing? It was all part of the evening's entertainment, part of the theater of the thing! He smiled his smile—surely they understood this! It was all just a fantastic romp!

"I see, sir," the detective answered in his uninflected voice. "And the gentleman you later accompanied to the Sharon Hotel, where I believe they are pleased to rent rooms by the hour, was he too one of your friends from uptown?"

His smile felt as if it had dried on his face.

"And the following night, Mr. Paolo Costa of Mott Street—" he was again consulting his notebook—"is he too a friend from society?"

"Go to the devil!"

"And the following night, Mr. Walter Beamis come over from Brooklyn. A friend?"

"Let us halt this charade," Ryckman said in a voice that made no attempt to hide its venom. He leaned into the table. "You and your fine clothes, Drexel. Your fine manner, your damned watercolors. What you are is a pervert, and the worst sort. An invert, a fairy, a nancy. In the *parlance*," he added with a nasty smile. "And if you do not within twenty-four hours tell my daughter that you return to New York, and that you will never see her again, I will destroy you."

"Destroy me?" Franklin found himself repeating. He could feel his chin quivering. The walls of the room were turning liquid.

"Nor do I mean to merely inform my daughter of your character and of your inclinations, but to publish it to the world. You are a favored subject of the society columns, I believe? What d'you suppose TOWN TOPICS and the other scandal rags would do with the information Mr. Crowder is ready to impart to them? And Mrs. Auld, and Mrs. Lydig, and your great friend Mrs. Belmont, what will they do when they learn who you are? Learn the name you go by down there? Eh?" And a look of exultation spread across his features. "Twenty-four hours, Mr. Drexel! *Deborah!*" he said.

~I have just experienced the most mortifying half-hour of my young life. William is having a great laugh over it, says I am conducting myself like a character in an *opera buffa*.

I was in my room reading when I heard the downstairs door-knocker rap, and then the door open. But with the seven of us, and the servants, comings and goings in the house are never-ending, and so I thought nothing of it. But some time later Mother came to my room and informed me, with something of the old worry on her face, that Father wished to see me in his library. Oh, the school-boy fears that raced through me at the summons! Had someone informed Father of what I had been obscurely fearing all summer long? That his bookish son had been hanging about the Newport hotels like a pickpocket?

I went down, knocked quietly at the door of the library, and upon entering found Father seated at his usual desk, but in the chair across from him, where usually William or I underwent the paternal examination, a man I did not recognize. He had turned at my entrance so that he observed me from the *contrapposto* posture with his great beard lying atop his shoulder. I wondered at him a moment, wondered indeed at what seemed a too appraising look he directe'd at me, and then in a horrible instant I knew who he was.

I went and stood before them. Father waited to introduce us as if he wished to see whether my reaction indicted or exonerated me. Or perhaps he wished, in his jolly way, in his assurance that no evil can come into the world if we do not ourselves invite it in, perhaps he wished just to enjoy my discomfiture.

"Mr. Taylor," he said finally to the man, "I don't believe you have quite—" he shaded the "quite" with his sense of humor—"*quite* met my son Harry."

"I have not," said the man.

"Harry, may I introduce Mr. Taylor of Waterbury, of the American Brass Works."

"Mill," the man corrected.

"The American Brass *Mill*," repeated Father.

I bowed and—stupidly!—clicked my heels as we had learned at Geneva. Mr. Taylor in his turn inclined his head to me. He was a most massive man, with a most massive beard, and a broad forehead, and a monocle through which he viewed me as if he meant to dissect me. Whatever humor Father seemed to find in the situation he evidently did not share.

"Won't you be seated, Harry?"

I lowered myself into a chair and waited. Father brought his fingertips together in that way he has when contemplating the angels perched among the cobwebs in the corner of a room. He then turned his face full to me.

"Mr. Taylor informs me you have been making love to his daughter."

He said this kindly, with a small smile above his beard, as if he supposed it a mere matter of fact that yet needed to be agreed upon. There was a column of books on his desktop that looked perilously close to toppling.

"Do I have that right?" he said to Mr. Taylor.

"I have not used those words. But you have my sense, sir."

Father bowed his head slightly, as if he appreciated this distinction between the rind of the words and the core of their meaning. Just in front of him, on its pewter plate, sat the canister ball that had nearly killed Wilky.

"Have you, Harry, been making love to Mr. Taylor's daughter?" he asked when I did not speak. "Alice, I understand her name to be. Glorious apparent coincidence!" he thrilled, adding as an afterthought, for he has learned that people do not always follow him: "*Apparent*, I say, there being none such." At which he smiled, sure we appreciated this nicety of the divine.

"I have had the pleasure," I hazarded, and trying to get my stammer under control, "of making the acquaintance of Mr. Taylor's daughter Alice, and of his wife, and their young son." I crossed my hands in my lap. "His name is Harry," I added so as not to be delinquent in this fact. Father's eyes widened behind his spectacles and he gazed at Mr. Taylor as if upon a miracle.

"We discover gifts and correspondences all about us," he said in his deep-throated way, "do we not?"

"I am not after gifts and correspondences," Mr. Taylor said with a penetrating look. "I am after understanding what your son's intentions be toward my daughter. We are not in the habit of our Alice going about with young men."

Father looked as if he meant to pose the great swoop of his forehead against Mr. Taylor's own large brow. "And we in turn are not used to our Harry trifling with the hearts of young ladies. I'll ask again. Harry, have you spoken of love to Miss Taylor?"

"I have not, sir," I said.

"And should you have?"

I sat in silence for a minute, crossed and uncrossed my legs. I understood Father to be asking whether my behavior, in order for it to be honorable, needed to be followed by a declaration of love. I looked from one man to the other, and then threw myself into telling Mr. Taylor—oh, that I had to speak all of this in front of Father!—that I had a great admiration for his daughter and that I valued her friendship. That she seemed to me an altogether fine young lady. Intelligent, charming, with a finely developed moral sensibility. That I believed the portrait that Mr. Hunt was making of her caught with the sympathy and plenitude of art the luminescence of her character. That I accounted her a friend in the best sense of that relation. But that I believed I had never spoken to her in tones that might be construed as being those of the language of love. Did I understand that Miss Taylor had informed her father otherwise?

To this Mr. Taylor roused himself. "I have not spoken to my daughter on the subject, but her mother has apprised me of your conduct. I do not know how it is in Newport, but in Waterbury, when a young man goes about with a marriageable girl, it generally means one thing."

"Ah!" I said, hoping the word would diffuse into the room other possibilities.

"You are not, I think, immune to the world's expectations!"

"I had not," I quietly said, "thought the world was paying much attention to me."

"You had better think so, when the reputation of a young lady is at stake!"

At this Father leaned in with his elbows on his desk and fixed his sympathetic eyes on me. He said he was surprised to hear me speak so of a young lady. If she truly was as fine as I said, if her qualities so pleased me, and if I found her moral sense so commendable . . . after all, I was twenty years old, he said.

And there it was, the question that had so vexed me, so hounded me, voiced not just in the cloister of my mind but aloud there in Father's study! I stammered something, some question as to whether Miss Taylor maintained that I had conducted myself in the person of (I could barely get the words out) "a young man courting a young lady?"

"My wife says your attentions to our Alice have been extensive and continuous. That you have taken it upon yourself to show them about the city. That in addition to excursions with my wife and son, you have gone walking alone together. Is my wife mistaken in any of this?"

I stared at the thing so baldly put before me, then let my gaze sink into my lap.

"Harry?" said Father.

"I cannot," I found myself saying.

"But if she is a fine young lady . . ."

"I cannot," I said again, and at the words I felt flood through me a humiliating and yet liberating certainty. It was as if I, at last, *knew*.

There ensued a most horrible silence. Though I did not look at him, I felt Mr. Taylor draw himself up as if some suspected flaw, some fault line in my character, had been revealed. But he lay this exultation aside, and when he spoke, it was to Father, and in a voice colored with a new tone.

"I have not until recently been acquainted with your name, Mr. James. I attend to an altogether different sphere than do you. But I am led to believe you have some fame in literary circles?"

Father seemed to hear a compliment in this. "I have been known to scribble a thought or two," he said with what I imagined was a smile (for I could not look at him).

"That, in addition to books, you express yourself in the newspapers? You take part in the issues of the day? Your name is not unknown to the reading public?"

I heard more quickly than did Father the import of this, and before Mr. Taylor could unveil further his threat I quickly inserted myself.

"If I have done wrong without realizing it," I blurted out, or some hurried words to that effect, "I am willing to attempt to rectify things, if needs be by suffering a stain upon my own reputation." My eyes darted quickly between the two men. "If you feel that I have compromised your daughter's reputation, if my behavior has not been what I thought it was, what I intended it to be, I would be willing to subscribe to an action that would allow Miss Taylor to remain unreproached, with no tarnish attaching to her. Namely, I would be willing to allow the world to think I had asked for, and been turned down by, your daughter. That I had wished to have, but had not, her favor."

"Harry!"

"It most gravely injures me to think I have caused her pain."

"But the way to heal pain is not through prevarication and duplicity! Dear Harry!"

Mr. Taylor let this submission draw itself out, this victory, this enrichment. And then he stood and rather magnificently said: "Do you think my daughter would agree to such a notion? To such—" and he seemed to wait for a curtain to begin to fall—"to such *perfidy?*"

"I cannot marry her," I simply said.

"Marriage!" he cried, as if the word, coming from me, shocked him. "That, sir, is quite out of the question." And then, with the full richness of his exultation: *"Now!"*

3rd Day

Well, I have done it. Whether it be the thread that leads me out of the labyrinth I know not, but I have taken myself down from the Cupboard, chipped tho' I may be, and have placed myself upon the Board of the world.

Straight after morning chores (and before I could lose the will to Action I had worked up yesterday out on Doubling Point), I put on my cloak and walk'd down to the harbour's edge and then out Pettibone's Wharf to the small ship-lapp'd building that stands attach'd to the Warehouse of John Pettibone (the Father, I mean) and serves as his Counting-house. They were surpriz'd to see me there, entering as I did without knocking, and a girl. I ask'd if I might speak to him alone, at which he could not keep the surprize from his face, but he begg'd me to be seated, and I did so in a rude chair that faced the stool he sat on. The two men who were with him went out by the Warehouse door.

I told him that I came to him in my Father's place. That if my Father had not been lost, it would be he who was calling on him. Or it would be my Mother, if she had not too been lost. Did he understand me in this? I ask'd. He said he did, tho' there was still about him a look of confusion. I said he must treat with me as he would my Father, and he said he would.

I told him then that I wish'd to marry his son. That I said this in as even a voice as I did, as if I were a man of Business come to him to suggest a venture, amazes me now in a way that it did not at the time. I said the one simple sentence and did not weaken it by explanation or excusal but simply waited for a response.

Marry his John? was all he could say. He look'd at me with his gray eyes and through his beard (as I may say), still in surprize. I told him yes, that that was what I had come to him to propose. It was then that his manner chang'd, not to one of Agitation or of Anger but, it seem'd to me, of Embarrassment. There came onto his face the Discomfort of considering how he was going to say no to me.

He said that John was not of marrying age, and nor was I. And it was a very bold thing I was doing. It was a very bold thing for a young girl to say. A maiden does not act so, he said.

I told him I did not have anyone to speak for me and so must speak for myself. I told him I was not acting as a maiden. I was acting as my Father would do were he here. I told him the times forc'd me into acting beyond what I was. To which he said that I needed to be careful in so acting, lest I become beyond what I am. I repeated that there was no one to act for me, that I had Dorcas and our household to look out for. That no one would look out for us if I did not.

At these words he did soften some. He rubb'd his eyes, and tried to smile upon me in that way people have of smiling and not smiling at the same time. He said that he and his Wife had always admir'd Father. That he was a good Captain, and a reliable one, and a fair Trader. That it had Distress'd them greatly when Mother died. And that they admir'd me for conducting myself during this time of Trial as a young woman of Sense and Ability. He hoped I would take what he said to Heart. Yet, the fact remain'd, his John was not of marrying Age, no more was I, and if my Father were here—well, he would not be here, was the point, he said. For there would be no need for this Marriage if Father were alive. So tho' I might contend that I acted as Father would, I did not.

I answer'd him then that it was true we were young. Yet there were those of our age who enter'd into Marriage, were there not? He had perhaps heard that a Match with an older man of our Meeting had been propos'd to me. If I was old enough to marry under those Circumstances, why was I not under these I now propos'd?

He allow'd that there were those who married at my age, but they did not marry one another, he said with a great emphasis. Such a union was foolhardy, he said. It would be like what we hear of the Crusade made of Children, he said. To which I answer'd that in six months I would be sixteen, and in eighteen months I would be seventeen. The Doubt attendant upon our ages, I said with my own smile, was readily cured by time.

He seem'd on the point of gently laughing at this, as if we might for the moment forgive our Difference, but the door to the Counting-house open'd and in came John's sister Miriam, who was at school with me. She had with her the basket lunch she brought her Father every Noontide. At the sight of me she stopp'd, and her face could not make up its mind whether to wonder at my presence or to smile at it. We had a brief friendly Exchange, but she seem'd to understand all the same that something was in the Air that was not for her, so with a kiss of her Father's cheek she left her basket and went back out the door. At that, one of the men who had earlier left enter'd by the Warehouse door (he having heard the other door shut and supposing me gone), but at the sight of me, he turn'd and went back out. This was all as a kind of Comedy, and it left us in Silence for a good minute.

In time John's Father said he was surpriz'd it was not John who had come to speak to him of this Matter. Why had he not spar'd me this difficult Interview? he wonder'd.

I told him John did not know of it, and when he seem'd to understand me to mean that he did not know of my coming that morning, I felt call'd upon to say that his son did not know I wish'd to marry him.

This took him anew with Surprize. Had we not spoken of it between us? he wanted to know. Had we not confess'd love between us? I told him again to remember that I came as my Father, that these were but the Praeliminaries of a Marriage. That when the Families had agreed, then the Children might be consulted. He was amaz'd at this, amaz'd at me, he said. This was brazen indeed! Did I think my Father would countenance me acting in so brassy a Manner? I told him then, and for the first time my voice betray'd me, told him that I believ'd my Father would be proud of me. That the Winds of the world had turn'd against me and that I had taken steps to trim Sail and to come about. And more than that, that I was proud of myself. If it was not to be my hand upon the Tiller, I ask'd, whose was it going to be? Would he have me wait until I and mine were ruin'd? Or would he have me marry a man thrice my age?

This did seem to take some of the wind from his sails and he luff'd where he sat, saying no more about brazen and brassy. But it could not be so, he said all the same. He was sorry for me but his John was still a boy. He had as yet no Trade. And he would not have him go out to work at the Ropewalk or in the Distillery merely because he had an untoward Wife to support. His John was fitted for higher things. In due time he would go out as a ship's Mate, and he would learn to master Sailing, and in due time he would have his own Ship. In due time, he repeated, with a meaning look.

I told him I had not this time he spoke of.

I cannot give it you, he answer'd.

July 6

I have been down to view the maps. I went under a Ruse of preparations for my Spies, yet all aflame with the thought of making it through the Countryside to the Jewess. And hardly a Ruse it was, for we do make several plans for forays into Rebel territory. Under that guise I studied the southerly lay of Massachusetts, located the town of Taunton, looked for likely routes. I had gone with the idea that I might plan a Reconnaissance thither, but I quickly perceived the town was too far, too within the Rebel's country, too far from any of our Agents, and withal not of a military Consequence for any plausible Expedition. Still I copied out a map, committed to memory some various Ways, calculated the time it would take, selected a town to which I might plausibly direct a Foray. And from thence? (What a Boldness it would be!)

The others act differently toward me. I do not think it is my Conceit.

Rumor is about. They have heard something and now are pulled back in their looks and their Intercourse. It half pleases me. That they might have the Suspicion that I caused Smithson's death, that I engineered it, and did so because he had stepped into Affairs that were none of his. Let them know me for this. I have then the best of both worlds, done the Deed and so known as one not to cross, and yet still free, untaken.

'Tis now late at night. The lights winking upon the Harbour water put me in a Strange mind that I care not what happens to me. In such a mood if they came to me and asked the questions the Board asked, then I might answer them. I have, I know, strange Recesses in my being. I know not what to make of them at times.

Smithson is missed. He at least had wit. These others go about as feelingly as clods of Turf.

What strange gods led her to a town named Taunton that the very word might Mock me! And how this afternoon did the sight of that word, the Town formerly unknown to me but now Freighted with thought of her, how it beckoned to me! Like a besotted School-boy I caressed the paper where it was written, imagining the narrow Village streets, the paths that lead out to the fields, the stone walls, the leafy trees. Aye, somewhere within the Neighbourhood of that printed word she lies abed, dresses in the morning, thinks of me. 'Tis Summer there as well as it is here. The same Clouds pass overhead. At night is the Sky lit with the same Stars.

Sandy had his ticket. One of five hundred. It had sat on the painted bureau in his room for a week with its crisp, elegant printing. *Champagne at Windermere, 4–6 p.m., September 3rd. All proceeds to benefit the Redwood Library.* He had tried to pretend that he didn't know whether he would go or not, that at some point he must quit, stop, pull up stakes—why not now?—but all along he intuited that this was his best chance. If she was there—and she *would* be there, unless she was seriously, seriously ill—if he could just see her, could plant himself in her presence, the body, the face, the smile she had loved: would she not talk to him?

There was the question of how to dress. The tourists might come in shorts and halter tops, Alice had said, but not the family. She had picked out a diaphanous white thing for herself—her Emily Dickinson winding-sheet she called it—did Sandifer own a jacket and tie?

When the time came, he again parked the Indian several streets over and walked the couple of blocks to the house. He got there just as one of the Bellevue Avenue trolleys pulled up outside. At the gate one of the Salve Regina girls—the other one, the one with the terrible haircut—was taking tickets. He held back until the last of the tourists had gone through and then went up to her.

"Hi," he said, handing his ticket over and directing a smile down at her.

"Hi," she said.

"Mitten, right?" he said. That was her name. Mitten. "They've got you taking tickets, I see." Again, the winsome smile.

"Yeah."

He gazed inward across the lawn. Through the trees he could see the bright-striped tent, the people milling about. He hesitated a moment, wondered how he might manage this, what to say, what tone to take?

"Everyone's stationed somewhere," he mused, still looking across the lawn. "Tom in his dinner jacket, eh? Margo under the tent." This, even though he was too far away to see them. "Where's Alice?" he asked after a moment in as nonchalant a voice as he could manage. The girl didn't answer.

"Seen Alice?" he said again, pointed this time.

"We're not supposed to talk to you," the girl said.

He turned back to her. It was as if his dark imaginings—what had seemed a kind of crazed paranoia when he was alone in his room, when he was out walking at night and thinking up all sorts of stuff—had stepped out into the sunlight.

"You're not supposed to talk to me?" he repeated.

The girl looked down. "You probably shouldn't be here."

"Who told you you shouldn't talk to me?"

She turned her homely face up to him and there was a kind of pleading there, like she was asking him to not make her do this.

"Look," he said, and he tried again to smile. Had he not always been friendly to her? "I just need to know what's happened."

The girl shook her head no. He spread his palms in a gesture of innocence.

"Why won't anyone tell me what's happened?"

"You shouldn't be here," the girl said, still not looking at him. "You'll make things worse."

"Tell me what's happened and I'll go away."

She screwed up her mouth, still wouldn't look at him.

"Mitten," he said, and he reached out, touched her on the forearm. Another trolley was pulling up. "I love Alice," he said in a warm, sane, honest voice. "I need to know how she is. I need to know what's happened."

Part of the bad haircut was that she had these bangs that would fall like an apostrophe in one eye. It would have been sort of cute and wayward if the girl were otherwise cute, but she wasn't. She brushed the bangs aside, pursed her lips as if on the verge of something, looked up at him. The trolley disgorged its passengers.

"She knows," she said finally.

"What does she know?"

"She knows about you and Aisha. Now you have to go."

"What does she know? How does she know?"

"You said you would go."

"*How* does she know? Who told her?"

But she had to turn to the line of tourists, deliver her rehearsed "Welcome to Champagne at Windermere!" She took their tickets, said thank you to each, but she found a moment to shoot a look back at Sandy, importunate, a little angry, like she meant to hold him to his word. But he merely said his own thank you and began walking in under the camouflage of the tourists.

There were already several hundred about the lawn, under the tent, going in and out of the maze or strolling down toward the water. He saw Tom at the center of a group, Margo standing beside the servers at one of the champagne tables. He wanted to hold off being spotted for as long as he could, so he moved away, headed up the walk toward the house.

Inside, he went methodically from room to room, from the breakfast room to the library, into the formal and the informal living rooms, to the billiard room, the dining room. He checked every possible nook, smile at the ready, but she was not there. There were only the tourists, champagne flutes in hand, and a security guard himself moving slowly from room to room. Coming back down the hall, he stopped at the wide staircase that led up to the second floor. It had a velvet cordon draped from banister to banister, a black-and-gold PRIVATE sign hanging from it. He looked upwards at the vacant second floor. Could he not simply step over the cordon and go up? Find her in her bedroom? Speak at last to her, explain himself, have her understand?

He went again down the wide hall, blindly in and out of the rooms. She was there, on the floor above; he could *feel* her. He had only to get up the nerve. In the doorway of the library he stood and stared at the table where she had shown him her photograph albums that night—her mother and grandmother, the maze being laid out, the 1978 Mercedes under the porte cochere—and then he was back in the hall, affecting a purposeful stride, a proprietor's stride. When he got to the staircase—he couldn't believe how nervous he was! the hole in his stomach!—he looked once for the security guard, and then, with as relaxed an air as he could manage, unlatched the cordon, unhurriedly relatched it, and with the tourists pausing to look and wonder at him (good move with the coat and tie!) climbed resolutely up the staircase and onto the second floor.

He expected to find the door to her room shut, that she would be within in some state or other, but as he went down the hall he saw that her door was open. He called "Alice" quietly, gently, that he might not startle her. But there was no answer. He looked into the room, waited, listened, then stepped inside. She wasn't there. It took a moment to register—he had so often pictured her wasting away in bed—but she was quite simply not there.

He went back out, stood in the hall for a moment thinking what to do, then checked the bathroom, the other bathroom, the TV room. He looked into Aisha's room, then went back into Alice's, opened the closet, opened her drawers. They were filled with clothes still, her things—her pedal pushers, her biker-babe outfit, and over on her nightstand her Marian the

Librarian reading glasses. He picked up a sweater, a cashmere thing with butterflies on the front, lifted it to his face, tried to smell her in it.

Back in the hall he went down to the solarium with its semicircle of leaded windows. The place with its limed wicker furniture where she had put *Tristan und Isolde* on the stereo and slit her wrists. He looked out at the lawn below, at the striped tent and the people. There was a croquet game set up but no one was playing.

Was she out there somewhere? Smiling and thanking everyone for coming? Or was she in New York? Santa Fe? In a hospital somewhere?

Back outside he gave up trying not to be seen. He zigzagged from group to group, stepped into the big, open-sided tent pitched on the croquet lawn, then—of course!—went into the maze. But when he reached the center, there was just some lawyerly looking couple raising their glasses to him in congratulations. Coming back out, he passed within ten feet of Margo, didn't return her look, headed instead toward the Orangery. If Aisha was there, damn it, he'd demand to know what was up, enough pussyfooting around. But the closer he got to the glassed-in building, the more he sensed that it looked different, wrong. He tried the door but it was locked, and when he looked in through the dirty panes, he saw the inside was empty. All Aisha's stuff, even the acetylene tanks, packed up, gone.

"Hey, champ," he heard behind him. He turned to see Tom in his white dinner jacket bearing down on him. Fifty yards behind, Margo was coming too.

"Where is she?" Sandy said.

"Aisha?" Tom said with a look at the Orangery. "It's Labor Day weekend. The end of summer. She always heads back to Brooklyn about now."

"Alice."

"Ah, Alice!" he said, like silly me. He let a little smile settle on his face, paused to wait for a group of tourists to pass, then: "She doesn't want to see you."

"I want to hear *her* say that."

"She *has* been saying it. You're just not listening."

"Where is she?" he asked again, and then, when Margo drew up, said it to her: "Where is she?"

"Hello, Sandy," said Margo.

"Sandy was just leaving."

"Where is she?" he said again. Tom made this gesture, like can you believe this guy?

"Newport, New York, Santa Fe, Planet Alice," he said. "Wherever she is, she doesn't want to see you."

"Why don't you let me handle this?" Margo said to him.

"Nothing to handle. Sandy was just leaving."

She gave her husband a little pat on the stomach. "Why don't you go back to the guests and let me handle this. Send a security guard our way if you like."

He hung fire a moment, gave Sandy a look of something like contempt, and then shook his head. "Bad form, champ," he said, and he turned and started back up the lawn. Margo watched him go for a minute and then leaned her back against the side of the Orangery. Sandy swung around to face her.

"You're not going to get anything out of me," she said, holding her hand up like a traffic cop. "So don't even start."

"I just want to know where she is. Is she all right? Why can't I just talk to her?"

She did the traffic cop thing again. "But here's a lesson you might take away from all this. When laying traps for heiresses, it's better not to sleep with the heiress's best friend."

"That was all before."

"If you say so," she said.

"And I wasn't laying any traps."

"If you say so."

He closed the distance between them, leaned in to her. He remembered Alice telling him that Margo would be lying in wait for him. "Was it you who told her?" he asked.

"Me?" And she shot him a look, crossed her arms pointedly: how could *she* have known about Aisha? "Not me," she said. "One of the college girls took it upon herself. She must have—" and again she gave him a look, made a to-hell-with-you gesture—"she would have seen the two of you together. I think she thought she was protecting Alice. She thought Alice ought to know what kind of guy you are."

"What kind of guy am I?"

"Evidently the kind who fucks the best friend while he's also fucking the sister-in-law," she said with her eyes glowing in a way he'd never seen.

"That was all before," he said again.

"Whatever," she said, and for a full minute they just stood looking at each other. A trio of guests came toward them, champagne flutes in hand, looked in the windows of the Orangery, and then veered off toward the water.

"Look," Margo said finally. She let out her breath so her shoulders dropped, looked away, turned back. "Sandy," she said as if appealing to some residue of their time together. "It's not going to happen for you. You need to see that. You need to accept that. And you need to leave. I don't mean just here, now, but Newport." And she peered up at him like did he get that? He just stood there, hard, ungiving. "You said you were looking to sell the Indian," she tried. "Is that right? Haven't sold it yet? Because I'd be interested in buying it. Add to my image around town," she said with this smile, and when he didn't smile back, dropping the pretense: "We'll give you fifty thousand." She let the extravagance of the offer sink in; and then, even more extravagantly: "Fifty thousand if you'll get on it and—" And she made a gesture of him riding into the sunset.

"Too late," he said. "It's no longer for sale."

At which she closed her eyes, seemed in the instant to regret having had anything to do with him.

"As you wish," she said after a minute, opening her eyes and looking up the lawn. "There's the security guard coming." Sandy kept himself from turning to look. "He's overweight and out of shape. I'm sure you can take him." And she pushed off the Orangery, began walking back up the hill. "Please don't come around again," she called over her shoulder.

He watched her go. And then he looked up at the facade of the house, at the windows of the third floor. *Immured. Lost to the world.* He started up the lawn, obliquely, away from the house so he'd skirt the security guard.

When he reached the gate onto Bellevue, Mitten was still there, though the guests were mostly done arriving.

"So it was you," he said to her. She looked blankly at him.

"What?"

"It was you who told Alice about Aisha and me."

"Not me!" she protested. "Rachel—it was Rachel."

"Margo said it was you," he had the wits to say.

"No," the girl answered. "Honest! It was Rachel. Aisha tried to get me first, but I wouldn't. So she got Rachel."

He blinked. What had he just heard? "Aisha tried to get you?" he repeated.

"She thought Alice ought to know. But she couldn't tell her herself. So she tried to get me to do it, to tell Alice that I'd seen you guys together this summer, but I wouldn't. So she got Rachel."

He closed his eyes, looked at the blackness behind his lids. He had to ask again. "It was Aisha's idea?"

The girl bit her lip and nodded. "She thought Alice ought to know."

~I have had a note from Miss Taylor. It reads simply, most exquisitely: *I am so very sorry! Please forgive us.*

She leaves Newport soon.

I must somehow have her understand.

July 7

Do I mean to do it?

What Madness!

I toy, I toy! I can turn back at any moment, or rather not turn back but simply not go on! For I may make all Provision for going yet is it all done under the Guise of my directing the Eastward party. At any instant I can choose to not continue and I will but appear to have been doing nothing save my Duty. I can accompany the Foray up past the rebel Redoubts and across the Bay. I can interview & devise, plan & instruct, and I will have done nothing out of the ordinary of my Charge, have taken no step that obliges a further step. All such further steps are but in my Thoughts, unreal to the World. Only at the instant of Return will I need to decide. 'Tis only then that the Phantoms I work up must be brought to Life or quietly killed.

Yet I must make all necessary Preparations as tho' I have already decided. Yea, when the time comes to Plunge, I may instead step back from this Verge and render my Preparations for Naught, yet I cannot be heedless in the making of them. I must plan as if I mean to do.

And what is it I mean to do? Aye, there lies the Question and the Rub all in one! For I have let fly the fullest Fancies! Do I trifle? Do I flirt with myself? These Phantoms of my Brain: do they have the joints and wires of Marionettes, or do they breathe with Life?

I have played upon my Reputation (that I extemporize upon Danger and enjoy going about with my spies in their Colonial garb) and have convinced the Staff that I must needs accompany Flanders & Southwick on the planned foray to Rehoboth. That the state of these modern Revolutioners changes daily now that they are heartened by the news from France, and that it is a necessary Risk that I be upon the spot to direct and alter Matters as they develop &c. And so it is that we make Preparations to accompany a Patrol up the Island until we reach the Rebel fortifications from whence we may be ferried further Northward and across to the Massachusetts shore. Once at Rehoboth I must ensure that I am Quartered by myself, in the local inn if needs be, while Flanders & Southwick are housed by our agent. Perhaps a Ruse of not calling attention to ourselves by our number may be employed. Then we may go about our Business, yet at some opportune moment I must plausibly vacate my Quarters, leaving behind some Note upon which I will write my Intentions of pursuing some secret Charge, that I will be for some three days at the Wayside Inn of a nearby Village, and that they are to continue with their local business and await my return. I might leave some of my things in my room that they may provide Evidence that I am only transiently absent. I must beforehand engage a horse. Then I must make it the eight miles to Taunton.

It is then the Chess-player's plan ends and the game steps off onto Squares beyond the Sixty-four. For I know not (nay, not even yet! so hard upon!) what exactly I mean to do when I have gained this taunting town. Lying abed at night the most theatrical Fancies populate my Brain. Sometimes I am my old self and the Campaign is still the one I began back in the Winter, namely to checkmate Da Silva and have his Daughter. I will have her in the fields about Taunton and then, promising her some Fidelity or Future, I will return to Newport with her Virginity like a Scalp in my waistband. In this near Fancy I cook a story of how I was taken by the Rebels and held and questioned for some days (however long it takes me to lay Siege to the Jewess's Maidenhead) and that I escaped and am returned among them only to swagger the more. On Squares further from the board I remain in Taunton and have her over and over, still with the Prospect that I may return, only with a more harrowing story of Capture and Escape. And still further: that we swear to one another that we are as Man & Wife, and flee her Step-Mother's and go to some likely town along the Post road, perhaps even to Boston, where we may endure the War together and from where I might dispatch a Letter to one of our Agents, requesting that he endeavor to deliver it into the hands of Gen¹ Pigot's staff, and by which I might plausibly story how I was captured and am escaped and am in Boston incognito and Fate having washed me up here might I not serve as a Spy in the very Nest of the Rebels? Thereby might I have both the Cake of my Desertion and the eating of it.

These are my thoughts at Night, when the world Dissolves and there are only the Planets of the Brain.

In all of this there plays the Accompanyment of her dark eyes, of her pale skin, of her unbound Bosom, her falling hair.

If I am taken by the Colonials, I will be shot. If I am discovered by my own, I will be hanged.

I have heard no more from Gen¹ Waring. Am I quit of this damnable business? Or will I return from Rehoboth (scalp or no scalp) to find myself undergoing a Court-martial?

All the more reason to take the girl and fly with her to Boston or Salem or Halifax, not to stay but rather to sail from thence to Kingston or San

Juan and then on to France, Italy, Arabia—I care not! For that is what my furthest Fancy so impossibly dreams of!

6th Day

How things fall apace! For this morning Miriam Pettibone came to me and in a Secrecy told me that John had sent her and that he wish'd to see me. I question'd her on this, ask'd had her Father spoken to John, but it seems he had not. Rather she herself had told John of my visit to the Wharf, and that there had been some talk between their Father and their Mother, and there was Confusion about the house, and they had guess'd it was a great ado over me. And so he had sent her as his Messenger that we might meet.

What strange freedom I feel! For having trespass'd once, it is easier to trespass a second time. Once the Boundary walls of life as they are given us are broken, then perhaps we may find our way from without the walls. So it is that I am become my own Ariadne. So may I lead not just myself, but Dorcas, and Ashes and Spearmint, out of this Maze our lives!

I have told Miriam I will meet her brother tomorrow at sunrise out on the Harbour breakwater where we did play as children.

The day after Labor Day Sandy took the train from Providence to New York. He had two addresses with him—the du Ponts' apartment on the Upper East Side and Aisha's place in Brooklyn. What exactly he was doing, he wasn't sure, but it was all he had, the only way forward.

He went uptown first into the East Nineties, but Miss du Pont, the doorman informed him, was still away at Newport. And no, he had had no word when she might be returning, or whether she might be going straight to Santa Fe, but he would be pleased to take a message.

So it was off to the Ninety-Sixth Street station and the 6 train down to Union Square, and then the L line over to Bushwick. Aisha had led him to believe that she lived in some cutting-edge neighborhood, just ahead of the gentrification curve, but when he got there he was struck by how ugly and dirty and noisy the area was. He didn't know what he had expected— some SoHo-y, East Village vibe, he supposed—but what he found was a grim industrial street, graffiti everywhere, and along the curb groups of Spanish-speaking kids who didn't bother to look at him.

Next to her buzzer was a handwritten *Aisha (Brown) DuMaurier— Goldwork Variations*. "Brown" was her real name.

He steadied himself and rang the buzzer. When the door opened, it was not Aisha but a college-aged girl who gave him a look from behind her bangs and then led him down a concrete-floored hall and through a fire door into the studio. There was another girl there, and Aisha, both of them bent over their stations, pliers and files and carousels of miniature grinding wheels surrounding them. They were all three of them thin, under their aprons barely clothed.

Again he didn't know what he had expected. Some look of surprise, dismay, guilt. What he got was a barely raised brow, a wry *Well, well*, and then her back turned to him while she finished whatever it was she had been doing. Neither of the assistants gave him a second look.

When she was done she said, "Time for a break," to the girls, and then, "Coffee?" to Sandy. He waited while she took off her apron, and then the tam she wore to keep her dreads out of the way, and then followed her back out into the hallway and onto the street.

"Strange to see you here," she said as they walked; and when he didn't answer, almost to herself: "Two different worlds."

He weighed what to say. He had rehearsed it on the train all the way from Providence, but what he was about to accuse her of: how did you start?

"You left without saying good-bye," he said finally.

"I thought we were done saying good-bye," she answered in a toneless voice.

"Still," he said, "you left unexpectedly."

She didn't respond.

"Hastily," he added.

She stopped walking so that he had to turn around, take a step back to her. She peered directly up into his face.

"What's with you?" she said.

"Killer instinct," he answered.

She grimaced, shook her head. "Sandy, if this is some ex-lover's re-proach scene—"

"No scene," he said. "I just want to know a few things."

She crossed her arms, kept her eyes on him. There were cars going past, people on the sidewalk. They'd come only a hundred yards from her building. They were not going for coffee. "What things?" she said.

"How was Alice when you left?"

"Why ask me? You've been seeing her more than I have."

"As I think you know, I have *not* been seeing her more than you have. I haven't been seeing her at all."

He thought he saw on her face a wavering intelligence, as if she was trying to read him. How much did he know?

"I haven't seen her in a week, ten days," she said finally.

"And when you *did* see her?"

"What?" she said and she raised her shoulders in interrogation. "It was like always. What are you after? What do you want from me?"

"Not texting her? E-mailing her?"

"I don't know," she said. "I haven't heard from her. We go through spells."

He took a step toward her, leaned over her. She was so small, so slight, and he with his big athlete's body.

"Is that how she took it?" he asked.

"What?"

"Is that how she took it?"

Again, the peering at him like what was with him? "I don't get it," she said. "What're you talking about? What's happened?"

"What's happened?" he repeated. "You mean other than your telling Alice you and I were sleeping together?"

For a moment she simply stared up at him, pulled into herself, with something like revulsion on her face. And then she turned and began walk-ing back toward her building. He had to skip a few steps to catch up to her.

"I didn't tell her," she said in a thin, angry voice as he walked alongside her. "One of the college girls did. The bitchy one. Rachel."

"You got her to tell. It was you, Aisha. You got her to tell."

"Don't be stupid."

"It was you," he repeated. "You wanted her to know but you couldn't tell her yourself so you got Rachel to tell her."

"Why would I do that? After all that time, all the trouble of keeping it secret. Why would I do that?"

"Because it was worth a try."

"A try? A try for what? What are you talking about?"

"You thought it might send her over the edge."

"Exactly!" she said. She was walking faster. "Exactly! Why would I do that?"

"It would wreck everything you had with her. Get you kicked out of the Orangery, out of Newport altogether."

"Exactly!" she said again.

"But that was a risk you were willing to take."

"Again, why would I do that?"

"Because," he said and he grabbed her by the elbow, made her stop. "Because if it *did* send her over the edge, you stood to inherit Windermere."

Her body hardened. Her eyes, her face, her lips—everything against him.

"Windermere and its trust fund," he said.

She raised her hands—for an instant it seemed as though she meant to hit him—then closed her eyes, shuddered, turned her hands palm out in a gesture of refusal, of rejection. "I can't listen to this," she said and she began walking again. "I have nothing to say to you."

"And what I want to know is—" he went on, keeping pace beside her; he barely recognized his own voice—"is when did you first get the idea? When did it first come to you?"

She kept her face from him, again made the gesture of disavowal, of pushing him away.

"Did it only dawn on you when I started seeing Alice? Or was it there right from the start. Even that first day in the Orangery. You told me Alice thought I was the most beautiful man she'd ever seen. Did you get the idea then?"

They were nearing her building. She got her keys out.

"Sandy Alison the babe in the woods being set up?" he prodded.

She started to open the door but he grabbed hold of her, held her by the wrists.

"Sleep with the tennis guy. Figure out a way of getting him involved with Alice. And then pull the plug. Was that it?"

She had turned her eyes hotly, furiously on him. "Let go of me."

"Why else would you get Rachel to tell her?"

"Let go of me!"

"Why else?" he said, and he tightened his grip on her wrists, pulled them toward him so that with a little cry she had to go up onto her toes. For a good half minute they gazed fiercely at each other, and then he threw her wrists down. She pressed herself back into the door behind her. Another minute passed.

"You have *seriously* gone off the deep end," she whispered finally.

He closed his eyes, tried to even out his breathing, and then, in a low, precise, painstaking voice, said: "One more time: why did you get Rachel to tell Alice about us?" And he held out a hand in his own gesture of rejection: "And don't tell me you didn't."

But she still didn't answer, kept her gaze on him hard and ungiving. They stayed like that for some time, for too long, but he wasn't going to give in. Eventually she let out a long breath, dropped her eyes, and turned away, turned so he could only see the back of her head, her dreads where they draped over her narrow shoulders. A car passed in the street, and then another. When she turned back, a bitter smile had come onto her face.

"Am I not allowed to have a guilty conscience?" she asked.

He was pulled up by that. "What?"

"The lying, the secrecy?" she said. "Which was all my idea, I admit. But I didn't like it. I never liked it."

"That's not it," he said, and shook his head.

"She *had* to know. I *had* to tell her."

He shook his head again. "Why not just come clean with her, then? Why get the college girls?"

"Because I was ashamed!" she said. "She was my best friend!"

"No," he said, and he had to remind himself that this was who she was, cool, duplicitous, calculating: wasn't she? "It was all you, Aisha. The tactics, the strategy, Windermere."

And at that she closed her eyes, made her hands into little fists, and pressed them over her ears. She seemed to sway where she stood. When at last she spoke, it was in a voice low and strained, almost strangling with anger.

"I don't ever want to see you again, Sandy. Do you understand?"

He just stared at her.

"Don't come around. Don't call me. Don't text me. Do you understand?"

"I know what you were doing, Aisha," he said. "I'm the one who knows."

She had turned to finish unlocking the door, but now whipped around on him. "You?" she cried in a voice rich with disgust. "Sandy Alison, the Southern Gentleman? It was *you* who was trying to get her money! It was *you*, Sandy, not me! I *had* to tell her!" And she started to back through the doorway, still with her eyes fixed on him. "Evil to him who thinks evil," she said, and then, with her voice thrilling: "As your *former* fiancée liked to say!"

And with that she shoved the door open and disappeared inside.

Franklin did not know where he was. His lovely shoes were ruined. His legs could go no farther. It was night and the ocean was somewhere off to his right, south, he guessed that was. But there was fog now, and he had left whatever path he had been on hours ago and now there was nothing around him but a waste of scrub bushes and sandy soil, and the occasional whooping of some nighttime bird to frighten him.

So great had been the shock he'd received that upon leaving the Ocean he had walked as if only half alive, first down along the wharves so that he might be away from Bellevue, and then onto the Point, then in and out of the gravestones in the Jewish cemetery, and then through the mews and couloirs where the great houses had their stables (and where two summers ago there had been that lovely boy—lost! all lost!), walked in a kind of aimless panic until he had found himself on one of the paths leading out of town, going past the fort with its great berm and into the meadows and marshes and scrubby thickets beyond. He had been heading, he now vaguely supposed, toward the breakwater as if somehow—by necromancy, alchemy, hoodoo—he might find there the secret crux of the matter and so begin to think his way out. But the sun had set and he had gotten turned about—could he not simply follow the damned ocean?—and now he was tired and lost and it had begun to drizzle and his lovely shoes were soiled and wet through.

He found a rock and sat down and for the hundredth time tried to calm himself.

Oh, how his mind had ranged, how it had bolted, dreamed, hallucinated! But there was simply no way out, neither a way forward nor a way back. He could neither call Ryckman's bluff—the man would not hesitate, even if it meant his daughter must bear up under the ensuing scandal, to do exactly as he said—nor could he go to the woman, explain himself, beg her forgiveness. And the idea of simply withdrawing—a delightful cousin was getting married in Vevey: had he neglected to tell everyone? Bah! it was all theater! the wild imaginings of Franklin Drexel upon the stormy heath! And theater would not do, not this time.

How *could* he have been so foolish? He who had been so unfailingly strategic! There had been only a few months to make it through! Could he not have walked the straight and narrow until it was safe and Windermere secured? How foolish, reckless, blind! Hobson, Parrish, Briggs—they had all played at being rakes, wastrels, *bons vivants*. But he had always thought himself superior. He was not playing, he *was*, and they, poor toddlers . . . !

And the woman, he thought with a horrible laugh. She loved him! Laughably, ludicrously, she loved him and now she would suffer her own humiliation, her own stripping away!

What his mind kept returning to was this: if he did exactly as Ryckman demanded, if he ceased to pay his attentions to the woman (with whatever excuse!), and assuming he could trust Ryckman to keep his word, then he would be saved from absolute ruin. The nature of his life, his *secret* life, would not be exposed. So at first blush it seemed he was stymied only in the moment. The loss was confined to this particular campaign—Mrs. Newcombe, Windermere, the house on Sixty-Second Street. Ah, well:

farewell to a dream! But he could begin again next summer, couldn't he? A little more shoe polish on the gray. There would be another Mrs. Newcombe, wouldn't there be? This time, preferably without a father.

But each time he thought it, each time he beat his wings against that particular glass globe, a second, deeper, harder, more bitter realization set in. For there was Mrs. Belmont. Mrs. Belmont with her pugilist's face. For him to leave the field of battle so inexplicably, to let fall Mrs. Belmont's colors, was to commit a kind of social suicide. The mother-in-law of the Duke of Marlborough would never forgive him. More than that: she would cast him out without a second thought. Her house would be closed to him. Her patronage, her society. If he withdrew from his pursuit of Ellen Newcombe after Mrs. Belmont had selected him for her, he could not simply return to who he was before. There was no *status quo ante* available to him. He could not go back to being Franklin Drexel the lapdog, the gay gadabout. Having been crossed by him, Alva Belmont would drop him as if he were a sprig of poison ivy. He would never again be invited up Fifth Avenue, by her or by anyone else. He would be relegated to the second circle, perhaps even the third circle, where he would be a kind of curiosity, the man who had once made the Four Hundred laugh, who had sat in his evening clothes at their glittering dinner tables, stood on their lawns in his pale green suit, accompanied them to Bailey's Beach in a top hat!

Two kinds of ruin to choose from, one the ruin of the loud and obscene, the other of silence and exclusion.

All of which left him—he had arrived here again and again the whole wretched night—left him washed up on the shore of a trembling possibility. The *impossible* possibility, he said to himself now.

For if there was no way out, if it was all going to fall down around him, if he was going to be cast out, his name made unspeakable, then why not vanish? Give over all this gilding, this pretense, this duplicity, and without telling anyone cancel his life, change his name if he had to, and vanish. Zurich, Marseille, Constantinople, Marrakech: could he not go and live somewhere the life of a bohemian? He had seen men like himself in Paris, had he not? Artists, writers, social reformers who seemed to live openly, in acknowledgment of who they were. Could he not make do with just a room and a suit of clothes and his watercolors if it meant freedom? If it meant he might wear his thoughts out loud, *breathe* out loud? For a moment he stood giddily on that precipice—life as who he was!—but in the next instant it crumbled beneath him as it had the whole night. It would be one thing if he were truly an artist! But he was not. There was no such substance that might be depended upon, that remained whatever else might vanish. Indeed, what *was* he if not gilding? He was the very soul of gilding—Franklin Drexel the Gilded Man!

And yet, and yet . . . Might it not be possible, even for a gilded man? If there was, after all, nothing else! To step into the shadows of the demimonde and stay there. To step behind the arras, to be done with duplicity, to enter the maze *of who one was* never to leave!

July 10

We have made Rehoboth and I am in my room at the Inn. 'Tis night, and quiet, and there is a great fog lowered upon the world, so it seems but half there.

I have left behind in my Quarters at Newport my Regimentals and casual Possessions. And I have left behind a sum of money which, should I not return, will argue against any Appearance that my going was premeditated. The Sum is not what I would have wished in the Ideal execution of my Scheme, but wherefore I go (should I go!) and whereof I hope (should I hope!) I know not, only that I will need Gold & Silver for whatever it be.

If one may not vanish in the midst of War, then when may one vanish?

I concoct Tales, whole Novels of Incident and Deceit, of lives that run Parallel to this my own, of Rebel jails and escapes, of versions of myself as in a Glass. I would almost welcome a Court-martial, that I might set this Theater to spinning like a Whipping-top!

Eight miles from here the Jewess sleeps in her innocent bed.

I will not be a Coward.

Tomorrow I step off the Chess-board.

~I have finally written to Miss Taylor. Without directly alluding to what transpired in the Hebrew cemetery, I expressed my sorrow that there had been a misunderstanding between us, or if there had not been a misunderstanding, apologized for having behaved in such a manner as to allow first her and then her father to misunderstand me. I then said that I had greatly enjoyed the pleasure of her company these several weeks, that I esteemed her a young lady of fine intelligence and character, and that I wished her every happiness in life. I said I hoped she would remember me with some fondness, as I surely would her. And I bid her *adieu*.

Wherever the life of a writer takes me, I hope I will never again write so false a thing.

After I sent it off, I picked up and went out walking so as to be away from the world. I set off southward and as soon as I could turned down some of the less-traveled paths. But instead of an exorcism (how the scene in Father's library plays through me like a nightmare!), I spent the whole time reliving the episode (all the while tramping about in the mud; Mother says I have quite ruined my shoes), tried in short to explain myself to myself and to Miss Taylor as if she were somehow invisibly with me, until finally I found myself composing a second letter in my head. It was the letter I would have written if one could, in the heart of one's heart, truly *be* oneself! I will do my best now (though it is late and I am indeed tired), my best to write out some version of what I composed and recomposed as a way of settling my mind and, perhaps, of forgiving myself.

My dear Miss Taylor,

The first letter I wrote you I composed to satisfy the requirements of our noontide lives. This I write to satisfy those lives we live as if in the gloaming.

You are the first friend I have, as it were, earned. All others who I might account friends come to me through my family, are my cousins, or are the children of friends of my father. You alone have I acquired purely on my own, from the proceeds of my own worth, if that is not too bold a way of saying it. For the kindness you have shown me this summer in keeping me company, and for the honor you have bestowed upon me (you know of what I speak), I am, and will always be, deeply grateful.

I approached you in falseness. You were, for me, a model I allowed into the atelier of my nascent literary imagination. I looked to sculpt you into dramatic form, to subject you to slights and flaws and false positions that I might make a story of you. For, as I once obliquely admitted, my "research" into the lives of the resort hotels was not for some journalistic purpose, but rather the first toddling steps toward acquiring a novelist's stride. But at every turn, from our first colloquy in the Jewish cemetery, to our wordless, yet confiding, hike to the breakwater, up to our last remarkable meeting, you have confounded my imagination. How sorry a literary inventor I turn out to be! And how the noontide tumult of reality embarrasses the thin inventions of romance!

Ah! My dear Alice, I mistook life for art!

I am guilty, I believe, of what Mr. Hawthorne calls the unpardonable sin. I have looked, and watched, and observed, and noted, as if the world were but an experiment in a philosopher's laboratory. I have, in short, attempted to peer into the sanctity of the human heart (or what seems to me to be perhaps worse: attempted to imagine the sanctity of a human heart) without sympathy, without an extension of my own heart, without the warm and ruddy coal-fire with which Mr. Hawthorne says we must leaven the moonlight of our intellects. That I treated you as if you were the lead I would turn into gold (that for all my observing I could be so blind that I did not see you were already gold!) is the chief lesson of this summer of so many lessons.

Unpardonable, yet you have (it seems) pardoned me.

Here is what I will never forget: the image of you (if only I had Hunt's talent!), you in your simple white dress, crossing the aisle to the Confederate wounded, and going from bed to bed while the rest of us pretended not to see. That was the moment my stories dried up and fell like dust at my feet. The nobility with which you faced life! How you shamed us! And how beautiful you were in the shaming!

Why, then, as my father asked me in the presence of your father, if I find you so fine, can I not marry you? Why cannot Harry James, recently turned twenty years old, marry Alice Taylor, and live with her the searching, experiential, committed life she wishes to live?

I do not know how to answer this. Everything I might say, everything I have known myself to think on this matter, is cloaked in a kind of fog. Whether the fog is made of that which is inchoate in me, or unnamable, or unsayable, I do not know. But I have come to understand—and the realization has cost me and freed me in equal measure—that I will never marry, that I am not made to be a husband to a woman, father to a child. I cannot explain this, even to myself, yet the certainty has at last come and is now as absolute, for me, as day and daylight. Some things, even in the honesty of our hearts, even in the confines of a letter which will never be sent, never be read, must be left unsaid.

My dear Alice, I cannot live my life out loud. If I am to have a life at all, it must be one of indirection, of deflection, of slanted truth. (I once played a game of chess with Alice—our Alice—and when the progress of the game turned against her she began to move her pieces off the board, because (she explained) there were squares out there too, you just couldn't see them!)

I wish to live my life on the squares out there. I wish to be free to observe life (I hope with the warmth of heart you have shown to me), and to translate what I see into something that might be called Art. For from out there I hope to be able to see in here. To see not just the artifacts of individuality (the different hats and hems and hairstyles we wear), but to see that which unites us, that which we share au fond. That this living of a life out there dooms me to being alone, casts me in the tragedy you foresaw that afternoon in the cemetery, terrifies me. But it must be so.

It is something I have difficulty reconciling, this sense I have that the hundreds of millions of us who breathe upon the earth are each a unique flame, that we are each uniquely composed within the caskets of our bodies and our minds, that each has an experience of the world as different as that of a fishwife's from a foundryman's, and yet we all live the same life (millionaire, artist, soldier, slave), we each of us strive to understand who we are, why we are here, to love and be loved, and that for all that striving, we are each of us lost in the mystery of our own heart.

Here is the story I would make of you, dear Alice, if I had the talent.

A young lady lives in a resort town (Newport, Saratoga, Vevey) which is yearly visited by the wealthy and the famous. She is something of an oddity in the town, with a beauty of her own which not all can see, yet she is marred by innocence (as one may be, I believe). To this resort town comes a young man of some report (he has proved himself, let us say, in some field of endeavor), he comes to the resort, makes the acquaintance of our local young lady, but because of a flaw in his nature, he cannot see her as she is. He is struck by her unusual beauty, by the fashions she wears, by her curious behavior, finds himself inexplicably drawn to her, delights in observing her, but all the same he cannot see her. And in the end he does not realize that something in his observing, in his actions (I shall have to develop this), acts as a blight upon our girl, upon her goodness.

She is, tragically perhaps, shorn of her innocence.

This is what I fervently hope, that I may someday write such a story and that by writing it I may have, at last, a genuine relation with you. Ah! my dear Alice: grant me the artist's hand, the poet's voice! That I might make your story partake of that imperishable bliss I know to be the empery of Art, and so be myself assumed into the great Circle of life! For that is how you can save me!

On the train back from New York Sandy watched the nighttime landscape going past, the lighted interior of the passenger car overlaid like a ghost on the world, the reflection of his half-lit face slipping across the Connecticut countryside, across the dark trees and bushes, the buildings in the distance, the moon behind the clouds.

He had given up trying to understand. Whether he had just done something unforgivable, accused someone of motives so vile, so outrageous, so—there was no other word for it!—so *evil*, that there was no way to cleanse himself if he was wrong; or whether he had, in fact, *seen* something, seen how one human being had used another, had used *him*: well, he had given up. All the way from Brooklyn back to Grand Central, and from Manhattan to Bridgeport to New Haven, he had wrestled with it, accusing himself, accusing Aisha, laying out the evidence—Mitten, Rachel, Margo—but there was no way to truly know, no center of the maze he might eventually reach, and he had sunk into a kind of stupor. He, Sandy Alison, with his sun-bleached hair, who everyone liked to have around. For miles and miles he had sat there looking out the window at the other Sandy traveling parallel to him in the dark.

Somewhere out there was Alice du Pont, damaged, hurt, in love with him though he didn't deserve her, but out there somewhere. Even now, after everything, couldn't he find her—surely, there was *some* way—find her and save her, save himself?

He lifted his face to where the moon kept pace with the train. Cold, calculating, *strategic*, he had called Aisha. Maybe she was, maybe she wasn't. But Alice, Alice was somewhere in the world. At Windermere still—hadn't the doorman said so?

But he'd no sooner felt a stirring inside him than he sank back in his seat, closed his eyes. She didn't want to see him. Nothing could be clearer than that. *Don't come around again, Sandy.* They'd both said that, Margo and Aisha, the exact same phrase, both of them. And Alice—just like Tom had said—was she not saying it as well?

Out the window he could see the dark plain of the Sound and the ragged line of white where the waves broke against the shore. For a mile, two miles, he just listened to the *clack-clack* of the rails.

Okay, fine, it was hopeless—but didn't he still have to try? If only as a way of cleansing himself? Maybe a real letter this time, not an e-mail. Get Mary the cook to give it to her, or maybe walk around the Salve Regina campus until he spotted Mitten's bike in some bike rack. He could station himself there until the girl showed up. Heck, he could do both, Mary *and* Mitten. He'd leave the envelopes unsealed so they could read the letter, see that he meant no harm, see that this was *love*. Surely one of them would manage to get it to Alice.

Couldn't he do that? One last try?

She had been right. He *was* Mr. Winterbourne—blind, shallow, always facing in the wrong direction. He would tell her that in the letter. But he would tell her too that she had opened things in him, deepened him in ways he was only now beginning to understand. He would tell her that he had not realized that the life she had imagined for him that wonderful night in the library—the kids, the house, the gift of the world—that that life so removed from who he was, who he had always been, was the life he wanted, but now he could not rid himself of it. And he would tell her that he had this picture of the two of them: Alice du Pont a bright red spinnaker aloft in the wind and Sandy Alison her anchor. He would not deny that her money and her house and her privilege made it all the more enticing, but it was she, she with her lovely eyes and her manic depression and her bowling shirt, that he wanted. He would not give her up.

He would wait for her on the breakwater at sundown. Starting the evening of the day she received the letter, he would be there. He would be there day after day, week after week, waiting for her. On the breakwater, he would tell her in the letter, where she'd said that first day that sometimes just being alive was enough. It might take a week, two weeks. It might take a second or third letter. Or him arranging for a taxi to pull up at Windermere every night just at sundown with express instructions to carry Miss du Pont out to the Newport breakwater, where a marriage proposal awaited her. But in the end, she would come, wouldn't she? Was it not at least worth a try?

With his eyes closed, the train rocking him, he jotted down in his memory phrases he might use in his letter. He could see it all in his mind's eye, the breakwater, and the pounding surf, and the sun lowering in the west, the distant sailboats glinting in the last light. One night, two nights. One week, two weeks. But she would not be able to resist. A night would come—after he'd watched hundreds and hundreds of cars approach along Ocean Drive only to pass him by—a night would come when a taxi would appear with its lighted sign and begin to slow down. His heart would give a little leap as it came to a stop at the side of the road. What would she be wearing? her bowling shirt? her Woodstock fringe jacket? Perhaps she would tell the taxi to wait as a sign she had not given in yet, had not yet forgiven him. But he would go to her, wordless, and he would lift her half-broken body in his arms and carry her out onto the rocks as he'd done that first day, and there he would tell her he loved her and he would ask her to marry him. It would be something they would tell their twenty children. (He'd put that in the letter.) Sandy Alison the tennis pro proposing to the heiress Alice du Pont on the Newport breakwater, at sundown, with the world a golden blaze behind them. And how she had said yes.

These were the phrases he jotted down in his memory as he watched the dark landscape go by: *bowling shirt . . . cloaked in a kind of fog . . . a spinnaker in the wind . . . breakwater at sundown . . .*

7th Day

At first I thought he would not come. For I stood upon the Breakwater at sunrise in a most deathly Fog and waited and waited. I fear'd something had miscarried. Or that he had chang'd his mind, had been work'd on by his parents or his friends. But then a figure took shape out of the gray coming toward me over the rocks. My heart leap'd and I moved toward him until we stood face to face, John Pettibone and Prudence Selwyn. The Fog was so thick that it was as if Newport had vanish'd and there was just our selves, and the near rocks, and the gray of the water receding into a gray Nothing behind us. It embolden'd me, this Sense that there was no World but ourselves, and I spoke to him in a Manner I could never have done before.

I told him I needed a Husband. I told him I had always lik'd him, and that it was he I wish'd to marry. I said all this without a blush about me, in an extremity of Honesty. I told him it was a like proposal that I had gone to see his Father about, and that his Father had said that he was too young to marry. Now I wish'd to hear it from himself. I told him I had a House of my own, with no lien real upon it, and that I own'd a servant too. That these came with me as a kind of Dowry, and that he was not like to do better. Then thinking that this was too brassy a thing to say, I smiled and said that he must watch out, for I was accounted a good Business woman these days, and that he must look to himself if he enter'd into a Transaction with me.

Then I said I hoped he did not mind me speaking so plainly. I said that we were of the Society of Friends, and as such might we not conduct ourselves with a plainness that went beyond our manner of dress? Might we not speak plainly as well? If not, then I ask'd him to forgive me this straightness, but that he must needs understand that, for me, the time for Coyness had pass'd.

He said then that I quite took his breath away. That he had overheard his Mother and Father speaking and had come with an amaz'd conception of what had taken place between his Father and me, but to hear me speak so, he said it amaz'd him further.

I told him to not be too amaz'd, lest the time pass him by. Thee hast heard of Edward Swift's offer? I ask'd, not because I thought he had, but so that he might learn of it then. And that it might throw a Fear into him if he did not act.

He then gave out with a beautiful Rush of things! How he had always lik'd me. And that he thought of me often. And that hearing of this Business with his Father had made his heart run, and that he had been awake the whole of the night with the thought of seeing me and of what he might say. He did go on so, and there was none of the halting Speech I knew him for, so that I found myself in a Fury of feeling. Aye, we were young, he said. And it did worry him, he said. He would confess that, for it had worried him the whole of the night. As a man, he said, it came down to him. But he suppos'd he might get work with the woodcutters or out at the Ropewalks. Or he might go to the Sailmakers, or to one of the Distilleries. But he said these things in a way that I could see he was troubl'd. Would there be no help from his Father? I ask'd. Might he not forgive us and accept us and help us? We did then swirl around so with Possibilities and Ploys that in time I felt turn'd about and altogether lost. So I ask'd him what his own Hope was, what did he wish for himself? And I saw it disturb'd him to answer me, but answer he did. He said he was made for the sea, that it was in his family to go to sea, as it was in my family. That he wish'd someday to be Master of his own ship and sail in the trade with the Islands and along the coast, perhaps even to London or Portugal. That was what he had been brought up to and what he wish'd, and what he would throw over that he might have me. I ask'd was there no chance that this might still be, no chance that we could fit together a Livelihood until he became a Master? There was not, he said, even if his Father could be brought around, for the training was too long. He must go first as common hand, and then as a lowly Mate. He would have to work his way upwards and there would be no real livelihood for years. How many years did he think? I ask'd. With a look most desolate, as though he had betray'd me, he said it might be as many as six or seven.

I held him then by both wrists that I might bring him back to me. And I ask'd him did he want to marry me. These other troubling Matters aside, did his Heart want it? Did he wish me to be his Wife?

He said he did.

I ask'd again: would he marry me if there was a way to be found? Would he be my Husband?

He said he would. And he said it with an oath that shock'd my ears, and yet made the blood rush through my parts.

Then thee art mine! I told him, and I stretch'd up and kiss'd him there in the fog with the water at our feet. For I know a way, I whisper'd in his ear, and I held him to me and felt in my breast a great burst of love for Ashes and Spearmint and the whole lighted world! I know a way how we may get through the first seven years!

Acknowledgments

I would like to thank Laura Goering, Bonnie Nadzam, and Scott Carpenter for their insightful readings of earlier drafts of this book and for their many helpful suggestions.

And for their expertise and faith, I extend my gratitude to my agent, Barney Karpfinger, and my editor, Carole DeSanti.

And finally, I would like to acknowledge the generous support of the National Endowment for the Arts and Carleton College.

A PENGUIN READERS GUIDE TO

THE MAZE
AT WINDERMERE

Gregory Blake Smith

An Introduction to
The Maze at Windermere

I have read somewhere that curators of antiquities have discovered that oftentimes parchments of the Dark Ages have underneath their present writing an older writing incompletely effaced, and that by careful investigation, the older writing can be read beneath the newer. Such a layering of writing is called . . . a palimpsest. Ah, to be able to read both the surface and *that which is below the surface!* (pages 69–70)

The Maze at Windermere takes us on a dazzling narrative odyssey across five intersecting stories, each set at a distinctive moment in the history of the renowned seaside town of Newport, Rhode Island.

In 2011, handsome and easygoing tennis pro Sandy Alison is surprised to find himself falling for Alice du Pont, heiress to the legendary Newport mansion known as Windermere. Alice does not look like the women to whom Sandy is usually drawn, and Sandy is forced to examine what his motives are in pursuing Alice. Does he love her, or the world that she is attached to? More than a century earlier, in 1896, a closeted gay man with nothing but a sharp wit and impeccable taste schemes to secure a life of comfort and luxury by marrying the wealthy widow who owns Windermere. In 1863, young Henry James, soon to make his mark on the world, discovers his muse in Alice Taylor and strikes up a friendship with her. His attentions, however, are misinterpreted as romantic pursuit, and James must make a decision about what he is willing to sacrifice for his art. In the midst of the Revolutionary War in 1778, an aristocratic British officer stationed in Newport is consumed by his desire to seduce—at whatever cost—a young Jewish woman. Finally, in

1692, an orphaned Quaker girl looks to find a path forward for herself, and the slave she has inherited, without losing her chance at love and happiness.

Beautifully written and unforgettable, these five interwoven stories reflect and refract one another, demonstrating both the ever-changing landscape of Newport across history and the enduring landscape of the human heart in all its love, ambition, and duplicity.

A Conversation with
Gregory Blake Smith

*How did you arrive at the inspiration for the protagonist of this
novel, philandering former tennis pro Sandy Alison? In this era of
autobiographical memoir-novels, you seem to have written the opposite.
Was that a conscious decision? What went into creating these varied
characters?*

For me the power of fiction lies in the way it allows us—even requires
us—to break through the parochial limits of our own selves and live
imaginatively in the skin of others. *The Maze at Windermere* has gay characters, African-Americans both free and enslaved, a Jewish-Portuguese
immigrant, a character with cerebral palsy, a stunningly handsome tennis pro—none of whom even remotely resembles me. What I tried to do
in the novel is weave together diverse threads of American history into
stories that were *locally* different (dressed in the concrete details of a specific era, sexuality, race, class) and at the same time transcended those
local limitations to show the ways in which we are fundamentally similar
in our hopes and desires, and yes, in our duplicity. And to do that I
needed to invent a rich and varied cast of characters.

So where do these characters come from? I'm not sure I can fully
answer that, but here's how one got herself born. I had just returned from
Newport, Rhode Island, where the idea for the novel had first bloomed
in me, and I was wandering in a kind of creative delirium through the
Boston Public Garden, dreaming of the this and that of the novel-to-be,
when I happened to see a young woman with cerebral palsy walking near
the Swan Boats. I only saw her for a short time, but in those few seconds
the character of Alice du Pont came alive in my head. I saw her as if

complete: the encumbrance of her disability, the fierceness with which she lives her life, her wit, her daring, her moral courage. Okay, no doubt that's not literally true—the complete character must have come later in the writing of Alice—but that moment, the sight of that young woman walking with her strained, beautiful grace, set in motion the story of Sandy and Alice. It was like a gift from the writer gods.

So, what drew you to Newport as a setting?

I don't think there's another American city its size that has as remarkable a history as Newport. From its Quaker beginnings, through the part it played in the slave trade, to its utter devastation by the British during the American Revolution, and then its rebirth as a playground for the fabulously wealthy—it's really an extraordinary little city. I first came to know Newport through my interest in eighteenth-century furniture—I like to think of my character Spearmint as a predecessor of the great Townsend-Goddard cabinetmakers—but it took me years to realize that it was the perfect setting for a novel that layered history like a palimpsest. For me the greatest compositional kick came from the way the story in one era mirrors or inverts or qualifies the story of another era. Scenes take place in the "same" location only in different centuries. The Jewish merchant Isaac Da Silva's house (where the bigoted aristocrat Major Ballard attempts the seduction of the young Judith Da Silva during the Revolution) becomes a restaurant in the contemporary story where Alice and Sandy take their first steps toward one another. So, too, the Newport breakwater and the city's cemeteries and the maze at Windermere itself are the settings for scenes in different centuries that bear a provocative resemblance to one other. These parallels, mirror reverses, plot inversions, are like Easter eggs for the reader to discover and enjoy.

Within that rich and privileged milieu, you make a point of illuminating the lives of those who might be considered marginal to it—from the Jewish community that had a long history there, to a gay man, to an heiress with a disability that has shaped her life. How did you think about "otherness" and marginality as you were composing the novel?

There's a scene in the opening of Steven Spielberg's *Lincoln* where two black soldiers confront Daniel Day-Lewis and give him what for. To my ears it's a completely implausible scene, an example of what Edmund White has recently called "dressing up modern characters in historical drag," which is to say, retroactively giving the historically marginalized the power and moral consciousness of twenty-first-century people. That strikes me as not just historically fake, but artistically immoral. So that's what I *didn't* want to do with my characters. Rather, I tried to show how each of them is caught in the web of their era, whether the paternalistic seventeenth-century world of Prudence, my orphaned Quaker girl, or Aisha trying to make her way in the new gilded age of our own twenty-first-century America. It's in seeing how these characters work their lives against the historical and social realities of their times that the pleasure of the novel—and I hope, its honesty—resides.

The author Henry James is a prominent character in the book. How did you make that choice? Can you comment on how you worked to evoke the inner life of another writer, particularly one who looms so large in the history of American letters?

I had my choice between Henry James and Edith Wharton and James won out. Mostly because he lived in Newport during the Civil War whereas Wharton lived in Newport during the Gilded Age, and that era was already spoken for by my charming conniver Franklin Drexel.

But here's the thing. There's no evidence that James ever had a sexual, or even romantic, relationship with anyone, male or female. At the end of *The Ambassadors* there's a scene where the elderly Lambert Strether advises a young man: "Live all you can. It's a mistake not to." I find that moment chilling. It's as if the older James is speaking to his young self in regret, warning him. In *The Maze at Windermere* I wanted to dramatize the moment when the young James—he's only just turned twenty—arrives at that tragic renunciation, that moment of withdrawal with its accompanying vision of a life of celibacy, a life spent observing other people living (and writing brilliantly about them, it has to be said) but not fully living himself.

The attention to detail in The Maze at Windermere *is astounding, from descriptions of different parts of town over time to the specific way Prudence dates her entries. How would you describe the process of weaving a tale that is at once timeless, yet so rooted in specific periods?*

In the fiction workshops I teach I regularly get student writers who claim they didn't want to describe what their main characters looked like, or how old they were, or even what gender they were, because they wanted them to be "universal." It's at this point that I get up from my chair, go out into the hallway, and look for the nearest window to jump out of.

Because those students so misunderstand where the magic of fiction lies. They don't get that it's *through* the particular, the concrete, the specific, that we catch a glimpse of the universal—the sight of Anna Karenina's black hair against her white shoulders, both its own lovely self and a timeless figure for the allure of female beauty. The great pleasure of writing *The Maze at Windermere* was in depicting the rich variety of its historical eras and the ways in which the town itself, its people, its language, its values, changed from era to era. The synagogue used as a hospital during the Revolution, the antique grass tennis courts at the Casino, the lime rickeys consumed in the summer shade, the slave barracks down along the wharf: it's details like these that create the reality of a novel's world and carry its felt life.

Every character in the book is layered, but Sandy Alison may be the most mysterious. He seems at once conscious of his former womanizing ways, and both relieved and simultaneously disappointed that that period of his life has come to an end. How would you describe Sandy's conflicts in this day and age? How do they reflect the rich history you illuminate in this novel, and speak to present day concerns?

Is Sandy a womanizer? Or is he womanized? Which is to say, is he the sexual hunter or the hunted? The evidence of the novel seems to suggest the latter. And yet, and yet . . . for all his personal warmth, his good looks and easygoing ways, there's something wrong about Sandy's involvement with the women of Windermere. There's a kind of emotional blindness to him, a limitation to his moral sight that requires the reader to constantly re-evaluate him, especially regarding to what degree he is responsible for what happens to Alice. When he kisses her in that scene in the library at Windermere, is he succumbing to the duplicitous motives that lie at the heart of so many of the other characters in the novel? Or is it a moment when he begins to reach beyond conventional ideas of female beauty, of personal worth, and begins to grow both morally and emotionally? And to what degree is he "set up" by Aisha, or has he simply misread her motivation all along? In each of the novel's eras the reader is confronted with similar questions of culpability: Is Franklin Drexel's scheme to marry a rich woman he can never love excusable because he lives in a world that has no place for him as a gay man? Should Henry James have seen sooner that his attentions to Alice Taylor might be misinterpreted? And is even the despicable Major Ballard redeemed by his beginning to love the young woman he had only meant to seduce? None of these questions are simply answered, but they are the many-hued threads out of which the novel is woven.

QUESTIONS FOR DISCUSSION

1. At one point in the novel Alice du Pont tells Sandy Alison that in France there's ". . . a crime called *abus de faiblesse*. Which is exploiting someone's frailty or weakness for your own gain. A kind of killer instinct" (page 60). Who is doing the exploiting in this novel, and who is being exploited?

2. In one of their early conversations Sandy and Aisha discuss money and motive: "When that kind of money was involved, that kind of privilege . . . could anybody really be sure of their motives?" (page 90). Do you agree with the idea that one's motives can be obscure even to oneself? Beyond their stated motives, what do you think each main character—Sandy Alison, Franklin Drexel, Henry James, Major Ballard, and Prudence Selwyn—truly desires?

3. Major Ballard writes that he sometimes feels "as if I am standing outside the World and looking in, as if I am on the Edge of the world's Orchard and I can see the Fruit hanging on the trees but am denied them" (page 116). Other characters in the novel share this experience of feeling that they don't quite belong. Major Ballard's impulse is a determination to "eat of the fruit of that Orchard, violently if that was what it took" (page 117). How do other characters respond to their experience of being on the margins of their world?

4. Certain phrases, themes, and places surface and resurface across the different eras in this novel. Did you notice any in particular? What is their significance? And, in general, what do you make of the way in

which ". . . the rich past underlies the present" (page 69) in *The Maze at Windermere*?

5. Sandy takes Margo at her word when she offers to write him a recommendation. When Alice hears of this she laughs, surprised by his innocence, and tells him he should pass on it. "You don't see it because it's not inside you and so you don't recognize it in others" (page 198). Is this an accurate assessment of Sandy? Is Sandy as innocent as others believe him to be? As he believes himself to be?

6. In part three the structure of the novel shifts, and we begin to switch more rapidly and fluidly between narrators. What is the purpose and effect of this?

7. As the author says in his Q&A, in each of the novel's eras we are confronted with similar questions of culpability: Is Franklin Drexel's scheme to marry a rich woman he can never love excusable because he lives in a world that has no place for him as a gay man? Should Henry James have seen sooner that his attentions to Alice Taylor might be misinterpreted? And is even the despicable Major Ballard redeemed by his beginning to love the young woman he had only meant to seduce?

8. There is some uncertainty as to what path some of the characters will choose to take as the novel draws to a close. Indeed, the author seems to be encouraging the reader to "step off the chessboard" of the novel and imagine how those paths will unfold. What do you see the future holding for each character?

9. And finally, consider the maze motif in the novel. In what ways do the characters find themselves in figurative mazes? Does the reader find him- or herself in a maze as well?